PRAIRIE HEARTS

M. J. CONNER

BARBOUR
PUBLISHING

Circle of Vengeance © 2001 by M. J. Conner
Mariah's Hope © 2006 by M. J. Conner
Joanna's Adventure © 2007 by M. J. Conner

ISBN 978-1-60260-493-3

Scripture quotations are taken from the King James Version of the Bible.

This book is a work of fiction. Names, characters, places, and incidents are either products of the author's imagination or used fictitiously. Any similarity to actual people, organizations, and/or events is purely coincidental.

Cover model photography: Jim Celuch, Celuch Creative Imaging
Cover image: Jim Richardson/National Geographic/Getty Images

Published by Barbour Publishing, Inc., P.O. Box 719, Uhrichsville, Ohio 44683, www.barbourbooks.com

Our mission is to publish and distribute inspirational products offering exceptional value and biblical encouragement to the masses.

ecpa Member of the
Evangelical Christian
Publishers Association

Printed in the United States of America.

Dear Readers,

Thank you for selecting *Prairie Hearts* to read. You now hold in your hands a collection of three stories set in and around Cedar Bend, a fictitious nineteenth century small town in western Kansas. The lives of three women, Carrie Butler, Mariah Casey, and Joanna Brady are intertwined as each of their stories is told.

The idea of a young man bent on seeking vengeance for a supposed wrong came to me one day, so I told my sister, Jean Norval, that we should write a book. She agreed. The next two months, we concentrated on writing the best story we possibly could, and *Circle of Vengeance* became our first book written under the pen name, M. J. Conner.

Later, we decided that Carrie's father was probably lonely after Carrie had married and left home. Since Carrie gave up teaching school to focus on this new chapter of her life, Cedar Bend needed a new schoolmarm and Mariah Casey needed a change of scenery. Why not put those three needs together along with a little orphaned girl who needed love? We did, and *Mariah's Hope* began to take shape. This book was almost finished when my sister, Jean, died after a short bout with cancer. In fact, she never knew *Mariah's Hope* had been accepted for publication. I quickly wrote the conclusion and wished I could tell her that our second book would be published. Maybe she knows.

To complete the tale of our little Kansas town, I finally brought Clay Shepherd back to Cedar Bend and to the one girl he had never forgotten—Joanna Brady. *Joanna's Adventure* is more harrowing than anything I would ever want to experience, but I hope you enjoy reading each of these stories, woven together into a heartwarming tale of prairie life in the late 1800s.

My prayer is that as you read *Prairie Hearts*, you will follow Carrie, Mariah, and Joanna's example and gain a deeper relationship with our precious Lord. Always allow Him to be Lord of your life.

I love to hear from my readers. You can contact me through Barbour Publishing by sending in the short, one-page form at the end of this book, or through my Web site at www.mildredcolvin.com.

God bless you,
Mildred Colvin

CIRCLE OF VENGEANCE

Dedication

Dedicated to Lester Conner.

"Blessed is the man that walketh not in the counsel of the ungodly, nor standeth in the way of sinners, nor sitteth in the seat of the scornful. But his delight is in the law of the Lord; and in his law doth he meditate day and night" Psalms 1:1–2. Thank you, Daddy, for daily allowing us to see God in your life. We love you more than can be expressed in these few brief paragraphs. It would take volumes.

Jean and Millie

Prologue

Western Kansas, 1880

The sharp report of gunfire filled the night as the boy knelt on the floor beside the lifeless body of his mother. The man crouched at the window, the old Henry he'd taken from a dead Union soldier at Shiloh clutched tightly in his hands.

He returned their fire as best he could, but they both knew—the man and his twelve-year-old son—that his effort was hopeless. There were too many of them.

A blazing torch arced through the darkness and landed with a soft thud on the roof, igniting the dry shingles.

The man left his post at the window to kneel beside the woman. He unfastened a locket from around her neck, then gently removed the wedding ring from her finger. He slipped the ring onto the heavy gold chain, then reached across the body of his wife, and clasped the locket around the boy's neck.

His big, rough hand rested for a brief moment against the soft velvet of the boy's face. "Lucas, I want you to climb out the back window."

Wordlessly the boy shook his head.

"Yes, son! You must. I'm goin' out the door. While I draw their fire I want you to run."

"But, Pa! I can't. I can't leave you."

"You must, son." The man's voice came out harsh with emotion as he struggled to his feet.

A shower of sparks fell around them as the boy leaned down to kiss his mother's pale cheek. Then, his father half carried, half pulled him to the window. He caught him close in a desperate final hug before lifting him onto the sill of the open window.

"As soon as I open the door I want you to run. Run, Lucas, and don't look back. Don't never look back. And, always remember—vengeance belongs to the Lord."

"You comin' out, reb, or you gonna stay in there and fry." The disembodied voice came from the darkness in front of the house and cut off anything else the father might have said to his son.

Darting around the small fires that had flared up, the man burst through the door. A barrage of gunfire sent him sprawling backward into the burning room.

The boy hesitated for only a moment before dropping to the ground. He ran, darting from one shadowy spot to the next.

He didn't stop to look back until he reached the deep shadows. The flickering flames revealed a half-dozen men standing together, watching the burning house. He didn't recognize any of them.

While the boy watched, the roof fell in, sending up an illuminating flare of light. In the shadows cast by the big tree, behind and to one side of the huddled men, the boy caught a glimpse of a man on horseback. Then, the fire died down and the cover of darkness concealed the man once more.

The boy knew that man. There was no mistaking him. His broad-shouldered height and the tall bay horse he rode set him apart. He'd been harassing them ever since their family came here from Tennessee a year ago. Cutting their fences. Running off their cows. Muddying their water hole.

Hatred for the big man welled in the boy's heaving chest. His hands clenched at his sides, as the desire for revenge became a living thing inside him.

"Someday I'll be a man," he whispered through clenched teeth. "And when I'm strong enough, I'll come back. Someday you'll pay for what you've done."

A wall crashed into the blazing inferno. Once more the flames leaped high, illuminating the big man and briefly revealing the umber silhouettes of several mounted figures behind him.

The man turned his head toward the boy's hiding place. In the brief moment before the fire died back down, the boy memorized the big man's face. Then, choking back sobs, he turned and ran into the darkness.

Chapter 1

Western Kansas, 1892

Despite the gloomy sky overhead, Carrie whistled softly as she prepared to leave the ranch house. Fearing the coming storm, Papa had been reluctant to let her go. He gave his permission grudgingly, only after she explained to him the importance of this trip to town. She promised him she would hurry and assured him that Gretchen would be with her most of the way. After she excused herself to get dressed, Carrie overheard her papa telling one of the hands to hitch up the buggy for her.

She hesitated for a moment when she saw the bay filly tied to the hitching rail. She was high-strung, and Carrie didn't quite trust her. Still, Gretchen would be with her, and if she said anything to Papa, he might change his mind about letting her go.

The wind whipped Carrie's long skirt around her legs as she untied the horse. The little filly rolled her eyes and pranced to one side.

Carrie was used to the wind that blew almost continuously on the Kansas prairie, and paid it little mind as she climbed into the buggy, took a firm grip on the reins, and settled into the seat. "You'd better calm down before Papa, or Mac, or Cyrus see you," she said softly.

The bay did seem to grow calmer in response to her voice. By the time they reached the end of the lane, she was plodding along as sedately as an old plow horse. As soon as they turned onto the main road—and were out of sight of the ranch house—Carrie loosened her hold on the reins. The filly tossed her head and broke into a smooth trot. Carrie relaxed and began composing a mental list of the errands she needed to attend to in town.

If Lucille weren't in such a hurry to get married, they wouldn't be so rushed to get everything done. As it was, Carrie and Gretchen had only a month to get their dresses made, in addition to taking care of the myriad details that were their duties as bridesmaids.

At twenty, Lucille was two years older than Carrie and Gretchen. Carrie smiled as she thought of her friend, then laughed aloud as she remembered the last night Gretchen and Lucille had spent with her. They always stayed at Carrie's house because Gretchen had so many little brothers and sisters there was no privacy, and Lucille's mother was so finicky they couldn't have any fun at her house. It had only been a few months ago.

Wearing long white flannel nightdresses and heavy winter robes, the three friends went out to the kitchen, popped corn and made hot chocolate. At least Gretchen and Lucille did; Carrie didn't know the first thing about cooking. Back in Carrie's room, they sat cross-legged on the bed drinking chocolate and eating popcorn. Talking about clothes and men, they giggled until they were breathless.

Then Lucille, who was overly dramatic, rolled her huge green eyes and flung herself back on Carrie's bed. Crossing her arms over her bony chest, she intoned, "This is how I shall live, and this is how I shall die. An old maid schoolteacher, unsullied by the hand of man."

They giggled and pummeled each other with pillows until Mac banged on Carrie's door and told them to quiet down, or he was going to make them sleep in the barn.

Now, after a whirlwind courtship, Lucille was going to marry Jedidiah Smith, the new owner of the livery stable. And Gretchen would be next if Billy Racine, Cyrus's top hand, ever worked up nerve enough to ask her.

"I'll be the only one left." Carrie sighed.

It wasn't that men didn't like her. They did. Jake Philips had been in love with her ever since he sat behind her in first grade. She liked Jake, too. He was comfortable. Like an old pair of shoes. She knew everything about him. She even remembered how he used to wet his pants because Miss Finch wouldn't let him go to the outhouse. She wrinkled her pert little nose. She'd rather be a spinster and die "unsullied by the hand of man," as Lucille put it, as to marry a man she knew as well as she knew Jake.

Not that she didn't like men. It was just that she had yet to meet the man of her dreams.

From the year she turned fourteen, Carrie had often daydreamed about the man who would one day win her heart. His hair was brown—golden brown with a stubborn lock that tumbled over his forehead. He had gentle blue eyes, and his square chin had a slight cleft.

Gretchen and Lucille knew all about him. When they were younger the three girls called him "The Mysterious Stranger," and they spent hours dreaming up adventures in which he was constantly rescuing Carrie from some terrible danger. He was always fearless, courageous, daring, and heroic. In spite of the fact that he could shoot straighter and ride faster than any other man, he was gentle and compassionate. He was also extremely romantic, and the stories always had a happy-ever-after ending.

Carrie sighed. The other two girls had long ago forgotten "The Mysterious Stranger," that paragon of masculine perfection. But Carrie hadn't. She thought of him when she was alone, or had nothing else to occupy her mind. Jake Philips—in fact, all the men she knew—paled in comparison to her dream lover.

The Braun ranch buildings loomed ahead, and Carrie urged the little filly into a faster trot. She hoped Gretchen was ready. The wind seemed stronger, and she didn't want to get caught in a storm. Papa would never again let her go out alone if she did.

Gretchen was watching for her and came running out the door as Carrie brought the buggy to a halt in front of the house.

She climbed up and plopped on the seat, making the buggy bounce. Her bosom heaved as she caught her breath. Gretchen was blond and tall—even taller than Carrie, who was six inches over five feet—and voluptuous. Her mother had a new baby every two years, regular as clockwork, and Gretchen was always in a hurry and breathless from chasing after so many younger brothers and sisters. Though she said she loved babies, she often told Carrie she never wanted as many as her mother had. In her opinion, three or four were plenty.

Carrie's mother died when she was young, and even though she never suffered from a lack of love, she had been a lonely, only child. She thought the noisy, rambunctious Braun clan was wonderful. Besides, she adored Gretchen's mother. Having been raised by her father and his two partners, she sometimes wondered what she would do without Hilda Braun's wise and sensitive counsel, especially when it came to some of the more intimate aspects of growing up.

Carrie flicked the reins, and the bay took off like she had just heard the starting gun. Gretchen clutched the side of the seat with one hand and clamped the other hand down on her bonnet. "What's wrong with her?" she gasped.

"She's skittish and only about half-broke, I think," Carrie said as she struggled to bring the buggy under control. Finally the little bay slowed to something between a trot and a gallop, and Carrie relaxed enough to say, "I don't know, but I think Papa must have had that new hand Cyrus hired hitch the buggy for me."

"You mean the one that kept wanting to court you? The one you told you didn't keep company with the hired help?"

Carrie nodded, and Gretchen said, "Perhaps you should have been more tactful."

Tactfulness wasn't one of Carrie's strong points. A faint blush touched her smooth cheeks. "I tried," she said, "but Jess didn't seem to understand the word no."

The girls spent an hour at the dressmaker's choosing fabric and a pattern from the latest issue of Vogue and being measured for their dresses.

When they came out, the wind had picked up and ominous black clouds were rolling in from the southwest. They hurried through their other errands, then climbed in the buggy and headed out of town.

"Mrs. Wright has been after me to wear a corset ever since I was fourteen. I've always managed to talk her out of it before, but this time she pulled the tape so tight around my waist she almost cut me in two." Carrie wrinkled her nose. "I just know she's going to make my dress so small I'll have to wear one of those awful contraptions to get into it."

Gretchen laughed. "Carrie, you're the only girl I know who has never worn a corset. They really aren't that bad," she soothed. "I've worn a corset since I was thirteen."

Carrie gave her a dubious look. "I don't know." The color rose in her face. "Besides. I don't have one. And I don't know how I'm going to ask Papa." Her face brightened. "Maybe I could borrow one from you."

Gretchen shook her head. "My goodness, Carrie, you can't wear one of my corsets. Not that I wouldn't be happy to loan you one, but you surely noticed when Mrs. Wright measured us that my waist was twenty-four inches. And I'm wearing a corset. Yours was only twenty-two inches without one."

Carrie sighed. "I guess I'll just have to ask Papa."

By the time they reached the Braun's place, thunder rumbled overhead, and the black clouds were hanging so low they could almost reach up and touch them.

"You'd better come inside and wait out the storm." Gretchen said.

Carrie shook her head. "If I don't get on home they'll worry about me. Besides," she inclined her head toward the filly, "she's finally figured out who's boss."

Gretchen collected her purchases and stepped out of the buggy. "I don't know," she said with hesitation lacing her voice. Carrie followed her gaze to see the little bay rolling her eyes and prancing nervously.

"I'll be all right," Carrie said. She touched the reins lightly to the filly's back, and she bolted forward.

The sky darkened to a threatening black, and lightning flashed in the west as she pulled onto the main road. Carrie thought about turning back to wait out the storm, as Gretchen had suggested. But, when the bay tossed her mane and picked up speed, Carrie realized it would be impossible to turn her; she had her hands full just trying to keep her on the road.

The wind jerked her bonnet off, and long strands of auburn hair blew across her face and eyes. Just then, an especially powerful bolt of lightning streaked down, striking a large tree along the side of the road directly ahead of them. The little bay danced backward, crying out in fear, then bolted off the road.

Carrie was thrown back against the seat as the buggy cleared the ditch, but she quickly righted herself. Realizing she had lost all control, she hastily wrapped the reins around the stock, and concentrated on staying in the buggy until the filly ran herself out.

A jagged streak of lightning struck the ground nearby, and a deafening clap of thunder ricocheted across the prairie. A wild scream tore from the bay. Beside herself with fear, she reared on her hind legs pawing the air, then jumped to the side, dragging the frightened girl and rocking buggy straight toward a deep gully. Carrie squeezed her eyes shut and hung on for dear life. When she opened her eyes, she saw a tall man on a big black horse riding out of the storm.

He raced past the out-of-control buggy. Then, his gloved hand reached out and grabbed the bridle, turning the bay away from the edge of the gully, and bringing her to a trembling stop.

He looked back at Carrie. "Are you all right, miss?"

"I am now." She watched as he dismounted. He was tall and broad shouldered. A pearl-handled Colt 45 Peacemaker in a black holster was tied low on his right hip.

As he began to stroke the bay's nose and whisper soothingly to her, Carrie climbed from the buggy. He looked at her and his blue eyes lit up. "I'd say you're more than all right." He grinned.

Chapter 2

Carrie had seen appreciation in men's eyes before when they looked at her and paid them no mind. But this man was different. She blushed and tried to brush her auburn hair into some semblance of order.

"Thank you for rescuing me," she said.

"The pleasure was all mine." When he smiled and removed his hat, a lock of golden-brown hair fell across his forehead. "You must have been frightened out of your wits." He reached out and took her hand. "Look how you're tremblin'."

She had been frightened, and she was trembling, but not from fear. He hadn't shaved for a couple of days, and through the light growth of whiskers she saw a dimple in his square chin.

"What took you so long?" She felt the color rising in her face. "I mean where did you come from? I don't remember seeing you before. Are you from around here?"

"Nope." His grin revealed strong, white teeth. "I'd reckon you could say I'm just a stranger passin' through."

The sky had lightened some, and Carrie realized the sound and fury of the storm had passed. She quickly pulled her hand from his. "I'm sure someone will be out searching for me, Mr. . .Mr. . . I don't believe I caught your name."

His blue eyes crinkled at the corners when he smiled at her. "Thornton," he said. "John Thornton."

"My name is Carrie. Actually, it's Caroline. I was named after my mother."

"Caroline. A beautiful name for a beautiful young lady." His soft drawling accent caressed her name, and sent shivers chasing up and down Carrie's spine. "I think you had best get back inside the buggy, Miss Caroline. I just felt a few drops of rain, and I wouldn't want you to get wet."

Carrie hadn't even noticed the big drops splattering around them. She couldn't let him get away. Not now. Not when she'd only just found him. "Our place isn't too far from here," she said. "If you'll follow me home, I know Papa would like to thank you."

"Why, Miss Caroline, I have no intention of lettin' you drive home alone. If you don't mind, I'll just tie Jet to the back of the buggy, and we'll see you safely home."

14

"No, I don't mind." She couldn't contain a jubilant smile. "As a matter of fact, I'd appreciate it. I'm still a little shaky."

"Just as soon as I help you into the buggy we'll be on our way."

Before Carrie realized his intent, he put his hands around her waist and lifted her into the buggy. Then he tied the big black gelding to the back and climbed in beside her. By the time he had the buggy turned around, the rain was coming down in a torrent. The downpour lasted less than two minutes. The clouds had moved to the east, and the sun was shining brightly when they bounced through the ditch and turned onto the main road.

When Carrie saw three mounted men approaching at a gallop, her heart sank. "That's Papa, and Cyrus, and Billy," she said. "I suppose they're coming to look for me."

John guided the buggy to the side of the road and stopped.

He studied the men as they approached. They were all three wearing loose-fitting slickers, but he could see that the man in the lead was tall and broad shouldered. The second man was considerably older, shorter, and of a more stocky build. The man bringing up the rear looked to be around John's age. He was extremely tall and lanky, and sat his saddle with loose-jointed ease.

The first man reined in and dismounted before the big Appaloosa came to a complete stop. He leaned against the buggy, and John saw that, beneath his deep tan, he was pale. "Carrie, are you all right?"

Carrie leaned forward to look around John. "Of course I am, Papa. The storm frightened my horse, and she—"

"I still can't believe that any one could be so irresponsible as to—"

"Oh no, Papa! I thought I could handle her. Really I did."

"I'm sure you did." Her father raised his wide brimmed Stetson and combed his fingers through his thick auburn hair, before clamping the hat back on his head. "We'll discuss your part in this later. Right now I'm talking about Cartwright giving you that filly to drive. If he hadn't got a dose of conscience and gone to Billy when that storm blew in, it's hard telling what might have happened."

Billy, who had remained mounted, winked at her. Carrie thought of pointing out to her father that John Thornton had rescued her, not Jess Cartwright's conscience. But she knew her father and wisely kept her mouth shut.

The older man dismounted and walked around to the other side of the buggy. He patted Carrie's arm. "You sure you're all right, young'un?"

"I'm a little shook up, Cyrus. Otherwise, thanks to Mr. Thornton, I'm fine."

"Well, you don't have to worry about young Cartwright no more. Soon as he told me what he done, I sent him packin'."

"You fired Jess?" Carrie felt a pang of guilt. If she hadn't been so rude to him, none of this would have happened. "I don't think he meant to hurt me."

"That's what he said." Cyrus snorted. "Said he was jist playin' a little joke on you. Well, I let him know in no uncertain terms that we didn't think it was funny."

Cyrus patted Carrie's arm once more before stomping around the buggy and pulling himself into the saddle.

"The main thing is that you're all right." Carrie's father pushed away from the buggy. "But, I think you might as well know now, we're going to make some changes."

"Please, Papa, don't. . . ."

He frowned. "We'll talk about this later, Carrie." He started to walk away, then stopped and looked at John. "My daughter said your name was Thornton, didn't she? Mr. Thornton, would you mind driving Carrie home?"

The younger man had smiled at him, but this was the first time either of the older men had acknowledged John's presence. "No, I wouldn't mind at all," he said, picking up the reins.

"Good!" the other man said, curtly. "I want to talk to you when we get back to the house."

John nodded and guided the little bay back out onto the road. The three men on horseback fell in behind the buggy.

"Oh, boy!" Carrie muttered under her breath. "Now I'm going to get it."

John glanced at her. "Your pa won't whip you, will he?"

Carrie looked at him with wide brown eyes. "Whip me? Papa? Of course not. Mama used to whack me once in a while, but since she died. . ." She shook her head. "If anybody laid a hand on me, Papa would have their head mounted on a stick."

John grinned. "That's good 'cause I'd hate to go up against your pa. He looks like he can handle himself."

"Well, you don't have to worry about that. He isn't going to whip me, but he's going to do something just as bad."

"What can be as bad as a whippin', Miss Caroline?" He grinned at her. "If I remember right, my pa could make an old peach switch beat a pretty snappy tune on my backside."

"Your pa whipped you?" Carrie gasped. "How terrible!"

John threw back his head and laughed. "He only whipped me when I really needed it, and that wasn't too often. I loved Pa, and I rarely disobeyed him."

"I love Papa, too." Carrie said.

"Who's the old man? Your grandfather?"

Carrie shook her head. "Goodness no. I guess I never had a grandfather. Cyrus and Mac are Papa's partners. Oh, dear!" Carrie sighed. "Mac is really going to have himself worked into a lather."

"Why didn't he come with the others?"

"He can't ride. His horse rolled on him about ten years ago and crushed his leg. Since then he's been our biscuit shooter. Maybe you can stay for supper. Mac is a wonderful cook."

"Much as I'd like to, Miss Caroline, I have a job waitin' for me, and I'm afraid I'll have to be movin' on."

They chatted about inconsequential things the rest of the way to the ranch.

A wispy little man wearing Levi's and a plaid flannel shirt hobbled out of the house as soon as the buggy rolled to a stop. "Where you been, little lady? I walked close to ten mile this afternoon, jist worryin' 'bout you, and with this gimpy leg thet's a fur piece." He glared at John. "Well, air you jist goin' to set there gawkin' or air you goin' to help the little lady down?"

John jumped down and ran around the buggy. He reached up and lifted Carrie from the buggy as effortlessly as though she weighed next to nothing.

Her father and Cyrus walked around the buggy to join them. "Mr. Thornton, in all the excitement we forgot to introduce ourselves. The young fellow back there is William Racine. These are my partners, Cyrus Groves and Mac McDougal." Billy grinned and gave a little salute. The other three men shook John's hand.

"I'm Sherman Butler."

John's hand dropped back to his side, and the smile died on his face.

"I have a job offer for you, if you're interested," Butler said.

Of course, they would need someone to replace Jess! Carrie's face lit up.

Surely John would forget the job he was going to and stay. Mac grasped her arm. "I baked somethin' special fer you, little lady. Jist come on inside while they's talkin' business."

Carrie tried to catch John's eye as Mac hurried her away, but he refused to look at her.

That night, John left the bunkhouse and walked out to the corral. After he checked on Jet, he stood in the shadows and looked toward the sprawling ranch house. A couple of hours ago, sixteen men had gathered for supper around the long table in the kitchen. Billy told him that Sherman Butler and his foreman rarely ate with the men—preferring to dine with Butler's daughter—but tonight both he and Cyrus had been present, one at either end of the table.

Funny how things worked out. If a wrangler hadn't been snubbed by Miss Butler and chosen to get revenge. . .If it hadn't stormed. . .If he hadn't just happened to ride along when he did. . .

He had expected it to take days to track down Butler. Instead, Sherman Butler had been dumped right into his lap. Not that he was so crazy about the job he'd accepted. Playing nursemaid to Butler's daughter wasn't going to be easy.

He hadn't seen Caroline after the little man dragged her off to the kitchen. Billy said she didn't fraternize with the hired help. Well, that suited him just fine. She was too beautiful for her own good. Certainly too beautiful for his good. If he wasn't careful, Miss Butler could lead him down roads he would not allow himself to travel.

One by one, the lights in the house were extinguished. John turned and headed back to the bunkhouse.

Chapter 3

When Carrie woke the next morning, she stretched luxuriously, then curled down under the covers. Last evening, watching from her window while John turned his big black gelding into the corral with the other horses, she knew he was staying.

She also knew Papa didn't want her to mingle with the hired hands. He said it would only cause trouble. She had spent the evening trying to think of a way to make Papa see that John was special, and they should spend time together, without letting him know how much she liked him.

It was funny how it had all worked out without her having to do anything.

Last night when Papa had come to tuck her in, he had sat down on the side of her bed and had taken her hand in his. "Caroline Abigail, you could have been killed today. You have always come and gone as you pleased, but from now on, you are not to go out alone. Do you understand?"

She understood all right. Papa had called her by her full name. That meant she wasn't going to like what he had to say. She knew he was going to take away her freedom. And all over some vengeful, love-struck cowboy. It wasn't fair! "But, Papa, it wasn't my fault. Jess Cartwright—"

Papa cut her protests short with a shake of his head. "While Jess Cartwright is mostly at fault for what happened today, you must accept your share of the responsibility. You made some very poor decisions, little girl. When you saw that filly at the hitching rail, you should have asked the boys to hitch up another horse for you. Having failed to do that, you should have taken shelter at the Brauns's until the storm was over."

"But, Papa, I thought I could handle her. Really, I did."

A slight smile tugged at the corner of his mouth. "I'm quite sure you did. But, you must realize that you can't always handle things. Sometimes an older, wiser head is required. That's why I've hired John Thornton. He is to escort you everywhere you go."

After all her scheming and plotting it was to be this simple?

Her father patted her hand. "I'm sorry, Carrie, I know how much you value your freedom, but this is the way it's going to have to be from now on."

Carrie scooted down in bed and turned her face into the pillow. "Does he have to go with me every morning when I ride Brandy?"

"I'm afraid so, honey." Her father stroked her arm as he spoke. "I don't want you to go anywhere without him. Tomorrow morning, I'm sending him out with Billy. After that, Mr. Thornton will be at your beck and call."

He had kissed her, told her again how sorry he was, then left the room.

Just thinking about John Thornton this morning brought a smile. In fact, she'd probably smiled all night while she slept. She jumped from bed and ran to the window. John and Billy were just riding out. Well, Billy could have him today, but after that, he was all hers. Carrie twirled away from the window. As soon as she got dressed, she thought she'd go for a ride.

John and Billy rode all morning, checking cattle, and looking for breaks in the fence. About noon, they stopped at a line shack. "We might as well sit at a table to eat." Billy grinned.

John shrugged his shoulders. "I'd reckon it beats eatin' on the ground."

They left the horses to graze, and John followed Billy into the cabin. Two bunks were built against one wall. A rickety table and two straight chairs occupied a second. A wood-burning stove with a pile of firewood took up the third wall beside it.

"All the comforts of home," Billy said, brushing a spider off the table, along with a thick layer of dust.

"I've seen worse." John set the sack of hardtack and beef jerky Mac had given them that morning on the table. Then he pulled up one of the chairs.

He started to reach for the sack, but stopped short when Billy bowed his head. Last night at supper he'd been surprised when the men joined hands around the table while Butler prayed. Then, this morning, Butler hadn't been there, but one of the other men prayed. Now, Billy was praying. John shook his head. He couldn't figure what Butler was trying to pull. Trying to pass himself off as a God-fearing Christian, he supposed. Well, he might be able to fool some people, but he couldn't fool John Thornton.

Billy looked up and grinned. "There's a few don't hold much with prayin' and Bible readin'. Cyrus, he's the foreman, don't require it, but him and Mr. Butler and Mac is all believers and so is most of the men."

"My folks set quite a store on the Bible and prayer, too," John said.

"That so?" Billy's dark eyes reflected his interest. "Your folks is Christians then?"

"Yeah." John took a big bite of hardtack and washed it down with a swig of water from his canteen.

Billy chewed for a minute. "My pa wasn't much on religion, but my ma took us young'uns to church ever Sunday."

John kept eating.

"I didn't listen to her much after I got a little older," Billy continued. "Guess I kinda figured all that church stuff was for women and little kids. Then, one night I went out with a bunch of fellas. We started drinkin' and shootin' up the town. We didn't mean no harm—we was just havin' ourselves some fun—but the sheriff and his deputies took the destruction of public property serious. Anyway, they shot one of the fellas, and the rest of us ended up in jail."

"That's too bad," John said, interested in spite of himself.

"Yeah! Well, I didn't kill my friend, but I felt responsible for his death. Sittin' there in that jail cell I finally realized if I kept to the path I was on, I'd end up on a coolin' table just like him. When I got out of jail, I decided it was time to make a fresh start. I come here to the Circle C lookin' for work. When they told me they didn't allow no drinkin', nor swearin', nor gamblin', that was fine with me. Drinkin' was what got me in trouble in the first place. I never wanted to see a bottle of whiskey again as long as I lived."

He took a swig from his canteen then wiped his mouth on the back of his hand. "Anyway that was six years ago. It took me a while to start goin' to church, but finally I begin ridin' in with Mr. Butler and the other men. One Sunday mornin' I made a decision that changed my life. I sure wasn't plannin' to walk down that center aisle, but seems like the Spirit just reached out and shook me, and this voice inside me said, 'Now's the time, Billy Racine,' and the next thing I knew—"

"This is all very interestin'." John pushed his chair back from the table. "But I think it's time we were movin' on."

Billy grabbed up the empty sack and followed him outside.

The two men mounted up and rode west. The sun was warm on their heads, and a gentle breeze stirred the tall grass. John turned and looked at Billy. "Butler's got hisself a good size piece of ground here."

Billy nodded. "Four hundred square miles, or thereabouts, I reckon."

Two hundred fifty-six thousand acres. John stared straight ahead, his eyes hard, his face set. "Men like Butler are driven by greed. The more they've got, the more they want, and they don't care how they git it."

"Some, maybe," Billy said. "But, not Sherman Butler and his partners. They started out with nothin', just like me and you. They worked hard for ever'thing they got."

"That so?" John raised a disbelieving eyebrow.

"Sure is," Billy said. "They hitched up together after the war and drifted to

Texas. You're a Texan yourself, ain't you?"

John nodded but offered no additional information, and Billy continued with his story. "Anyway, they stayed in Texas awhile, gathered up a herd of longhorns, and drove them up the Chisholm Trail in '71. Land here was pretty easy to come by then, and this is where the market was, so they just stayed. Mr. Butler had left his wife and baby in Texas. After a year he had a cabin built and was settled in, so he went back for them. His little boy died when he was three. His wife, Miss Caroline, never was real stout, and she died before I come here. Miss Caroline was a real lady, I reckon, and Mr. Butler loved her somethin' fierce. The Circle C's named after her, you know. They've expanded over the years, but I don't reckon it's come easy."

John had listened without comment to Billy's narrative. Now he said, "Well, I reckon we don't all see Butler the same way."

"Sherman Butler is one of the finest men I ever knew." Billy defended his boss.

"I'd reckon there's people in Texas would disagree with you," John said, spurring his horse forward.

They spent the rest of the afternoon mending fence and checking cattle.

They made a good team. Billy liked to talk, and John didn't mind listening.

Late in the afternoon, Billy shaded his eyes and squinted toward the sun. "Must be 'bout four o'clock. Guess we'd better be headin' back. Mac don't take kindly to folks bein' late for supper."

John nodded, and the two men mounted up.

They hadn't been riding long when they topped a rise, and John saw a small grove of trees. He pointed. "Looks like an old homestead."

Billy nodded. "Yep, it is. Wanna take a look?"

John shrugged. "Sure. Why not?" He nudged Jet forward, and Billy followed.

When he drew closer, he saw that the trees were an orchard. He dismounted by the ruined foundation of what had been a small house. A huge tree a short distance from the house provided pleasant shade in the summer.

Billy followed him when he walked over and looked up into the spreading branches of the tree. "Looks like a kid might've had a swing here," he said, pointing up at some frayed scraps of rope swaying in the breeze. John nodded, then turned, and walked away. He paused beside a bed of iris that had been planted against the burned-out foundation of the house. "I wonder how long ago the house burned."

Billy lifted his hat and scratched his head. "Ten or fifteen years ago, I reckon."

He replaced his hat. "It was before I come here. I reckon the folks didn't live here more than a year or so before the house burnt. They must've planted the orchard. The apples just begin bearin' a couple a years ago."

John nodded, then began to walk to the orchard with Billy tagging at his heels.

"The people that lived here is buried right over yonder," Billy said. "Come on! I'll show you."

This time Billy led the way. John stood beside the fence that surrounded the well-tended grave and looked down at the tombstone. "Who put the stone here?"

Billy scratched his head. "I don't rightly know. Mr. Butler, I reckon."

John read the inscription aloud. "In memory of the Nolan family. John. Mavis. And their son, Lucas. Died—August 21, 1880."

John turned, and he and Billy walked back to their horses. The two young men mounted up, nudged their horses into a gallop, and without a backward glance headed toward the bunkhouse and supper.

Chapter 4

After watching John and Billy ride out, Carrie quickly made her bed and straightened the room, then dressed in a soft, tan, full-sleeved shirt, and a brown, ankle-length, divided skirt. She plaited her long, auburn hair into a single braid, and pulled on riding boots. Snatching up a cream-colored, roll-brimmed Stetson, she went to the kitchen.

Mac's sleeves were rolled up past his elbows, his hands and forearms submerged in a large pan of soapy dishwater when she came through the door swinging her hat by the chin strap. Andy Clark, the gangly teenage boy who helped him in the kitchen, was taking the clean dishes from the rinse water, drying them, and then putting them away. They both turned and looked at her. Andy's slightly blemished young face was suffused by an expression of unabashed adoration.

Mac frowned. "Where you think yer goin' in thet git-up, little lady?"

"I'm taking Brandy out for a short run." Carrie grabbed for a biscuit, and Mac slapped at her hand with a soapy spatula.

"You set yourself down there to the table and eat yore breakfast proper, young lady," he growled.

"Haven't got time." Carrie put her hand with the biscuit behind her back, out of Mac's reach.

"You got all the time in the world." Mac dried his hands on the dish towel and reached for a clean plate. "Set down, and I'll rustle you up some grub."

"All I want is some of your delicious apple butter for my biscuit." Carrie looked at him appealingly. "Please, Mac."

"What kind of breakfast is thet fer a growin' girl?" Mac grumbled as he handed her a clean spoon.

"I haven't grown an inch in the last two years," Carrie reminded him, as she moved to the table and spread a generous layer of apple butter on the biscuit.

"Thet's why yer so skinny," Mac said. "If you'd eat proper you'd put some meat on them scrawny little bones."

"I'm not scrawny, am I, Andy?" Carrie smiled at the boy, and his face turned bright red all the way up to the roots of his sandy hair.

"No, ma'am! I think you're the purtiest girl in the whole world."

"Purty is as purty does," Mac growled. "And you ain't goin' nowheres, little lady. Didn't yore pa tell you from now on you ain't leavin' the place 'thout John Thornton goes with you?"

"He told me. But Mr. Thornton rode out with Billy a while ago."

"Then I reckon you'll jist have to wait 'til he rides back, won't you?"

"Papa said Mr. Thornton would start riding with me tomorrow morning. If I go out this morning, I'll have to go alone."

Carrie knew her father had left the ranch earlier so felt perfectly safe adding, in an aggrieved tone, "If you don't believe me you can ask him."

"I ain't questionin' yore word, little lady, but we talked 'bout this yesterday, and we's in agreement you wasn't to go anywheres alone. Yore pa never told me nothin' 'bout yore goin' out alone this mornin'. But I'd reckon if you don't go fur. . ."

Carrie knew the battle was won, and she threw an affectionate arm around the little man's shoulders. "Thanks for the biscuit, Mac. I won't be gone long." She leaned down slightly and planted a kiss on his bristly cheek.

"You don't have to go gettin' all mushy on me." He rubbed the spot she'd kissed. "I reckon it'll be all right this time, if you don't go fur."

"I'd be right proud to go with you, Miss Carrie," Andy said.

"I know you would, and I really appreciate you offering." Carrie's arm dropped from Mac's shoulders. "Maybe some other time." She reached up to pat the boy's cheek as she walked past. "You're turning into a right handsome young man, Andy."

Andy stood next to Mr. McDougal, and together they watched as Carrie went out the door munching on her biscuit.

" 'She walks in beauty like the night,' " Andy murmured.

"What's thet you said?"

The boy's face colored. "Nothin', Mr. McDougal. Just somethin' I read in a book."

" 'She walks in beauty as the night,' " Mac said softly. "Yep, I reckon she does. And so did her ma." He turned his face away for a moment before turning back to scowl at Andy. "I ain't payin' you to gawk at the little lady and spout nonsense from sum book. Now get back to work!"

An hour after she left the ranch, Carrie slid from Brandy's back beside a small pool of crystal-clear water. This was her oasis. Her secret place. She had stumbled across it a couple of years ago and had immediately claimed the spot for her own. A sparkling stream, running swiftly through a grove of trees, cascaded over the rocks in a shimmering waterfall. The dancing water hesitated only long enough to feed the deep pool before spilling over the side and passing swiftly on its way. Carrie found something almost magical in the calm pool with the madly rushing water on either side. The pool was a constant in her life, a circle of serenity.

She knelt on the thick, velvety moss and leaned over. The pebbles on the bottom seemed to lie just below the surface of the water, but Carrie knew the pool was much deeper than it appeared. Once she had tried to measure the depth with a long, slender stick, but had been unable to touch the bottom.

The reflection of the drooping willows formed a frame for her face. Carrie had never been overly concerned with her looks, but now she carefully studied each feature. She liked her eyes. They were big and dark with long, sweeping lashes. The same eyes that looked back at her from the framed portrait of her mother that hung over the fireplace. Her mouth was shaped like Mama's, too. Only it was wider and her lips were fuller. She decided she didn't like her mouth. It was too big. Her nose was short, straight, and pert. She didn't like her nose at all. She had inherited the deep dimples in her softly rounded cheeks and her auburn hair from her father. She liked the dimples and had always thought her hair was nice, but today she wondered if it was too red.

She sat back on her heels and sighed. There was nothing she could do about her face. You just had to take what God gave you and make the best of it. Andy had said she was pretty. She wondered if John thought she was pretty. He'd seemed to think so yesterday, but maybe he'd only been nice because she was—as Lucille always portrayed her in the stories they used to make up—a damsel in distress.

Brandy nudged her shoulder and she scrambled to her feet. "I know," she said, as she took up the reins, "it's time to go home."

The next morning John and Carrie rode together. Some distance from the house they topped a rise. Carrie stopped to let John, who had been trailing several feet behind, catch up. She swept her arm in a wide arc. "Don't you love the view?"

He looked out over the valley below but remained silent.

"The ranch house and all the outbuildings look like a child's toys from up here, don't you think? Look," she pointed to the right of the Butler ranch, "that's the Braun's place over there. Gretchen is one of my best friends. Lucille Jacobs is my other best friend, but she's marrying Jedidiah Smith next month. Gretchen and I are going to be bridesmaids. I was coming from the dressmaker when you saved my life."

Unnerved but undaunted by his silence, Carrie babbled on. "I've known Gretchen and Lucille practically forever. Lucille has an older sister. Her mother is so prissy about everything, but Gretchen's mother is wonderful. She has ten children! Isn't that a lot? Gretchen's the oldest. You know Billy?" She giggled. "Well, of course you do. You spent the whole day with him yesterday. Well, anyway, Billy and Gretchen are sweethearts." Carrie paused to catch her breath.

John turned his head and looked at her with eyes as clear and blue as the sky overhead. "Oh, really? Billy talks almost as much as you do, and he never mentioned a sweetheart to me."

"He didn't?" Carrie frowned. "I certainly won't tell Gretchen. It would break her heart if she knew he wasn't talking about her. She would think he didn't love her."

His gaze returned to the scene spread out before them. "Men have private thoughts, Miss Butler."

Carrie's dark eyes flashed. "Are you implying that women don't have private thoughts?"

"I don't know, do they?"

Carrie's face flamed. She kicked Brandy in the sides. The mare was a full sister to the runaway bay, and didn't need any encouragement to run. Before John realized what was happening, Carrie was racing down the opposite side of the hill.

He watched for a moment as Brandy streaked across the prairie with Carrie leaning low over her neck. "Well, Jet, I reckon we'd better go get them before that fool girl breaks her neck."

Carrie heard the thunder of hoofbeats behind her and urged Brandy on. Glancing over her shoulder, she saw them bearing down on her. She knew Brandy, good as she was, was no match for the big black. Sitting up, she reluctantly reined in.

Jet shot past her then slowed. John turned him with a motion of his body and brought him back to stand beside Brandy. "There's no way that little bay could ever beat Jet, no matter how long her pedigree is."

Carrie's pert little nose shot up in the air. "We could have beat you. We just didn't want to."

His laugh was mocking. "I've never seen anything—thoroughbred or otherwise—that could beat Jet. Certainly not that little fancy-dancy mare."

Carrie drew herself up to protest, and John interrupted. "We'd better get back to the barn, so I can rub these horses down."

"I take care of Brandy myself, thank you." Carrie pulled the little mare around and headed for home.

John trailed behind, watching her erect back. She sat well in the saddle, poised and alert to her mount. Carrie Butler was more woman than he had first suspected.

They rubbed the horses down in silence. When they led them out of the barn, John said, "If you've had your fun for today, I'm goin' to work."

"Fine." Carrie smiled up at him. "Since tomorrow is Sunday, we won't ride, but you will be expected to have the buggy hitched at eight-thirty sharp and escort me to church."

"I don't go to church, Miss Butler, so I'm afraid I must refuse your polite request."

She realized she had sounded a trifle bossy and flushed. "I'm sorry I was rude, but Papa said I was not to go anywhere without you. How am I supposed to go to church if you refuse to escort me?"

"I've heard that almost everybody here goes to town for church on Sunday morning, Miss Butler." He tipped his hat. "I would suggest you ride with your father." He gave her a jaunty little salute and walked away.

Carrie glared at his retreating back. Things certainly weren't going as she had planned. Yesterday when she met him, he seemed interested in her. Today he didn't act as if he even liked her. Her face lit up as a slow smile spread from her full lips to her eyes. John Thornton was the man she was going to marry, whether he realized it or not. And sooner or later he would take her to church.

Chapter 5

As soon as Butler and the entourage from the Circle C left for church the next morning, John saddled Jet and rode out to the west. He watched carefully for familiar landmarks until, topping a gentle rise, he looked down on the old homestead he'd visited on Friday.

He reined Jet in, hooked his leg around the saddle horn, and studied the peaceful scene below him for a short time before kicking his foot into the stirrup and urging Jet down the slope. He dismounted beside the ruins of the foundation and let the reins drop to the ground. The big black lowered his head and began to graze on the tender new grass.

Taking his knife from the scabbard at his waist, John knelt and dug up three of the irises growing beside the old foundation stones. He carried them carefully through the orchard. The fence that enclosed the grave had been put there to keep cows out; it was not so high that he couldn't step over. He knelt and planted the irises. When he was finished he stood looking at the tombstone for several minutes, then stepped back over the fence.

The black gelding was where he had left him. He mounted and rode up the slope the way he had come.

Carrie could hardly wait to tell Gretchen and Lucille about John Thornton. But by the time Mac had parked the buggy, the church bell was pealing out, calling the faithful to worship.

Lucille was on the other side of the church, seated between her parents and Jedidiah. She glanced up when the Butlers slid into their pew, and Carrie waved. Lucille raised her hand in a discreet salute. Mrs. Jacobs frowned at Carrie and poked a sharp elbow into her daughter's ribs. Lucille quickly dropped her hand and turned her attention back to the pulpit.

Carrie, settling down between her father and Mac, wrinkled her nose. Mrs. Jacobs was such a grouch. Poor Lucille! No wonder she'd been in such a hurry to get married. Living with that woman would be practically impossible.

Only one pew separated her from the Brauns. Billy was sitting with Gretchen almost directly in front of her. If only it weren't for the pew between them, she could whisper to Gretchen when they stood for the opening hymn. Since that was an impossibility, she'd have to write a note and figure out some way to pass it to her.

When her father, who was seated next to the aisle, went forward to pass one of the collection plates, Carrie began to rummage through her small handbag for a pencil. Mac nudged her gently and when she glanced up, he scowled at her. She tried to look as innocent as possible, but Mac shook his head slightly before taking her purse and putting it on the seat between him and Cyrus.

Carrie sighed in defeat, then picked up her Bible. She'd just have to wait until after church to tell Gretchen and Lucille about John. Wouldn't they be surprised!

From the number of amens and praises uttered that morning, Brother Carson must have preached a rousing sermon. Carrie wouldn't have known. Although she tried to look attentive, her mind was elsewhere.

After church, Lucille's mother whisked her away before Carrie had a chance to talk to her. And by the time she made her way through the congregation to Gretchen, the Brauns were ready to go. She managed to pull her friend away from Billy only long enough to say, "I've met him, Gretchen! The most wonderful man in the world. The man I'm going to marry."

"Oh, Carrie, how exciting. I wish I had time to hear all about it, but Billy's coming to our house for dinner." One of Gretchen's little brothers grabbed her hand and tugged toward where Billy and the rest of her family were waiting. "I'm going to have to go before Karl pulls my arm off. Come over as soon as you can, and tell me all about it." And with those few words, Gretchen was gone.

Things hadn't worked out at all as she had planned, and Carrie was feeling decidedly grumpy when her father lifted her into the buggy beside Mac. The Circle C crew, including her father and Cyrus, was merely a cloud of dust in the distance by the time Mac pulled out of the churchyard.

"I wish I could ride Brandy to church instead of being stuck in this poky old buggy." Carrie knew she sounded like a whiny five-year-old, but she didn't care.

"Yer jist a might peevish today, ain't you?" Mac looked at her from beneath beetled brows.

Carrie scowled back at him. "Nothing went right this morning."

"Thet ain't true, little lady." Mac shifted the reins to his left hand and made a sweeping gesture with his right arm. "Jist you look at all the beauty the Lord has surrounded us with. And, if'n thet ain't enough, He's allowed us to spend these last few hours in His house. They's lots of people would give their eyeteeth to have what we enjoyed today. Ain't thet right?"

Carrie shifted restlessly on the buggy seat. "Yes, Mac. I am thankful for all that I have, but still. . ."

Mac took the reins in both hands, and they rode in silence for the next mile. Finally, Mac said, "Thet was a mighty fine sermon Brother Carson preached this mornin'." He glanced at Carrie. "Didn't you think so?"

Carrie squirmed in her seat. "Yes, it was. Very inspiring," she murmured.

"If it were so inspirin'," Mac said as his faded blue eyes seemed to look into her heart, "what was it about?"

"You mean the topic?" Carrie looked everywhere but at the old man. "Well, I think it was about Jesus and. . .and. . .Nicodemus," she finished triumphantly. "It was about being born again."

Mac grunted. "You was either payin' more attention than I thought, or you jist made a lucky guess."

"I was listening," Carrie muttered.

"No you wasn't. You did more squirmin' round than a flea on a hot stove. Church is fer worshipin', little lady, not fer woolgatherin'. You'd best be rememberin' thet."

Sunday was a bad day for Carrie. Mac scolded her. She didn't catch a glimpse of John all day. And worse even than these things, she hadn't been able to talk to her friends. She knew she would burst if she didn't tell Gretchen about the wonderful turn her life had taken only four days ago.

Monday morning started off on a promising note. John was almost civil when Carrie told him of her plans to go to the Brauns'. Though he didn't say anything to her on the ride, she was encouraged.

When she turned in at the Brauns' gate, John followed. She stopped at the hitching rail and dismounted.

John stayed in the saddle. She tipped her head back and looked up at him. "Aren't you going to get off your horse?"

"I'll be back for you in a couple of hours." John turned Jet and started back down the lane.

How were Gretchen and her mother going to see him if he just dumped her on the doorstep like some unwanted parcel and rode away? "I thought you'd wait for me."

He glanced back over his shoulder. "I reckon you thought wrong, Miss Butler. I'll be back in two hours."

Carrie wrapped the reins loosely around the hitching rail while she watched him ride away. "Sometimes I'd like to shoot him," she muttered in Brandy's ear.

Gretchen's mother—an older, plumper version of Gretchen—opened the door, a small baby cradled in one arm. She reached out and drew Carrie inside with her free arm. "Gretchen told me last night that you had met someone special." She peered over Carrie's shoulder. "Where is your young man going? I thought you'd bring him in to meet us."

"He had some things to do. Perhaps when he comes back for me. . ."

The baby had been fussing, now he began to howl. "You'll have to excuse me, Carrie. This one wants his breakfast. Gretchen's in the kitchen feeding the little ones."

Carrie found her friend shoveling oatmeal into a balky two year old, at the same time she was urging two towheaded little boys to eat. "I can talk as soon as I get these three fed," she said, as she hurried by on her way to the stove. "Katy is overseeing the bed-making. Soon as she's finished she'll take over here, and we can visit." She plopped a steaming cup of tea on the table. "Here, sit down and drink this while you wait. And try not to spill it."

Carrie sat sipping her tea while her friend dashed around, alternately shoveling food into her little sister's mouth, wiping up the two boys' messes, and washing dishes.

Carrie didn't know how Gretchen did it, but by the time her tea was finished, she had fed all three children, washed and dried the dishes and put them away, and had the kitchen in order.

Fourteen-year-old Katy came to relieve her, and Gretchen and Carrie escaped to the bedroom Gretchen shared with Katy and the two year old. The room was already in order, so Gretchen dropped into a chair. Not seeming to know what to do with her idle hands, she picked up a crochet hook and a ball of thread and began to work on a half-completed doily.

"So, tell me all about him!" she said.

Carrie quickly told Gretchen how she met John. Then, she concluded by saying, "He rode out of the storm and rescued me, and I knew as soon as I saw him that he was the man I would marry."

Gretchen had been listening very carefully and without comment. Now she laid her crocheting to one side. "I don't know, Carrie. You say he's very handsome. Are you sure you aren't just drawn to him because he's good-looking?"

"Of course not." Carrie drew herself up indignantly. "I'm not a flighty female who falls in love with the first man who looks her way."

"I didn't say you were," Gretchen said. "It's only that this man is a stranger to you. You didn't even know he existed four days ago."

Carrie laughed. "But that's the wonderful thing. The first time I saw John I felt this flash of recognition. It was like I had known him forever."

"But you haven't, Carrie." Gretchen leaned forward and fixed her luminous blue eyes on her friend. "Where did he come from?"

"Texas." Carrie replied, promptly. "See! I do know something about him."

"But, not enough. Does he have any family? For all you know he could have a wife. And, if he is from Texas, what brought him here?"

"I think God brought him here so we could meet. And if that's true, then he couldn't have a wife. Now, could he?"

"That brings up the most important question of all. What are his beliefs? Is he a Christian?"

"I don't know. I only know that I love him. I thought you'd be happy that I had finally found someone."

"Oh, Carrie, I love you. And I want to be happy for you. But, please! Please! Ask some questions."

Carrie nodded. "If you think it's that important, I will."

The two girls spent the remainder of their two-hour visit talking about the wedding. Katy tapped on the door to announce, "There's a man on a big, black horse outside, Carrie. Is he for you?"

"Yes, he's for me," Carrie answered and grabbed her hat. "Now, you'll see him," she told Gretchen, "and when you do, you'll understand why I love him."

But by the time the girls came out on the porch, John was already halfway to the main road. He appeared to be waiting for her, but not too patiently.

At the end of the lane he fell in behind her and remained there until Carrie reined Brandy in and turned in her saddle to look at him. "Why don't you ride up here so we can talk?"

He stopped a horse length behind her. "We have nothin' to talk about, Miss Butler. Besides, I was told that you didn't fraternize with the hired help."

"I don't usually, but if we're going to spend time together, it would be nice if I knew something about you."

"We aren't keeping company, Miss Butler. I'm being paid to do a job, and I'm doing it. If my work isn't satisfactory, perhaps you should find someone more to your liking."

Every one of his carefully enunciated words struck at her heart with the force of a physical blow, but she managed to smile. "I find you quite satisfactory, Mr. Thornton." Then, remembering Gretchen's admonition to find out more about him, she said, "But there is one thing I would really like to know."

He cocked an eyebrow, which she interpreted as permission. "Are you married?"

"No, Miss Butler, I am not, nor have I ever been married. A man in my line of work can't afford the worry of a family."

She wanted to ask what his line of work was, but before she had the opportunity, he said, "Miss Butler, I suggest we head back to the ranch. I have work to do, even if you don't."

She nudged Brandy, and they galloped the rest of the way home a full fifty feet ahead of the man on the big black gelding.

John left Carrie at the barn rubbing down the little bay and rode to the west. He spent the remainder of the day mending fence and checking what cattle he came upon. There was always a threat of fire on the dry prairie, but the danger was intensified in the spring when the high winds could fan the smallest spark into a raging inferno and send it sweeping across hundreds of acres in a matter of hours, destroying everything in its path. He had seen several prairie fires and kept a constant watch for smoke.

Of necessity, John had lived a solitary life. He had never minded the loneliness before, but today the image of a beautiful redhead with a mouth made for kissing was never far from his thoughts.

That evening after supper, John sat in the bunkhouse listening to the other men talk. They had tried to draw him into conversation the first couple of days. He had been polite enough, but at the same time, he held himself aloof, rarely speaking unless addressed directly.

Only Billy still went out of his way to be friendly. The others had taken in his appearance. The short-barreled Colt Peacemaker 45 with the well-worn grip tied low on his narrow hip. The Winchester .44.40 with the calibrated rear sight he carried in the scabbard on the big black gelding. The steely watchfulness of his blue eyes. His taciturnity.

They considered all these things and put him down as a man with a past he was trying to forget. A gunfighter. Or, a man on the run. Most of them had been in the same position at one time or another and, without animosity, allowed him his privacy.

When one of the men picked up his guitar and began to strum a familiar tune, John felt the room closing in on him. Feeling as though he were suffocating, he walked out the door.

He paused to breathe in the cool, early spring air. Then, as a man began to sing, he walked to the corral. The words followed him. "Amazing grace how sweet the sound. . ."

Jet came to the fence and nudged his shoulder. He stroked his horse's neck and Jet whoofed contentedly. Even over the soft sound of the horse, he heard the familiar words.

Pushing away from the corral, he walked to the barn where he could no longer hear the guitar or the sound of the man's voice. But the words of the old hymn were not so easily escaped. From the deepest depths of his memory a sweet feminine alto sang: "The Lord has promised good to me; His word my hope secures; He will my shield and portion be as long as life endures."

He regained his composure as he stood in the shadows watching the ranch house. One by one, the lights were extinguished. He thought of the girl in one of those darkened rooms. And, he thought of her father, and of the job that had brought him here. Finally, he returned to the now silent bunkhouse.

Chapter 6

Determined to put John Thornton out of her life, Carrie gave up her morning rides. For the remainder of that week, she stayed close to the house, only leaving to ride into town with her father on Sunday. During her self-imposed exile, she caught glimpses of John and silently berated herself when her heart leaped. She was a fool! John Thornton would never love her. He didn't even like her. By week's end, she knew that, while she might put the good-looking wrangler out of her life, it was not going to be so easy to put him out of her heart.

Sunday night after her father tucked her in and put out her light, she decided her room felt a bit stuffy and got up to open the window. Breathing in the clean air, she lifted her eyes to the heavens. It was a beautiful night. Millions of pin-point diamonds of light lit the dark velvet sky.

The spring after her mother died, her father had been too wrapped up in his own grief to comfort her, so Cyrus and Mac had stepped in to fill the void in her life. She remembered sitting on the porch on Cyrus's lap. They had talked about Mama and about heaven where Mama lived now. While they talked, he had pointed out the different constellations to her.

Now, ten years later, she remembered and searched the heavens for the constellations. The Big and Little Dipper were easy. Some of the others were more difficult, but finally, using the Big Dipper as a reference, she found them. Leo, the lion. Gemini, the twins. Arcturus. And, lastly, Virgo, the virgin.

As she turned away from the window, a small movement in the shadows beside the barn caught her eye. Someone was standing there watching her window. Instinctively, she knew that the figure was John. She waited for several minutes before returning to her bed.

Early the next morning, her resolve to win John's love rekindled, she burst into the kitchen where her father sat eating his breakfast. "Papa, Mrs. Wright told me at church yesterday that our dresses are ready for the first fitting. I need John to escort me into town this morning." She bent and kissed his cheek. "Will you have him hitch the buggy for me?"

He set his coffee cup down. "Sit down and eat, Carrie."

"But, Papa, we need to go early and. . ." She dropped into her chair. "Those pancakes do look delicious. I guess I have time for one, Mac."

Mac turned from the stove and frowned at her. "You been moonin' round here all week like a dyin' calf in a hailstorm. No more than you been eatin' one pancake ain't even a start, little lady." He limped over and set a steaming stack in front of her. "You clean these up!"

She grinned up at him. "If I eat all these I'll be too fat for my dress for sure."

The old man cuffed her affectionately, then limped back to the stove.

A huge pat of yellow butter was already melting and running down the sides of the golden-brown stack of pancakes. Carrie added warmed sorghum.

Between luscious mouthfuls, she talked. "Just wait until you see me in my dress, Papa."

His pride was evident in his smile. "I'm sure you'll outshine the bride."

"Papa!" She scolded. "That wasn't nice. Lucille is really quite attractive."

"I was not passing judgment on the bride's beauty, little girl. I was simply remembering your mother and thinking how much you look like her. Caroline was the most beautiful woman in Texas. I never could understand why such a fine lady agreed to hitch up with a penniless wrangler like me."

"I know why, Papa." Carrie's voice was subdued. "And I'm glad you think I look like her. But I'm also glad I have your red hair and dimples."

Cyrus chose that moment to come in the back door. He patted Carrie on the head. "Did you leave anything fer me, young'un?"

"There's plenty left, but I ain't goin' to wait on you." Mac grunted, and sat down at the table.

Cyrus took a heaping plate from the warming oven and joined them. "Well, I reckon they won't kill me," he said.

"Them are the finest pan cookies you'll ever put a fork to," Mac grumbled. "If you'd stuff your mouth 'stead of runnin' it, you'd know that."

The two old friends exchanged several insults before they bowed their heads and offered thanks. Carrie, remembering she hadn't prayed, dutifully bowed her head.

When she raised her head, her father was looking at her. She smiled sheepishly. "I guess I was so excited about going to town I forgot."

"Seems to me you've been fergettin' a lot lately," Mac muttered.

The three men exchanged glances. Then her father said, "You will be stopping by for Gretchen, won't you?"

"Oh, yes! She'll need to try her dress on, too. That's why I forgot—about praying, I mean—I was excited about spending the morning with Gretchen."

She looked down at her plate. "There's one more thing, Papa." A faint pink tinged her cheeks. "I have to have a. . ." She raised her head and looked from her father to Mac to Cyrus, to Andy—who had been sitting across the table gazing at her with worshipful eyes ever since she sat down—then back to her father. "Mrs. Wright says I have to have a. . .a corset."

Andy's face was even redder than hers as he got up and hastily left the room.

"Is that so?" Her father shook his head. "What's Mrs. Wright trying to do? Make a grown-up lady of my little girl?"

Carrie glanced at Cyrus and Mac, expecting some comment, but they were suddenly busy with their pancakes.

"It's the dress, Papa. I tried to convince her to make it looser, but she insisted that wouldn't be stylish. I won't be able to button it at the waist without one."

Her father's expression grew thoughtful. Carrie had only been eight when her mother died, but she had come to recognize that faraway look in her father's blue eyes. He was thinking about Mama. "When Caroline knew the end was near, she had me pack some things to keep for you until you were older."

The thought of her mother thinking of her while she lay dying brought tears to Carrie's eyes. She impatiently brushed them away.

"I'll go tell John to hitch the buggy. While you're gone we'll put the trunk in your room. If what you want isn't there, I'm sure Mrs. Wright can supply the necessary item of apparel."

Carrie pushed her chair back. "You finish your breakfast. I'll find Mr. Thornton."

John wasn't difficult to find. He was leaning against the barn picking his teeth with a straw.

She greeted him with a wide smile. "You are to hitch up the buggy and escort me to town."

He straightened and threw the straw aside. "Certainly, miss." He tipped his hat. "I live to serve your every whim."

Her smile faded. "Hitch up the little bay. The one I was using the day of the storm."

"Really?" His smile was insolent. "Sure you can handle her?"

She had intended to ask him to drive her, but his arrogance brought out her stubborn streak. An angry flush tinted her smooth cheeks. "You aren't being paid to question my orders," she snapped, and immediately wished she could recall her hasty words.

A muscle jerked in his cheek as he choked back an angry retort. Turning on his heel, he stalked to the corral. Taking a coiled rope from the fence post, he effortlessly lassoed a placid brown mare.

She started to make a caustic remark about his lack of ability with a lasso, but bit back the words and stalked into the ranch house while he hitched the mare up to the buggy and saddled Jet. On the drive to the Brauns', he rode just far enough behind the buggy to make conversation difficult, if not impossible.

When they reached the Brauns', John dismounted and handed Gretchen into the buggy. He even smiled at her. A nice friendly smile, not the superior smirk he reserved for Carrie. Then, he resumed his silent vigil several hundred feet behind the buggy.

As soon as he was out of earshot Gretchen clutched Carrie's arm. "Oh, Carrie! I can't believe it." Her blue eyes danced with excitement. "He is 'The Mysterious Stranger.' Right down to the dimple in his chin. Only he's even more handsome than we imagined."

Carrie glanced at her friend. "I didn't want to say anything before for fear it would be prejudicial, but you can see it, too." She turned her attention back to the road. "The only problem is, I don't think he likes me much."

"Oh, Carrie!" Gretchen squeezed the other girl's clenched fist. "Of course he likes you. How could he not? After all he is 'The Mysterious Stranger.'"

"I don't know." Carrie shrugged. "Everything I say or do makes him angry."

"Oh, I see." The other girl smiled knowingly. "You had a little tiff."

It wasn't little, and it was much more than a tiff. But Carrie straightened her back and lifted her chin. "Gretchen, if it's the last thing I do, I'm going to marry John Thornton."

"Oh, I don't know about that, Carrie." A slight frown creased the other girl's smooth forehead. "I mean the 'Mysterious Stranger' was just made up, like in a fairy tale. John Thornton is a real, live person."

"I know," Carrie giggled. "Isn't it wonderful?"

"But like I said before, Carrie," Gretchen said, glancing over her shoulder at the man trailing their buggy, "you don't know anything about this man."

Carrie laughed. "Of course I do. After we left your house on Monday, I asked him about himself, just like you told me to."

"Oh, good." Gretchen visibly relaxed. "Then he is a Christian."

Carrie shifted in the seat. "Well, that's not exactly what I asked him."

"Why not?"

"Well, my goodness, Gretchen, that's a pretty personal question." She slanted a glance at her friend. "Don't you think?"

"I most assuredly do not think so." She shifted in the seat to face Carrie. "Exactly what did you ask Mr. Thornton?"

"I asked him if he was married. And he's not." She favored the other girl with a triumphant smile. "So there."

"If John Thornton doesn't share your faith, you'd best just forget him. After all, he's not the only man in the world."

"No," Carrie's brown eyes were serious. "But he's the only man I will ever want."

"Carrie, you know what it says in the Bible about being unequally yoked together with unbelievers."

"You worry too much, Gretchen." Carrie reached out and patted the other girl's arm. "We've never had an argument in our life. Let's not quarrel about this."

She flicked the reins and the horse broke into an easy canter.

———

John watched until the two girls were in the dress shop before leaving to attend to some personal errands.

Carrie tried her dress on first. No matter how much she sucked in her breath, it failed to meet around the waist.

Mrs. Wright clucked disapprovingly. "You simply must have a corset if your dress is to fit properly, Carrie."

"I know and I will have one," Carrie promised. "I'm going to look for one in Mama's trunk this afternoon."

"Caroline was a beautiful lady. She wouldn't have dreamed of venturing out without a corset." The dressmaker's plump face relaxed in a relieved smile.

"I'm sure she had several."

"We will turn up the hem and pin it today. When you come for your final fitting be sure and bring the corset." She adjusted a few gathers. "I think this will do quite nicely once you have the proper foundation garment."

Carrie twirled in front of the long mirror, being careful to not step on the unhemmed skirt. "I think it's lovely, don't you, Gretchen?"

"Yes, it's very pretty," Gretchen agreed.

"Try yours on while Mrs. Wright turns up my hem!"

When Gretchen stepped out from behind the screen, Carrie caught her breath.

"You are so beautiful, Gretchen."

The other girl blushed. "You've just never seen me in anything this fancy."

The dressmaker stepped forward and made a few minor adjustments. "You see what a difference a corset makes in the fit?" she said.

Even with a corset, Gretchen's waist was a couple of inches larger than hers, but Carrie nodded her head. The corset did make a difference. "You've done a wonderful job, Mrs. Wright."

The dressmaker beamed her appreciation.

Chapter 7

John was just riding up when the girls emerged from the dressmaker's shop.

"Where have you been?" Carrie asked as soon as he dismounted. Though it was obvious from his freshly shaven face where he'd been.

"I've been to the barbershop, Miss Butler." His blue eyes were cold. "I didn't realize I needed your permission to go for a shave and a haircut."

"No. . .no, you don't," she stammered. "I just meant you look so. . .so. . ." Breathtakingly handsome was the phrase that came to her mind. "Much nicer," she finished lamely.

John scowled at her, then turned to the other girl with a smile that rivaled the noonday sun.

"Miss Gretchen?" He handed her into the buggy, then putting one foot in the stirrup, swung lightly into the saddle, leaving Carrie standing in the street.

He tipped his hat. "As soon as you are ready, Miss Butler, we'll be on our way."

She climbed into the buggy and picked up the reins with trembling hands. The buggy moved out into the street, and John fell in behind.

It began to sprinkle just as they rode into the Butler's barn lot, and it showered intermittently the rest of the afternoon. That night the heavens opened, and rain fell for several days.

Confined to the house, Carrie's dark mood matched the stormy weather. Her father had brought her mother's trunk in and left it in the corner of her room. She found the corset on top, underneath a large Bible, but she didn't have the energy to explore further. She removed the corset, replaced the Bible, and closed the lid.

She spent the rest of the week sleeping and moping around the house. She whiled away one whole afternoon sitting on the couch gazing at the portrait of her mother that hung above the fireplace. In the portrait, her black hair was loose and cascaded down over her shoulders in shimmering waves. Her smooth dark skin, large soulful eyes, and high-bridged nose spoke of the touch of Spanish blood that flowed through her veins. A hint of a smile played at the corners of her well-shaped mouth.

Carrie tried to remember her. She had fragments of memory of her mother before she got sick. But most of her memories were of a beautiful, frail woman who spent most of her days in the big bed in Papa's room. She could remember the soft silkiness of a nightdress. A light flowery scent mingled with a medicine smell. The gentleness of a thin hand on her hair. Her mother had slept more and more that last winter. Then one morning she didn't wake up. A week later she died.

She couldn't remember the funeral. Only that she had cried and cried. And Papa hadn't. He had drawn his grief around himself like an impenetrable cloak. Finally, he had gone away for a week. When he came back, except for the sadness that still lingered in the depths of his blue eyes, he was the attentive, loving Papa she had always known.

Where had Papa been that week? She went to the only person she thought might give her an answer.

Mac was sitting in a rocking chair in front of the massive fireplace with his bad leg propped up on a footstool. She pulled up a chair facing him and sat down.

He laid aside the newspaper he'd been reading and peered at her over the round wire-rimmed glasses that perched on the tip of his nose. "You look like you'd been sent fer and couldn't go. What's ailin' you, little lady?"

"I've been looking at the portrait of Mama. When Papa left after Mama's funeral, where did he go?"

Mac took off his glasses, reached into his pocket, and pulled out a large bandanna. First, he scrubbed at his eyes then polished his glasses until they shone. "That fireplace must be smokin' agin."

He pushed himself out of the chair and picked up the poker. Carrie sat patiently while he poked at the fire.

Mac put the poker back in its stand by the fireplace, and hobbled over to the cabinet. "When we first come here we cooked in thet fireplace. We didn't have nothin' like this here stove back then."

Carrie knew the huge black and chrome range was Mac's pride and joy, but she didn't want to hear about it. "Where did Papa go, Mac?"

"I got work to do, little lady. Why don't you just have a slab of this here chocolate cake I baked in the oven of my nice range, and forget them questions?"

"But, I really want to know where. . ."

"Your pa took his Bible and a jug of water and went up to one of the line shacks. Now, get you a piece of this here cake and quit pesterin' me."

"Forevermore, Mac! I'm not a child. I want to know, what did he do up there? Please, Mac," Carrie's big brown eyes begged. "You're the only one who ever tells me anything."

"Humph!" Mac snorted, but there was a pleased expression in his faded blue eyes.

Carrie pressed her advantage. "What did Papa do at the line shack?"

"I'd reckon he found somethin' he'd been a-lookin' fer a long time." Mac tied a large white apron around his skinny middle. "If'n yer goin' to stay here pesterin' you might as well peel spuds."

Carrie pushed her chair back under the table. "I'll just leave," she said, and swept majestically from the room.

The rain ended the next afternoon, and the warm May sun made its welcome appearance. Carrie found John in the small corral with a bronco. The animal was already snubbed down to the breaking post, and John was standing in front of the big red gelding, stroking his neck, and talking softly to him.

Carrie hadn't seen this gentleness in John since the day he rescued her, and she stood quietly watching, until he looked up and saw her. He ambled across the corral to her. "Is there somethin' I can do for you, Miss Butler?"

"Gretchen and I need to go into town. Will you hitch the buggy up, please?"

"I'll have it ready in half an hour. I would like to clean up a bit before we go. If that's all right with you."

Carrie nodded, and went in the house to wait. He hadn't seemed overly happy to see her, but at least he hadn't been rude. Maybe John had missed her this past week, as much as she had missed him.

Gretchen and Carrie spent the night before the wedding with Lucille. They were too excited to sleep, and the three friends laughed and talked until well into the night.

The next morning, Lucille's mother hovered over her daughter, helping her dress. Carrie, knowing that her own mother would never see her in her wedding dress, felt a twinge of sadness, but she quickly put her selfish thoughts aside. This was Lucille's day.

Gretchen laced Carrie's corset so tight she protested. "Gretchen! If you pull those strings any tighter, my eyes are going to pop out! Then I'll never trap John."

The other two girls giggled, but Lucille's mother clicked disapprovingly. "Young ladies do not trap husbands, Carrie."

She turned to the other two. "Lucille, you and Gretchen are dressed. I would like to speak with Carrie in private. Would you mind going into the spare room to finish your primping?" She glanced at the small clock on her daughter's dresser. "We will only be a few minutes."

"Yes, Mama." Lucille gathered up her skirt and left without a backward glance.

Carrie rolled her eyes. This wasn't the first lecture she had received from her friend's mother.

Gretchen smiled at her sympathetically before pulling the door closed behind them.

"Carrie, it has been my intention to speak to you for some time, but with planning the wedding and all. . ."

"I know we've all been very busy," Carrie murmured in agreement. "But you most of all," she added hastily. "I know most of the work has fallen on your shoulders, and you've done a marvelous job."

Flattery might work with Mac and Cyrus and her father, but Mrs. Jacobs was made of sterner stuff. "Your mother was a beautiful woman, Carrie."

"Yes, she was," Carrie agreed.

"Caroline was not merely beautiful on the outside, she had a beautiful spirit as well. Your mother loved the Lord with all her heart, Carrie. She was a good and faithful servant right up to the day she died."

"That's what Mac told me," Carrie said.

"I feel very fortunate to have been friends with your mother, Carrie." Mrs. Jacobs lifted a delicately embroidered hankie to the corner of her eye. "Did you know Caroline led me to the Lord?"

Carrie shook her head. She hadn't known.

"Well, she did. Then I was able to bring Nels, and later our two girls to a saving knowledge of Jesus Christ. I will be forever grateful for what Caroline did for me and my family."

Carrie thought of the Bible in her mother's trunk. "I think I remember Mama reading her Bible."

"I'm quite certain you do. Caroline read her Bible faithfully. She was the one who impressed on me how very important it was to find time every day to read the Word and pray. A quiet time, she called it. A time to be alone in communion with our Savior." She patted Carrie's arm. "That is one of the things I wanted to talk to you about, Carrie. I know your mother would want you to follow her example. How long has it been since you sat down and really read your Bible?"

"I read my Bible," Carrie protested. "Maybe not every day, but I don't always have time."

"You are an avid reader, Carrie. You find time to read novels. You find time to ride. You always have time to visit your friends. Why do you have time for the wood, hay, and stubble of this life, but no time for the gold and silver? The things of eternal value."

"I go to church every Sunday."

"Yes you do. And, that's a credit to your father and his two friends. Sherman has done a wonderful job of raising you, Carrie."

Carrie dug the toe of her slipper into the rug. "I love Papa, and Mac, and Cyrus."

"I'm quite sure you do." Mrs. Jacobs took Carrie's dress from its hanger. "I'll help with your buttons while we finish our little talk."

She slipped the dress carefully over Carrie's upswept hairdo. While Carrie adjusted the folds of the skirt, the older woman stepped behind her and began to work the tiny buttons through the looped buttonholes.

"They love you too, Carrie. So much so, that they can't see your faults. Therefore, I feel it is my duty to have this talk with you. I doubt that you have ever cooked a meal in your life. Your housekeeping duties consist of making your own bed. And, worst of all, I fear church has merely become a place you go to socialize. I was there when you and Gretchen went to the altar. My heart rejoiced when you two girls were saved. Gretchen has matured into a fine Christian young woman, but you, Carrie. . .I don't believe you have grown in your faith one iota."

Carrie glanced pointedly at the clock.

"Yes, we have to go in a few minutes." Mrs. Jacobs slipped the last button through its loop. "You are of a marriageable age, Carrie. Surely you want a husband and babies. . .every woman does."

She put her hands on Carrie's shoulders and turned the girl to face her. "It takes more than a pretty face and figure to attract a suitable husband. A man wants a wife with a sweet, submissive spirit—a godly woman he can depend on to manage his home and raise his children."

Mrs. Jacobs began to gather up her things, and Carrie sensed freedom. "Thank you for talking to me, ma'am. If you are finished, I think I'll go see if Lucille needs me." Her hand was on the doorknob when Mrs. Jacobs reached out to put a restraining hand on her arm. "There is one other thing, Carrie—this John Thornton you are so infatuated with."

Carrie groaned inwardly. She should have known she wasn't going to get away so easily.

"I haven't seen young Mr. Thornton in church even once since he's been here."

"John is a good man," Carrie protested weakly.

"Good is not enough." Mrs. Jacobs frowned. "We, as Christians, are not to be unequally yoked together with unbelievers. It is best you forget this man, Carrie."

She released the younger woman's arm, allowing Carrie to escape at last.

Finally, dressed in their wedding finery, they rode to the church in the Jacobs' buggy.

While the bride and groom exchanged vows, Carrie's thoughts drifted to John. Would they ever stand where Lucille and Jedidiah were standing now? Would John ever look at her with love in his eyes, and promise to cherish her forever? Lucille's mother said men like to feel protective toward a woman. She said if Carrie ever wanted a young man to love her, she was going to have to behave in a more ladylike manner. Maybe Mrs. Jacobs was right. Maybe she would have to learn to act helpless, and flirt, like some of the girls she had gone to school with, such as Becky Colton. She certainly had no trouble attracting any man who caught her eye.

"You may kiss the bride," the minister's voice interrupted Carrie's musings.

She watched as her friends exchanged a tender kiss, and her determination to become a lady was strengthened. As soon as she got back to the ranch, she was going to introduce John Thornton to the new Carrie Butler.

John was on the way to the breaking corral when he saw the Butler's buggy coming up the lane. He stopped in front of the barn to watch as Butler reached up and lifted Carrie down. She scanned the barn lot, then walked slowly toward him. As she came closer, he saw that she was wearing something frilly and green. The dress set off her upswept red hair and flawless, lightly tanned skin to perfection. He couldn't control the rapid beat of his heart, but he managed to keep his face an expressionless mask.

She greeted him with a wide smile. "Oh, Mr. Thornton, you should have been at the wedding."

"I've been to weddin's, Miss Butler. In my experience they are all pretty much the same."

"Oh, but this one was different." Her eyes sparkled. "You'll never guess what happened."

It was almost impossible to not respond to her, but he managed. He'd spent a lifetime hiding his feelings. "No, I don't reckon I will. I was never good at playin' games, Miss Butler."

Carrie refused to let his indifference dampen her spirits. "Billy proposed to Gretchen and she accepted." She hugged herself and her joy bubbled over. "Isn't that the most romantic thing you ever heard of?"

A long denied emotion stirred inside John. He struggled against it. And won.

"Romantic?" He lifted an arrogant eyebrow.

Carrie caught her breath. He was the most exasperating man she had ever known. "Yes, romantic. Gretchen caught Lucille's bouquet, which means that she will be the next one married. And Billy walked up to her right then and there and asked her to marry him. Right in front of all the wedding guests. Practically the whole town was there."

"Practically the whole town, huh? Well, I guess with that many witnesses old Billy is hog-tied, and as good as branded." An amused smile tugged at the corner of his mouth before he could suppress it. "I'll be sure to give the poor fellow my condolences."

Carrie was sure she had seen him smile. Just a hint of a smile. But a smile nevertheless. Remembering her resolve, she batted her eyes and giggled. "Why, Mr. Thornton! What an absolutely horrible thing to say."

John looked at her a bit strangely. "If you don't need me, Miss Butler, I have a wild bronco waiting for me." A sudden, overwhelming urge to show off for her gripped him. "Perhaps you'd like to come watch."

Carrie's heart jumped, then she remembered. A real lady would never hang on a corral fence cheering on a broncobuster. "My goodness, Mr. Thornton." She fluttered her eyelashes at him. "The breaking corral is no place for a lady."

"Fine. Have it your way, Miss Butler." He tipped his hat and started to turn away.

"Mr. Thornton." He turned back to face her. "Please be careful," she said softly.

The gaze of her dark eyes caught and held his for one precious moment. Then he touched the brim of his hat and walked away.

Chapter 8

Carrie watched John climb over the corral fence before turning toward the house. She wished she could have gone with him. But since she couldn't, her top priority at the moment was to change into some more comfortable clothes.

As soon as she was in her room, she began struggling and straining to undo the row of tiny buttons down the back of her dress. She'd had misgivings about wearing a corset, but the spark of interest she had detected in John's blue eyes made it seem worthwhile.

She finally unbuttoned the last button and slipped the dress off her shoulders, letting it fall to the floor. She looked at herself in the mirror and was pleased with what she saw. She realized the corset emphasized her small waist and full bosom, but besides the fact that it was terribly uncomfortable, she couldn't wear anything she couldn't put on by herself. Mrs. Wright had said her mother wouldn't dream of leaving the house without her corset. In this womanless household, how had Mama managed to lace herself up?

"Of course," a faint blush touched her cheeks, "Papa must have laced her corset."

She reached behind her back and struggled to undo the laces that Gretchen had pulled so tightly. She breathed a sigh of relief as she folded the corset, and laid it on top of Mama's trunk to be put away later. When she hung her dress in the wardrobe, she rifled through the other garments hanging there. She hesitated over a navy riding skirt, then selected a more feminine green gored skirt and a matching shirtwaist in a green print.

She had just finished dressing when the activity outside drew her to the window. She pulled the lace curtains aside. A billowing cloud of dust rose in the breaking corral. A group of men sat on the weathered rail fence, or leaned against it, calling encouragement to the man on the wild bronco.

Captivated by the excitement, she sank to the floor in front of the open window. With her arms crossed on the low windowsill, she was able to catch only an occasional glimpse of the man and the horse. The breaking of wild broncos was as much as part of ranch life as roundups and branding. She had sat on the corral fence watching dozens of horses broken with never a thought for the man in the saddle, but this time was different. Even knowing this must be the final breaking of the big red gelding, she expected the rider to be thrown at any moment. A thrill of fear passed through her along with a silent prayer, *Please, Lord, don't let John be hurt.*

John stuck to the saddle like glue—the breaking rope wrapped around one gloved hand, the other hand uplifted—while the horse twisted and turned in a futile attempt to remove the man from his back.

Finally, the bronco came down in a series of stiff-legged, bone-jarring leaps that failed to unseat the rider. Cheers rose from the watching men as the big gelding trotted around the inner periphery of the corral. Someone swung the corral gate open, and the horse and rider—the conquered and the conqueror—galloped through and disappeared in a cloud of dust.

The crowd around the corral broke up as the men returned to their duties. Carrie saw her father, Cyrus, and Mac walking toward the house, and quickly moved back, letting the curtain drop. The three men were involved in earnest conversation as they approached her window and Carrie unabashedly eavesdropped.

Her father said, "I'd say that young man has proven his abilities."

Cyrus nodded. "He knows his job all right, and seems to enjoy it."

"Enjoys it too well, if you ask me. I wouldn't trust him fur as I could throw 'im, and with this gimpy leg that ain't fur," Mac grumbled.

"Have you had trouble with him?" Sherman frowned down at Mac.

"Nuttin' you could put yore finger on," Mac admitted grudgingly. "I jist don't like the way he looks at the little lady when he thinks nobody ain't watchin'."

"You been hangin' over that fancy stove too long." Cyrus snorted. "The heat's affectin' your brain."

The men stopped walking almost directly in front of the window where Carrie stood hidden behind the lace curtains.

"Carrie seems so pleased with the arrangement, I guess I never thought he might be thinking of her as more than just a job," Sherman said. "But I'm her father, and sometimes I forget she's not a little girl anymore."

He sounded worried, and a trill of fear shot through Carrie. What if her father took John away from her?

"You ain't got a thing to worry about," Cyrus scoffed. "I've been watchin' Thornton when he's with Carrie. He's no more interested in her than Billy is."

Carrie wrinkled her nose. Cyrus was half-right. Billy at least liked her. Sometimes John Thornton treated her like she was his worst enemy.

"This old fool's been readin' too many of them dime novels," Cyrus said.

"Wouldn't hurt you to do a little readin'," Mac growled. "Might broaden yore horizons."

Ignoring his friend's final remark, Cyrus said, "Young Thornton's been here a month. He's proven himself a fine hand. I'm thinkin' it's time we told him he had a job."

"Yer the foreman," Mac growled. "I'm jist a biscuit shooter. Reckon yer the one with the final say. But I still says there's somethin' not quite square 'bout that young man."

"Then that's settled." Carrie's father sounded relieved. "You talk to him first chance you get, Cyrus. You might keep an eye on him when he's with Carrie," he added almost as an afterthought.

"I ain't worried 'bout Thornton's behavior with Carrie," Cyrus said, over a mumbled remark of Mac's. "But I will keep an eye on him. There's things about him that jist don't add up. Fer instance, you know I always tried to take care of the Nolans' grave." The men began walking away, and Carrie only caught a fragment of the next sentence. "Well, somebody's been messin' around out there, and I got a hunch. . ."

The three men moved out of earshot, and Carrie whirled away from the window. Dropping down on her bed, she lay back and spread her arms wide. Mac said John was interested in her as more than just a job. Her heart sang.

She lay there for several minutes thinking of ways she could get John to declare his feelings for her. Although she had grown up in a household composed of men, she knew so little about them. Lucille's mother had chastised the way she acted and said she needed to be more feminine. And she was willing to try, but there had to be more to catching a man than that. She remembered Gretchen's mother saying the way to a man's heart was through his stomach, but Mrs. Braun was a wonderful cook. Carrie couldn't boil water.

She sighed. It might take years before she learned to cook. If only her mother were here. Papa had adored Mama. But she remembered him saying one time that her cooking left something to be desired.

Carrie sat up on the bed. Her mother had been gone so long she sometimes seemed like only a dream, and Carrie seldom thought of her unless she was going through some totally female crisis. Lately, however, she had been thinking of her a lot.

She saw the corset lying on the trunk. Papa said Mama had left special things for her. Maybe there was something in the trunk that would help her.

She rose from the bed and dropped to her knees in front of the leather-bound trunk. Almost reverently, she lifted the lid. A scent of roses and lavender wafted out from the sachet bag tucked in the corner of the trunk, and the light fragrance brought with it an especially vivid memory of her fragile, dark-haired mother.

A large Bible rested on top of the trunk's contents. With deliberate care, Carrie opened the book to the inscription page and read that her father had presented it as a gift to her mother on their first wedding anniversary. Carrie discovered inside the Bible's flyleaf a heavily embossed envelope on which her mother had written, *My Beloved Daughter*. She withdrew the card from the envelope and read, *"To everything there is a season, and a time to every purpose under heaven."*

Carrie replaced the card, then ran her hands lovingly over the rich leather cover before laying the Bible to one side.

She took a small box from the trunk, opened the lid, and lifted out a pale blue, embroidered silk reticule. Three things were inside the dainty handbag. A pressed rose. A dance card filled with men's names—none of them her father's—and another cream-colored envelope with Carrie's name inscribed on it with her mother's delicate script. The card inside proclaimed, *"A time to dance." My first grown-up party. Houston, Texas, April 6, 1865.*

She lifted the next item from the trunk and her eyes widened in wonder. It was her mother's wedding dress. She stood holding the white satin and tulle garment at arm's length, then crushed it to herself, and turned to face the full-length mirror. What would John think when he saw her in Mama's dress on their wedding day? Would he think that she was beautiful?

She turned to lay the dress across the bed and noticed another cream-colored envelope on the floor. It must have been concealed in the folds of the dress. Carrie's name was written on the front. She opened it and read, *"A time to love"—June 9, 1869.* The day her parents were married. She returned the card to the envelope, and laid it on top of the dress.

The next item was a tiny white christening dress with a matching bonnet. She began searching for an envelope with her name on it this time and saw it almost immediately. The card inside said, *Sherman Matthew—March 10, 1871.* And, below that her name and birth date. *Caroline Abigail—March 16, 1874.* Then, *"A time to be born."*

The final envelope—this time edged in black—contained a dark, silky, lock of hair tied with narrow, black ribbon. The card read, *A curl from Matt's first haircut.* And, beneath that, *"A time to mourn"—December 9, 1873.*

Carrie knew about the brother who had died of pneumonia three months before she was born. Had even seen a photograph of the chubby, dark-haired baby. But, until she held the lock of hair in her hand, he had never seemed real to her.

Now, a pain stabbed through her heart at her own sense of loss, and the realization of her mother's anguish at losing her firstborn. She wiped her eyes before beginning to replace the items in the trunk.

Finally, she closed the lid, but remained on her knees beside the repacked trunk. Surely, Mama had left her these things for a reason. Was it to bring her comfort? What had Mama meant by the cryptic messages she had left behind? If only she were here to explain.

Overwhelmed by an almost unbearable yearning, Carrie rested her head against her mother's trunk and wept.

Chapter 9

One bright June morning, instead of following their usual route, Carrie turned to the west. After a few miles, John rode up beside her. "You headin' somewhere in particular?" he asked.

She gave him a sunny smile. "As a matter of fact I am. Just over that far rise, there's an apple orchard. About this time of year I like to check on the apples."

He scowled. "Why?"

"I like to see how big they are. When they're ripe I pick them. Mac makes apple butter and the most delicious pies you ever tasted."

"I can save you a trip. It's too early for apples to be ripe."

"I know that, but I like to go there, anyway. There's something peaceful about the orchard." She slowed Brandy and turned in the saddle so she could look at him. "Is there some reason you don't want me to go?"

He shrugged. "It's no concern of mine where you go."

"Good!" A roguish grin flashed across her face, as she forgot her resolve to be more ladylike. "Bet I can beat you there." She kicked Brandy in the ribs and shot ahead of him.

John watched her long auburn braid swing against her slender back as she bent low over Brandy's neck. She had a good head start before he whispered, "Go get her, Jet!" and gave the big gelding his head. Effortlessly, Jet closed the distance between them.

For the blink of an eye, they rode side by side. Then John nudged Jet forward and left Carrie behind. He didn't slow until they topped the rise, and he looked down on the old homestead.

He was leaning nonchalantly against the trunk of the large high-branched tree when Carrie rode up and slid from Brandy.

"You won!" She laughed, and her dimples flashed. "We had a bet. What is my penalty to be?"

John grinned mischievously. "I'll think of something suitable." Then he remembered who she was, and his smile disappeared. "If you're going to look at the apples, you'd best be doing it. I haven't got all day."

His sudden shift in mood hit Carrie with the force of a blow. Trying to regain the playfulness she'd seen in his eyes before that blue curtain of indifference lowered, she said, "I bet you didn't know that's the hanging tree you're leaning against."

"The hangin' tree?" A spark of interest softened the coldness of his eyes. He stepped away from the tree and looked up at the wide-spreading limbs above his head. "Billy never said anything about it."

"Well, he probably doesn't know." Carrie's eyes were on his face. "It happened a long time before he came here."

"What happened?"

"I'm not really sure," she said, her voice reflecting her eagerness to hold his attention. "But I know some men were hanged here."

"What did they do?"

"I don't know." Carrie's voice faltered, as the old familiar mask of indifference began to descend over John's features. "I don't believe I ever heard."

"Probably owned a piece of land some rich man wanted," John said.

A chill ran down Carrie's backbone at the expression on his face. "I'd better go look at the apples," she said. She turned quickly and walked away.

John watched her go, and the pain in his heart was almost more than he could endure. It had been years since he had allowed himself to love, but he knew that he loved Carrie Butler. He also knew that she could never be a part of his life. As soon as he finished the job he had come here to do, she would want no part of him—would in fact, hate him—and he would move on.

Until then, he had to stay away from Carrie.

He lifted his head and saw her walking among the apple trees. Every now and then, she lifted her hand to pluck a tiny apple from a tree. There was something so completely feminine, so familiar about her gestures that a lump formed in his chest and rose into his throat. How many times had he seen his mother walk through their orchard back home in Tennessee, exactly as Carrie was doing now? Thinning, she had called it. Removing the small, malformed fruit from the tree so that the perfect little apples would have room to grow.

A longing for his mother welled up within him. He passed Carrie without so much as a glance and went to the grave. He stood by the fence and looked down at the roughly carved words on the tombstone.

"This grave has been here for as long as I can remember." Carrie's soft voice startled John, but he didn't give any outward indication that he was aware of her presence.

"Cyrus takes care of it," she said. "I didn't know he had planted flowers though." She stepped around John and knelt at his side. Reaching through the fence, she sifted the dirt through her fingers. "They really need a drink," she said, "especially the rosebush. See how dry the soil is?"

John, still not trusting himself to speak, nodded.

"Will you bring some water?" She stood and looked up at him with pleading eyes. "I hate to see anything die. I think there's an old well here somewhere. If we can find it, we can water them."

John turned without a word and walked to the well that was hidden by the tall grass. He pushed the heavy plank cover aside and dropped the rusty bucket into the wide well. It landed with a splash.

While he pulled the bucket up, he admired the workmanship of the well. The man that was buried in the orchard, and his son, had spent many hours digging the well, then collecting the rocks that lined it. In silent testimony to the skill and integrity of his craftsmanship, the rocks stood as straight and solid as the day they had been laid.

Something his father had said about the workman being worthy of his hire came to John's mind. Must have been from the Bible. Pa had been a great one for reading the Bible and often quoted passages of scripture. Well, there was only one passage in the Bible that concerned John.

"Whoso sheddeth man's blood, by man shall his blood be shed." Those words had become his creed. He was still a young man, but he had spent a good portion of his life seeking vengeance for people like the Nolans. Fighting fights that were not his. Dispensing justice where justice had been denied.

"Need help?" He hadn't heard her come up, but Carrie stood at his side, a hopeful smile lifting the corners of her soft, full lips.

"I can manage alone." John said brusquely as he swung the bucket from the well onto the rock casing that extended several inches above the ground, forming a low wall.

She followed meekly as he carried the full bucket to the grave, and stood beside him as he let the clear water pour slowly out.

"They're already perking up," she said as the last few drops soaked into the parched earth. "Papa says that's what the love of God does to our souls. It flows over us, soaking into the dry hurting places, and giving new life."

"I'm sure your papa would know all about that," John said, lifting the bucket over the fence.

He started to turn away as she said, "I don't remember anything about what happened to the people that lived here, but Mama was friends with the woman."

He turned back and looked down at her. Encouraged by the spark of interest she detected in his ice-blue eyes, she babbled on. "I was little when the Nolans died, and I've never heard Papa speak of them, but I remember coming here with Mama a few times. She said they were a good Christian family."

"I thought you didn't remember anything about them," he said.

"Well, I don't. Not really. I mostly remember Lucas, the son." Her cheeks flushed. "I know you're going to think this is silly, but I was really sweet on Lucas. He was mostly outside with his father, but one time he came in for a snack. I remember there was only one cookie left in the cookie jar, and he gave it to me. Then he patted me on the head and smiled at me, and I was absolutely smitten." A gentle sigh lifted Carrie's shoulders.

"I don't even remember what he looked like, except for his eyes. He had the most beautiful, gentle blue eyes. I remember telling Mama on the way home that when I grew up I was going to marry Lucas Nolan." She smiled a bit sheepishly. "I told you it was silly." She shrugged her shoulders. "I remember I cried and cried when Lucas died."

John looked down at her. "Do you remember anything about the night of the fire?" he asked hoarsely.

"Strangely enough, I do remember that night—although my memories are hazy—because Papa left without kissing me good night. Mama put me to bed and told me to go to sleep. I tried to stay awake, but I finally gave in to sleep. It was almost morning when I heard Papa come in. I remember the sky was starting to get light. I heard Mama and Papa talking in the kitchen. I climbed out of bed because I wanted my good-night kiss. When I got to the kitchen Mama was crying, and I heard. . ."

She paused, trying to remember, and John prompted. "And, what? What did you hear your father say?"

She shook her head. "I don't know exactly what Papa said. I guess he told Mama about the fire. It's what Mama said that I remember. She was crying. I rarely saw her cry and her tears frightened me. I stopped in the shadows just outside the kitchen door. Papa had his arms around Mama. Trying to comfort her, I guess. She was saying, 'I told you it would come to this, Sherman. I told you it had been over for fifteen years. I begged you to let the hate go, but you wouldn't. Now, all those people are dead. That boy! Oh, Sherman, the Nolan boy was only twelve years old.' "

Carrie's hands went to her face and her eyes widened. "Oh, no!"

"What is it? Did you remember something else?"

She nodded. "It was horrible. The most horrible sound I have ever heard. And it frightened me even more than Mama's tears."

"What was? What frightened you? What happened?" He fought the urge to reach out and shake the information from her.

Finally, the words came out. "Papa cried."

Chapter 10

The expression on John's face changed so suddenly it was as though a shutter had been slammed closed. His eyes, which only a heartbeat ago had been alight with interest, went cold.

Turning on his heel he stalked away. Numbly, Carrie followed him.

On the ride back to the ranch house, a million questions raced around in Carrie's head.

What had she said? What had she done? She loved this man, of that she had no doubt, but she didn't understand him. And she doubted that she ever would. Why did he have to be such an enigma?

She looked at his broad-shouldered back, for this time he was in the lead, and she had to push Brandy to keep up. She recalled the avid expression on his face when she told him about the hanging tree. Except for the orchard, there was only that one tree at the old Nolan homestead. How had it become known as the hanging tree? Had there actually been men hanged there? Or was it only a story started by a group of cowboys huddled around a lonely campfire? Something based loosely on fact, and exaggerated with each telling until it lost all resemblance of the truth?

She had never been the slightest bit curious, but now she wanted to know. Not just for John, but for herself as well.

That night when her father came to tuck her in, he sat down on the edge of her bed. "And, how was your day, little girl?" he asked, as he had every night for as long as she could remember.

"I rode out to the old Nolan homestead this morning." She pushed herself up against the pillows.

"How are your apples coming along?"

"I think we're going to have a good crop." She plucked at the light blanket that covered her.

His hand closed over hers, stopping its aimless movement. "Is something bothering you, little girl?"

She looked up at him. "Papa, why do they call that big tree the hanging tree? Were some men really hanged there? Or is it just—"

"Forget it, Carrie!" he said harshly, and took his hand away.

58

"But, Papa. . ."

"That happened a long time ago, little girl." He leaned over and kissed her cheek. "Let it lie."

He put out the light, and left Carrie alone in the dark with a new set of unanswered questions.

Why did Papa avoid the Nolan place? She had asked him to go with her to gather the apples a couple of years ago, but he had said he was too busy. As far as she knew, he had never been to the burned-out homestead. Why? What had happened there? And why didn't he want to talk about it?

She scooted down in bed and turned on her side, facing the window. Through the lace pattern of the curtains, she saw the twinkling stars. She wondered briefly if John was leaning against the barn watching her window, but she didn't get up to look.

The next morning when she went out to saddle Brandy, Cyrus was leading his own horse out of the barn.

"Looks like you got a mighty fine mornin' fer your ride, young'un," he commented.

"Uh-huh," she answered absently.

Cyrus frowned. "Somethin' botherin' you, Carrie?"

"There is something I'd like to know, if you have a minute."

"I've always got time fer you, young'un." He patted her arm. "You go right ahead and ask. I'll tell you anythin' you want to know."

Carrie took a deep breath. "I want to know about that old tree out at the Nolan place. The one they call the hanging tree. How did it get its name?"

His face went still and his eyes hooded, closing her out. "It happened a long time ago, Carrie. It don't concern you none. Leave it be, young'un."

"But—" Cyrus cut Carrie's protest short with a shake of his head.

"I got work to do, young'un." He led his horse out the open door, then turned, and added over his shoulder, "Maybe you best stay away from the Nolan place."

Carrie watched him mount up and ride away. There was one more place to go. She knew she could persuade Mac to tell her what she wanted to know.

⸻

"Battin' them big brown eyes ain't gonna get you nowheres with me, little lady." Mac frowned at Carrie. "Whut happened over to the Nolans don't concern you. Now you set yourself down here an' have a glass of milk an' some of these here molasses cookies. They's yore favorite, and I jist took 'em outa the oven of my nice range."

She'd had to wait until afternoon before she was able to catch Mac alone. Now, he refused to tell her anything.

Carrie stomped her foot in frustration. "I'm eighteen years old, Mac. Why do you all still treat me like a child? I can't see why you're all so secretive about what happened. And I don't want your stupid cookies and milk."

She turned on her heel and slammed from the room.

Several times during supper, Carrie caught Papa or Cyrus glancing covertly at her. She picked listlessly at her food. If Mac and Andy hadn't been busy in the kitchen feeding the men, Mac would have been scolding her for not eating.

Finally, she laid her napkin to one side. "I'm not hungry. May I be excused?"

Her father didn't answer but merely nodded his permission. Carrie saw the worried look that he and Cyrus exchanged as she rose from the table and left the room.

An hour later when her father looked in on her, Carrie was already in bed and asleep. He crossed the room and kissed her soft cheek. Then he turned out the light and slipped quietly from the room.

Sometime later Carrie's empty stomach woke her. She hadn't eaten since breakfast. Thinking about Mac's molasses cookies, she slipped on her robe and padded barefoot to the kitchen.

". . .gonna keep askin' questions, 'til somebody tells 'er whut she wants to know."

It was Mac's voice. Realizing he was talking about her, Carrie stepped back into the shadows and listened.

"The only one that would tell her is you," Cyrus said.

"I ain't tellin' her nothin'," Mac said, "but I think mebbe she oughta be told."

"No!" That was her father's voice. She inched closer. "She wouldn't understand. Carrie must never know what happened that night."

"Wal, I think yer wrong, Sherman. Carrie loves us. Ain't nothin' gonna change thet."

"I don't know, Mac. What we done wasn't wrong, but things is different now. The young 'un might not understand."

"I reckon the little lady would fergive us, whether she understood, or not."

"That's not a chance I'm willing to take."

There was a moment of silence, then a chair scraped back. She heard Mac limp across the floor, then a rattling sound, and him limping back to the table. She smelled the coffee as he refilled their cups, and her empty stomach twisted.

Finally, Mac said, "I'd reckon young Thornton will be squirin' the little lady to thet party the young folks is havin' for the newlyweds Saturday night."

"I talked to him about it this afternoon. I told him he was to drive the buggy, and leave that big, black gelding at home."

Carrie had so many things on her mind she had forgotten Lucille's party. John was actually going to escort her instead of trailing behind! All thoughts of her empty stomach and of the hanging tree vanished. She crept back to her room and crawled into bed.

It was important that she look her best Saturday night. She mentally inventoried the contents of her closet. Nothing would do, except the green dress she had worn to Lucille's wedding.

She sighed and snuggled down on her pillow. Her dreams that night were sweet.

Carrie knew she was going to need help dressing for the party, so when Billy drove the wagon to town for supplies Saturday morning, she rode as far as the Brauns' with him.

She and Gretchen spent most of that afternoon getting ready. The curling iron never had a chance to cool as they tried several different hairstyles before finally settling on one.

Gretchen's mother found a few free minutes to spend with the girls while they were getting dressed. She sat in a chair watching as they took turns lacing each other's corsets.

"After Lucille's wedding I swore I would never again wear this thing," Carrie gasped, gripping the bedpost as Gretchen pulled the laces tighter.

"You have to get Mr. Thornton's attention somehow," Gretchen said through clenched teeth as she gave the laces an extra hard yank.

"I hope this works, because nothing else has. I even tried to be ladylike for a while." Carrie felt as though her ribs were about to meet her spine. "Stop, Gretchen! That's enough. I want his attention. But I don't want to die to get it."

"I thought you were going to marry young Mr. Thornton," Gretchen's mother said.

"I am." Carrie was studying her reflection in the mirror. "He just doesn't know it yet."

"I see," Mrs. Braun said, but it was clear from the expression on her face she didn't.

"I knew the first time I saw him that John Thornton was the man I would marry." Carrie wrinkled her pert little nose. "Unfortunately, I don't think he likes me much. But, he will. I'm going to make him love me."

Mrs. Braun shook her head. "You can't make someone love you, Carrie. Love is either there or it isn't. God has given John Thornton a will of his own—just as he has all of us—and this young man's love is a gift only he can give. Even more importantly, Carrie, I don't think Mr. Thornton is a believer. You know the Bible says, 'Be ye not unequally yoked together with unbelievers: for what fellowship hath righteousness with unrighteousness? and what communion hath light with darkness?' I've seen unions like that, Carrie, and they brought nothing but pain and suffering."

The baby began to cry, and Mrs. Braun went to see to his needs.

Carrie knew Gretchen's mother was right. She couldn't force John to love her. Sometimes she wondered why she even wanted to. He was surly, and uncommunicative, and often downright rude. But she had seen occasional flashes of the man underneath.

There had been his open interest the day he rescued her. His gentleness and patience with the broncos he was breaking. The warmth she had seen in his blue eyes the day he won the race.

She loved that man. She had known that first day she saw him that he was her destiny. Nothing that had happened thus far had changed that. The dance would be the first time they were together in a social situation. Billy would be driving the Brauns' little runabout, leaving Carrie and John alone in her buggy during the ride to and from town. And they would be together for several hours at the dance.

Surely tonight, John would see her as something more than a distasteful job.

Chapter 11

The evening didn't begin as Carrie had hoped. Billy helped Gretchen into their buggy, then, when John made no move to climb down and assist her, he handed Carrie into her buggy.

The sun was setting in a magnificent blaze of color when they followed Billy onto the main road.

"It was thoughtful of the Grange to wait until Jed and Lucille were settled in their new home before throwing this party for them. Don't you think?"

He didn't reply or give any indication he was aware of her presence, despite the fact that her arm brushed against his every time the buggy swayed.

"Gretchen looks really pretty tonight, doesn't she?" Carrie paused long enough for him to answer. When he didn't, she chattered on. "She's wearing the dress she wore to Lucille's wedding." She smoothed down her light green dress. "So am I."

When he still didn't answer, she turned her head away from him.

He stole a furtive glance at her. The setting sun washed over her, transforming her into a red-gold vision. Her dangling earrings captured the light and released it in dazzling prisms of color. Her dress had a scooped neck that revealed just enough golden-touched skin to be intriguing. Her upswept hair was a glory of red-gold curls. The tendrils that escaped and curled on the back of her slender neck caught his attention. There was something about those wispy curls that moved him as nothing else had. He realized his thoughts were taking him to a place he couldn't afford to go, and he forced his attention back to the road ahead.

When they pulled in next to Billy and Gretchen's buggy at the hitching rail, John jumped down and walked around to the horse's head. He expected Carrie to climb down as usual; when she didn't, he started around to help her.

Before he reached her, a handsome young man walked up to the buggy. "Carrie, I thought this was your buggy." He reached up and lifted her down. "I've been watching for you."

"Jake, I'm so happy to see you." Carrie wore a syrupy sweet smile as she spoke.

"You're not with anyone, are you?"

"I am now." John saw Carrie throw a quick glance his way. "Feel free to enjoy yourself, Mr. Thornton. I'll let you know when I'm ready to go."

When she took Jake's arm, Billy, who had been standing to one side with Gretchen, gave John a puzzled look. Then, the two couples walked across the dirt street to the brightly lit Grange Hall.

Jealousy seared through John like a white-hot brand. For a moment, he considered going up the street to the saloon and waiting until she was ready to go. But he didn't. He had never been a drinking man, and didn't enjoy being around men who were. So he squared his shoulders and marched across to the Grange.

He hung his hat on the rack then stood inside the door for a moment scanning the crowd. He had no trouble spotting Carrie. She was talking to another couple—the guests of honor he presumed. She looked up at the young man at her side and made some comment. He laughed and put his arm around her shoulders in a brief hug.

John felt a light touch on his arm and looked down into a pair of laughing blue eyes. "I'm Becky Colton. My friends dared me to come over and introduce myself." She turned and waved saucily to a group of giggling girls, then looked back up at him. "I haven't seen you before. Are you new in town?"

John smiled. "I've been out at the Circle C for a couple of months."

The fiddler took his place on a raised platform and began to warm up for the first set of the square dance. "Would you care to dance, Miss Colton?"

If his smile didn't reach his eyes, she seemed not to notice. "Why, sir, I don't even know your name." She fluttered her long, dark lashes at him.

"My name is John. Now, would you care to be my partner?"

"I would be delighted to, John."

He caught a brief glimpse of Carrie's flaming hair as he guided Becky across the room.

Even though Becky was small, pretty, and a good dance partner, he had only intended to dance one dance with her. However, she did not allow him opportunity to escape, and he'd lost sight of Carrie in the crowded room by the third dance.

When he finally did spot her, he couldn't believe his eyes. She seemed to be having a wonderful evening without him. As the night wore on, he saw Carrie dancing with several different men. However, the young man she called Jake was obviously monopolizing her time.

Watching Carrie partner with yet another apparently unattached man, he excused himself from Becky and tried to dance with several other women as well. When he saw Jake escort her to the dance floor for yet another dance, John could no longer pretend to enjoy himself. He excused himself from his latest dance partner and went outside. Leaning against the buggy, he nursed his smoldering jealousy. Finally, he stalked back into the Grange Hall.

Carrie was at the refreshment table with Jake. He crossed the room to them.

When she saw John heading their way, Carrie's heart skipped a beat. He was easily the most attractive man in the room. She turned back to Jake, forcing a laugh at the joke he had just told.

"Miss Butler." Carrie turned and looked up at John. There was fire in his blue eyes. "I'm takin' you home."

She wanted to reach out and brush back the wayward lock of hair that lay on his deeply tanned forehead. "I'm not ready to go home, Mr. Thornton."

"I didn't ask you if you were ready, Miss Butler. Get your things together and tell your little friend good-bye. We're leavin'."

"Just a minute, Carrie." Jake put a restraining hand on her arm. "If your driver wants to go, I'll be happy to take you home after the party is over."

Carrie hesitated, and John snapped. "Miss Butler came with me and she's leavin' with me."

"It's my understanding you were hired to be Miss Butler's driver," Jake said. "I think you're a bit out of line, fella."

John's fists clenched at his sides. "Would you like to step outside and settle this, kid?"

Jake looked John up and down, assessing the breadth of his shoulders and the strength in his muscular arms and chest. He shook his head. "You're bigger than I am, and you have probably done a lot more fighting. I'd be a fool to go up against you." He tightened his grip on Carrie's arm. "But you don't have to go with him, Carrie. He's only a hired man, and I will see you home."

Carrie was aware they were quickly becoming the center of attention. "It's all right, Jake; I'll go with Mr. Thornton."

Jake shrugged. "It's your decision. I'll walk you to your buggy."

The crowd parted as they passed through, followed by John.

Billy intercepted them at the door. "John, if you could spare a minute, I need to jaw at you."

Jake and Carrie walked across to the buggy, and he lifted her into the seat.

"Carrie," Jake took her hand in his. "You know I've loved you ever since first grade. I was wondering if I could come calling on you."

"Oh, Jake! I love you, too, but I'm not in love with you. I never could be. I'm sorry."

Jake released her hand, and shrugged. "Well, you can't blame a fella for trying." He dug the toe of his boot in the dust, then looked up at her. "You're sweet on Thornton, aren't you?"

Carrie blushed. "Was I that transparent?"

"Couldn't keep your eyes off him." He chuckled. "Well, I see him coming, so I guess I'd better be going before he pounds me into mincemeat." He started to walk away, then turned back and said, "By the way, I think he's a little sweet on you, too, Carrie."

The two men met in the middle of the street, nodded stiffly, and walked on. John climbed in beside Carrie and picked up the reins. A stony silence settled over the two occupants of the buggy as he backed out and turned toward the Circle C.

They were almost to the ranch when John pulled the buggy to the side of the road. They sat for a time before Carrie turned her head and looked at him. He was staring straight ahead, but in the light of the full moon she could see a muscle in his jaw jumping. She knew he was angry—though she didn't know exactly why— and she clasped her hands in her lap.

"Well, if you have something to say you might as well say it," she said.

He continued to stare straight ahead. "I guess you know you made quite a spectacle of yourself tonight."

She felt the first small prick of anger. "What's that supposed to mean?"

He turned to face her, resting his arm on the back of the seat. "You know very well what I mean. You flirted outrageously with Andy. That poor little kid would jump off a mountain if he thought it would impress you."

She felt her face growing warm. "Andy is just a kid. I danced with him once. What's really bothering you, Mr. Thornton?"

"All right. You asked. I'll tell you." He leaned toward her. "You flaunted your-self like a cheap saloon girl."

"I flaunted. . ." He was being so unfair. The anger rose in her, choking off her words.

"You hung all over that kid Jake, and he couldn't keep his hands off you."

"Jake is my friend."

"Well, I was almost forced into beating your friend into a bloody pulp to defend your honor."

"My honor! My honor!" Carrie spluttered. "My honor was never in need of defending, Mr. Thornton. Besides, what was I supposed to do? Stand in the corner and watch you dance with every unattached female under the age of a hundred? Except me. You never once asked me to be your partner."

"It was my understanding I was being paid to escort you, Miss Butler. I didn't realize my duties included being your lover as well."

Anger washed over Carrie in a blinding wave. She raised her hand, and he caught it before it connected with his face. His other arm slipped around her shoulders, and he pulled her to him. Then he did what he had wanted to do since the first time he saw her.

Carrie had never been kissed before, yet instinctively her lips responded to his. Her arms slipped up around his neck, and she melted against him.

John didn't know what he had expected. But not this. Never this. He broke off their kiss and pulled her head down on his shoulder. "Caroline. Caroline." He whispered the words. "My sweet Caroline."

"I love you, John." The words, muffled against his neck came clearly, bringing him to his senses.

He put his hands on her shoulders and held her away from him. "Is that what you wanted, Miss Butler?" he said mockingly. "Well, you can't say John Thornton doesn't do his job."

Her face went dead white, and she slapped him hard across the cheek. "Take me home!"

"The lady's wish is my command." He picked up the reins, and the buggy once more moved down the road. "But, then, I reckon I just proved that."

As soon as the buggy rolled to a stop, Carrie scrambled down and ran into the house. John drove into the barn. He sat for a time, his head bowed, his cheek stinging, his heart aching. Finally, his movements stiff and mechanical, he climbed slowly down, unhitched the buggy, and put the horse in a stall.

Then, feet dragging, he walked to the bunkhouse.

Chapter 12

Spring roundup began the Monday morning following the party. Long before daylight, Mac pulled himself up on the seat of the chuck wagon, picked up the reins, and headed out. Carrie, riding Brandy, and Andy, on a steel gray cow pony he called Sidewinder, rode alongside the wagon. A wrangler followed with a remuda of two hundred horses.

Half asleep, Carrie slumped in the saddle. She had always looked forward to the roundup, but this year if she could have found a reason to beg off—short of telling her father the truth—she wouldn't have come. She had always thought tears were a sign of weakness, but Saturday night she had cried herself to sleep.

Her spiritual life had been sketchy these last few weeks to say the least. Now, with nowhere else to turn, she prayed, *Father give me strength to face John, and hold my head up after what happened Saturday night. And, please, Lord, don't let me cry when I see him.*

The sun was just coming up when Mac hollered, "Whoa," and the covered chuck wagon came to a rattling halt. "Reckon we'll set up here fer now," he said.

Andy unhitched the horses. Then, he and Carrie turned them, along with Brandy and Sidewinder, out to graze with the remuda.

Mac and Andy began to set up camp.

"What can I do to help?" Carrie asked.

"I figgered you'd be goin' out to hunt strays like you always done." Mac looked at her from beneath grizzled brows.

Carrie shook her head. She didn't want to take the chance of running into John Thornton. "Not this time. I thought I'd hang around camp and help you."

"Wal, I reckon while me an' Andy's settin' up, you kin grab one a them baskets an' gather up some cow chips."

Carrie wrinkled her nose. "I'll do that, Miss Carrie," Andy offered.

"No, I'll do it. You help Mac."

The task wasn't really all that bad since she had on gloves and the chips were dry. When the basket was full, Andy helped her carry it back to camp.

One of the Circle C beefs had been butchered to supply meat for the roundup. Mac made a pot of sonofagun stew and hung it on a tripod over the fire. "Don't never boil it," he said. "Jist let it simmer nice and slow fer two or three hours."

Cooking was easier than Carrie had imagined. "What do we do next?"

"I'd reckon I'll mix us up a mess of sourdough biscuits."

"Let me do it," Carrie said.

"Mebbe you'd best watch me make a batch afore you attempt it yoreself, little lady." Mac climbed into the wagon and Carrie followed. The inside was outfitted with cabinets where food, dishes, and supplies were stored. A baking table was on one side and, across from it, the narrow cot where Carrie slept.

Mac measured potato water into a bowl, then stirred in flour and sugar. "We'll jist set thet aside to rise," he said. "When it doubles, we'll finish up our biscuits."

By the time the first gathering of bawling cattle were driven into a milling circle several hundred feet from the chuck wagon, the meal was nearing completion. Mac had added salt, pepper, and hot sauce to the stew, along with small pieces of chopped sweetbreads and brains. The biscuits were in the Dutch oven. A large pot of coffee hung over the glowing embers.

Limping a few feet from the wagon, Mac banged a large spoon against the bottom of a dishpan. "Come an' get it!" he bellowed, setting off an immediate horse race from the holding grounds.

The men jostled and exchanged good-natured insults as they gathered around the washbasins Mac and Andy had set out for them. After they washed the dirt from their faces and hands, they formed a ragged line.

While all this was going on, Mac and Andy set up a long table. Tin pie pans and cutlery were stacked at one end so that they were within easy reach of the men. Next was the large pot of stew, then a pan of biscuits, and lastly the pot of coffee flanked by large tin cups.

Cyrus stepped to the head of the line. When he removed his hat, the men became silent, pulled off their own hats, and bowed their heads. After Cyrus prayed, he joined Carrie's father at the end of the line. The men slapped their hats back on as they started to move down the serving line.

Mac ladled stew into their plates, Carrie added a couple of biscuits, and Andy filled the cups.

After the last plate was filled, Carrie looked toward the milling herd and saw John. When some of the men saddled fresh mounts and headed back to work, she knew the men riding watch would be coming in to eat. She quickly filled her plate and climbed into the chuck wagon.

After she finished eating, she lay down on the cot. She only intended to rest a few minutes, but when she woke, the branding for that day was over, and it was almost suppertime.

Supper that night was roast beef and brown gravy with quartered potatoes that had cooked alongside the meat in the rich broth. Carrie once more took her place between Mac and Andy to serve the biscuits that were left from the noon meal. John went through somewhere near the middle of the line.

His blue eyes captured hers and held her captive for a heartbeat—before she managed to look away. Billy, who was behind him, clapped a big hand on John's shoulder. "That was some mighty fine ropin' you was doin' today."

"This was just a good day."

"You ever do any of the fancy stuff? Fig'r eights and such?"

"I know a few tricks, but all a man needs to know is the head and heel catch." John picked up a cup of coffee. "Where I come from, if a man tried anything more than that on the job he might as well pack up his gear."

"Yeah, it'll get you fired here too, but sometimes we like to do a little showin' off after work. Wanna show us what you can do later?"

Carrie's hands were trembling by the time the two men walked away, and she didn't hear John's reply.

Andy, standing beside her pouring coffee, said, "I bet I can do something Mr. Thornton can't."

"I doubt there's anything Mr. Thornton can't do."

"He can't do what I can, Miss Carrie," Andy boasted. "Me and Sidewinder can do somethin' nobody else can."

"And what can you do?" Carrie wasn't really interested, but the men who had gone through the line earlier had been teasing Andy about being a cook. They had called him a grease belly and wanted to know when he was going to be grown enough to do a real man's work. The boy seemed so eager to impress her she felt sorry for him.

"I get way back. Then I run up behind Sidewinder and jump on. Old Sidewinder takes off like a scared jackrabbit and runs somethin' fierce. Want me to show you?"

Carrie shook her head. "I don't want you to do that trick, Andy. It's too dangerous. If you should miss and fall, your horse could kick your brains out."

The boy laughed. "Shucks, Miss Carrie, I ain't gonna fall. There's a trick to it, you see. I tie a knot in Sidewinder's tail. I just put my foot on the knot and jump right on."

"That's even worse. If you should slip, you could be dragged. Promise me you won't ever do that trick again, Andy."

Andy didn't promise, but when he didn't mention it again, Carrie forgot about it.

By Friday, the roundup had moved to the banks of a shallow creek in the far corner of the Circle C. After breakfast, while the men were out making the morning gather, Carrie walked down to the creek with a bar of soap, a towel, and a blanket. Screened by a stand of cottonwoods, she stripped down to her sleeveless, knee-length, cotton knit union suit, and gingerly stepped into the cold water. She waded slowly out to the deepest spot, which was only a little more than chest high, and lathered up. She swam for a while, rinsing off the soap, then washed her hair.

When she waded out of the water she felt clean and refreshed. She dried her hair, then wrapped the towel around her head. Holding the blanket around her, she gathered up her clothes. When she got back to the wagon, she put on clean clothes from the skin out and hung the wet union suit and her towel on a line inside the wagon to dry. After combing and braiding her damp hair, she climbed out of the wagon to join Mac and Andy as they put the finishing touches on dinner.

Early that afternoon, the last of the herd was branded, castrated, had their ears notched, and were released. With the hard work of the roundup ended, the men trooped down to the creek, as Carrie had done earlier, to scrub a week's worth of dirt and sweat from their aching bodies.

Early Saturday morning, they would head back to the ranch, but the rest of Friday was theirs to enjoy. When they returned from their baths they were clean-scrubbed, dressed in fresh clothes, and ready for fun.

They immediately convened a kangaroo court and began to try some of the cowboys for various crimes. No matter how eloquently the accused man argued his case, he knew he was going to be found guilty. The penalties were mainly harmless nonsense, carried out amidst laughter and catcalls. Finally, a young cowboy called out, "I accuse John Thornton of bein' too good at ever' thin' he does."

"Guilty," the man acting as judge called out, not giving John the opportunity to defend himself. "What'll his punishment be?"

"We got it right over yonder," one of the men called out, pointing to a wild-eyed steer staked out a short distance from camp. "Saved that killer 'specially fer ol' John. I'm thinkin' he can't stay on thet feller's back fer more than five seconds."

Carrie had been standing with her father, Cyrus, and Mac, enjoying the tom-foolery. Now her eyes grew wide. "Don't let him do it," she said. "Please, Papa! Cyrus! You've got to stop him."

"Looks like we can't do anything about it," her father said. John, surrounded by a group of men, was already striding toward the red-eyed, snorting animal.

"If he didn't think he could handle it, he wouldn't attempt it," Cyrus said. "John's a good man. I'd reckon he's got sense enough not to try somethin' he don't think he can do."

Carrie had spent the past week avoiding the tall, good-looking cowboy. After the mean, hurtful things he had said to her Saturday night, she had told herself she hated him. Now, watching the other men hold the wild-eyed steer immobile with their ropes while he prepared to lower himself onto its back, she knew she could never hate him. She would love John Thornton until she took her dying breath.

The men released the steer and beat a hasty retreat. Carrie watched in horrified silence as the crazed animal used every move in the book to rid himself of the man on his back. When it seemed he had exhausted his bag of tricks, he lowered his head and bucked his hind legs into the air. Close to doing a complete somersault, he suddenly corkscrewed his massive body.

Carrie clapped a hand over her mouth to stifle a scream when she saw John slipping toward the wildly pitching steer's head. Knowing he was going to be impaled on the wicked-looking, razor sharp horns, she squeezed her eyes shut and turned her face against her father's chest.

His arms closed around her. She felt the steady thudding of his heart. Then, a mighty groaning roar went up from the men.

Chapter 13

The shout became a cheer.

"He's all right, Carrie," her father said.

She opened her eyes and turned to look. Miraculously, John had regained his seat.

Cyrus held a stopwatch in his hand counting off the seconds.

It seemed to Carrie that John had been clinging to the back of the steer for an eternity before Cyrus said, "Five seconds." However, the hand of the watch indicated ten seconds, before John threw his leg over the steer's back and slid off. He landed running. The steer chased him several feet before tossing its head and trotting away. All the men, including her father and Cyrus, rushed forward to crowd around John. Feeling as though her bones had turned to water, Carrie sank to her knees and wrapped her arms tightly around herself. Her head dropped forward, and she could feel tears running down her cheeks.

"You all right, little lady?"

She felt a gentle touch on her shoulder. Lifting her head, she looked into Mac's worried eyes. "Oh, Mac! Why do I have to feel like this?"

"I'd reckon not even old Solomon with all his wisdom could answer thet question, little lady."

"He said such cruel hurting things to me, but it's as though ever since the first time I saw him I've known him. The real him, not the face he shows the world, but the kind, gentle man he is inside."

"I know, little lady. I know." He reached a hand down to her. "Here, let me help you up from there."

She took his hand and scrambled to her feet. "Were you ever in love, Mac?"

"I wuz, an' still am. I reckon I'll allus love Emily."

Carrie had never thought that Mac might have had a life before she knew him. A life she knew nothing about. "What happened?"

"She died of the cholera durin' the war. Her and our little baby boy." He pulled a red bandanna from his pocket and blew his nose.

Tears filled Carrie's eyes. "Oh, Mac, I'm so sorry."

"Now don't you go gettin' all weepy on my account." He stuffed the bandanna in his hip pocket, and cleared his throat. "It wuz a long time ago, an' I reckon I'll be seein' 'em agin afore long."

Carrie wiped her tears away on the sleeve of her shirt. "Were you ever sorry, Mac? Did you ever wish you'd married someone else? I mean since Emily died."

"Nope. Fer some of us they's only one love, little lady."

"I know I'll never love anyone else."

Mac reached out and patted her arm. "In thet case, I wish I could tell you jist to foller your heart. But, I cain't, little lady. I jist cain't."

Since Mac wanted to get as much packing done as possible that evening, supper was served early. Carrie stood between Mac and Andy putting corn bread on plates heaped high with cowboy beans. There had been a couple of horse races after the kangaroo court, but all the men could talk about was John's ride. Billy and John were together near the middle of the line. Carrie smiled at Billy. "Congratulations on your race. That Cayuse can really run."

He smiled. "Thank you, Miss Carrie, but compared to what John here done, the race was small potatoes. Did ya see him ride?"

"I saw him," Carrie said, noncommittally.

"What did you think of my ride?" It was the first sentence he had spoken to her since Saturday night, and she supposed she should have been thrilled, but. . . "I stayed on double my time."

There was something in his manner that seemed so cocky—so utterly male— he infuriated her. He had frightened her half to death. Now he was standing here preening before her like a peacock. Did he expect her to flutter her eyelashes and tell him how wonderful he was?

"Was that intentional?" She plopped a piece of corn bread on his plate. "I thought you just didn't know how to get off."

Before he had a chance to reply, she snapped, "You're holding up the line. Move on!"

Mac chuckled. "Thet's tellin' 'im, little lady."

Andy said softly, "You wasn't very nice to Mr. Thornton, Miss Carrie."

"Mr. Thornton hasn't been very nice to me."

"But he's a hero."

"Hero." Carrie snorted. "I thought you knew the difference between a hero and an idiot. Mac and Cyrus are heroes. They fought in the Civil War. There wasn't anything heroic about what John Thornton did today. It was foolhardy and show-offish, and I wasn't impressed."

"In my book, any man that can stay on the back of a buckin' steer, with jist a rope to hang on to, is a hero. Just wait till you see my trick with Sidewinder."

"I told you to forget that stupid horse trick. In the first place, you can't do it. In the second place, if you try, you're likely to get your neck broken. And, in the third place, I don't care." She slammed a piece of corn bread on the last plate, then tore her apron off. "Grow up, Andy!" She stalked away.

"I don't care what Miss Carrie says, when I do my horse trick the men'll quit callin' me grease belly."

"There ain't nothin' wrong with bein' a cook. Ever'body knows an outfit travels on its belly. Besides, life's a precious gift God gives to us," Mac said. "An' the little lady's right. Real heroes don't risk their life 'less they's a good reason fer 'em to do so." He handed Andy a plate. "Now come on an' eat. We got a heap a dishes to warsh tonight, an' I don't reckon the little lady'll be back till she's cooled off some."

The dishes were done and packed away when Carrie joined Mac and her father beside the chuck wagon. Billy and John were performing a series of fancy moves with their lariats. Approximately twenty-five feet separated the mounted men as they faced each other, matching trick for trick. What they were doing was more an exhibition than a contest, and Carrie settled down next to Mac to watch. She didn't even miss Andy until he called out her name. "Watch me, Miss Carrie!"

She turned her head and saw Sidewinder. Andy, his bare feet throwing up little puffs of dust, was already running toward the horse. She clutched Mac's arm, and they both started up. Before they had time to call out, Andy jumped. His foot slipped through the knot and kicked the horse's rump. Startled, Sidewinder leaped forward. While they watched in horrified silence, the frightened horse ran toward the opening between John's and Billy's horses, dragging the struggling boy with him.

Two lariats shot out. Both loops settled around the runaway's neck. He ran another twenty feet or so before the loops tightened, bringing him to a stop. The two men had already made a few dallies around the saddle horn, now they locked the rope with a half hitch and dismounted.

Carrie ran to Andy and knelt to put her arms around the frightened boy. "Oh, Andy, you could have been killed."

John, who had been sawing through the horse's tail with his knife, freed the boy's foot before turning on Carrie. "This was all done for your benefit. Anyone with any sense would have discouraged him from tryin' such a dangerous stunt. But you egged him on, and you almost got him killed."

"I didn't. . ." Carrie started to protest, then jumped up and pushed through the men gathered around Andy.

When her father started after her, Mac put a restraining hand on his arm.

"Let 'er go, Sherman. The little lady needs to be alone, an' I'm a-goin' to have a little talk with young Mr. Thornton."

John was helping Andy to his feet. Mac hobbled over to him. "Somebody else will take care of the boy. You an' me is a-goin' to have us a little confab."

Billy stepped in to help Andy, and John followed Mac in the opposite direction Carrie had gone. Away from the creek.

As soon as she was out of sight of the men, Carrie began to run. She ran until her chest ached. Then she made her way slowly to the bank of the creek, sat down on a fallen log, and buried her face in her hands. Tears stung the back of her eyelids, and she blinked them away. Carrie had spent so much time alone, she had become accustomed to speaking aloud to herself. "You will not cry, Caroline Abigail Butler! Tears never solved anything," she said sternly. "Do you hear me?"

She began to pray softly to herself, begging God for his guidance. She remembered Gretchen's mother telling her that she couldn't force John to love her. Then, she recalled something she had overheard Cyrus tell one of the wranglers last summer.

Cyrus had been quite a gambler before his conversion twelve years ago, and he sometimes used the gambler's vernacular when making a point. The man had been having trouble reaching a decision concerning some land he had a chance to buy. Cyrus had advised, "Well, Cole, it's like this—you've got to study the situation real close. If you think you got a good hand, stay in. But, if your cards is bad, you'd best just throw them down and get out of the game." Cole had evidently been holding a winning hand; he had his own little ranch now.

Carrie lifted her head and looked out at the water. "You don't have even one good card, Carrie Butler," she said softly. "It's time you threw down your hand and got out of the game."

The sun was just sinking beneath the horizon when John found Carrie. Her back was slumped and he knew she was crying. Guilt washed over him. Mac had given him a good dressing down, and he had deserved every word the fiery little man said. He walked around the end of the log and stood, hat in hand. "I've been lookin' for you," he said.

She glanced up at him. She wasn't crying. But there was a guarded, watchful expression in her dark eyes.

"Andy's scraped and bruised some, but he'll be all right." He hesitated a moment. "Mind if I sit?"

She shrugged and turned her face back to the creek.

He sat down a couple of feet from her and looked down at the hat he was twisting in his hands. "I owe you an apology," he said, darting a quick glance at her. She hadn't moved.

His gaze moved to the creek. "I'm sorry for the things I said to you back there. I thought, well, I knew the kid was sweet on you, and I reckon I thought. . ."

Because he had been showing off for her, he had assumed the boy was, too. But that wasn't something he could admit. Not even to himself. "Andy told me you warned him not to try that stunt, but he thought the men would be impressed."

She still didn't move.

"I want you to know I'm sorry for what I said the night of the party. There was nothin' wrong with the way you behaved. I was just. . ." He couldn't tell her he had been jealous. No more than he could admit he'd stayed on the back of that Idaho brainstorm longer than was necessary because he knew she was watching.

"All I can do is ask your forgiveness, Caroline. Miss Butler. I'm truly sorry, and I'm ashamed of the way I behaved."

She turned her head and looked gravely into his blue eyes. "You're forgiven, Mr. Thornton." She stood up and brushed her dark riding skirt. "But I want you to know one thing. Men who risk their lives for no reason do not impress me. Men like Papa and Cyrus and Mac are my heroes."

She turned and walked hurriedly away.

A bullfrog boomed, calling for his mate. A distant warble answered the nearby trill of a mockingbird. A fish leaped to catch an errant dragonfly skimming over the surface of the water, then splashed back into the creek. John Thornton sat alone in the gathering darkness.

Chapter 14

The Monday after they returned from the roundup, John and Carrie resumed their daily rides. By the beginning of the second week, everything appeared to be as it had been before, but John sensed a wariness in her. A holding back.

He tried to convince himself this was what he wanted.

He had come to Kansas to execute Sherman Butler. His resolve was no less than it had been.

In the quiet loneliness of the night, he told himself that he had already lingered too long. He needed to complete his mission and move on.

The next morning when he rode beside Carrie over the gently rolling prairie, the hot dry wind rustled through the tall thirsty grass. The passage of their horses flushed a covey of quail. The startled birds skimmed across the prairie with a whir of wings.

Carrie turned to him with a delighted smile, and his heart whispered, *How can I leave her?*

"If I had been carryin' a shotgun we would have had quail for supper," he said.

"Oh, no!" Carrie's soft brown eyes widened. "They still have young ones. Mamas shouldn't be taken away from their children."

He smiled. "They're only birds."

"Even little birds need their mamas. Do you have a mother, John?"

He looked away from her. "Not anymore."

She couldn't see his eyes, but she saw the set to his jaw. "You miss her, don't you?"

He shrugged. "Sometimes."

She dared one more question. "Are you an only child?"

He glanced at her. "I had a younger brother, but he died."

She saw the curtain descending over his blue eyes. "I had an older brother," she said, "but I never knew him. He died before I was born."

He didn't reply. This brief glimpse of John Thornton's past was all she could expect today.

She turned Brandy toward the Nolan place. "I want to see about the apples," she said. "Besides, it's so dry I know the flowers on the grave need water."

Carrie walked beside him from the well to the grave, and stood quietly while he poured the water slowly over the cracked earth.

"I wasn't quite eight when Mama died," she said. "She was mostly in bed the last year, and I don't remember her very well, but I know she loved flowers."

He lifted the bucket over the fence. "That should take care of them for today."

She nodded. "We'll have to come every day and water them."

They walked slowly back to the well. Carrie pushed her soft tan Stetson back and let it dangle by the chin strap. She raised her face to the cloudless blue sky. The wind snatched at the loose strands of hair that had escaped her braid and now blew them across her face. "Cyrus says we're ripe for a fire," she said.

John pushed his hat to the back of his head and scanned the horizon. "It's dry enough for sure," he said. "And the way that wind's blowin'. . ."

He left the sentence unfinished as he lowered the bucket into the well. He pulled it up, filled to the brim, and set it on the well curbing.

"Would you like a drink?"

He picked the bucket up and held it for her while she drank deeply. She wiped her mouth with the back of her hand while he drank. When he set the bucket back down, she dipped her cupped hand in and splashed the cool water over her flushed face and neck.

Watching her, he smiled. She looked up and saw the gentle expression in his blue eyes. *I've known him forever,* she thought.

To cover her confusion, she turned and walked to Brandy. Slipping her foot into the stirrup, she swung herself into the saddle. He mounted Jet and they turned back toward the ranch.

They hadn't ridden far when she said, "Mama loved Papa enough to die for him."

He looked sharply at her. She blushed. "I have a habit of talking to myself."

She reached a gloved hand down and patted Brandy's neck. "I was thinking about something Mac told me the other day."

"I wouldn't think that was something Mac would talk about."

She straightened up in the saddle. "Real men do use the word love, Mr. Thornton."

He felt her moving away from him. Closing him out. "No, that isn't what I meant. I just. . ."

She turned in the saddle to face him. "Mr. Thornton, I told you after the roundup that I wasn't impressed by showy bravado. Now, I'm going to tell you what I do admire."

They reined in their horses. John hooked his leg over the saddle horn and turned enough to see her face while she talked. She sat straight-backed. Prim. Proper. Ladylike. Her eyes straight ahead. "Mama was a descendant of Sam Houston on her father's side," she said. "And the Spanish conquistadors on her mother's side. She was born to wealth and privilege." She shot a sidelong glance at him and saw his quick grin. "That is the way Mac said it," she defended.

She relaxed, and turned to face him. "I'm not sure how they met—Papa says he was just an ordinary cowpoke—but they fell in love. Her family didn't approve of him from the beginning, but Mac says Mama was strong-willed. They finally agreed to let them marry, but when she insisted on following Papa to Kansas they disinherited her. Mac says she was like fine china. Fragile and easily broken. But, Mac says, that didn't stop her. She came here with Papa and she worked right alongside him and Cyrus and Mac to build this place to what it is today. Mac says when Mama knew she was going to die, she told him she would rather have had fifteen years with Papa than a lifetime in a fine mansion with any other man. Mac told me that Mama knew when she left Texas she wasn't strong enough for life on the frontier. He says she knew she was facing a death sentence when she came here, but still, she loved Papa enough to die for him."

John knew how hard life could be for women who left comfortable homes to follow their men into uncharted territory. He supposed there was an element of truth in the story the old man told Carrie. But why would any woman follow a cold-blooded killer like—

"Mama died a few days before my eighth birthday." Carrie's soft voice called his attention back to her. "Papa grieved something terrible. I felt like I'd lost both of them for a while."

He saw remembered sorrow in her soft brown eyes. "Mac and Cyrus stepped in. After Papa got well, the three of them raised me. They washed my face and combed my hair. They sat beside my bed when I was sick. They scolded me when I misbehaved. Not one of them was ever afraid to say the word love."

She looked down at her hands, which rested lightly on the reins. "They did something else. They taught me that the Bible is the inspired Word of God. They told me that the Old Testament shows us where sin leads. The New Testament shows us the way out of sin. They taught me that the teachings of the New Testament are to be our guidebook for this life. I have never known Mac, or Cyrus, or Papa to compromise their Christian beliefs."

She raised her eyes to him, and he saw tears clinging like dewdrops to her long, dark lashes. "I gave my heart to Jesus Christ when I was twelve years old. I promised He would always be the Master of my life. That's something I seem to have forgotten these last few months."

She took up the reins. "We'd best be getting home."

He dropped his leg down and kicked his foot into the stirrup. They rode slowly and silently across the prairie. The ranch house was in sight before she spoke again. "Mac and Cyrus have done their best to take Mama's place, and I love them and Papa with my whole heart. But sometimes I'm so lonely."

He didn't reply, but she hadn't expected him to. She urged Brandy forward.

John dropped a few paces behind. Watching her slender, straight back and the swinging auburn braid of her hair, he felt his heart swell and crowd up into his throat. He wished there was some way to spare her the pain to come, but he knew there wasn't. Tomorrow, or the next day, or some day very soon, he was going to finish what he had come here to do, and Carrie would be faced with a new sorrow.

They rubbed the horses down in silence. When they came out of the barn, Carrie said, "I won't be riding in the morning. Gretchen is spending the night, and we have plans for tomorrow."

He watched her walk away, then went to the corral and selected a fresh mount. A few minutes later he rode out.

The next morning John rode the fences checking for breaks. He was thinking about Carrie when he topped a slight rise and saw a rider in the valley below him. He recognized the big man astride the Appaloosa. Reining in, he slipped from the saddle, and led Jet into a copse of scrub oak. He slid the Winchester from its scabbard and flipped up the calibrated sight.

The man dismounted and knelt to examine something on the ground. Butler's broad back was to him. John lifted the rifle to his shoulder and sighted down the barrel. There was no way he could miss.

Carrie's face appeared between him and her father's back. "I love Papa with my whole heart," she said.

He lowered the gun and shook his head to clear it. He once more lifted the rifle to his shoulder. "I've been so lonely," Carrie's soft voice said inside his head.

Again, he lowered the rifle. Then, for a third time he raised it to his shoulder. Butler's back was still turned to him. All he had to do was pull the trigger. Still he hesitated.

He'd killed men before. But not like this. He'd never shot an unarmed man. Always before they had been facing him. They'd gone for their guns first. No matter how vile their crime, they'd had a chance. He had walked away because he was faster than they were.

He lowered the rifle. He couldn't kill Butler like this. He wanted him to know why he was dying.

He took the few steps to Jet and slipped the rifle back in the scabbard. He put his foot in the stirrup and swung into the saddle. As he turned Jet away from Butler, he saw a wall of smoke rising in the southwest. Driven by the wind, it was moving swiftly across the prairie in their direction.

John broke out in a cold sweat, and his heart began to pound. He fought the urge to run. To put as much distance as possible between himself and the fire. Butler was still in the valley. He turned back and urged Jet down the rise toward the big man.

Chapter 15

By the time the two men reached the ranch house to sound a warning, then raced to the fire, the greedy flames had crossed the barbed wire southern boundary of the Circle C and were moving fast.

The crew from the Circle C were joined by the Brauns and their hands, as well as the men from several surrounding ranches. Buckboards from the various ranches, carrying barrels of water, were pulled up and left at a safe distance from the fire. Between fifty and seventy-five men spread out along the northeast perimeter of the fire, beating at the flames with wet gunny sacks.

Carrie helped Mac fill the barrels of water in their buckboard, then rode out with him. After Mac parked a safe distance from the fire, they both climbed down to join the line of men. They no sooner got the fire stamped out in one spot than the wind urged it to life somewhere else.

When Carrie ran back to the wagon to dip her sack in water, she searched the line of soot-blackened men for John. But she didn't see him.

Meanwhile, John was several hundred feet away fighting the fire, as well as a much more formidable adversary. He had faced danger most of his life. Few things frightened John Thornton, but fire terrified him.

John turned to go back to the wagon and found himself facing a wall of crackling flames. He turned to his left and flames shot above his head. He turned to his right. More flames. A sudden shift of wind had sent the fire back on itself, trapping him in the center of a blazing inferno. A circle of death.

An agonizing scream tore from his throat, as he ran blindly back and forth searching for a way out. He imagined he could smell his hair singeing, was positive he could hear the sound of his skin beginning to fry like fat bacon in a hot skillet. Blind panic seized him. He screamed again and again.

Suddenly a huge, shapeless figure burst through the fire. Steam rose from it, and he knew Death had come for him. It reached out for him. Doubling his fists he backed away. Something crashed into his chin. Then there was only blackness.

John struggled to escape the darkness. Slowly, inch by painful inch, he pulled himself up out of the inky black pit, and forced his eyes open. Carrie was bending over him. Her face was pale and smudged with black. He wanted to wipe the soot from her face, but he hadn't the strength to life his hand.

"I love you, Caroline." The words were a painful croak.

She smiled and he felt her hand on his hair. He struggled to stay awake, but he was so tired. Slowly his eyes closed.

"I love you, too." He heard her softly spoken words, as he began the slow spiral back into the darkness.

———

When he next woke, he was lying between clean sheets in a shadowy room. He heard water running and turned his head toward the sound. Rain was streaming down the windowpane. His throat hurt, and his tongue felt as if it were glued to the roof of his mouth.

A strong arm slipped around his shoulders and lifted him to a sitting position. The rim of a cool glass touched his cracked lips. Ignoring the soreness of his throat, he drank greedily. "More!" he demanded hoarsely.

The arm lowered him back onto the pillow, and the glass was taken away. "Not just yet," a man's voice said.

John's eyes were adjusting to the dim light, and he could make out Sherman Butler's features, as the big man bent over him. "Where. . .?" His throat hurt when he tried to talk, and he couldn't complete the sentence.

"You're at the main house. We brought you here so we could look after you. You gave us a scare, but you're going to be fine. You swallowed quite a bit of smoke, so your throat may be sore for a while. And, your lips are cracked some from the heat."

"The little lady smeared so much ointment on you thet you look like you oughta be entered in a greased pig contest." Mac appeared beside Butler, and looked down at John. "You'll be jist as purty as ever in a couple a days, but right now, yore a mite blistered."

John wondered where Carrie was. He raised his hand to the gold chain around his neck. His hand moved down over his bare chest to his waist. He was wearing some sort of light trousers. He felt clean, and knew someone must have bathed him. Surely, she hadn't been in the room when they put him in bed.

"Afore Sherm sacks out, you want us to help you take a little walk, air would you ruther use the commode?"

John shook his head. "No! No commode."

Mac chuckled. "I thought not. They's an outside door here. If'n we hurry you won't even get damp."

The cool, damp air felt good on John's face and chest, but he was glad to be back in bed. Butler left, and Mac lit a lamp and settled down in the circle of light with a book.

John lay looking at the ceiling and trying to remember what had happened after he was trapped. A man—for now that the panic was gone he knew it had been a man wrapped in a wet blanket—had braved the flames to rescue him. It must have been Billy. He raised a hand to explore his jaw and winced. Old Billy packed quite a wallop.

"Yore jaw's a mite sore, ain't it?" Mac chuckled. John moved his head so he could see the old man. His book lay open on his lap. His faded blue eyes twinkled as he regarded John over the top of the wire-rimmed spectacles perched on the end of his nose. "Sherm's got a right like the kick of a mule, don't he?"

John frowned. It had been Butler that carried him to safety? He turned his face to the wall. Slowly the darkness closed around him once more.

It was still raining when he woke again, but it was daylight. Carrie stood beside the bed looking down at him. He yanked the sheet up to his chin, and she laughed. "Who do you think put you to bed yesterday afternoon, Mr. Thornton?"

She laughed again. A light, happy laugh. "You can relax. They wouldn't let me see you until you had Papa's pajama trousers on and were all tucked in. Ready for some breakfast? I brought you a tray."

He suddenly realized he was ravenous, and, clutching the sheet around his neck, pushed himself up against the pillows.

She set a lap tray across his legs. "However, I did rub ointment all over your chest and face, Mr. Thornton." She winked. "In my opinion, you haven't got a thing to be ashamed of."

She took a napkin off the tray and shook it out. "Would you like me to feed you?"

He scowled. She smiled and handed him the napkin. He remembered opening his eyes yesterday and seeing her bending over him. Her face, beneath the soot and dirt, had been pale and frightened, but she hadn't cried. He recalled thinking how much he loved her. Surely, he hadn't spoken the words aloud.

"I've already had my breakfast, so I'll sit over here in the chair while you eat. If you want anything, let me know."

He grunted and picked up his fork. The eggs were perfect, the bacon was cooked to a turn, the gravy was thick and creamy, and the biscuits were so light, they seemed to float from the plate. He washed the meal down with a pitcher of cold milk. When he was finished, he wiped his mouth with the napkin and lay back against the pillows. When she came to take the tray, he ventured, "Did you cook breakfast?" and was pleased to find he was only slightly hoarse.

A startled expression crossed her face, then she shook her head. "No, Mac did."

He managed a teasing grin despite his sore lips, "I'd ask Mac to marry me if he wasn't so ugly."

"I don't think he's exactly what you'd want in a wife, Mr. Thornton."

"I'd reckon you're right, Miss Butler. But, pretty faces are easy to come by. A good cook, on the other hand, is a priceless jewel. My mother used to make the best Southern pecan pie and her apple pies would melt in your mouth."

Carrie gazed thoughtfully at him, then she picked up the tray and left the room.

It continued to rain, but several of the men stopped in, one or two at a time, to visit him. None of them stayed longer than five minutes, and John told Billy he was beginning to feel like a malingerer, lying in bed while the other men worked. Billy laughed and said none of them was doing anything much because of the weather. He should just enjoy the rest and the nice soft bed while he could.

He hadn't seen Carrie since breakfast, and now it was almost noon. When Butler came in to check on him, he said she was involved in some secret project in the kitchen. John wondered what she could possibly be doing that would keep her occupied all morning. When she brought him his noontime meal, he noticed a smudge of flour on her nose.

"Here's your dinner," she said, setting the tray across his lap, and handing him his napkin.

She perched on the edge of the bed watching him put away a huge rib-eye steak, and a heap of golden-brown fried potatoes. As soon as he was finished, she took the tray.

"I made you something special for dessert," she said, and left.

When she came back, she was carrying a huge slice of apple pie on a small plate. She handed him the pie and a fork before once more sitting down on the edge of the bed.

John looked at the pie. It didn't look like his mother's. Hers always had a neat fluted edge. This one didn't really have an edge. It looked a little bit as though she had stood back and thrown the top crust on. He suppressed a smile at the mental image. At least the crust was nicely browned. He looked from the pie to Carrie. She was watching him with an expectant smile. "I made it as a surprise for you," she said.

He smiled at her, then poked a forkful of pie in his mouth. He was surprised all right. She must have used salt instead of sugar. He grabbed the glass of water from the table beside the bed and swallowed it in one gulp. "More!" he gasped.

Carrie picked up his fork. He shook his head and thrust the glass in her hand. She took a tiny nibble of the pie and handed him the water pitcher. While he drained the pitcher, she put the pie on the bedside table, then buried her face in her hands.

He returned the empty pitcher to the table. She was still sitting with her face hidden by her hands, but he could see her shoulders shaking. His heart ached for her. She'd worked so hard, and she had done it for him.

He put his hand on her shoulder. "Don't cry, darlin'! I don't care that you can't cook. I still like you better than Mac."

She dropped her hands from her face and turned to him. "Well, I should hope so," she chortled. He pulled her into his arms. They hugged each other, and laughed until tears streamed down their faces.

After their laughter died away, Carrie remained in his arms, leaning against his chest. Her hand reached out to toy with the locket suspended from the heavy gold chain around his neck. "This is beautiful. Where did you get it?"

"It belonged to my mother. My father gave it to her on their wedding day." His arms tightened around her for a heartbeat, then he released her.

She sat up to examine the locket more closely. It was an intricately engraved two-by-three-inch oval. He took it from her and pressed a hidden spring, then handed it back to her open. "This is my Ma and Pa."

Chapter 16

Carrie studied the images in the locket. The dark-haired young man was wearing the uniform of the Confederacy. The girl's hair was light, and she was very pretty. "You look like your father," she said softly.

Finally, she handed the locket back to him. He snapped it closed. "A picture of Mama in her wedding dress hangs above the fireplace," she said. "I'd like for you to see it sometime."

He didn't reply. She looked at him and saw that his eyes were closed. She leaned over and kissed him gently on the lips, then scooted off the bed. She brushed the lock of hair back from his forehead. "Sweet dreams," she whispered, and tiptoed quietly from the room.

When John heard the door close behind her, he opened his eyes. What was he going to do? His sole purpose in coming to Kansas had been to avenge the death of his family. Hatred for the man who killed Ma and Pa, and stole Lucas's life, had driven him for twelve years. Now, he was lying in his enemy's bed, sheltered by his roof, wearing his pajamas.

Worse yet, he was in love with the daughter of the man who had murdered his family. What was he going to do? He squeezed his eyes shut, and two tears rolled slowly down his cheeks. "What should I do, Pa?"

He saw in his mind his father and mother sitting at the kitchen table. Pa's Bible lay open before him.

Pa read aloud. " 'But I say unto you, Love your enemies, bless them that curse you, do good to them that hate you, and pray for them which despitefully use you, and persecute you.' "

Pa reached a hand out to Ma. "Mavis, we must pray for Sherman Butler and these other men. They are wanderin' lost through life, tryin' to avenge somethin' that's been over for fifteen years." He reached his other hand out to Lucas. "Come, pray with us, son. And, I want you to remember one thing, Lucas. Vengeance is a circle. If you let it, it'll just go on from generation to generation destroyin' endlessly. Someone's gotta break the circle, son."

They had joined hands around the table and prayed for the salvation of their enemies. That night, Sherman Butler had come with his men. His gentle, peace-loving pa had died. And, Ma. And, Lucas had been destroyed, too.

Where had God been when his family was being slaughtered? While his family lay in the ground, Sherman Butler had grown powerful and rich. Where had God been the last twelve years? God had told Cain the voice of his brother's blood cried out to Him from the ground. Surely, the innocent blood of his family had a voice. Cain had been punished for his crime. Sherman Butler had prospered. It wasn't just. If God wasn't going to punish Butler, then he had to.

The vision of Carrie's beautiful face interposed itself on the back of his eyelids. He blinked his eyes open. His feelings for Butler's beautiful red-haired daughter went far beyond mere physical desire. He had known other women. But always he had been able to leave them and ride away without a backward glance.

Carrie was different. His feeling for her went far beyond the attraction he had felt when he first met her. He loved her. The kind of love that called for a visit to a preacher, and led to a home and children. 'Til death do us part love. The kind of love his parents had shared.

His hand went to the locket lying against his heart. He could no longer deny his love for Carrie. But no matter what the cost, his family's murderer must pay for their deaths. He had to finish what Sherman Butler had started twelve years ago.

The next day it quit raining. John moved back to the bunkhouse and returned to work.

One morning Carrie and John rode out to look at the damage from the fire. Already new grass was pushing up through the black stubble of the burned off pasture. "Isn't it wonderful how nature renews itself?" she asked.

He nodded in agreement, but his eyes were on her. Carrie had always been beautiful, but since the fire, she was incandescent. He knew he was responsible for the glow that emanated from her, and while he told himself it would be better if she didn't love him, some basic instinct buried deep in him was proud that she could love him so much.

"I want to show you something," she said, and turned Brandy toward the creek.

They rode for some time before they entered a grove of trees. Carrie reined Brandy in and slid from the saddle. John dismounted and moved to her side. She reached out and took his hand. "This is my secret place," she said. "I've never told anyone about it, not even Gretchen and Lucille. I come here when I'm sad or lonely. I never wanted to share it with anyone before, but I want to share it with you."

Her brown eyes were innocent and soft with love. John knew she was offering a very special part of herself to him. He also knew he wasn't worthy of her trust. He should turn and walk away. His fingers closed around her hand. Side by side they walked through the trees.

The Garden of Eden couldn't have been more beautiful than Carrie's secret place.

She looked up at him. He slipped his arm around her waist, and pulled her close. His heart pounded in his ears, drowning out the sound of the waterfall, as he bent his head to her. The kiss they shared beside the serene little pool spoke of a lifetime of loneliness and yearning. When he released her, she laid her open hand against the side of his face, then smoothed back the curl of golden-brown hair that dropped over his forehead. He traced the line of her soft, full lips with a gentle fingertip as he memorized every feature of her face.

Neither of them spoke when they once more joined hands and walked back to their horses.

As soon as they rode into the ranch yard, they noticed a crowd had gathered at the side of the smaller corral, where the horses were broken. They caught a glimpse of a man lying on the ground.

"It's Papa!" Carrie jumped from Brandy and ran toward the corral. She was already kneeling on the ground beside her father when John walked up and joined the other men.

He moved over to stand by Billy. "What happened?"

Billy turned a worried face in his direction. "He was breakin' a bronc and that sidewinder run him into the fence. His leg's broke, but Cyrus thinks it's a clean break. Mac went to the house fer a blanket. They sent Abel to town after the Doc. Soon as Mac gits back we're gonna carry him in the house."

When Billy turned to say something to the man on the other side of him, John looked at the man on the ground. Butler was at least two inches taller than John's six feet two inches, and easily weighed two hundred fifty pounds. Not an ounce of it fat. Sherman Butler was a big, muscular man. A powerhouse of a man. And, looking at him lying helpless on the ground, John realized that he was still a young man. Just into his forties, he reckoned, and not really looking even that.

Carrie smoothed the thick auburn hair back from her father's forehead. "Does it hurt terribly, Papa?"

"Nah!" he said. "But, I'm getting old, little girl. Five years ago something like this wouldn't have happened."

"You're not old," she protested. The men parted, and she looked up. "Here's Mac now. They're going to carry you inside and put you to bed."

Carrie scrambled to her feet and stepped back while Mac spread the blanket out beside her father. The men lifted him as gently as possible and laid him on the blanket. He didn't make a sound, but his face paled, and beads of sweat broke out on his forehead. John knew it must have hurt terribly, and admitted a grudging admiration for the big man.

Carrie walked beside the improvised stretcher, holding her father's hand, while they carried him to the house. The other men trailed along behind and John went with them.

They laid him on the big bed in his room, blanket and all. Cyrus took a knife and slit the left leg of his denims. An ugly red and purple bruise discolored the leg from the knee down. They pulled the boot from his right foot. Then Cyrus flicked open the knife and moved to his left foot.

"What do you think yer a-doin'?" Mac growled.

"I'm cuttin' his boot off." Cyrus scowled. "What's it look like I'm doin'?"

"Well, what's he s'posed to do with only one boot?" Mac demanded.

"I don't know, Mr. McDougal, I reckon you jist might have to dig into your cookie jar and buy him a new pair." Cyrus brandished the knife while the two elderly men argued.

Butler raised up on his elbow, "Am I going to have to get out of this bed and whip both of you?" he thundered.

"I jist don't see no use a-ruinin' a perfectly good pair of boots," Mac grumbled.

"Well, what do you want me to do, jist yank it off him?" Cyrus shouted, waving the knife around his head like a saber.

"Forevermore!" Carrie's voice rose above the men's. "Cut that boot off before his leg swells up, and you can't get it off."

While they yelled at one another, John saw something he hadn't allowed himself to see before. These four people—the sweet gentle girl he loved, her father, and the two crusty old cowpokes—were a family. He didn't know how Butler and the two older men had come together in the first place, but he had no doubt of one thing. The four of them were bound by something stronger than blood. In spite of all the yelling—or perhaps because of it—it was plain to see how deeply they loved one another.

He turned and walked out of the house. Jet and Brandy were still where they had left them. He took Brandy in the barn and rubbed her down. Then he mounted Jet and rode toward the west.

It was twilight when he came back to the ranch. Billy was standing by the corral when he turned Jet in with the other horses. He leaned against the fence beside him.

"How'd it go?"

"Carrie stayed right at her pa's side while the Doc set his leg. He'll be laid up awhile, but he'll be good as new when the leg heals."

John glanced at the other man. "How'd she take it?"

"Carrie?" Billy shrugged his shoulders. "She done fine. Carrie's a strong little gal. By the way, she said she wanted to see you when you got home. She's waitin' fer you in the house."

John thought about refusing, but he wanted to see that she really was all right. He turned on his heel and walked to the house.

He found Carrie in the spacious main room. She was sitting on a large, leather-covered couch and looking up at the portrait that hung over the massive rock fireplace.

He hesitated at the door, and she turned her gaze toward him, then rose, and crossed the room to stand in front of him. She slipped her arms around his waist, as if it were the most natural thing in the world to do, and rested her head against his chest. Instinctively, his arms went around her, and he held her close.

Chapter 17

She stepped back and took his hand. "I'm glad you're here."

"How is he?"

"The doctor gave him laudanum for the pain, and he's asleep. Come, sit with me for a while." She urged him toward the deep leather couch.

John quickly glanced at the open beams above his head. The rough cream-colored stucco walls. The massive sandstones that framed the large fireplace and soared to the roof peak. The bookcases that filled most of one wall.

He had been in the parlors of a few rich folks, and this was nothing like those rooms. There was no silk, or satin, or brocade here. No delicate furniture a man was afraid to sit on for fear he'd break it. Instead, the massive couches and chairs were deep, inviting, and covered in leather. Woven wool rugs with Indian designs were scattered over the polished hardwood floors. Those fancy parlors looked cheap and tawdry compared to this.

They sat down on the couch. "This is Mama," she said. "Wasn't she beautiful?"

John looked up at the woman in the portrait. "She was very beautiful," he said. And she was. But not nearly as beautiful as Carrie.

With a contented sigh, she snuggled against him. He put his arm around her, and she rested her head on his shoulder. There was comfort in their silence. Finally, she said, "I miss her so much, John. Today when I saw Papa on the ground, I was so scared. I don't know if I could bear to lose him, too." Her hand was toying with a button on the front of his shirt. "I'm so glad you are here with me. I've been so lonely, John. So. . .very. . .very. . . ." Her hand dropped away from his shirt.

He saw that she had fallen asleep. He eased her down and covered her with a blanket that was folded over the arm of the couch. Then he stood and looked at her. Her long dark lashes shadowed her flushed cheeks. Her soft, full lips were slightly parted. She looked young, innocent, and terribly vulnerable. Tears stung the back of his eyelids. Blinking them back, he slipped quietly from the room.

John didn't see much of Carrie the remainder of that week; she devoted all her time to caring for her father. He hadn't expected her to go to church on Sunday morning, but when the Circle C wranglers rode out, she was in the buggy beside Mac. Cyrus trailed along behind with the other men.

John watched them drive down the long lane before he went back to the deserted bunkhouse to gather his things. Then, he strapped on his gun belt, and walked slowly to the house. He slipped through the kitchen door and walked carefully down the hall to Sherman Butler's bedroom.

Butler was propped up against the pillows asleep. John eased into the big chair across from the bed.

He sat for half an hour, trying not to think about Carrie, before Butler stirred and opened his eyes. He gave a little start when he saw John, then smiled a greeting. "I thought I was alone," he said. "What can I do for you, John? Or did you come to visit?"

John rose and walked slowly across to stand beside the bed. He looked directly into the big man's eyes. "My name is not John Thornton," he said, "and I have come here to kill you."

"I don't understand." The man's eyes were questioning, but there was no fear in them. "Who are you? Why do you want to kill me?"

"My name is Lucas Nolan. On the night of August 21, 1880, you murdered my mother and my father."

"Lucas?" Butler's eyes searched his face. "Lucas was killed with his parents. Is this some sort of hoax?"

Lucas reached up and pulled the locket to the outside of his shirt. "Have you seen this before?"

Butler nodded. "I saw it when we put you to bed the day of the fire."

Lucas flipped a switch and the locket sprang open. He held it where Butler could see the pictures inside. "This is my mother and father. She was standing in front of the window when you came with your men. A defenseless woman. A sweet, gentle woman who never hurt anyone." He fought against the tears he felt crowding into his throat. "She was clearing the supper dishes from the table when you killed her. The house was already burning when Pa put her locket around my neck. He boosted me out the window and told me to run. I waited until you shot him then I ran. Now, I'm back. And, you're going to pay for what you did."

Lucas snapped the locket shut and dropped it back inside his shirt.

Butler shook his head. "Thank God you're alive," he said. Then he buried his face in his hands and wept.

Lucas shifted from one foot to the other, unsure of what to do next. He had been prepared for Butler to beg for his life. He hadn't expected this.

Finally, the big man lifted his head. "Cyrus always said you weren't there, but I thought he was wrong. I didn't see how you could have escaped." Before Lucas realized what he was doing Butler reached out and grasped his hand. "I didn't kill your parents, Lucas. But I was at least partially responsible for their deaths. Please, sit down. Let me tell you what happened that night."

Lucas's eyes never left the big man's face as he sank slowly down on the bed at his side. What he had to say wouldn't change anything, but Butler had the right to defend himself.

"Your father fought in the Confederate Army. My father was a Union soldier. I know that doesn't seem like a reason to hate a man. But I hated anyone who fought on the side of the South. When you moved here, I wanted you out. I didn't personally cut your fences, or foul your water hole, or run off your stock. But some of the men from nearby ranches did. And I looked the other way."

He leaned forward. "You must understand, Lucas, Kansas was solidly behind the North during the war. There were a lot of old Jayhawkers still around. Men who thought John Brown was a hero. August 21 was a Saturday night. A bunch of good-for-nothings had gathered at the saloon in town. They got a few drinks in them—they weren't the most sterling characters at best—and six of them decided to burn your folks out."

"You were there," Lucas interrupted. "I saw you."

"I was there. We all three were. Me. Cyrus. Mac. One of the men that worked for us was at the saloon. He rode out here and told us what was happening. We got our men together and rode over there as fast as we could. We were too late to save your folks, but the six drifters were still there. Then several of the other ranchers showed up."

He passed a hand across his eyes. "There was no doubt they were guilty. We hanged all six of them in that big tree."

"Caroline told me she didn't know why it was called the hanging tree."

"She doesn't. Mac has always thought we should tell her about the hangings, but I never wanted her to know. I was afraid she wouldn't understand."

Lucas knew Sherman Butler was telling the truth.

Everything he had believed the past twelve years was a lie. Half his life he had hated an innocent man. He struggled to his feet. "I'm sorry."

"Don't be. I understand, Lucas. More than you will ever know, I understand."

"I'll be goin' now." He turned at the door. "Tell Caroline—" He shook his head. "Never mind. It isn't important."

"Don't leave, Lucas!" Sherman reached out a beseeching hand. "Your folks' place belongs to you. Please stay."

"No!" Lucas said harshly. Then his voice softened. "I can't."

He turned his back on Sherman Butler's pleas and walked away.

Lucas was tying his bedroll on behind the saddle when Carrie and Mac drove into the ranch yard, followed by Cyrus on horseback.

Carrie jumped down from the buggy and ran to him. "John, where are you going?"

He finished securing the bedroll before turning to face her. She was wearing something pink. His heart ached until he thought it would burst. "I'm leaving."

"Leaving?" She clutched at his arm. "You can't leave me. Please! Don't leave me, John."

"I have to." He gently removed her clinging fingers from his arm, and held both her hands tightly in his. "There is no John Thornton, Caroline. There never was. It was all a lie. Everything was a lie. I am a lie."

"No!" Tears were streaming down her face. "I love you and I know you love me. That isn't a lie. I love you. It doesn't matter who you are."

"I don't even know who I am, darlin'." He felt the wetness of his own tears. "I have to find out."

He released her hands and swung into the saddle. "Good-bye, Caroline."

He turned Jet and they galloped away to the west. Carrie ran to the house. She collided with Cyrus coming out the back door. He reached out to steady her. "Your pa told me ever'thing. Don't worry, young'un. It's goin' to be all right."

He patted her arm, then hurried to his horse, mounted up, and followed Lucas.

Carrie flung herself on her bed. Her mother's Bible was lying beside her. She clutched it to her, and sobbed until there were no tears left. Finally, she lay quiet and exhausted. "If you were here, Mama, what would you tell me?"

There was no answer. "You didn't let anything keep you from Papa," Carrie whispered. "I'll go after him. I'll follow him to the ends of the earth if I must, but I won't let him go. I'll never let him go."

She pushed herself into a sitting position. When she laid the Bible on the bed beside her, the cream-colored envelope fell out. She opened it, took out the card, and read the words her mother had written. *To every thing there is a season, and a time to every purpose under the heaven.*

She returned the card to the envelope. On a whim, she opened the Bible to the place her mother had marked with the frayed ribbon marker. At the beginning of the third chapter of Ecclesiastes, she saw the words her mother had written on the card. She read the first eight verses. Then read them again. Suddenly what Mama had been trying to tell her was crystal clear.

"Not my will, but Thine," she whispered. "Oh, Lord, forgive me. I've been a headstrong selfish fool. Lord, take my life. From this day forth I belong completely to You."

She lay for several minutes praying and crying. Prayers of surrender and submission. Tears of repentance and joy. With recommitment came renewal, and a deep peace engulfed her.

She got up from the bed, straightened her clothes, washed her face, and smoothed her hair.

Mac tapped on her door. "Air you all right, little lady?"

"I'm fine," she said, and knew that she was now. "I'm just fine, Mac."

"Wal, yer pa and me got somethin' to tell you if you feel like talkin'."

She glanced at her mother's Bible lying on the bed. "Thank you, Mama," she whispered.

She opened the door and kissed Mac's worried face. Then she linked her arm in his, and they walked down the hall to her father's room.

Chapter 18

Lucas walked through the orchard, stepped over the low fence, and knelt beside his parents' grave. Only one perfect red rose still bloomed on the bush he had transplanted when he first came to the Circle C.

"The last rose of summer," he murmured. The lines of the old Thomas Moore poem came to his mind. He snapped the rose from its life-giving stem and scattered the petals over the grave. " 'When true hearts lie withered and fond ones are flown, Oh! who would inhabit, this bleak world alone?' "

"You don't have to be alone, Lucas."

He started, and jumped quickly to his feet, his hand on the gun at his side. When he saw who it was, he relaxed. "That's a good way to get yourself shot, Cyrus."

Cyrus chuckled. "Yeah, I reckon it is. I had better sense than to walk up behind a man with a gun in my younger days. Reckon I'm gettin' careless in my old age."

Lucas stepped over the fence. "What're you doin' here?"

"Sherman sent me because he can't come hisself. He wants you to stay."

Lucas shook his head. "Didn't he tell you I came here to kill him?" he asked, and started to walk away.

Cyrus followed him through the orchard. "Yep! He told me you was aimin' on shootin' him, but you never could."

"You don't know how close I came the day of the fire." Lucas caught up Jet's reins. "I had him right in my sights. It was just luck I didn't kill him."

"Maybe." Cyrus nodded. "But more likely it was the grace of God stayed your hand."

"You can call it whatever you want. All I know is, I came here seekin' justice for Ma and Pa. You all took care of that twelve years ago. Now it's time I was movin' on."

"Is that what you really want, to jist keep movin' from place to place? Driftin' until you meet someone that can draw faster or shoot straighter? Is that the way you want your life to end, Lucas? Layin' dead in some dusty street with no one to care? I left a little girl cryin' her eyes out—"

"I don't want to talk about her," Lucas interrupted. "Leave Caroline out of this."

"You can't leave her out." Cyrus pulled on his ear. "Do you think when Carrie finds out what brung you here, she'll quit carin' about you? Cause if that's what you're thinkin', you don't know our Carrie very good."

"It isn't just that." Lucas put one foot in the stirrup to mount. "Everything I am was shaped by my hatred for Sherman Butler. I trained for the day I would come back to face him, just as a soldier trains to do battle. I thought about little else. And it was all a lie. Somewhere between the hatred and the lies, Lucas Nolan was lost. I don't know who I am any more. Butler told me this morning that he understood. But he doesn't. Nobody does." He swung into the saddle. "Until I know the truth, I have nothing to offer Caroline."

Cyrus put a hand on Jet's bridle. "Sherman said he told you everything, but I reckon he didn't."

Lucas's eyes narrowed. "What do you mean? Did he have more to do with my folks' killing than he said?"

"No, he told you straight enough about what happened here, I reckon." Cyrus pulled on his earlobe. "I'm talkin' about what happened before that. Sherman weren't old enough to fight in the war. Ain't you a mite curious about how come he hated the rebs so much he didn't even want your pa livin' close by?"

Butler had said he hated the Confederacy. It hadn't even occurred to Lucas, until now, to wonder why. He stepped down from Jet. With Cyrus leading the way the two men walked over and sat down on the sandstone foundation.

Cyrus began to talk. "Me and Mac was with Sherman's father during the war. Jim was a good man. He got killed at Shiloh. Before he died, he asked me and Mac to see about his wife and boy. We promised him we would. It was three of the longest, most miserable years you can imagine before the war ended, but we kept our promise."

His eyes took on a faraway look as he peered into the past. Lucas waited impatiently for him to continue.

"We found the place right off," Cyrus said. "The house was powerful in need of paint. But the fields was plowed, and things looked to be well cared fer. We couldn't raise nobody, so we jist set down on the porch and waited. Along about twilight, this tall, gangly, redheaded kid comes in with a team of mules hitched to a plow. We knowed soon as we seen him he was Jim's boy. He was surprised to see us, but when we told him we was friends of his pa, he invited us to stay fer supper. He told us Abigail—that was his ma—had died some time ago. He didn't tell us how she died. Not until later."

"How old was Mr. Butler?" John asked.

"He wasn't more than fourteen, just a young'un, and all alone. I didn't have no kin to speak of, and Mac's wife and little boy had died with cholera durin' the war. We kinda threw in with the kid, and we stayed there fer a year or so." Cyrus kicked at the hard-packed earth with the toe of his boot.

"To make a long story short, the boy was restless and so was we. He sold the farm fer what he could get—which was precious little—and we commenced to roam. We finally ended up in Texas, which was no place fer a young'un with a grudge agin the South, which is what Sherman was. He hated Johnny Rebs worse than anyone I ever seen. You see the war was over fer me and Mac. We jist wanted to fergit it. But it hadn't ended fer Sherman. One night he told us why."

Cyrus paused in his narrative to collect his thoughts before he continued.

"Seems Abigail had been at the house alone when a bunch of Reb foragers come along. They violated her and they tortured her, then they stole everything they could carry, and they left. When Sherman come in from the field that evenin' he found his ma. She was still alive, but they wasn't nothin' he could do fer her. She died that night. Sherman buried his ma, but he never buried his hate fer the men that killed her. It festered and grew inside him fer six years. Then we come to Texas. He was eighteen years old, and he wasn't a skinny kid no more; he was full-grown. Texas had been on the side of the South. She was crawlin' with Johnny Rebs itchin' fer a fight. Sherman never started a fight, but he never backed down from one neither."

John looked at the other man, "So, Mr. Butler was a gunfighter?"

Cyrus nodded. "I reckon you could say that. He's good with a gun, Lucas. Real good. Best I ever saw, and I seen plenty. He got quite a reputation. Then he met Miss Caroline Houston. The gunfighter and the lady. They fell in love. Her folks wasn't what you'd call real happy about the match, but Caroline had a mind of her own. They had a big, fancy wedding. I reckon the Houstons thought they could break Sherman to lead, and make an acceptable son-in-law out of him. When they found out they couldn't, they tried to get Caroline to leave him and come home."

"Carrie said her mother loved her father enough to die for him," John said.

Cyrus' face grew thoughtful. "That she did." Then he chuckled. "Caroline had spunk. She stayed with Sherman." He pulled on his earlobe. "Sherman fergot about hatin' Johnny Rebs fer a while. He begin to work real hard at providin' fer his family. I reckon he didn't want Caroline to think she'd made a mistake stayin' with him instead of movin' back into that big mansion with her folks. After the war, there was a lot of cattle roamin' free. They didn't wear no brand, and nobody wanted them, so we rounded us up a good-sized herd. We waited until Caroline had Matthew, then, soon as we knowed everything was all right, we trailed them cows to Kansas. Like I said, Sherman had quite a reputation in Texas; now that he was a family man, he thought it might be best not to go back. There was plenty of land here. So we decided to stay. Soon as we got a cabin built, Sherman went fer Caroline and the baby."

"So that's the story?" Lucas asked.

"Not quite," Cyrus shifted a bit on the stone they were sitting on. "I ain't told you the most important part yet.

"Caroline was a Christian, and soon as the church was built her and Mac—he'd been a believer since he was a young'un—started goin' to church. She gentled Sherman down some, but she never could git him to go to church with her. Then your folks moved in, and the hate in him flared up again. Oh, he never done nothin' to hurt your pa directly, but we sat by while other folks did. Then they was killed.

"My shame at what we'd done—or more rightly what we hadn't done—drove me to my knees. But not Sherman. The guilt gnawed at him somethin' awful, but he hardened his heart. Then Caroline got sick. He never let hisself believe she'd die. When she did, he pushed everybody away, even little Carrie, and closed the pain up inside."

John felt a sharp pain for the small girl he barely remembered. "It must have been a difficult time for Carrie."

Cyrus nodded. "Yes. It was a hard time for all of us. Anyway, to get back to my story. Finally, Sherman took a Bible and a jug of water and went to one of the line shacks. I was afraid he'd harm hisself, and I wanted to go after him. Mac said no. He said the time had come fer Sherman to make a decision. He said we'd be a heap more help stayin' home prayin' than we would followin' and interferin' in the Lord's work. I was kinda new at the prayin' business, but Mac weren't. So, that's what we done." Cyrus drew a deep breath before he continued.

"There'd always been a lost look in Sherman's eyes, even before Caroline died, but when he come home that look was gone. We knew then that he'd found what he'd been searchin' fer."

When Cyrus fell silent, Lucas stood up. "Thanks for telling me, Cyrus. My pa said vengeance was a circle, and I reckon he was right."

"It's a circle only as long as nobody steps out. But, that's what you done today, Lucas. You stepped out. The circle of vengeance is broken. There's a place for you here. Carrie loves you, and I'm askin' you to stay."

"I can't." He turned and walked to where Jet was grazing, and Cyrus followed. He picked up the reins. "For the first twelve years of my life I was Lucas Nolan. For the last twelve I've been John Thornton. Half my life I've carried a load of hate inside me. Now the hatred is gone, and there's a big empty space where it was. I feel like an empty shell, Cyrus. I have nothin' to offer Carrie."

"I reckon we're all empty shells, son, until we meet the Lord."

"Don't you understand, Cyrus? Carrie doesn't know Lucas Nolan. She knows John Thornton. And, John Thornton never existed. The whole last twelve years has been a lie." He put his foot in the stirrup and swung into the saddle.

Cyrus put a hand on the younger man's knee. "Do you think you're the only man that's ever changed his name? Sherman Butler never existed until twenty years ago. I told you he was a gunfighter when we was in Texas. He had a different name then, Lucas. If I was to tell you what it was, you'd recognize it jist like you recognize the name of Bat Masterson, or Wyatt Earp, or Doc Holliday, or Wild Bill Hickock, or any one of a dozen others that lived by the gun. Sherman wasn't that different from you, son. In many ways you put me in mind of him."

Lucas leaned over the saddle horn and looked down at the older man. "There's somethin' I want you to know, Cyrus. I was never a gunfighter. The first eight years I was on my own, I did what I had to do to survive. Mostly muckin' stables, and then later, when I was old enough, wranglin'. I tried never to do anything that would shame the memory of my pa and ma. The last four years, I was a Texas Ranger."

Cyrus brushed an invisible mist from his eyes. "I know your folks would be right proud of you, Lucas."

"I like to think so." Lucas blinked the haze from his own eyes.

Cyrus cleared his throat. "Well, like I wuz sayin', when we come here, he wanted a new start, so he took a new name. But, changin' names don't change a man, son. It was what happened in that line shack eight years ago that changed Sherman.

"I see that same lost look in your eyes as I used to see in his, and as I used to see in my own when I looked in the lookin' glass. We all got that empty space you was talkin' about, Lucas. Don't none of us really know who we are 'til we let the Lord fill us with his love and forgiveness. Your ma and pa was Christian folks. They'd want you to follow their lead, boy."

Lucas looked out over the vast, beckoning prairie. "I know they would, Cyrus. And, maybe someday I will. But, right now, I can't."

The older man sighed, "Well, I reckon I understand how you feel, Lucas. But one of these days the Lord's gonna speak to you, boy. When he does, don't you run from Him."

"I've got to be on my way." Lucas reached out and the two men shook hands.

"I'll be prayin' fer you, son. We all will. And when your roamin' days is over. . ." Cyrus squeezed the young man's hand before releasing it. "Jist don't fergit where home is."

Lucas raised his hand in a final farewell, then nudged Jet into a gallop.

Cyrus stood watching until they disappeared from sight. Then he mounted up and headed back to the Circle C.

Chapter 19

For the next few months, Lucas drifted, never staying in one place more than a few days.

For twelve years, he had allowed himself few friendships and no attachments. It had been a hard, lonely life, but one he deemed necessary, and he had adapted. Now, he felt as barren as the desolate land he rode across and as empty as the vast sky that stretched over his head. Carrie was never far from his thoughts, and the loneliness cut through him like a knife.

He spent the fall in Colorado and Utah. When he woke to find the first snow blowing across his bed, he drifted south to Arizona, then New Mexico, and finally back to Texas.

One morning he woke to the sound of birds singing. The sun was shining and billowy white clouds drifted lazily across an azure sky. It had been almost a year since he rescued Carrie from the runaway buggy. It seemed an eternity since he rode away from her. It was time to move on. That night he gave notice to the foreman, and left the Texas ranch where he had worked the past week.

He wandered aimlessly northwest. It was late afternoon when he rode into a small town in Oklahoma. He tied Jet to the hitching rail in front of the saloon and went inside. Twenty minutes later he came out, untied Jet, and swung into the saddle.

"Well, boy, looks like we might get us a job at the Bar X. The bartender said they were hiring. We just follow this road five miles. He says we can't miss it."

On the edge of town, a large tent had been set up. Wagons, buggies, and saddled horses crowded the surrounding field.

"Looks like they're havin' themselves a revival meetin'," Lucas said, and started to urge Jet on. Then a familiar tune drifted from the tent, and a woman began to sing.

The day Lucas rode away from her, Carrie left her girlhood behind. She had been led—by the cryptic messages her mother left for her—to read the complete passage from the Bible. In reading it again and again, she had come to understand what her mother was trying to tell her. *To every thing there is a season, and a time to every purpose under the heaven.* A time to love and a time to let love go.

When her father and Mac told her what had happened at the Nolan place twelve years earlier, she knew why John Thornton had so exactly matched her mystery man. "The Mysterious Stranger" had been created—not from the fantasies of a lonely young girl—but from her memories of Lucas Nolan. When she was a small girl, she loved twelve-year-old Lucas Nolan. When John Thornton appeared, that love was rekindled.

She had lost Lucas twice. The first time when she was five, and again when she was eighteen. Now, she was nineteen, and she knew Lucas wouldn't be back this time. It had taken much prayer, and a lot of soul-searching, but she had finally accepted that she would spend the rest of her life alone.

Lucille hadn't returned to her position in the small school, and Carrie had offered to fill in. She taught the entire term, and she loved it. Seeing the expression of wonder on young faces when they finally grasped the solution to a difficult problem, or realized for the first time that they were actually reading, had proved fulfilling beyond her expectations. She had always loved children. Since she would never have her own, perhaps God was calling her to teach other people's children.

Now that the school term had ended, she found herself at loose ends. One warm spring day she rode out to her secret place. Leaving Brandy on the edge of the grove of trees, she walked to the pool. The spring rains had swollen the creek and sent the water roaring over the waterfall, before it rushed on its way. Still, the small pool was as peaceful as ever.

Carrie pushed her hat off and let it dangle down her back. Kneeling on the edge of the pool, she leaned forward to examine her face in its placid depths. It was the same face that had looked back at her a year ago, yet there were subtle differences. A new serenity. A peacefulness. A maturing of the girlish features.

Another face appeared above hers in the mirror-smooth waters. A lean, masculine face, with a lock of golden-brown hair falling over the wide forehead, and a slight dimple in the square chin. A face she had thought she would never see again.

She sprang to her feet and flung herself against his broad chest. His arms closed around her. She felt the strong beat of his heart. She lifted her head, and stepped back enough to look at him. Lines of fatigue etched his tanned face. He was dusty from the trail and he needed a shave. She didn't notice those things. They didn't matter.

She searched his eyes, and found what she was seeking in their blue depths. They were no longer John Thornton's cold, hurting eyes. These were the gentle eyes of the boy who had given a small girl the last cookie in the cookie jar. They were Lucas Nolan's eyes.

"You've come home to stay, haven't you?"

"If you still want me I have," he said, and there was a question in his blue eyes.

She raised her face to his. The kiss they shared answered all their questions, and erased the months of loneliness.

<hr>

Later, they walked slowly along the bank of the creek, leading their horses. She told him about her pupils and Gretchen and Billy's December wedding.

He told her of his life in the months after he left her.

"Always before, I read everything I could get my hands on," he said. "Yet, when I was involved in someone else's life, I forgot how lonely I had been in those days."

Carrie understood. She had whiled away many lonely hours reading. She squeezed his hand in silent understanding.

He returned the gentle pressure of her fingers. "This time all I could think about was you," he said, "and what I had left behind."

"I prayed for you every day," Carrie looked up at him, and her brown eyes glowed. "But I didn't think you'd ever come back to me."

"I had nothing to give you, Caroline."

"You had yourself. That's all I ever wanted, Lucas."

"I couldn't even offer you myself. I was lost." He released her hand and put his arm around her shoulders. "A little over a week ago—in a small town in Oklahoma—I found myself. I'd like to tell you about it."

She slipped her arm around his waist and rested her head against his shoulder. "I'm listening."

"I was lookin' for a job when I passed a big tent. I figured they were havin' a revival—an' I for sure didn't want no part of that—so I started to hurry Jet past. Then, someone began to play the piano and a woman started singing 'Amazing Grace.'" He shot a quick glance at Carrie before he continued.

"When I was a boy, the first thing I heard every morning when I woke up was my mother singing hymns as she fixed breakfast. 'Amazing Grace' was her favorite, and it was always one of the songs she sang."

They stopped walking, and Carrie looked up at his face as he talked. "It was like somethin' was drawin' me to that tent. I thought it wouldn't hurt anything to sit outside and listen 'til she was through singin'. Next thing I knew I was walkin' in. I found a seat in the back and sat down. They sang a few more hymns, then the preacher got up. He was a big strong-lookin' man. Reminded me of your pa." The corners of his eyes crinkled with a smile as he looked at Carrie.

"I remember he took his text from Matthew 18:11–14. But I couldn't tell you what he preached. Somethin' about the lost sheep, I reckon. All I remember is when the sermon was over he gave an invitation. It was like an invisible hand was pulling me forward. Next thing I knew I had taken the sawdust trail, and was kneelin' at the altar in front of everybody, sobbin' my heart out."

Tears were trickling down Carrie's cheeks. He cupped her chin in his hand. "I know who I am now, darlin'. I'm Lucas John Nolan, a child of the King. I'm not empty anymore, Caroline, but without you, I am incomplete. I still don't have anything in the way of material possessions to offer you; everything I own is tied on Jet's back—"

Carrie interrupted. "I don't care, Lucas, all I ever wanted was—"

He put a silencing finger across her lips. "I'm not finished yet, darlin'. I've been rehearsin' this speech for hundreds of miles. If you'll let me finish, you can talk all you want. All right?"

She nodded, and he removed his finger. "Now, where was I? Everything I own is tied on Jet's back, except for one thing." He dug down in the watch pocket of his denims and brought out a small velvet bag. He loosened the drawstrings and shook a wide gold band into the palm of his hand. "This was my mother's wedding ring. I know she would be proud to have you wear it."

"Yes," Carrie said.

"Now wait a minute, I haven't asked you yet. I want to do this proper like."

"Of all things, Lucas Nolan! I've been waiting for this day since I was six years old. I don't care anything about proper."

"But I do. I want this to be a day you'll tell our granddaughters about." He dropped to one knee and took her hand in his. "Caroline, I can't offer you much. All I have is myself. But my heart belongs to you, and it always will. Will you be my wife?"

Her face was wet with tears, as she stood looking down into his eyes, but she didn't say anything.

"Well, will you marry me, or not?" Lucas finally demanded impatiently.

She wrinkled her nose. "I'm thinking about it."

"Thinkin' about it! You already said yes." He scrambled to his feet. "You have to marry me, Caroline. I love you. I can't live without you. Without you my life wouldn't be—"

"Now, that's what I consider a proper proposal." She grinned up at him. "Yes, Lucas Nolan, I will marry you. And I will love and honor you all the days of my life."

He frowned at her. "What about obey?"

She gave a saucy toss of her head. "That's negotiable, Mr. Nolan."

Chapter 20

If it had been left up to Carrie, they would have been married the week after Lucas came home. However, Lucas and her father had other plans. When they finally selected the date for their wedding, it seemed far in the future to Carrie. Much, much too far. But there was so much to do, and they were so busy, the months passed swiftly.

Carrie woke before daylight on the first Saturday morning in August. Today was the day. At two o'clock this afternoon, she would become Mrs. Lucas John Nolan. Her mother's wedding dress was hanging in the wardrobe, pressed, and ready for her to wear. Despite her happiness, tears welled up and rolled slowly down her cheeks. If only Mama could be here to see her in the dress she had worn on her own wedding day.

She sat up and lit the lamp on the table beside her bed. Last night, when her father came to tuck her in, they had talked for over an hour. Then, he had taken a familiar cream-colored envelope from his pocket. "Your mother wrote this that last evening." He cleared his throat before he was able to continue. "The next morning she didn't wake up."

He tucked the letter inside the front cover of her mother's Bible. "Caroline asked me to give this to you the night before you were to be married. She wanted you to read it first thing on the morning of your wedding."

When he leaned over to kiss her good night she put her arms around his neck and clung to him. "I love you, Papa, and I'm going to miss you so much."

"I love you, too, little girl." His voice clogged with emotion as he held her close. "But Lucas is a good man, and you're only going to be a few miles away."

They had talked a few more minutes about Lucas, and about the house he had helped Lucas build for her that summer. Then, he had kissed her once more, turned off the light, and left her to her dreams.

Today was her wedding day. The Bible lay in the soft circle of lamplight. She reached out and opened the front cover.

Propped up against the pillows, she studied her mother's spidery script on the face of the envelope. *For my precious Carrie on her wedding day,* she had written. Tears welled up in Carrie's eyes. She brushed them away on the corner of the sheet, and ran a fingernail under the flap of the envelope. The dried glue separated easily. She unfolded the thick sheets of paper and began to read.

My beloved daughter,

her mother had written.

> *Today is your wedding day.*
> *How happy and excited you must be. And perhaps a little sad also because I cannot be there to see you in my wedding dress. Oh, Carrie, Darling, I do hope you are going to wear my dress. It is such a beautiful dress. But it doesn't really matter what you wear. Only that you are happy.*
> *By this time, I am certain you have examined the items in the trunk that I left for you. When I had your papa pack them away, I enclosed little notes explaining the significance of each item. Today, I had your papa bring my little lap desk so that I might explain more fully.*
> *The first thing you come across will be my Bible. This is the foundation you must build your new home on, Carrie. If Christ is truly the head of your family, your marriage will be strong and endure.*
> *The second thing will be the tiny handbag I carried to my first dance. It is a symbol of the carefree days of youth.*
> *The third thing is my wedding dress. It signifies the joy of earthly love.*
> *The fourth item is the tiny christening dress both of my babies wore. It represents the miracle of life.*
> *The last item is the lock of hair from Matt's first haircut. It is representative of the uncertainty and sorrow that is a part of every life.*
> *I am ready to make my final journey, Carrie. In these last weeks of my illness, the first eight verses of the third chapter of Ecclesiastes have gained a precious significance for me. I firmly believe there is a season and a time to every purpose under heaven. I have had a wonderful life, Carrie, now it is my time to die. And even though I regret that I must be parted, even temporarily, from you and Sherman, I am eager to join my Savior.*
> *I want you to know, my darling, that my love encircles you this day and every day of your life.*
>
> > *Love,*
> > *Mama*

Her mother's last conscious thought had been of her. Tears blurred Carrie's vision as she folded the two sheets of paper and returned them to the envelope. "Thank you, Mama," she said softly. "I do know what you were trying to tell me. I believe I have known ever since the day Lucas went away."

The sky in the east was growing rosy when she slipped the letter between the pages of the Bible. A tap on the door, and Mac's gruff command to get up brought her from her bed.

"We're a-waitin' breakfast on you, little lady," he said. "You'd better be a-shakin' a leg if you want yore pa to drive you to Lucille's place. You ain't wantin' to be late fer yore own weddin', air you?"

She was going to get dressed for the wedding at Lucille and Jed's house in town. "I'll be right there, Mac." Carrie pulled her robe on and opened the door. She planted a kiss on Mac's whiskery cheek and linked her arm in his. Together they walked down the hall to the kitchen where Cyrus and her father were waiting.

"Ease off some, Gretchen," Carrie gasped. "You're squashing my innards."

"Hush!" Gretchen ordered, giving a final yank on the corset's laces. "There, we're done."

"I swore I'd never wear this awful contraption again," Carrie said. "But Mrs. Wright refused to let out any seams."

"You look so slim," Lucille said, hoisting her swollen body from the bedroom chair she had been sitting in. "I don't think I shall ever be slim again."

"Nonsense! Of course you will," Gretchen said. "Except for your belly, you're still skinny as a stick."

Gretchen carefully removed the sheet from Carrie's dress, and caught her breath. "Oh, Carrie! It's the most beautiful dress I've ever seen."

The two young women slipped the dress over Carrie's head, being mindful to not mess her hair, and arranged the full folds of the skirt around her. Then Lucille began the task of fastening the dozens of tiny satin-covered buttons that closed the back of the full-sleeved, scoop-necked bodice.

When she was finally finished, they both stood back and looked at Carrie. "You're beautiful," they breathed in unison.

She had chosen to wear her hair loose, caught back at the sides with silver combs that had belonged to her mother. Auburn curls spilled over her smooth shoulders and cascaded down her back in a copper waterfall to her waist. The friends' three-way hug was somewhat impeded by Lucille's eight-month pregnancy and their care to not muss Carrie's dress.

They laughed as they drew apart. "This is just like a fairy tale," Lucille said. "Who would ever have thought that "The Mysterious Stranger" was Lucas Nolan all along."

"Or that he would practically come back from the dead to save your life," Gretchen added, her blue eyes shining.

"It's so romantic," Lucille clasped her hands over her bulging belly.

"Now you'll live happily ever after," Gretchen said. "Just like the princesses in the stories."

Carrie shook her head. "If there's one thing I've learned, Gretchen, it's that there's no such thing as happily ever after. Lucas and I will be happy for the most part, but I'm sure we'll have our share of pain and heartache." She glanced at the small clock on Lucille's bedside table. "It's time to go."

As her friends adjusted the folds of her veil, Carrie remembered frail, thin hands stroking her hair. The light flowery fragrance of her mother's perfume still lingered in the dress she wore, and in that moment Carrie felt that her mother was with her.

A tap sounded at the bedroom door, and Lucille opened the door. "It's time, Carrie," her father said.

"I'm ready, Papa." Carrie turned to face him.

Tears came to his eyes. "You look so much like your mother did on our wedding day," he said.

Carrie smiled as she reached out to him. He took her hand in his, and they walked slowly from the bedroom followed by Lucille and Gretchen.

Lucas and Carrie joined hands, and he looked into her soft brown eyes as they repeated their vows. She was radiant, and his love for her swelled up into his throat.

This evening they would go home to the little house that he and her father had built for her on the foundation of his parents' house. There, on the site of so much tragedy, they would raise their family. The small house would grow as children were born until it became large and sprawling. A swing would hang from the outspread limb of the old tree in the front yard, and the sounds of laughter and childish voices would banish the last memories of the mob violence that had robbed him of his own childhood.

"Do you have the ring?" Had he lost the ring? Lucas felt a moment of panic, then Billy handed the wide gold band to the preacher, and he breathed a sigh of relief.

The preacher held the ring in the palm of his open hand. "I want you to notice that this ring is a perfect circle," he said. "As the circle has no beginning and no ending, so too, the love Caroline and Lucas share is never ending. Lucas, please take the ring and repeat after me, as you place it on Carrie's finger. 'I, Lucas, take thee, Caroline. . .'"

Carrie's eyes never left his face as Lucas repeated his vows. He was so dear to her. The last few months under Mac's expert tutelage had convinced her she would never be much of a cook, and housekeeping didn't inspire her. She prayed that he would forgive her inadequacies. She so wanted to be a good wife to him.

"With this ring I thee wed," Lucas said. She looked down as he slipped his mother's ring on her finger. It was a perfect fit.

Carrie repeated her vows, promising to love, honor, and obey. Then, feeling a bit inhibited by so many eyes watching, they shared their first kiss as husband and wife.

Carrie's father, looking proud and happy, but a bit teary-eyed, was sitting in the front pew of the packed church. Mac and Cyrus, wearing new black suits, were seated beside him. Their shirts were dazzling white; their boots polished to a mirror shine. Mac pulled a faded red bandanna from his pocket and wiped his eyes. When he noisily blew his nose, Cyrus scowled at him, then covertly wiped at his own eyes.

The three men followed the newlyweds up the aisle. Lucas opened the door, and the five of them stepped out into the bright August sunlight.

"Welcome to the family, son," Sherman said.

Lucas ignored his new father-in-law's extended hand and threw an arm around his shoulders. Carrie's heart sang with happiness as she watched the two men embrace.

Lucas reached out and drew Carrie and the two older men in. He gazed around the circle of happy faces. The five of them—Carrie, Sherman, Mac, Cyrus, and himself—were a family now.

His father had said vengeance was a circle. But so was love. He looked into his wife's glowing brown eyes, then down at the golden gleam of his mother's ring on her slender finger.

The circle of hate and vengeance had been broken by the most powerful force on earth. Love.

MARIAH'S HOPE

Chapter 1

Willow Creek, Ohio, 1893

W ho can find a virtuous woman? for her price is far above rubies.'" The minister's face was solemn as he closed his worn, black Bible and faced the handful of mourners standing around the open grave.

"We are gathered today to celebrate the home going of Margaret Casey, devoted wife of Charles, loving mother of Mariah. I never knew my predecessor, Pastor Charles Casey, or Mrs. Casey personally," the black-garbed pastor continued, "but I have been told that before the tragic accident that took her husband's life and left her an invalid, she worked tirelessly at Brother Casey's side ministering to his flock."

Mariah Casey, standing apart from the other mourners, the March wind whipping her black skirt against her legs, listened as the minister continued to expound on the virtues of the woman lying in the closed casket. A woman who, by his own admission, he never knew.

After the final prayer, Mariah left the cemetery and walked the short distance to her home. Turning in at the front gate, she strolled around the yard inspecting her flower beds. The yellow daffodils were already lifting their cheerful faces to the sun, and soon the tulips would be in bloom. By midsummer the yard would be ablaze with color. Mariah pulled a few weeds, then walked up the front steps, crossed the porch, and unlocked the front door. Stepping across the threshold from the bright spring sunshine into the perpetual gloom of the dark parlor, she hesitated for a moment, waiting for the querulous, demanding voice that had greeted her return home every day for the past eighteen years since her father's death. The house was silent.

Two days ago she had come home from school to find her mother lying dead on the floor. Now Margaret Casey rested in the cemetery beside a man she despised—her hateful voice forever stilled—and Mariah was free.

She went to her bedroom and changed into old clothes. After carefully brushing the black suit she had worn to the funeral and hanging it in the wardrobe, she sat down on the edge of the bed.

With her mother gone, she was free to rip down the heavy drapes and let the sunshine in. She could rehang the mirrors her mother had demanded she pack away after the accident. There were so many things she could do, but sitting alone in the gloom of her own bedroom, she knew she would do nothing to the dark, oppressive house. Though she had spent all of her thirty-five years in this house, it had never been her home. It never would be. Twin tears splashed on her clasped hands, and she impatiently brushed them away. Crying never accomplished anything.

She slipped to her knees beside her bed. *Father, please look on me with favor and hear my prayer. I'm not asking for a husband and children. I know it's too late for that, but please send me a friend. Someone who doesn't care that I'm tall and skinny and unattractive. Someone who can see beyond my outward appearance and love me for what's in my heart.*

Cedar Bend, Kansas

Walking out of Harris's Mercantile, Sherman Butler almost collided with Gladys Jacobs, who was hurrying into the store.

"Mr. Butler, I have the answer to your problems," she said without preamble. "This morning I was talking to the Lord about how your Carrie was getting married and how we were going to need a new teacher here in Cedar Bend. The solution to our problem came to me just as clear as day." She looked up at Sherman, her blue eyes magnified by the gold-rimmed glasses perched on the end of her sharp nose. "My cousin Mariah would be perfect for the position. I have her address right here."

Gladys Jacobs was a fine woman, but she had a tendency to be a bit overbearing at times. Sherman inwardly groaned as she extracted a scrap of paper from her handbag. "Mariah has taught at the same school in Ohio for almost twenty years."

He took the paper she thrust at him and glanced at it before putting it in his shirt pocket. "We have already contacted several highly qualified people about the position."

"Not a one of those people has responded, is that not correct?"

"Not yet," Sherman agreed. "But I'm sure we'll get a favorable reply soon."

"Time is running out, Mr. Butler." She straightened her narrow shoulders. "I spoke to Doctor Brady this morning. He feels my cousin Mariah would be perfect for us."

A wry smile twisted Sherman Butler's mouth. Gladys Jacobs was singleminded and tenacious when her mind was set on a project, but he had to admit, she got things done. "Your cousin may not be interested in giving up her present position and relocating to Kansas."

"I haven't seen Mariah since she was a small child, but we have corresponded for several years. I fear she is a lonely, unhappy woman." A thoughtful expression crossed Gladys's sharp features. "My uncle was a minister—a wonderful man to be sure—but more involved with feeding his flock than nurturing his only child. Mariah was a young girl when we left Ohio almost thirty years ago. Even then, Margaret—as vain and selfish a woman as ever lived—made no secret of the fact that her daughter was a disappointment to her. Many years ago my aunt and uncle were involved in an accident. Uncle Charles was killed and Margaret was badly injured. Since then Mariah has taught school and cared for her mother. She wrote me several months ago to tell me Margaret had passed away. Mariah has no family in Willow Creek and, reading between the lines of her letters, not a single friend."

She paused to catch her breath, and Sherman began to ease around her. "I'll keep your cousin in mind, Gladys. But I expect to receive a favorable reply from one of the people we've contacted any day now."

"If you write to Mariah this week she will have time to dispose of her property, resign her present position, and get settled in here before school starts."

Sherman grinned. "You are one determined woman, Gladys Jacobs."

"I am when the situation calls for it," Gladys agreed. "I'm quite certain my cousin would welcome a fresh start, Mr. Butler."

"I have a load of lumber on the wagon, so if you will excuse me. . ."

"How is Lucas and Carrie's house coming along?"

"It will be ready for them to move into by the day of the wedding."

"It doesn't seem possible. Little Carrie getting married, and my Lucille having a baby." Gladys sighed. "Only yesterday they were babies themselves."

"Yes, time passes." Sherman glanced up at the sun. "Speaking of time, I'd better be on my way." Tipping his hat, he took leave of Mrs. Jacobs.

"You contact Mariah this week," she called after him as he swung up on the wagon seat.

Sherman chuckled as he drove away. Gladys Jacobs wouldn't give him a moment of peace until the teaching position was filled.

The July sun beat down on his shoulders as he turned the matching team of bay workhorses toward the old Nolan place. It didn't seem possible Lucas and Carrie would be married a month from now, and she'd be moving away from the Circle C. A lump rose in his throat. She would only be a few miles away, but he was going to miss her something fierce. He wished Caroline could have lived to see the wonderful young woman their headstrong, spoiled little girl had become. She would be mighty proud.

When Caroline died twelve years ago, the pain had been so intense he felt as if his heart were being ripped from his chest. Time had tempered his grief to an occasional dull ache. He still loved her and always would, but more and more she was becoming a faded memory. He lifted his wide-brimmed Stetson and wiped a blue-chambray-clad arm across his damp forehead. Seeing Lucas and Carrie together aroused a longing in him he thought had been buried with Caroline. After all these years alone, Sherman was ready to remarry.

Lord, I'd sure appreciate it if You could send someone special my way. Someone I can love. Someone who will love me in return. A good woman I can share my heart and my life with. Lord, You and me both know I wasn't the husband I should have been to Caroline. But I'm a different man now. If it's Your will, Father, I'd like a second chance.

A drop of sweat trickling down the side of his face reminded him summer was half over. He should be praying for a teacher instead of a wife.

He pulled the piece of paper Gladys Jacobs had given him from his shirt pocket and read aloud the name and address written there. "Miss Mariah Casey, P.O. Box 103, Willow Creek, Ohio." He crumpled the paper in his hand, preparatory to throwing it away. "Regardless of what Gladys says, I doubt Miss Casey would be interested in moving to Cedar Bend."

Of the five letters he sent out in May, he had already received two rejections. Time was running out. "If I don't hear anything in the next week or so, maybe I should contact her."

He smoothed the paper and returned it to his pocket. He'd talk it over with Mac and Cyrus tonight and see what they thought about Gladys's cousin.

Sherman had been a gangly fourteen-year-old orphan when he came in from plowing one day to find two strangers sitting on his front porch. Mac and Cyrus told him they had been with his pa when he fell at Shiloh. He invited them to stay for supper, and they never left. He'd been a restless kid, and a few years after he threw in with Mac and Cyrus, he abandoned the southern Missouri farm where he had been born, and the three of them began to roam. He wasn't overly proud of some of the things he'd done in the following few years. Meeting and marrying Caroline had settled him down considerably and made him think about the future. He and Mac and Cyrus had put together a good-sized herd of cattle and trailed them to Kansas. From that humble beginning, with hard work and perseverance, they had built the Circle C.

A few hours later Sherman sat at the kitchen table with Mac and Cyrus. The three men discussed their day over a final cup of coffee as they had every evening for the past thirty years.

During a lull in the conversation, Sherman mentioned his meeting with Gladys Jacobs that morning. "Seems Gladys has a cousin in Ohio who's a teacher." He chuckled. "She's bound and determined this woman is the answer to our problems. She gave me her name and address and insisted I write to her immediately."

"Wal," Mac said, scratching his bristly chin, "might not be a bad idea to write to this woman."

"Time is runnin' short, Sherm," Cyrus added.

"I still haven't heard from the last three teachers I contacted."

"And you may not." Mac hobbled over to the stove and brought back the coffeepot. After topping off their cups, he returned the pot to the stove and sat back down. "It wouldn't hurt none to get in touch with this woman."

"If I don't hear anything by the end of next week, I've about decided to contact Gladys's cousin."

"In the meantime you might want to write to a few folks back where she lives," Cyrus suggested. "Wouldn't hurt to check and see what folks think of her."

"I reckon I could get some names from Gladys next time I'm in town."

"You best seek the Lord's guidance in this here matter, too," Mac suggested.

"I'll do that." Sherman pushed his chair back from the table. "Tomorrow is a busy day. I think I'll look in on Carrie, then turn in."

<hr />

Carrie's auburn hair hung in a braid over her shoulder. She looked like a little girl, propped up against the pillows in her long, white nightdress. A pad of paper rested on her bent knees, a stub of a pencil was clenched between her fingers. She had been making innumerable lists since Lucas returned to Cedar Bend two months ago and she began to plan their wedding.

Sherman shuffled a flurry of scribbled pages to one side before sitting down on the edge of the bed. "From the looks of things, you've been busy."

"I had no idea planning a wedding would be so much work." She gathered up the scattered sheets of paper that littered the bed and stacked them on top of the tablet. "But I think I'm almost finished." With a sigh of satisfaction she placed the tablet and pencil on the floor beside her bed. "It is going to be a beautiful wedding, Papa."

He took her hand in his. "I'm sure it will be, little girl." He cleared his throat. "I'm going to miss our nightly talks, Caroline Abigail."

"Me, too, Papa." She looked at him with her mother's dark, Spanish eyes. "But I won't be that far away. We can talk every day."

He wanted to say that it wouldn't be the same. That he would no longer be the most important man in his little girl's life. He wanted to tell her he was a mite jealous of the young man who was taking her away from him. He patted her hand before releasing it.

"Don't look so sad, Papa." Carrie's dimples flashed. "You know Mac's been trying to teach me to cook."

"Mac told me you baked a pie today."

"Did he tell you the crust was so hard we couldn't cut it?" Carrie giggled. "We gave it to Mutt, and he dragged it off and buried it."

"I believe he did mention something about that."

"You know I can't cook, Papa. Poor Mac has just about given up on me." She sighed. "He even told Lucas that if he didn't want to starve until I finally learned how to cook, he was either going to have to learn to do it himself or plan on taking most of his meals here. You will probably get so tired of seeing our faces across the table you'll run us off."

"I can't imagine that ever happening."

"Just wait until we come over dragging five or six grandchildren with us." A slight blush tinged her tanned cheeks. "Lucas and I are planning on a large family."

Sherman hadn't thought of his baby with babies of her own. But he decided he rather liked the idea of having young ones around. Being a grandfather might not be half bad.

"Did Hilda Braun talk to you about—" He pulled on his shirt collar. "You know what I mean."

"She did, Papa," Carrie said with a smile.

Sherman breathed a sigh of relief. The Braun family lived on the neighboring ranch. Their oldest daughter, Gretchen, and Carrie had been best friends since they were toddlers. After Caroline died, Carrie spent a lot of time at the Brauns'. He didn't know how he and Mac and Cyrus would have raised his little girl without Hilda Braun's guidance.

"You know Billy and Gretchen are going to stand up with us."

Sherman grinned. "Seems I heard something about that."

"I guess I do go on about wedding plans." Carrie pulled her knees to her chest and wrapped her arms around her legs. "I wish Lucille and Jed could stand up with us, too. But, I suppose since she's expecting, her mother wouldn't think it proper. I asked Joanna Brady to sing, but we haven't chosen the songs yet. What did they sing at your wedding, Papa?"

Sherman thought back to that long-ago day and shook his head. "I haven't the slightest idea, little girl. Something in Spanish, I think. I was so nervous I don't remember anything clearly except kissing your mama."

"That's so sweet, Papa." Carrie rested her chin on her knees. "I miss her so much sometimes. Do you think she knows about Lucas?"

"I couldn't say, Carrie."

"She would love him, wouldn't she?"

"She was fond of him when he was a young boy. I'm certain he would meet with her approval."

"I think she would be pleased that we're building our house on the foundation of Lucas's boyhood home, don't you?"

"I think she would."

"Our house is coming along really well, don't you think?"

"I do." Sherman shifted a bit on the bed. "I saw Gladys Jacobs this morning when I went into town for supplies."

Carrie wrinkled her nose. "What did she have to say?"

"Now, Carrie, Mrs. Jacobs means well." Sherman touched a finger to the tip of Carrie's nose.

"You know that I love Mrs. Jacobs." Carrie grinned. "She spent years trying to transform me into a proper young lady. Aggravated me to no end. Remember the sidesaddle, Papa? It was her final effort. After that failed she gave up on me."

"Not quite." Sherman grinned. "There was still the episode with the corset."

"She won that one." Carrie giggled. "Well, sort of. I wear a corset if I have to, but I still reserve the right to despise them."

"Mrs. Jacobs loves you, Carrie." Sherman gave the long auburn braid a gentle yank.

"I know she does, Papa." Carrie sighed. "Now that I'm older I realize everything she did was out of love. Love for me, but especially love for Mama. She tried to take Mama's place, but she couldn't. No one could ever take her place, right, Papa?"

"No," Sherman agreed. "No one could ever take Caroline's place."

"One time when I was about twelve, Mrs. Jacobs told me it would be nice if you remarried." Carrie's softly rounded chin took on a determined tilt. "I set her straight on that." She leaned forward and wrapped her arms around Sherman's neck. "I told her you were perfectly happy as you were."

Sherman savored the clean smell of her hair as he held her close. His life was going to be so empty without her.

She released him and leaned back against the pillows. "What did Mrs. Jacobs have to say?"

"Well. . ." Sherman cleared his throat and blinked back a sheen of wetness from his eyes. "She suggested I write to her cousin and offer her the teaching position."

"The old-maid schoolteacher in Ohio?"

"What do you know about Gladys's cousin?"

"Not much." Carrie frowned in concentration. "I think her father died when she was about my age. Ever since then she has taught school and taken care of her mother. Lucille says she is like Cinderella, except she isn't beautiful, and there will never be a handsome prince to rescue her from a life of dreary servitude."

Sherman stifled a chuckle. Lucille was imaginative and melodramatic. He'd learned long ago to take what she said with a grain of salt.

"Before Lucille met Jed, she said she was going to end up like her cousin. 'This is how I shall live, and this is how I shall die,' she always said. 'An old maid schoolteacher unsullied by the hand of man, just like Cousin Mariah.'"

Sherman stood. "Well, I believe I shall turn in." He leaned over to kiss Carrie's cheek. "Good night, little girl. Sweet dreams."

"Good night, Papa." Carrie pulled the sheet up to her chin as he walked to the door. "I think you should write to Mrs. Jacobs's cousin."

Sherman hesitated, his hand on the doorknob. "Why is that?"

"You know how teachers stay about a year then get married?" Carrie sat up. "I was just thinking. Mrs. Jacobs's cousin is close to forty. No one will want to marry an old maid like her. She could probably teach for years and years. Just think of all the trouble it would save the school board if they didn't have to search for a new teacher every year."

"Maybe you're right." Sherman tried to recall being so young that forty seemed old. "I'll certainly give it some thought."

Carrie turned out the lamp before snuggling down on her pillow. "I love you, Papa."

"Love you, too." Sherman closed the door behind him and turned his steps toward his own bed.

Chapter 2

Mariah woke early on the morning of her thirty-sixth birthday. Swinging her feet over the edge of the bed, she sat up. The heat was oppressive in the closed room. Her high-necked gown, worn thin, clung to her back. Tendrils of dark hair that escaped her thick, waist-length braid were plastered to her temples. She stood, crossed the room, and pulled back the heavy drapes. It didn't help much. The air was heavy with humidity.

A half hour later, freshly bathed and dressed in lightweight, white knit drawers and a low-necked, sleeveless summer vest, Mariah stood before her bedroom mirror and loosened her braid. Her lustrous, dark hair and smooth, flawless skin were the only features she had inherited from her dainty, feminine mother. Her sapphire blue eyes and lanky frame came from her father. Almost six feet tall, she was what most people called *plain*.

Even now on the brink of middle age, she blushed at the memory of the beauty cream she had sneaked into her room when she was sixteen. She still recalled word for word the ad that beguiled her: *"If nature has not favored you with that greatest charm and beauty, send for our product and you will be pleased over the result of a few weeks' time. Will make any lady beautiful as a princess."*

It took her months to save the necessary dollar and a half. After six months of faithful and unproductive use, her mother found the cream and threw it away. The harangue that followed still made Mariah's heart ache.

"You are a fool, Mariah," Mother scolded. "If it was meant for you to be beautiful, you would have been born that way. You were a long, scrawny, homely baby. I was ashamed to have my friends see you when you were a newborn, and time has done nothing to improve your appearance."

Mariah cried herself to sleep that night, not because Mother slapped her and threw away the beauty cream, but because she knew her mother didn't love her.

She pulled the brush through her hair a final time. The light caught on a single strand of silver. Mariah hesitated a moment before slicking the wavy tresses back and securing them in a large, no nonsense bun on the back of her head. Crossing the room, she opened the door of the massive wardrobe. She was too tall for ready-made and too impoverished to pay a dressmaker, so necessity dictated that she make her own clothes. Fortunately she was as efficient at the sewing machine as she was in the classroom. She perused the neat row of white shirtwaists and dark-colored skirts before choosing a faded calico housedress. This morning she would work in her garden.

Fully dressed, sitting alone at the oak kitchen table, she bowed her head and whispered a prayer before eating her customary breakfast: an egg boiled for precisely three minutes, a thick slice of homemade bread spread with jam, and one cup of hot tea.

After her few dishes were washed, dried, and put away, she sat in the rocking chair in the kitchen. Taking her Bible from the small chair-side table, she opened the worn leather cover. A slip of paper listed the number of chapters to be read each day in order to complete the Bible in one year. This morning she dutifully read the prescribed chapters in Jeremiah. With the completion of the final verse, she carefully placed the ribbon marker between the pages and closed her Bible.

On her knees in front of the rocking chair, she tried to pray but found it impossible to stay focused. In the first months following her mother's death, Mariah prayed daily for her life to be different. An excellent cook, she dreamed of having friends over to share Sunday dinner. She fantasized about a special woman friend. Someone she could share confidences with. God hadn't answered her prayers. Why had she expected Him to? When she was small, she prayed for a baby brother or sister. When she was older, she prayed for a husband and children. Always she pleaded with God to send her someone to love. God sat on His throne and turned a deaf ear to her entreaties.

When she stood, her sleeve brushed against a letter lying on the table. Her only cousin's most recent correspondence came yesterday, but she hadn't felt like reading Gladys's maternal ramblings about her two daughters and their domestic bliss. Now, as she picked up the thick packet, she discovered a second slim envelope beneath.

Mariah put on gold-rimmed reading glasses and sat down in the rocking chair. She first skimmed through the unexpected letter and then read it thoroughly. When she finished, she leaned back in her chair. Sherman Butler, president of the school board in Cedar Bend, Kansas, was offering her a teaching position. Gladys must have given Mr. Butler her address. She laid the letter to one side and opened her cousin's letter.

Gladys began with news of her family. Her younger daughter, Lucille, was expecting her first child any day. Mariah couldn't believe Lucille had been married long enough to be a mother, but after counting off the months on her fingers, she realized her young cousin had married well over a year ago. Time seemed to pass so quickly sometimes.

Gladys also wrote at length about a friend of Lucille's named Carrie Butler and her upcoming wedding. Carrie was the teacher she would be replacing if she accepted the position.

"You need to be with family, Mariah," Gladys wrote. "I know this is short notice, but please say you will come."

She read Mr. Butler's letter a third time. The salary he quoted was more than generous. She had never been more than ten miles outside the city limits of Willow Creek. Could this job offer be the beginning of the new life she longed for?

The clock in the parlor chimed six times, reminding Mariah there was work to be done. She laid Sherman Butler's letter on the table with her cousin's letter. In the serenity of her garden she would consider Mr. Butler's offer.

Mariah spent the morning working with her flowers. The months following her mother's death had been as lonely as the years preceding it. Women her age were busy with husbands and children. Those younger pursued their own interests, mainly finding the perfect man and becoming wives and mothers. It seemed no one had time for a lonely spinster.

Tears lingered just below the surface, but she refused to surrender to self-pity. In the year following her twenty-fifth birthday, when she accepted her spinsterhood as a permanent state, she shed her final tears. After all, what had those tears accomplished?

She gave a vicious yank at a stubborn weed. This morning when she discovered the strand of silver in her dark hair, she had considered yanking it out. "Vanity," she murmured as she pulled another recalcitrant weed.

Her mother had been vain. So vain she had let an all but invisible scar and a slight limp cut her off from the world. After the accident, Mother drew the heavy drapes, took down the mirrors, and cloistered herself in the gloomy house. Except for school, church, and occasional trips for food, in the dark months while her gardens slept beneath a thick blanket of snow, Mariah was forced to share her mother's prison.

Mother was gone, but the prison remained. Curly tendrils escaped Mariah's severe hairdo and plastered to her temples. She blotted the sweat from her face with a gloved hand. It was time to go inside. Still kneeling amidst the blossoms, she took a moment to consider the question that had been on her mind since she read Mr. Butler's letter. *Should I go to Kansas?*

She stood and surveyed her flowers. Eighteen years ago she had begun to cultivate her gardens and dream of a handsome prince on a prancing steed who would rescue her from a dreary life of loneliness. The gardens flourished until the yard of the former parsonage became a showplace. The prince, however, never appeared. Eleven years ago Mariah quit looking for him.

Should I go to Kansas? The tall hollyhocks growing against the fence behind her vegetable garden stirred gently in the faint breeze. A bee gathered nectar from the zinnias at her feet. As she walked to the porch, the roses nestled by the back steps perfumed the air. She stooped to breathe in the fragrance of the yellow blossoms before continuing up the steps. Sitting in a wicker rocker, screened from view by a lattice weighed down with morning glory vines, Mariah removed her gloves, then bent to unlace her shoes. Should she go to Kansas? She closed her eyes and rested her forehead against her knees.

She had been a young girl when the Jacobses left Ohio, but she remembered their kindness to her. Gladys had given her a fluffy yellow kitten the day they left. "Something of your own you can love and care for," Cousin Gladys whispered in her ear when she hugged her a final time. The Jacobses were scarcely out of sight when Mother took the kitten from her. Mariah blinked back scalding tears.

Why shouldn't she go to Kansas? Willow Creek held nothing but unpleasant memories. In Kansas she would be close to the only family she had left. If she remained in Willow Creek, when at last she was laid to rest in the churchyard beside her parents, there would be no family to mourn her passing. No one, except for a few former students perhaps, to remember her with fondness.

The job offer from Kansas was her means of escape. A chance for the new beginning she had prayed for. She pulled off her shoes and stood. For a moment she scanned the yard with its brilliant display of color; then she squared her shoulders.

There would be flowers in Cedar Bend. And maybe. . .just maybe. . . *Oh, please, Lord, let there be someone I can love.*

Chapter 3

Mariah closed her book and tucked it and her glasses into the large, leather Gladstone bag that had belonged to her father. Outside the coach window, undulating fields of grass, scorched golden by the early September heat, stretched as far as she could see.

Mariah leaned her head against the high back of the seat and closed her eyes. Today she would leave the train and board a stagecoach for the final miles of her journey. She had telegraphed Cousin Gladys from the last stop informing her of the stage's approximate arrival time. Would she be there to meet her?

Her seatmate—a plump, grandmotherly woman named Mrs. Sellers—woke with a start. "I musta dozed off." She yawned. "Lands sakes, seems as if I can't set down without noddin' off. I'd reckon I'm gettin' old. Where'd you tell me you was goin' to, dear?"

Mariah opened her eyes and turned her head toward Mrs. Sellers. "I didn't say."

The other woman laughed. "I'd reckon you didn't. So where are you goin'? Not that it's any of my business. I'd reckon I'm just an old busybody."

Mrs. Sellers *was* a busybody. Since she boarded the train yesterday evening she'd bombarded Mariah with an endless stream of questions. Not that she answered any more of them than civility demanded. Mariah didn't make a habit of sharing her personal affairs with anyone, least of all a stranger on a train.

"I'm goin' to stay with my daughter fer a few months." The older woman chattered on, her question about Mariah's destination seemingly forgotten. "She's feelin' poorly, you know. Not that Carl ain't a big help. It's jist that the poor man can't be expected to work all day then come home to take care of five youngsters, you know. Soon's the new baby comes and Sally's back on her feet, I'll be goin' home." A cloud passed over her cheerful face. "Not that there's much to go home to since my Abner passed away last year, you know. After forty years of havin' him always there it's mighty hard to be alone." She sighed; then her face brightened. "Of course, I've got a wonderful church family. You seen some of 'em when I got on the train. They insisted on comin' to see me off. The Lord surely has been good to me."

Mariah's minister and his wife were the only ones standing on the platform when she boarded the train. She turned to look out the window. Pastor Billings and his wife had been there out of duty, not because they cared about her. Even though he took her father's place in the pulpit almost eighteen years ago, he scarcely knew her. The thought brought tears to her eyes, which she quickly blinked away. She would not allow herself to indulge in self-pity.

Mrs. Sellers's soft elbow in her ribs interrupted her thoughts. "We're almost there, dear."

Two hours later Mariah traveled over the gently rolling prairie in a stagecoach. Clouds of dust thrown up by the horses' hooves drifted past the open window. She had given up trying to brush away the fine powder that settled on her black suit.

A husky man occupied the seat facing her. The other two passengers—boys in their late teens—had climbed on top with the driver. The man introduced himself as Karl Braun, then tipped his hat over his eyes. Moments later roof-raising snores began to emanate from his open mouth.

Mariah reached up to adjust her hat, at the same time discreetly removing a six-inch hatpin. If the man attempted anything improper, she would be prepared to defend herself.

Mariah took a book from her bag and settled down to do some reading. She had read *Little Women* countless times but still loved the story. An hour later she sighed as she turned the final page and closed the cover. She could only imagine having a mother like the March sisters'. A mother who loved her children even if they weren't pretty.

The man stirred and thumbed his hat off his eyes. "You from back East?"

"I'm from Ohio," she replied, her hand tightening on the hatpin now concealed beneath the folds of her skirt.

"Next stop's about a mile ahead." The man put a hand to the back of his neck and rolled his head. "Got a crick in my neck," he explained. "That your stop? Cedar Bend?"

"Yes." Mariah shifted a little on the unyielding seat in a futile effort to relieve the kinks in her aching back.

"I'd reckon you're gonna be our new schoolteacher. I'm on the school board. I knew Mr. Butler had contacted you, but I've been out of town on business the last three weeks and didn't know if you'd accepted the job. You are Gladys Jacobs's cousin?"

Mariah realized Mr. Braun was waiting for her to introduce herself. She made it a policy not to converse with strangers—especially men—but the gentleman across from her seemed harmless enough. Besides, in a manner of speaking, he was her employer. She slipped the hatpin back in her hat and extended her right hand. "My name is Mariah Casey, Mr. Braun. My father and Gladys's father were brothers."

The man's hand was callused, the handshake firm and brief. "I see a family resemblance. You put me in mind of Lucille."

"I have never met my cousin's younger daughter, and Clara, her eldest, was barely five years old when they left Ohio."

"We've had quite a time keeping a teacher. Last two didn't last no time 'til they got married. I'd reckon you gotta expect that with young girls. Especially the pretty ones." The man settled back in the seat. "I'm glad you accepted the job. Looking for a new teacher every year was startin' to get a mite burdensome."

Mariah, feeling the color rising in her face, turned her head to look out the window.

"That's Sherman Butler's land," the man observed. "He owns a big hunk of Kansas. His little girl, Carrie, was the teacher in Cedar Bend last year, but she got married a month ago. Carrie and my oldest girl, Gretchen, have been best friends since they were knee-high to a grasshopper. She's a pretty little thing, Carrie is. Sweet, too. You might think being raised without a mother she'd be a regular little terror, but she's not."

Mariah found herself listening with interest. After all, the people he was talking about were going to be her neighbors, and she hoped her friends.

"Of course I give my Hilda credit for most of that. After her mama died, Carrie spent a lot of time at our place. We have the ranch next to the Circle C."

"Do you have children that will be attending school, Mr. Braun?"

The man's hearty laugh brought an answering smile to Mariah's lips. "We have ten. There is Gretchen, our firstborn. She's married now. James just turned eighteen, and Tad is sixteen. They're the two riding topside. Katy is almost fifteen. The four oldest are through with school. Jay is almost fourteen; he will be in his final year. Then there is"—he counted off on his fingers—"Michael, Hugh, Little Karl, Abigail, and Paul. The two youngest won't go this year. Little Karl—we call him L. K.—is barely six. Hilda was thinking about holding him back a year, but he's been begging to go to school. She finally decided to let him go."

"I'm sure with so many older brothers to look after him he will do fine."

"They're good boys, Miss Casey. If any of them gives you the slightest bit of trouble, let me know."

"I have taught for eighteen years, Mr. Braun. I don't anticipate trouble."

"The kids in Cedar Bend have been raised to respect their elders, Miss Casey. I doubt if you'll have trouble with them. Still, boys can be high-spirited and mischievous. If you have a problem with any of the youngsters, mine or anyone else's, let one of the school board members know. We'll take care of it."

Mariah nodded, then turned her attention to brushing the dust from her jacket.

A few minutes later Karl Braun gave Mariah a hand down from the stagecoach. A slight woman with graying hair hurried up to her. "Mariah Casey, it has been twenty-five years, but I would know you anywhere."

Not knowing how to respond when the older woman embraced her, Mariah stood stiffly until her cousin's arms dropped away and she stepped back.

"You look very much like your father." A slender, slightly stoop-shouldered man moved to Gladys's side. "You remember my Nels?"

"Yes, of course," Mariah murmured, though in truth she remembered only their kindness to her.

"We're happy to have you with us, Mariah." Nels smiled and patted her arm.

Mariah nodded. "I am happy to be here."

"I'll collect your bags while you two women get reacquainted." Karl Braun walked to the small pile of luggage his sons were stacking beside the coach. "You boys load Miss Casey's things into Mr. Jacobs's buggy," he ordered.

While the boys made short work of loading the luggage, Gladys regaled Mariah with stories of her two daughters and their families. Mariah noticed Karl Braun walk over to a young woman standing on the boardwalk. She attempted to listen to her cousin, but her attention was on the young woman. She was tall and slender, with auburn hair in a thick braid that reached her waist. A wide-brimmed hat shaded her face, hiding it from view. Although she wasn't wearing men's clothing, she wasn't dressed like a lady, either. Her white shirt had full sleeves gathered into wide cuffs at the wrist. The skirt she wore was green and divided. Not exactly trousers, but close enough, it ended halfway between her knees and ankles. Even though the girl's tight-fitting boots covered her legs, Mariah thought the outfit unbecoming a lady.

A buckboard moved slowly down the street and stopped behind the stage. The Brauns climbed in with the lanky young driver. The buckboard made a U-turn in the middle of the street and headed back the way it had come.

"That was Billy Racine, Karl and Hilda Braun's new son-in-law," Gladys said, interrupting her own account of Lucille's new baby boy. "Oh, dear, in all the excitement I almost forgot Carrie." She took Mariah's arm and led her to the young woman. "Carrie Nolan, I would like to introduce you to my cousin Mariah Casey."

"I have been looking forward to meeting you, Miss Casey." The girl lifted her head, and Mariah found herself looking into the most beautiful face she had ever seen.

"Yes." Mariah felt awkward, tongue-tied, and homelier than usual. "Well, I am happy to be here."

"Papa is away on business, so he appointed me to help you get settled in." Her laugh was young, carefree, and bubbly. "You said in your letter that you would like a house of your own?"

"Nonsense," Gladys said. "Mariah will be staying with us."

"No, Cousin Gladys. It would be an imposition for you and Cousin Nels. Besides I have lived alone for some time, and I cherish my privacy."

"You are family, Mariah. We would love to have you."

"Mr. Butler informed me in his letter that the school provides a house. I will stay with you until my things arrive, Cousin Gladys. Then I will move into that house." When her cousin began to protest, Mariah shook her head. "Please, this is one thing I am adamant about. I will feel more comfortable surrounded by my own things."

"Would it be all right if I picked you up at the Jacobs's tomorrow morning?" Carrie asked. "I could show you the school. Also, Papa thought you would like to see the house. Would nine thirty be all right with you?"

"Yes. That would be fine."

"Good." Carrie smiled. "I better be getting home. Lucas will be starved."

Gladys placed her hand on Carrie's arm. "Have you tried any of the recipes I gave you?"

"A couple, Mrs. Jacobs. But mostly we eat at Papa's." Her happy laugh rang out. "I don't want to poison Lucas. Besides Mac loves to have us. I'll see you tomorrow, Miss Casey."

The girl untied a bay mare from the hitching rail, placed a small, boot-clad foot in the stirrup, and swung into the saddle. She gave a final wave before turning the horse. Mariah watched in disbelief as she galloped down the street. Astride!

Gladys seemed not to notice the Nolan woman's unconventional behavior. "Carrie is quite a girl. Those three men spoiled her rotten after her mother died." Gladys beamed. "Hilda Braun and I tried to advise her, not that we could ever take Caroline's place. Still, Carrie is a sweet girl. She's becoming quite a proper young lady, too. I like to think I'm partly responsible for that."

Mariah was sure there were many words one could use to describe Carrie Nolan, but in her opinion *proper* and *lady* were not on the list.

Chapter 4

At 9:25 Mariah walked to the edge of the porch and looked up and down the street. Not seeing an approaching conveyance of any sort, she sat down on the porch swing. Five minutes later she heard the clock in Cousin Gladys's parlor strike the half hour. After another quick check up and down the street, she returned to the swing.

A few minutes later her cousin joined her. "Carrie will be here by ten," Gladys said.

"She told me nine thirty."

"Well, things come up. You know how it is."

"No, I do not know how it is. Nine thirty means half past nine to me." Mariah found tardiness intolerable.

Gladys lingered for a few minutes chatting—mostly about Lucille and her new baby—before excusing herself and going back inside.

The clock in the parlor was striking ten when Carrie arrived. Mariah hurried down the walk and climbed into the buggy.

"Sorry to be late." Carrie's smile was dazzling. "We overslept. Then I had to see my husband off. I was sure you would understand."

"I understand, Mrs. Nolan." A quick glance assured Mariah that her companion was as perfect of face and form as she had thought her on their first meeting. This morning, clad in a blue-flowered dress and a white straw bonnet, the young woman was a picture of femininity. "However," Mariah continued, turning her gaze to the street ahead of them, "I have always prided myself on being a quarter hour early to any appointment. I have always believed that lack of punctuality indicates a lack of virtue."

She could feel Carrie's eyes on her. Words of apology for her harshness were on her lips when the girl giggled. "You sound like Mac. He always says, 'Little lady, you'll be late fer yer own funeral.' I apologize for my tardiness, Miss Casey. Please forgive me."

Mariah fidgeted with the clasp on her purse before taking a deep breath. "Your apology is accepted."

"Good. Now, which would you like to see first? The school? Or the house?"

"The school. Most assuredly, the school."

While Carrie secured the lines to the hitching rail, Mariah stood looking up at the freshly painted, white, rectangular frame building. The two windows that flanked the front door glistened, newly washed and spot free. "It appears well kept," she said.

"We are proud of our school." Carrie moved to enter the building.

Mariah followed Carrie up the three shallow steps and across the porch to the front door. "It isn't locked?" she asked, when Carrie turned the knob and swung the door inward.

"No one ever bothers anything." Carrie stood aside for Mariah to enter.

The room was not much larger than her second grade classroom in Ohio. The south wall contained a row of sparkling windows. The desks, though showing signs of wear, were polished to a soft shine.

Their heels clicked on the oiled wooden floor as they walked to the front of the room. Mariah stepped behind the battered desk with the blackboard to her back and rows of desks before her. There were six rows of desks with eight desks in a row. The smallest desks were next to the window, and they gradually increased in size to the largest ones against the windowless north wall. *Forty-eight children of different ages and different grade levels.* Uncertainty tempered Mariah's anticipation. *How will I ever competently teach so many children?* Mariah sat down in the chair and folded her hands on top of the desk.

"I know it looks rather daunting." Carrie stood beside the desk. "I was terrified the first time I sat behind that desk." She walked over to the first row of desks. "My second graders sat here. My third in the next row, and so on." She turned to two low tables surrounded by miniature chairs on Mariah's right. "My little first graders sat at these tables where I could keep an eye on them." She rested her hand on the back of one of the chairs and looked out over the empty classroom. "I love all of them, and I am going to miss them."

Mariah cleared her throat. "I have always made it a policy not to become attached to my pupils."

Carrie looked at her with wide eyes. "How can you not? Especially the little ones. They are so precious and so eager to learn."

"I have taught for eighteen years, Mrs. Nolan." She rose from the desk and walked to the bookshelves on the north wall. "In my experience it is better for all concerned if one maintains a distance from the children." She ran a long, slender finger down the spine of a book. "I see you have an excellent selection of reading material."

"We are not illiterate, Miss Casey."

She turned to face the young woman. "I never said you were, Mrs. Nolan. You misunderstood."

Carrie turned away. "If you are through here, I'll take you to see the house."

"Yes, I think I have seen enough." Mariah pushed the chair under the desk. "One more thing, Mrs. Nolan. The door is to be locked when school is not in session. I will require a key. No one else is to have access to the building, except the president of the school board, of course."

As she gathered her purse and gloves from the desk, Mariah saw the young woman roll her eyes. "I'll make it a priority to deliver your message to my father as soon as possible." Carrie turned and swept out of the room.

When Mariah climbed into the buggy, she ventured, "If it is permissible, I'll come back every day this week to prepare my lesson plans."

Carrie picked up the reins. "Do as you please, Miss Casey. With your vast experience I'm quite sure you know more than I what is necessary."

As they rode silently away from the school, Mariah sat stiffly beside Carrie. She had been intimidated by the young woman's looks from the moment she met her. As always when she felt threatened, she retreated behind a screen of false superiority. She had been hateful to Carrie Nolan, and she was ashamed of her actions. She wanted to apologize, but the words wouldn't come. Instead she prayed inwardly, *Dear Lord, I am so sorry for my actions. I didn't mean the things I said to Mrs. Nolan. You know how desperately I wish to change. To become a woman who is worthy of friendship. Help me to control my tongue in the future.*

Mariah fell in love with the white frame house with the yellow roses blooming beside the front gate as soon as she saw it. A leisurely walk through the five large rooms confirmed her first impression.

"I want to buy this house," she said.

"There is no need for that. The school board furnishes the house for you rent free."

"I would prefer not to rent, Mrs. Nolan. Who owns it? I'll talk to him or her personally."

"I believe Eli Smith at the bank is the owner, but it isn't for sale."

"Nonsense." Mariah heard the harshness in her own voice and attempted to amend it. "In any case it won't hurt to ask. If you will direct me to the bank—"

"I'll drive you. But this house is not for sale."

On Saturday, Sherman Butler returned from his business trip to Texas. That evening he sat down to supper with his two partners and his son-in-law and daughter. After they had thoroughly discussed his trip, Sherman turned to Carrie. "What did you think of the new teacher, little girl?"

Lucas laughed as he reached for the green beans. "I made the mistake of asking that question, Sherm. Prepare for an earful."

"Wait until you meet her, Pa." Carrie smirked at her husband.

"She had excellent references." Sherman frowned. "What's wrong with her, Carrie?"

"Everything. When I went to the Jacobs' to pick her up the morning after her arrival and take her to visit the school, the first thing she did was scold me for being late."

Mac chuckled. "How late was you, little lady?"

"Only thirty minutes, and I had a good reason, too."

"I allus did say if you was a half hour late you was early," the little man teased.

"Anyway," Carrie continued, choosing to ignore Mac's comment, "she was sitting on the porch swing looking like she was about to explode. I barely got the buggy stopped before she marched down the walk and climbed in. I apologized for being late. Do you know what she said? Well, do you?"

"I'd reckon since we wasn't there, young 'un, we couldn't know what she said."

"I know what she said, Cyrus." Lucas winked at the Circle C foreman. "But I can't tell this story with the same flair as my wife." He patted Carrie's clenched fist. "You tell them, sugar."

"She said that lack of punctuality indicated a lack of virtue. I didn't get angry. I wanted to, but I didn't. You would have been proud of me. That wasn't the worst, though. While I was showing her the school she said a teacher should maintain distance from her pupils. Can you imagine? I had to bite my tongue to keep from telling her what I thought of her."

"Now, little lady," Mac said, "you don't know this woman. Ain't I always told you, you cain't tell what's in a package by lookin' at the wrappin'?"

"I know what's in this package," Carrie said. "A hateful old maid with no heart. Oh, I almost forgot. Miss Casey said for you to have two keys made so she can lock the school when she's not there. The only other person who gets a key is you, Papa. Can you imagine that?"

"Simmer down now, young 'un. The lady more'n likely ain't never lived in a little town like Cedar Bend. She ain't used to trustin' her neighbors," Cyrus said. "Mac's right, much as I hate to agree with the old coot. You don't know the teacher well enough to pass judgment. I 'spect she feels a mite strange here. She'll probably be right nice once you get to know her."

"Wait until you meet her," Carrie grumbled. "You'll see."

"Did she like Eli Smith's house all right?" Sherman asked.

"She must have." Carrie snorted. "She bought it."

"I didn't realize it was for sale."

"Neither did Eli until Miss Casey walked into his office. She told him she had the money from the sale of her house in Ohio, and since Cedar Bend was going to be her home from this day forth, she wanted a place she could call her own. She frightened the poor man out of his wits. Or, I suppose I should say, out of his property."

Sherman chuckled. "Knowing Eli, I'm sure he didn't get hurt in the transaction."

"I guess not," Carrie agreed grudgingly. "But I still don't like her ways."

Sherman rolled over for the fifth time. What if they had made a mistake hiring Mariah Casey sight unseen? He punched the pillow, trying to mold it into a more accommodating shape. What had the letters of recommendation actually said? "Miss Casey is dependable. Reliable. Competent. Of high moral character." Even though she had been living among these people her entire life, they could have been writing about a stranger.

He would meet Miss Casey tomorrow after church. He sighed deeply and rolled over again. Come morning he would know if the new teacher was as bad as Carrie said.

Chapter 5

Mariah sat beside her cousin, her eyes fixed on the plump young woman standing at the front of the small church. "If you will turn in your hymnals to page 219, we will sing 'Near the Cross.'"

"The song leader is Joanna Brady," Gladys whispered to Mariah. "Her father is our doctor."

All around her, voices raised in praise. Mariah held the hymnal in front of her, silently mouthing the words of the beautiful old hymn. When she was small she loved to sing. Then one day Mother told her she sounded like an old crow in the corn patch, and the music inside Mariah died. The memory of that day, even though it had been almost thirty years ago, brought back a pain that stabbed through her like a knife.

As the congregation sang the final chorus, Carrie Nolan swept down the center aisle followed by a tall, broad-shouldered man. The young couple slid into the second pew from the front next to a white-haired gentleman that Mariah assumed was Mrs. Nolan's father. She frowned at the back of Carrie's head. If she didn't respect the Lord enough to arrive on time, she should have the decency to sit in the rear of the church where her entry didn't create a disturbance. Mariah realized that she was passing judgment on young Mrs. Nolan again and quickly asked the Lord to help her overcome her unkind thoughts.

After his sermon, the pastor made a few announcements concerning upcoming events. "In conclusion," he said, "I would like to introduce a special guest. Miss Casey, will you please stand?"

It took the sharp jab of Gladys's elbow in her ribs to bring her slowly to her feet.

"Miss Casey is our new teacher." The pastor smiled. "As you all know, a carry-in dinner is being held at the Cattlemen's Association building today in her honor. The ladies of Cedar Bend have prepared a bountiful repast as always. You will have an opportunity to enjoy some of the best food in the state at the same time you are making the acquaintance of our new teacher. Welcome to Cedar Bend, Miss Casey."

A round of applause brought a rush of color to Mariah's face. She knew they expected her to say something. The most she could manage was a murmured

"Thank you" before resuming her seat.

"Why didn't you tell me about the dinner?" she whispered to her cousin.

"It was to be a surprise." Gladys smiled and patted her arm as they rose for the final song.

Within minutes of their arrival at the Cattlemen's Association, Gladys had introduced Mariah to so many people her mind whirled. How would she ever remember so many faces and the names that went with them?

"Mariah, this is Joanna Brady," Gladys said. "You remember, she is our song leader."

"Of course," Mariah replied. "You have a lovely voice, Miss Brady."

"Thank you." The young woman smiled. "Miss Casey, may I introduce my father, Dr. Tom Brady?"

A lanky man moved to Joanna's side. "Dr. Brady is a member of the school board," Gladys said.

"Welcome to Cedar Bend, Miss Casey. I hope you will be happy here."

"I'm sure I will." There was a strong resemblance between the doctor and his daughter. They were both olive-skinned with dark hair and gentle, brown eyes. But, while he was tall and angular, Joanna was short and softly rounded.

"Say, Sherm just walked in the door." Tom Brady motioned to someone behind Mariah. "He's coming over. You haven't met Sherman Butler yet, have you?"

"I believe I saw him in church." When Mariah turned, she expected to see the silver-haired man Carrie Nolan had sat beside. Instead she found herself being introduced to a tall, handsome man with thick, curly, auburn hair and a well-groomed mustache. He didn't appear to be much older than herself. "Mr. Sherman Butler, may I introduce Miss Mariah Casey, our new teacher?"

"Miss Casey, welcome to Cedar Bend." His handshake was firm. "My daughter tells me you bought a house."

Mariah nodded. "It seemed a wise investment with the state of the economy and so many banks back East failing."

"I think you made a wise choice. One never knows what will happen in times like these. I hope President Cleveland is able to get a handle on things and this depression doesn't last too long."

"Papa, I've been looking for you." Carrie Nolan linked her arm through her father's. "Hello, Miss Casey. I should imagine you are prepared for tomorrow."

"It took the better part of the week," she said, "to put things in their proper order."

"I thought everything was in order."

Mariah looked into Carrie's beautiful face and read the disdain in her dark eyes. "Orderly, yes, of course, but not conducive to my methods of teaching."

"Well, I suppose you would know more about that than I." Carrie smiled sweetly. "After all, you were teaching before I was born." She tugged gently on her father's arm. "They're ready to begin, Papa. Come sit with us."

Mariah knew she had further alienated Mrs. Nolan with her sharp tongue. Why must she always be on the defensive? Carrie Nolan could no more help being beautiful than *she* could help being plain.

"I'm happy you are here, Miss Casey." The big man smiled as Carrie led him away.

"Would you sit with my father and me, Miss Casey?" Joanna Brady asked.

She turned to the nonthreatening young woman. "Yes. Thank you, Miss Brady."

Her smile lit up her sweet face. "Please call me Joanna."

"See what I meant about her?" Carrie slid into the chair beside her husband. "There was nothing wrong with my schoolroom."

Her father took the chair beside her. "Everyone has different ideas on how things should be done, little girl. I wouldn't judge Miss Casey too harshly."

They stood to pray before Carrie had a chance to reply.

While they ate, Sherman had ample opportunity to observe the teacher seated across the room. Several people stopped by the table to speak to her. Though she replied, there was nothing in her manner to encourage them to linger, and they quickly moved on. Was she shy or, as Carrie insisted, cold and hateful?

As soon as they finished eating, people began to circulate and gather in small groups to visit. Sherman saw Felicia Wainwright sweep through the door with two small girls. Her daughter, Callista, was dressed like a little princess in white ruffles with pink bows in her blond hair. Hope, her orphaned niece, wore an ill-fitting dress that looked as though it had been made from a flowered feed sack. The woman scanned the room until her sharp eyes came to rest on Mariah Casey. The two girls in tow, she bore down on the teacher.

Sherman knew that Felicia Wainwright had brought Carrie to tears on more than one occasion. He wondered how Miss Casey would handle the woman's demands.

"Excuse me. I am Mrs. Felicia Wainwright. Are you the new teacher?"

With a glance, Mariah took in the stout woman's elaborately styled blond hair and haughty expression. "Yes, I am Mariah Casey."

"My daughter will be in your second grade class this year." She rested a hand on the head of a miniature version of herself. "This is my darling Callista. Callista, precious, this is Miss Casey. She will be your teacher. Say hello to Miss Casey, dear."

The pudgy child stared silently at Mariah.

"Callista is very bright. You shan't have a bit of trouble with her." She laid hold of the smaller girl's arm and urged her forward. "However, I would like a few words with you about my niece. Callista, dear, I saw some of your little friends outside. Why don't you go play with them while I speak with Miss Casey?"

"I have to leave," Callista spoke in a high-pitched whine, "because she doesn't want me to hear what she has to say about Hope. Hope can stay because she's a dummy."

Mariah saw the same pain in the tiny girl's eyes she had seen reflected in her own mirror after one of her mother's barbed comments. Her heart ached for the defenseless child. "Go play with the other children, Callista."

Callista's eyes widened. Her lower lip trembled ever so slightly. "Now!" Mariah insisted. With a frightened glance the child dashed away.

"Don't get dirty, precious," her mother called after her. "I suppose I should apologize for my daughter." She smiled at Mariah. "But she is only a child. She hasn't yet learned to control her tongue."

Mariah frowned. "Children learn from the example that is set before them."

"Callista meant no harm." The woman managed a weak laugh. "After all, we have all heard the old saying, 'Sticks and stones may break my bones, but names will never hurt me.'"

"That is an erroneous saying, Mrs. Wainwright. Names break hearts and destroy spirits. I do not allow any child in my classroom to be abused, either verbally or physically."

"What Callista said to Hope couldn't possibly hurt her. My niece is deaf."

Mariah looked at the beautiful little girl. "Have you had her hearing tested?"

"I never saw the need. Hope is four years old, and she has never spoken a word. What other explanation could there be?" Mrs. Wainwright waved a bejeweled hand in a dismissive gesture. "My widowed sister died giving birth to Hope. I have done my Christian duty by the child, Miss Casey. My husband and I have given Hope a home. We have put food in her mouth and clothes on her back."

Mariah took note of the scuffed shoes and coarse, shapeless garment Hope wore. "What do you wish to speak to me about, Mrs. Wainwright?"

"I want to send Hope to school with Callista. She appears to be of normal intelligence. Of course I realize she will never be able to learn much, but I thought perhaps you could teach her something."

Mariah knew she should refuse—Hope was much too young to begin school—but the little girl's sad eyes tore at her heart.

"Mr. Butler is president of the school board. It would be necessary to seek his permission before allowing a child of such tender years to attend school."

"Of course. Come, Hope." Felicia Wainwright clutched the little girl's hand and set course in Sherman Butler's direction. Mariah followed in her wake.

Sherman saw Felicia Wainwright bearing down on them, followed by Miss Casey.

"Mrs. Wainwright is heading our way," Karl Braun said. "Wonder what she wants."

"I guess we'll soon find out," Tom Brady said.

"Guess so," Sherman agreed. "I only hope Miss Casey doesn't resign and head back to Ohio before the school year even begins."

The woman's breathless arrival precluded further conversation. Mrs. Wainwright fanned her perspiring face with a chunky hand. "Gentlemen, I'm glad you are all here. Miss Casey wants to speak to you."

"Is there a problem, Miss Casey?" Sherman asked.

"Mrs. Wainwright wishes to enroll her niece in school. I told her she would need your permission. Hope is only four years old."

"I delivered this little girl," Dr. Brady said. "As I recall it was late July. When is Hope's birthday, Mrs. Wainwright?"

The woman's face reddened. "July twenty-ninth."

"So she is barely four years old." Karl Braun shook his head. "Miss Casey will have her hands full as it is. A four-year-old child has no place in school."

"What is your recommendation, Miss Casey?" Sherman Butler asked.

Mariah looked down into the sad, blue eyes of the small girl. "I think Hope should come to school tomorrow."

"What do you think, gentlemen?" Sherman asked.

"Maybe we should discuss this in private," Karl Braun said.

The three excused themselves and moved a few feet away from the women. Mariah leaned down. "Would you like to come to school, Hope?"

"There's no use asking her what she wants, Miss Casey." The Wainwright woman's thinly arched brows drew together in a scowl. "I told you she's dumb as a post."

When the little girl looked up at her aunt, Mariah saw a dewdrop of moisture clinging to her long, black lashes. "Everything will be all right, Hope," she whispered in the child's perfect pink shell of an ear, hoping the girl could hear her after all.

After a few moments of earnest discussion the three men rejoined the women.

"Mrs. Wainwright, since Miss Casey is in favor of your niece attending school, Hope may start classes tomorrow with the other children." Sherman Butler's gaze shifted to Mariah. "This will be strictly on a trial basis, Miss Casey. We'll meet in one month and see how things are working out."

Mariah nodded. "Thank you, Mr. Butler. I am quite sure Hope will do fine."

"I hope so." Sherman glanced at Felicia Wainwright. "I sincerely hope so."

That evening in the large kitchen at the Circle C, Sherman Butler and his two partners enjoyed a cup of coffee.

"What'd you think of the new teacher, Sherm?"

Sherman remembered the gentleness in Miss Casey's eyes when she looked at Hope. He set his cup down. "I think she will be a fine teacher, Cyrus."

"Sad though," Mac said. "She's a woman bearin' a load of pain."

"She's a might bashful, I'd reckon," Cyrus said. "But I wouldn't say she's sad."

"She's sad." Mac hobbled over to the black range. "Anyone else want a cup of coffee?" When both men declined, he returned to his chair at the long oak table. "Miss Casey's heart has been plumb broke in two."

"You read too many of them romance novels, you old coot."

"Ain't got nothin' to do with my readin' material." Mac scowled at Cyrus. "A blind man could see that lady's hurtin'."

"You sayin' I'm blind?"

"I ain't sayin' nothin' of the sort." Mac took a sip from his cup. "But iffen the boot fits, wear it."

"I'm going to bed." Sherman pushed back his chair and left the two old friends wrangling over the new schoolteacher's heart, whether it was shattered or just nonexistent.

Chapter 6

Mariah stood facing her students. At least forty pairs of eyes looked back at her. Her pupils ranged in age from the diminutive Hope to a hulking young man who could barely squeeze into a desk. She had heard some of the older male teachers in Ohio talk about their experiences in backwoods schools. Sometimes older boys came to make trouble. A tremor of fear coursed through her.

Her father's Bible lay on the desk in front of her. She ran her fingers over the worn leather cover. "We will stand for the opening prayer," she said. "Then you may be seated during a short reading from the scriptures."

The children obediently rose to their feet.

Mariah tried to discern her new students' thoughts as she read the familiar passage. "'Weeping may endure for a night, but joy cometh in the morning.'" Mariah closed the Bible. "That concludes the first five verses of the Thirtieth Psalm. I will read a short passage to you each morning except Friday. I want each of you to memorize a Bible verse during the week and be prepared to recite each Friday after opening exercises. Yes, Callista?"

The blond second grader lowered her hand and stood beside her desk. "Can we say 'Jesus wept'?"

"I would prefer you put a bit more thought into it. Begin memorizing tonight."

"Miss Butler wouldn't let us say 'Jesus wept.'" Callista twirled a blond ringlet around her finger. "What about Hope? She can't memorize. Is she going to get a whipping because she—"

"Take your seat, Callista." Mariah glanced at the wide-eyed little girl sitting at the first grade table. Her scuffed, too-big shoes didn't even reach the floor. "No one is going to be whipped."

She picked up the attendance book. "When I call your name please respond by raising your hand."

Although it had seemed an insurmountable task, by the end of the week Mariah knew each student by name. As Karl Braun had assured her, although occasionally mischievous, they were well-behaved, obedient children.

Despite her efforts to remain aloof, the tiny girl at the first grade table tugged at her heartstrings. She found comfort in Hope and L. K. Braun's friendship. The sturdy six-year-old was very protective of Hope. Though the little girl didn't speak, Mariah noticed the two children always played together at recess.

Every spare moment, Mariah and Gladys worked on Mariah's house. They painted the dark woodwork sparkling white and covered the walls with colorful new wallpaper. Mariah hung blinds at the tall windows and topped them with white lace curtains. When they were finished, they stood back and admired their handiwork. Even vacant the house looked bright and cheerful.

"I like it," Gladys said.

"Mother would say it was garish," Mariah replied. "But I've lived in darkness for the last time, Cousin Gladys. I bought a new parlor suite after the auction of my parents' estate. Wait until you see it."

Mariah especially liked her bedroom paper with the full-blown red roses, and the small adjoining room she had designated as a sewing room and papered in a yellow floral. She papered the living room and dining room in blue stripes. The kitchen was done in green ivy.

In mid-September Mariah's belongings arrived, and she settled into her new house.

The following Sunday Joanna and Tom Brady invited her to dinner. Though she longed to become better acquainted with Joanna, she hesitated. If not for her cousin Gladys's insistence that she go, she would never have found the courage to accept the invitation.

A simple sign in front of the two-story house announced T. BRADY, M.D. A wide front porch, furnished with comfortable wicker chairs and a swing, spanned the front of the house.

Dr. Brady let the two women out, then turned the buggy toward the barn on the other side of the road.

Mariah followed Joanna across the porch and into a large foyer. "This is our waiting room," Joanna said. "Daddy's office and the surgery are on the right side of the hall. The parlor and dining room are on the left, and the kitchen is at the end of this hall." She gestured toward the staircase. "Our bedrooms are upstairs. You can leave your hat and gloves on the hall table if you would like."

After hanging her hat on a hook, Mariah folded her gloves and laid them on the table along with her purse. "Your home is very inviting."

"Thank you." Joanna smiled as she removed her own hat and gloves. "Since Mama passed, it sometimes seems empty."

Mariah followed Joanna down the hall to the cozy kitchen. "What can I do to help?"

"Everything is done unless you would like to slice bread while I make gravy. Then we'll get everything on the table. Daddy and I usually take our meals in the kitchen, but I thought since today is a special occasion we would eat in the dining room."

Carrying the platter of bread, she followed Joanna into the dining room. An empty invalid's chair sat in the corner. "It was Mama's," Joanna said. "She was an invalid for several years before God called her home. It was my privilege to care for her."

At first she thought the girl's remark facetious, but the tenderness of Joanna's expression when she looked at the chair dispelled that notion.

They placed the last bowls on the table as Tom Brady appeared in the doorway. "You may enter, sir," his daughter announced with a smile. "Dinner is served."

Joanna was a wonderful cook. Although the father and daughter's light-hearted banter was foreign to her, Mariah enjoyed the meal.

As they lingered over coffee and dessert, Dr. Brady asked her a few questions about her teaching experience in Ohio. Mariah gave each question careful consideration before answering.

"I realize it is different than what you were accustomed to, but do you enjoy teaching in a country school, Miss Casey?"

"It is very different," she agreed. "I taught second graders for many years. I'm not accustomed to older children." She laid down her fork. "I have one student—a young man named Mark Hopkins—who is twenty-one years old."

"I'm so happy that Mark is in school," Joanna said. "He's a couple of years older than I, but we started together. He was only there a few days before his father took him out to work."

"An eight-year-old child!" Mariah exclaimed.

"It isn't that unusual, Miss Casey." Dr. Brady leaned forward. "Ben Hopkins needed help proving up his land. Mark was his oldest child and only son."

"Mr. Hopkins should have realized the boy needed to be in school."

"Ben Hopkins is a good man. He only did what he felt was necessary."

"Mark is a sweet, gentle, hardworking young man," Joanna said. "Everyone loves him."

"Ben and Nora Hopkins have done an exemplary job of raising Mark and his sisters. They are all dedicated Christians." The doctor pushed aside his empty plate to rest his elbows on the table. Steepling his fingers under his chin, he said, "Not many families can make that claim."

"The Brauns appear to be another such family," Mariah remarked. "L. K.

Braun is only six years old, but he has taken it upon himself to be Hope's protector. The two of them are inseparable."

"Karl and Hilda Braun are raising their children to be compassionate, caring people," Tom Brady said. "I dare say they are well-behaved and respectful, as well."

At Mariah's nod of affirmation, the doctor smiled. "Karl Braun accepts nothing less from his children. Mr. Braun is strict, but he's also fair. Along with discipline, the Braun children receive a boundless supply of love."

"The Brauns' eldest daughter is a friend of my cousin Lucille," Mariah said.

"Gretchen Braun, Lucille, and Carrie Butler have always been—as you remarked about L. K. and little Hope—inseparable," said Dr. Brady.

"Carrie and Gretchen were in my grade at school," Joanna said. "Six of us graduated the same year."

"There are only two in this year's graduating class," Mariah said. "Henry Carson and Jay Braun."

"We had Gretchen Braun, Carrie Butler, Becky Colton, Jake Phillips, Clay Shepherd, and me. Three of us stayed in Cedar Bend, and three of us left. Becky is living with her aunt in Missouri. Jake went away to college." Joanna sighed. "I don't know where Clay is."

"Clay Shepherd's mother died when he was little more than a baby," Dr. Brady explained. "His father was a drifter. The year they spent in Cedar Bend was probably the longest Shepherd tarried anywhere. Clay spent a lot of time here." He glanced at the invalid's chair in the corner, and his face gentled. "My wife loved the boy, and I believe he was fond of her."

"It has been five years since I last saw Clay," Joanna added. "I still pray for him every day."

Joanna began to clear the table. Mariah rose to help her. As they worked in companionable silence, Mariah hoped that Joanna was actually enjoying being with her as much as she was enjoying the company of this tenderhearted young woman. A spark of belief that she had found someone to care about and who would care about her flickered in her heart.

Mariah had just concluded opening exercises the following morning when the door opened. Every head swiveled as the visitor stepped into the classroom. Mariah rose from her chair, her heart beating a staccato. "Mr. Butler, please come in."

"I thought I would drop in and observe your class for a few minutes," the auburn-haired rancher said with a warm smile.

"Of course. Please have a seat."

He walked to the front of the room and sat down in the chair in the corner. "Go on as usual, Miss Casey. Just forget I'm here."

Mariah took a deep breath. "All right, children. Get out your history books." As Mariah moved about the classroom, she tried to keep her mind off the man sitting in the corner. Her teaching had been observed before. She knew what was expected of her. With an effort, Mariah turned her attention to her students.

Sherman watched as Mariah stopped at each row of desks. As soon as she had the older ones settled, she moved to the table of first graders. Mark Hopkins came to the front of the room to join them. Sherman admired the young man. It must take a tremendous amount of courage to sit around a table with such small classmates, sounding out the words Miss Casey printed on the blackboard.

Sherman enjoyed the sound of the teacher's voice. It was soft and feminine but clear and easily understood. As she stood at the blackboard, a wisp of hair escaped her severe bun and curled against the back of her neck. He wondered why such an appealing woman wore her hair in such an unbecoming style. It was almost as though she were trying to make herself unattractive.

A short time later, he left the small school, thankful he had finally listened to Mrs. Jacobs and hired Mariah Casey. From what he had observed, she was more than competent as an educator. He was surprised to find himself also wondering what was hidden inside this teacher's heart.

That afternoon Mariah had her second visitor. Her last student had straggled out, and she was putting her desk in order when Felicia Wainwright barged through the door. "Miss Casey, how dare you punish my darling Callista!"

Mariah folded her hands on top of her desk. "Please have a seat, Mrs. Wainwright."

"I will not." The woman rested her hands on the desk and leaned forward until her face was inches from Mariah's. "Callista told me what you did to her. I will not allow it. Do you understand me, madam? I will not allow my precious baby to be humiliated."

The woman's face was red, and a blood vessel throbbed in her temple. Mariah rose and moved the chair from the corner. "Please sit down, Mrs. Wainwright."

The woman dropped into the chair placed beside the desk while Mariah went to the water bucket beside the back door and poured a cup of water. She thrust the cup into the woman's hand before returning to her chair behind the desk. "Why don't you tell me what this is about?"

The woman set the cup on the corner of the desk and fanned herself with a dainty linen handkerchief until she got her breath. "My baby told me she was forced to stand in the corner for fifteen minutes today."

"Did Callista tell you why she was punished?"

"She said that you don't like her."

Callista was not a likable child. No one in the classroom liked her. "I do not punish children because I do not like them. It is my responsibility to uphold integrity in the classroom. Callista copied off Jenny Carson's paper."

"I don't believe it." Felicia puffed up like a toad. "My child would never cheat. You're taking the side of the Carson girl because her father is the pastor at your church."

"Mrs. Wainwright, the truth is not always easy to hear." Mariah laced her fingers together on the desktop and took a deep breath. "Callista is still young enough to be malleable, but I fear if you do not take her in hand soon it may be—"

The woman's voice rose. "What do you mean 'take her in hand'?"

"Callista cheats, Mrs. Wainwright."

The woman began to sputter.

Mariah held up a hand. "Please hear me out. Your daughter lies. She torments Hope. She—"

"Hope!" The word burst from the woman. "This is all about Hope, isn't it? Callista told me you favored that little foundling over her."

"Callista's behavior has nothing to do with her cousin." An image of the tiny girl's huge, blue eyes passed through Mariah's mind. "Hope is an innocent child."

"You don't like the way I am raising the child."

"I didn't say that. I only—"

"You can have Hope." Her voice dropped. "Take her, Miss Casey."

People didn't give children away. Did they? Mariah leaned forward. "What are you saying?"

"I don't want her." Two fat tears rolled down the woman's face. "Every time I look at her, I see Carly."

"Your sister?"

"Mama and Papa never loved me after she came. Everyone always preferred Carly. They thought she was perfect. By the time she was fifteen, there were young men hanging around her like bees around a honeysuckle vine. I never had a suitor until Harry. When he asked me to marry him, I jumped at the chance. We moved to Cedar Bend, and five years after our wedding, God gave me Callista. Carly married when she was nineteen. After Mama and Papa passed away, Carly and her husband, Ned, came for a visit. They had been married less than a year, but already Carly was expecting. Everything always came so easy for her. Ned was killed in a riding accident—his horse threw him and his neck was broken. Two months later Hope was born and Carly died."

Mrs. Wainwright sat weeping into her handkerchief. Mariah quietly waited for the woman to regain control of herself. She didn't like Felicia Wainwright, but she knew what it was to be unloved. The woman drew a shuddering breath. She looked at Mariah through swollen, red-rimmed eyes. "The last words Carly spoke were to tell me she loved me and to ask me to take care of her baby." She twisted the damp handkerchief. "Every time I look at Hope and Callista, I see Carly and myself. I want to love Hope, but I can't. Please take her, Miss Casey."

Mariah looked down at her interlaced fingers. Hope was a child, a precious gift from God. She thought of the little girl's sorrow-filled eyes. A deep longing coursed through her. A yearning she could not deny.

"Harry has a job offer in California. We plan on leaving at the end of the week. You will never see us again, Miss Casey. Hope will forget us."

"Yes." Mariah's clenched hands trembled. "Yes, I will take Hope."

"You will?" Felicia Wainwright stood. "I. . .Oh, thank you! Thank you, Miss Casey. Harry will bring Hope and her things to your house this evening. I'll just collect Callista's books now. I think it would be best if she didn't return to school."

Mariah remained seated for several minutes after Felicia Wainwright left. Her father's closed Bible lay on the desk in front of her. *What have I done, Lord?* She ran her fingers over the worn leather cover. *I know nothing of raising a child. Please give me wisdom, Father.*

The parlor clock chimed seven times. Mariah moved the lace curtain aside to peer into the empty street. Felicia Wainwright had said her husband would bring Hope in the evening. Had she changed her mind? Mariah resumed pacing. In the room next to her own, the narrow brass bed was freshly made up and ready. She stood looking down at the four-patch quilt, then sank into the small rocking chair beside the bed. Hope wasn't coming. Felicia Wainwright was an overwrought, impulsive woman. She would never give up her niece.

A sharp knock at the front door brought Mariah to her feet. The slight man standing on the porch held his hat and a carpetbag in one hand. The other hand rested on the small girl's shoulder. "Miss Casey, I've brought Hope."

Mariah looked down into the little girl's wide, blue eyes. "Welcome home, Hope."

Chapter 7

Mariah felt a moment of panic after the door closed behind Harry Wainwright. Standing in the middle of the parlor floor with the carpetbag beside her, Hope looked as lost and confused as Mariah felt.

"Well, Hope, I am pleased to have you here." Mariah spoke to Hope, believing the girl could probably hear, but she also made gestures along with her words just in case Felicia Wainwright was correct about the girl being deaf. "Let's get you settled in." She picked up the little girl's bag. As small as the bag was, it was only half full. Hope followed her to the bedroom. "This will be your room. The bed was mine when I was a small girl. I didn't have time to decorate it for you, but we will do that later. I thought you might want to choose things for it yourself. Do you think you might like that?"

Hope watched while Mariah put away her few possessions. At the bottom of the bag was a package wrapped in brown butcher paper.

"What is this?" Mariah sat down in the rocking chair. Hope watched as she unwrapped a photograph of a young couple. The man was fair-haired and handsome. The girl had dark hair and large eyes that appeared luminous even in the sepia-toned photograph. "This must be your mother and father, Hope. See how beautiful she is. You look exactly like her."

An envelope with her name on it fell to the floor. Mariah picked it up and slipped it into her pocket. "I baked cookies for you this afternoon. Do you like oatmeal and raisin? How would you like to have cookies and milk for a bedtime snack?" Mariah held out the plate of cookies, and the little girl smiled brightly.

Sitting at the kitchen table, Mariah watched Hope eat a cookie. *Poor child! Mrs. Wainwright didn't tell her anything. She has no idea why she is here or what is happening. Father, please help me to make her understand.*

"Hope, I need to explain some things to you." The child gave no indication she heard. Mariah covered a small hand with her own. "You are going to live here with me, Hope."

The little girl looked up, her blue eyes questioning. "Forever," Mariah said.

Hope pulled her hand from under Mariah's. She took one of the two cookies that remained on the saucer and thrust it into Mariah's hand. It was on the tip of the woman's tongue to say she never ate cookies. She bit back the words and poured herself a glass of milk.

After the snack, Mariah helped Hope get ready for bed. When Hope was in

150

her nightgown, Mariah unbraided the little girl's hair. "You have beautiful hair," she said as she pulled the brush through the thick silken tresses. She braided her hair—loosely this time—and tucked her into bed. She read aloud from a Bible storybook that she had owned since she was a child until Hope's eyes closed in sleep.

For a time she sat in the rocking chair, looking at the little girl. The enormity of what lay ahead overwhelmed her. She put the book on the table at her side. Kneeling beside the small bed, she prayed for Hope to be healthy and happy. She prayed for her to grow up secure in the knowledge that she was loved and wanted. Most important, she prayed that she would come to know and love the Lord.

She forgot the letter in her pocket until she was preparing for bed. Sitting on the edge of her bed, she read Felicia Wainwright's letter. It was mostly a self-serving plea for understanding. She said she didn't want Mariah to think badly of her as she had done her best to give her sister's child a good home. "It was unfair," she wrote, "that Carly always had so much, while I had so little." At first, Mariah felt no pity for the selfish woman. But as anger began to form, a still, small voice reminded her that she wasn't as different from Felicia Wainwright as she wanted to believe. Pain from her own mother's sharp words still remained deep in her heart and caused her to say and do things she always regretted later. She dropped to her knees and prayed for Felicia Wainwright to find peace of heart and mind. She also found herself praying God would grant her the same.

———※———

Getting a four-year-old up, fed, dressed, and ready for the day was more time-consuming than Mariah could ever have imagined. By the time they arrived at school, more than half her students were standing on the porch waiting for her. Twelve-year-old Mabel Carson came to meet her. "Miss Casey, we were afraid you had fallen ill. Are you all right?"

"I'm fine, Mabel, but I appreciate your concern." Mariah unlocked the door and led the children inside.

After prayer and scripture reading, Mariah called the roll. When all eyes turned to Callista's empty desk, Mariah told the class that the Wainwright family was moving to California, and Callista wouldn't be back. No one asked why Hope was still present in the classroom, or why she had arrived that morning with the teacher.

Mariah noticed Hope hesitate beside Callista's empty desk as the children filed out to recess that morning. L. K. whispered something to her—he obviously thought she could hear, too—then took her hand, and the two children walked out the door together. When they came back inside, Hope passed her cousin's empty place without a second glance. Mariah saw no sign of the Wainwright family the rest of the week. Still, she was uneasy until she knew they had left town.

On Friday she dismissed school early and took Hope to Dr. Brady's office. After a thorough examination the doctor handed the little girl a peppermint stick and sent her from the room with Joanna.

"Miss Casey, have a seat." Mariah perched on the edge of a straight chair across the desk from the doctor. "I can find nothing wrong with Hope. There is no malformation of the ear. She reacts to sound."

"I knew it. I knew she could hear."

"As far as I can tell, she can also speak. It is my opinion that when she feels secure, she will speak." He adjusted a cup on his desk. "I understand the Wainwrights left this morning."

"Yes." Mariah breathed a sigh of relief. "I was afraid she would want Hope back."

"I never thought she would give the child up." The doctor's smile lit up his rugged face. "The Lord must have moved her heart."

Mariah thought of the letter Hope's aunt had left her. "He did indeed," she agreed. She then added to herself, *Her heart is not the only one God is moving. Thank You, Lord!*

Hope skipped along at Mariah's side as they walked to the mercantile.

Mariah had been to the store several times, but Mr. Harris had always been the only one in attendance. She cast around in her mind trying to recall where she had seen the cheerful woman who greeted her today.

"You don't remember me, do you? Now don't you be embarrassed, Miss Casey. You have had to get used to so many new faces. I'm Ettie Harris. I've seen you at church, but I don't believe we've ever been formally introduced."

"Of course," Mariah said. "You are the pianist."

"I'm also the pastor's mother-in-law, and I teach Sunday school, as well. From what I have heard, you are doing a wonderful job with all our children." The middle-aged woman beamed. "The Carson children are my grandchildren."

"Pastor Carson's children are a delight." Mariah smiled. "I don't know what I would do without Mabel."

"Yes, Mabel told me you chose her to help the little ones learn their letters. She tells me she wants to be a teacher just like you." After a brief exchange of pleasantries, Mrs. Harris got down to business. "What can I help you with, Miss Casey?"

"I need to buy some things for Hope." Mariah took a folded piece of paper from her pocket. "I have a list, but there may be other items that I have forgotten."

The woman took the slip of paper from Mariah. "My, this is quite a list."

"I want to replace everything she brought with her."

Mrs. Harris slipped Mariah's list into her pocket. "Fred is in the storeroom. I'll get him in here to wait on folks while I help you."

After Mrs. Harris turned the few customers in the store over to her husband, the two women selected underwear and stockings for Hope and piled them neatly on the front counter.

"Now," Mariah said, "we need to look at shoes."

"Certainly." Mrs. Harris led the way to a corner of the store. "You sit right here in this chair, Hope."

While Hope was being seated, Mrs. Harris went through a door leading to the back of the store and returned with two boxes. "These are the finest shoes made for children," she said, sitting down on a small stool in front of Hope. "Let's pull your shoes off, honey, and try these." Hope extended her feet. Mrs. Harris pulled off the old shoes and slipped on the new ones. "That appears to be a perfect fit. Let me get the button hook, and you can walk around in them."

Mariah noticed that Hope was responding to all that Mrs. Harris asked, and a warm feeling enveloped her heart. *Maybe she is beginning to feel secure—and loved.*

While Hope walked back and forth on the scrap of carpet, Mrs. Harris chatted with Mariah. "The shoes your little one is wearing are seventy-five cents a pair. I have a pair of higher quality that sells for a dollar sixty, but as fast as they grow at that age I would go with the less expensive pair."

"I am submitting myself to your expertise, Mrs. Harris. Though I have been with children most of my life, I must confess that I know very little of the practical aspects of raising them."

"Don't you fret, Miss Casey. You just follow your instincts and you'll do fine." She patted Mariah's hand. "I raised six children. If you have any questions don't hesitate to ask me or one of the other women at church. We will help in any way we can."

"Thank you, Mrs. Harris." Mariah's eyes were on Hope as she skipped across the rug. "I appreciate your thoughtfulness."

Hope climbed into the chair beside Mariah.

"Did you find the shoes comfortable, dear?" Mrs. Harris reached a hand toward Hope's feet. The little girl put her feet as far underneath the chair as possible. "Well," the woman said, laughing, "I believe she likes them."

A smile tugged at the corners of Mariah's mouth. "It would seem you have made a sale, Mrs. Harris. Is it all right if she keeps the shoes on?"

"Of course it is." The woman patted Hope's dark head. "You be sure and wear those pretty shoes to my Sunday school class. Your mama says you can keep them, honey."

At the word *mama* Hope looked up at Mariah. *Mama!* After one stunned moment, a feeling of joy washed over Mariah. "Let's look at some dress goods," she said.

"We have a wonderful dressmaker just a few doors down the street. You'll remember Eunice Wright from church," Mrs. Harris said.

"Yes, of course, but I brought my sewing machine with me from Ohio." Mariah stood. "I want to make Hope's clothes myself."

Mrs. Harris smiled understandingly and led them to a table piled high with fabric. Mariah and the shopkeeper selected a length of pale gray calico strewn with blue flowers, a blue plaid gingham, and a dark blue piece with multicolored flowers. A rack of ready-made dresses caught Mariah's eye. She looked through them and took one that appeared to be Hope's size from the rack.

"That one is seventy-five cents," Mrs. Harris said.

The dress was expensive—more than the fabric for the other three together—but she didn't have time to make Hope a dress before church Sunday morning. "Is there somewhere she could try it on?"

"Of course there is." She took the dress from Mariah. "Come with me, Hope. Your mama wants you to try this on." She took Hope's small hand. "We'll come back and surprise Mama."

Mama. Would she ever become accustomed to that word in relation to herself? *Thank You, Lord. Thank You. Thank You. Help me to be a good mama to this precious little girl You have entrusted to my care.*

"Well, now what do you think of us?" Mrs. Harris stood before her with Hope. The dress fit as if it had been made for the little girl.

"It's perfect in every way," Mariah replied.

Hope twirled around, causing the full skirt to flare out. Mrs. Harris chuckled. Mariah, no longer able to hold back, let her own laughter overflow.

"You get ever'thing loaded, Sherm?" The storekeeper leaned against the counter.

"I think that'll do me for this trip," Sherman Butler answered absently, his attention on the two women and the little girl at the back of the store.

The storekeeper followed his gaze. "Did you hear that Mrs. Wainwright gave that little girl to Miss Casey?"

"No, I hadn't heard," Sherman said.

"Yep. The Wainwrights moved to California. Left first light this morning."

The storekeeper leaned in closer. "Gave that little girl away like an unwanted puppy."

"Miss Casey took her?"

"Yep. They been in here the better part of an hour. The schoolteacher's buying the store out." He rested his hand on a pile of clothing. "This here is all for that little girl."

The women and the child moved slowly to the front of the store. Miss Casey's cheeks were pink, and her eyes sparkled. Sherman had always thought she was attractive, but today he realized how pretty she really was. He tipped his hat. "Mrs. Harris. Miss Casey. Who is this little princess?" He smiled down at Hope. "That is a very pretty dress you have on, sweetheart."

"She refuses to take her new dress off." Mariah laughed. "I am afraid she will insist on sleeping in it."

He found Miss Casey's laugh delightful. "I know what to do about that." He lifted Hope up and sat her on the counter. "Mr. Harris has some gumdrops here. Would you like some?"

Hope looked from the jar of brightly colored candies to Miss Casey then up at the tall man. "Give this young lady a penny's worth of gumdrops, Fred."

The storekeeper handed the small bag to Hope. "You mustn't eat any of these until after you get home and change your dress," Sherman said. "All right?"

Hope's lower lip stuck out the slightest bit, but she nodded. He couldn't resist hugging the little girl before he stood her back on the floor.

"Thank you, Mr. Butler, but it wasn't necessary that you buy her candy."

"It was my pleasure, Miss Casey." Sherman smiled. "Just don't let her have a candy until she takes off her new dress."

"No, I won't."

Sherman watched as Mariah counted out the money for her purchases. "You are never going to be able to carry all this home," Mrs. Harris said. "If you like, Fred can deliver it all after we close the store."

"Yes, I would appreciate that."

"If you don't mind riding in a buckboard, I'd be happy to see you and Hope home with your packages," Sherman offered.

The color rose in Mariah's face as she looked up at the smiling man. "Thank you, but I wouldn't wish to be an imposition."

"You wouldn't be. It's on my way." He picked up two of the bags. "I'll load this for you."

Mariah offered no further protest as she and Hope followed Sherman outside. He stowed her purchases in the buckboard, then lifted Hope into the middle of the wide bench seat before taking Mariah's elbow and assisting her onto the seat beside Hope.

"Miss Casey, are you getting settled in?" he asked as soon as they were on their way.

"Yes. I believe I am." Mariah glanced down at the small girl beside her. "My life has certainly changed in the last few weeks."

Sherman chuckled. "I should imagine it has."

After that, though Mariah responded briefly to his comments, Sherman's attempts at small talk seemed to fall on unreceptive ears, and the remainder of the short trip was completed in silence.

Soon they drew up in front of the neat, clapboard cottage. Sherman jumped from the buckboard and lifted Hope to the ground. When he extended a helping hand to Mariah, she hesitated for the briefest moment before placing her hand in his and climbing down from the buckboard.

Sherman continued to hold her slender, gloved hand even after she was standing in the street facing him.

"It was most kind of you to see us home, Mr. Butler." She blushed and gently extracted her hand from his.

"I'm glad I was there and could be of assistance." Sherman hurried to the back of the buckboard and carried Mariah's purchases up the steps of the front porch.

"If you leave the packages beside the door I will take them inside."

"I'll be happy to carry them in for you."

"No, please." Mariah glanced at the neighboring houses, and again pink tinted the delicate ivory of her face. "I can carry them in."

"As you wish." Sherman deposited the parcels beside the door and tipped his hat to the lady. "Good day, Miss Casey." He rested a hand on Hope's head. "Remember, little Miss Hope, no gumdrops until you have changed your dress."

Sherman whistled as he drove out of town.

Chapter 8

The Bradys were having dinner at Mariah's. There were so many last-minute details to attend to Sunday morning that Mariah and Hope were late for Sunday school. Though it was only a couple of minutes, for Mariah, who was unaccustomed to being late, it seemed like hours. After seeing Hope settled in her class, she slid into the pew beside Joanna Brady. The young woman smiled at her, and Mariah smiled back.

"Second Timothy, chapter 1," Joanna whispered.

Mariah quickly found her place and settled back to catch her breath. Hope hadn't looked too happy when she left her with Mrs. Harris, but Mariah refused to worry. The little girl was in good hands. She would be fine.

Pastor Carson was the teacher of the Sunday school class. *A very good teacher,* Mariah thought. After the reading of each passage, he encouraged discussion. It fell to Mariah to read the fifth verse. "'When I call to remembrance the unfeigned faith that is in thee, which dwelt first in thy grandmother Lois, and thy mother Eunice; and I am persuaded that in thee also.'"

"Every morning and evening my father read to us from the Bible," the pastor said, "but it was my mother who knelt beside our beds with us and taught us to pray. How many of you remember your mothers praying with you?"

Almost every hand raised. "Mama died when I was small," Carrie Nolan said, "but I remember her praying. When she knew she would be leaving me while I was still very young, she left a series of letters for me to read when I was older. Those letters, and her Bible with her favorite passages marked and the notes in the margins, mean the world to me."

"My mother always sang hymns while she prepared breakfast," Carrie's husband, Lucas, volunteered. "That is one of my fondest memories of her. Those early memories of Ma singing 'Amazing Grace' had a great deal to do with my own salvation."

"As you all know, Mama was unwell for many years," Joanna said. "The last few years she was an invalid, it was my privilege to care for her. We spent many hours together studying the Word, singing, and praying. That time with my mother is a priceless gift that I will always cherish."

Mariah listened quietly while several others in the class spoke of their early training times with godly mothers.

"Miss Casey," the pastor spoke, "do you have anything to add? I know your father was a pastor, but your mother surely had a tremendous influence on your life, as well."

Mariah looked down at the Bible lying open on her lap. Mother had surely influenced her life, but not in a way she could share with her Sunday school class. She looked into the pastor's caring gray eyes and said the only thing she could say. "My mother was a very beautiful woman. When I was small I idolized her."

When she said no more, the pastor went on to the next verse.

Mariah was walking out of church with the Bradys when a horse galloped up and a distraught-looking man flung himself from the saddle and rushed up to them. "Doc Brady, Lizzie's took sick. She needs you."

"Of course, Sid. You go on home. We'll be right behind you." He turned to Mariah. "I'm sorry about dinner, Miss Casey."

"It's all right," Mariah said. "We will do it another time."

"I'm sorry, Mariah," Joanna added to her father's apology. "Lizzie's labor is always difficult. We will probably be out there until sometime in the night."

Trying to hide her disappointment, Mariah assured them they would simply reschedule. She and Hope watched the Bradys' carriage turn onto the street.

"Well, Hope, it looks as though we'll have dinner alone."

"Not necessarily," a deep voice behind her said. Mariah turned and looked up into Sherman Butler's blue eyes. "Why don't you come out to the Circle C? Mac cooks enough for an army."

"I'd reckon we'd be happy to have you an' the little 'un." An elderly man Mariah assumed was Mac stepped from behind Sherman. "You an' the little lady kin ride out with me in the buggy."

Mariah was on the verge of refusing when she looked down at Hope. The little girl was looking up at her, blue eyes alight with anticipation.

"We accept your invitation." Mariah thought of the two pies at home. "Under one condition. That I be allowed to stop at my house and pick up dessert."

"I think that can be arranged." A wide grin revealed the strong, white teeth framed by Mr. Butler's full, auburn mustache. He escorted Mariah and Hope to the buggy, then mounted his horse and rode away with several other men.

"Lucas and Carrie will be long directly," Mac said, as he guided the horse out of the churchyard, "but we ain't waitin' fer 'em."

"Mr. and Mrs. Nolan will be there?"

"Yep! They'll be wherever there's a decent meal." The little man grinned. "I tried my best to teach Carrie to cook afore she wuz married, but she jist never seemed to have a knack fer it."

"I heard her tell Cousin Gladys she couldn't cook, but I thought she was being modest," Mariah said. "I imagined she could do anything."

"Carrie ain't never been known fer bein' modest 'bout her accomplishments." The old man chuckled. "And ain't nobody kin do ever'thing, Miz Casey."

"No, I suppose not," Mariah agreed, feeling somewhat better about spending an afternoon with Carrie Nolan. By the time Mac pulled the buggy to a stop in front of Mariah's house, Hope had become a soft weight against her. Mac put his arm around the sleeping child and cradled her head against his side. "You run on and git what you need," he said. "Me an' the little lady will be jist fine."

Mariah only hesitated a moment before climbing down from the buggy and hurrying inside.

———

"Sherm tells me you keered fer yer ma back in Ohio," Mac said, as soon as they resumed their journey.

"Yes, ever since I was eighteen." Mariah arranged the sleeping child so that she lay on the seat with her head cradled in her lap. "My parents were in a buggy accident. Father was killed. Mother's leg was broken, and her face was scarred."

"Missus Jacobs told Sherman that yer ma was left an invalid."

"The leg was badly broken and didn't heal properly. After the accident Mother walked with a pronounced limp. Then, of course, there were the scars."

The little man frowned. "I figgered it wuz worse than that."

"I'm sure Mother inferred that in her letters to Cousin Gladys, and for her it was devastating. My mother was a very beautiful woman, Mr. McDougal. Her life ended with the accident. It would have been more merciful for her if she had died with Father."

Mariah could hardly believe she was having such a personal conversation with a stranger. But there was something about Mac McDougal that inspired confidence. Still, she didn't like to remember the years she had spent trying to please her mother.

A quote from Shakespeare came to mind. *What's gone and past help, should be past grief.* She could do nothing to change what had happened the first thirty-six years of her life. Mariah ran a gentle hand over the dark ringlets of Hope's silky hair. The past was best left in the past. The future lay sleeping in her lap.

"You love that little gal a lot, don't cha?" Mac's faded blue eyes rested briefly on the sleeping child.

"Having Hope is a dream come true."

"Looks to me like yer doin' a mighty fine job with 'er."

"Thank you, Mr. McDougal, but I feel so inadequate." Mariah glanced at the little man before looking back down at the child. "I have always believed we learn our life skills from our parents. Mother wasn't an affectionate woman."

Mac pulled on his ear. "Wal, you ain't necessarily like yer ma." He glanced at Mariah. "You got a lot of love in you, Miz Casey. I kin see thet when you look at thet little girl, an' I'd reckon some things jist comes natural."

"Mother was ashamed of me." Mariah felt the pain crowd up into her throat. "She often said she didn't understand how she could have given birth to such a tall, homely child."

"No offense, ma'am, but I reckon yer ma was a right foolish woman." Mac cleared his throat. "You are tall, there's no denyin' thet, but yer fur from homely, Miz Casey. Don't you never let no one tell you otherwise."

The man's kindness touched her. Mariah looked away to hide the tears that threatened to overflow.

A few minutes later they left the main road and passed under an arched sign that read CIRCLE C RANCH. Hope stirred, sat up, and looked around with sleep-dazed eyes. "This here's the Circle C, little lady. The house is up there at the end of this lane."

The ranch house was a rambling one-story structure of cedar and native stone. Mariah had never seen such a dwelling, but she immediately liked it.

As soon as the buggy drew up in front of the house, Sherman hurried to meet them. "Welcome to the Circle C," he said as he gave Mariah a helping hand. When he reached for Hope she stood up on the buggy seat and leaped into his arms.

"Hope, don't ever do that again," Mariah scolded. "If Mr. Butler hadn't caught you, you could have fallen and been hurt."

"I wouldn't let her fall," Sherman said.

Hope looked at her, then tightened her arms around Mr. Butler's neck.

Mariah detected a mischievous gleam in the little girl's eyes. She turned away to hide her own smile. Mac was hobbling toward the house with her basket. She followed with Hope and Sherman.

"This here's my kitchen," Mac said, setting the basket on the table. "The ranch hands eat in here. Course with winter comin' on we ain't got a full crew."

Mariah looked around the large room. A huge fireplace, with a rocking chair and a small footstool in front of it, took up one wall. A long table surrounded by a dozen chairs stood in the middle of the wooden floor. A long counter, topped by shelves filled with dishes, glasses, and foodstuffs, lined one wall.

"We used to do all our cookin' in thet there fireplace," Mac said. "Thet was afore I got this here nice black range."

The black and chrome range—like everything else in the kitchen—was huge. The chrome was polished to a shine that reflected the room.

Mariah felt some comment about the range, obviously the little man's pride and joy, was in order. "It is a beautiful cookstove, Mr. McDougal," she said.

"Thet it is, Miss Casey." The little man smiled. "By the way, nobody ever calls me Mr. McDougal. I'm jist plain Mac."

Before Mariah had a chance to respond, Carrie Nolan swept through the door. "We're here," she announced. "Lucas will be in as soon as he's finished taking care of the horse. What's for dinner, Mac? I'm starving." She paused for a heartbeat when she saw Mariah. "I didn't know you were here, Miss Casey." She dismissed Mariah, and her gaze settled on the little girl clinging to Mariah's hand. "Hope, my goodness, don't you look pretty. Are you going to sit beside me at dinner?"

Hope immediately released Mariah's hand and clasped Carrie's hand. Mariah felt betrayed, though she told herself Hope was only a child. Why wouldn't she prefer the sparkling beauty of Carrie Nolan to her new mother's dull plainness? Still, no matter what she told herself, the pain in her heart was impossible to deny. The meal was delicious, but Mariah picked at her food. Mac and Sherman Butler tried to draw her into the conversation that flowed between Carrie Nolan and the four men, but she felt isolated and left out. She barely knew the people Carrie chattered on and on about. Worse yet, Hope kept looking up at the Nolan woman with wide-eyed fascination, hanging on every foolish word the young woman uttered.

At last the miserable meal was over. Mariah insisted on helping Mac clear the table, but he wouldn't allow her to do dishes. "I got me a feller thet does the cleanin' up, Mariah. You jist go in the parlor and rest."

"I have a better idea." Sherman smiled at Mariah. "How would you and Hope like to take a walk with me?"

He picked Hope up and set her on one arm. "Would you like to walk out to the corral and see the horses, Hope?"

Mr. Butler had been thoughtful to invite them to dinner. It would be impolite to refuse his offer. Besides, a walk was a perfect excuse to get away from Carrie Nolan. "A walk would be nice," Mariah said.

"Lucas and I will go with you," Carrie said, clasping her husband's arm.

"I don't reckon Sherm invited us along," Lucas drawled.

The color rose in Carrie's face. "Well, I happen to think—"

Mariah never had a chance to hear what Carrie thought. Sherman put his free hand on her elbow and guided her out the door. He set Hope on the ground and took her tiny hand in his. Mariah took the little girl's other hand, and the three of them walked across to the corral. Sherman picked Hope up and stood her on one of the higher rails of the corral fence. She draped her arms over the top rail and clung there as though it was an everyday occurrence for her.

"She's a natural-born rancher." Sherman laughed and put his hand on the little girl's back to steady her.

Mariah already had her hand around Hope's waist. When his hand touched hers, a tingle ran all the way to her elbow. Didn't he realize that her hand was resting beneath his? What was the proper thing to do in this situation?

She should pull her hand away. She should, but the feel of that big, work-roughened hand on hers felt so good. Finally he was the one to move his hand.

"You see the pony over there, Hope?" He pointed to a black animal with white stocking feet and a matching blaze on its forehead. "Next time you come to visit I'll let you ride her. That is, if it's all right with your mama."

Hope turned sparkling blue eyes on Mariah. The pony was smaller than the other horses but still looked potentially dangerous. "I don't know," Mariah said. "Hope is rather small to ride such a large animal."

"I'll lead her around the corral," Sherman said. "She'll be perfectly safe."

"We'll see," Mariah conceded. She lifted the little girl from the fence and stood her on the ground.

"There's something in the barn Hope might like to see." Sherman pointed out the long, low bunkhouse and several other outbuildings as they strolled in the direction of the barn.

In the dim, shadowy barn, the smell of fresh hay mingled with the earthy scent of manure and warm animals. Mariah heard the faint mewling of kittens. "They're in this corner." Sherman scooped Hope up with one arm. Mariah released the little girl's hand and followed.

The man reached a hand into the straw nest and lifted out a squirming ball of yellow fur. "They don't have their eyes open yet," he said. "Would you like to hold him, Hope?"

Hope nodded, and Sherman placed the small ball of fluff in her hands. "Don't squeeze him too tight," he warned.

Hope rubbed her face against the kitten's head. "Oh!" she said; then she laughed.

Mariah had never heard the child utter a sound. That single exclamation and the joyful laugh were an affirmation of her belief that Hope would one day speak. Tears filled her eyes and she quickly turned away. Sherman stood Hope down on the straw-littered floor and put his hand on Mariah's arm. She allowed him to lead her a few steps away from the little girl.

"She has never spoken before?"

Mariah shook her head. "No," she said softly. "But I knew she could. Sometimes when children are mistreated, they try to make themselves invisible."

"Well, in that case, Hope should be talking your ear off in no time." He wiped a tear from Mariah's face with his thumb. "You're doing a wonderful job with her, Miss Casey."

Mariah's breath quickened at the touch of his hand on her face. She couldn't recall anyone ever looking at her with the tenderness she detected in his blue eyes. For a heartbeat she allowed herself to believe Sherman Butler had feelings for her. Then she stepped back from him. "Raising a child is more difficult than I could have imagined." She looked at Hope cuddling the tiny, blind kitten. "It is also the most rewarding experience of my life."

"Well, did you have a nice walk?" Carrie's eyes were cold, her smile false. She, her husband, Cyrus, and Mac were sitting around the big kitchen table eating Mariah's pies and drinking steaming cups of coffee.

"Yes," Mariah said. "It was quite enjoyable. Mr. Butler showed Hope the kittens."

Carrie glanced at the little girl now sitting between Mac and Cyrus. "Papa is fond of children."

"This is mighty good pie," Mac said. "The crust is so flaky it melts in yer mouth."

The other men voiced an affirmation of Mac's compliment.

"I would like to show Miss Casey the house." Carrie stood and pushed her chair under the table. "May we be excused for a few minutes?"

"Certainly, if Miss Casey has no objection." Sherman's dimples deepened. "I think the two of you should get better acquainted."

Mariah was reluctant to go with Carrie, but there seemed no valid reason not to.

"I want to show you something in the parlor." Carrie led the way into a huge room with rough stucco walls and open beams overhead. Woven wool rugs were scattered over the polished hardwood floor. The massive, leather-covered couches and chairs were deep and inviting. Bookcases filled one wall. Mariah would have loved to peruse the volumes that rested there, but Carrie led her to stand before the enormous stone fireplace.

"This is Mama, Caroline Houston Butler. I'm named for her," she said. "Wasn't she beautiful?"

Mariah looked at the portrait hanging above the fireplace. The woman was beautiful, but it was the air of contentment the artist had captured that caught Mariah's eye. Caroline Butler was a woman who knew she was valued, and it showed in her face. Her dark eyes glowed with happiness.

"She is wearing her wedding dress," Carrie said. "There is one thing you need to understand, Miss Casey." She turned to face Mariah. "Papa loved Mama with his whole heart. In the years she's been gone other women have set their caps for him, but he has never been interested. Papa and Mama are bound together for all eternity. No other woman could ever take her place in his heart. I am telling you this so you won't make a fool of yourself."

Mariah felt the hot flame of humiliation burn her face.

"We had best rejoin the others," Carrie said. "I should imagine you will want to be leaving. One of the ranch hands will drive you back to town."

When they came back into the kitchen, Mariah collected her empty pie tins with downcast eyes, too shamed to look at anyone.

"Air you all right, ma'am?" Mac asked.

The concern in the old man's voice brought a lump to Mariah's throat. "I'm fine." She fought back tears. "Tomorrow is a school day. We need to go home."

"It is getting late," Carrie said. "We should be going, too. Do you want us to have Buck hitch the buggy, Papa?"

"That would be fine," Sherman said. "Have him bring it up to the house."

"It was nice of you to come, Miss Casey." Carrie leaned down to kiss Hope. "You, too, sweetheart."

Amid a flurry of good-byes, Lucas and Carrie left.

"I got somethin' fer you." Mac set a gallon of milk on the table, along with a cheesecloth-wrapped chunk of butter and a sack of eggs.

"Oh, I couldn't—" Mariah started to protest but was cut off by Mac's insistence that she certainly could.

"You might bring us a custard pie next time you come," he said.

"Well, I don't know." Mariah blushed. "It was nice of you to have us this time, but—"

"We were hoping you would come again," Sherman said.

Mariah was saved a reply by the arrival of the buggy. "Come, Hope, we mustn't keep the gentleman waiting."

Mac gathered up the eggs, milk, and butter and put them in Mariah's basket; then they all went outside. The horses were tied to the hitching rail. Mariah looked around for the driver, but there was no sign of the ranch hand Carrie had called Buck.

"You fergit somethin', Miz Casey?" Mac asked.

"No, I just—Mrs. Nolan said a ranch hand would drive us back to town."

"That ranch hand would be me." Sherman lifted Hope into the buggy, then assisted Mariah up before climbing into the driver's seat himself.

Sherman carried the burden of the conversation on the trip to town. Every time Mariah looked at him, she heard Carrie telling her not to make a fool of herself, and her stomach twisted. She kept her gaze fixed on Hope, the rolling prairie, the glorious gold and lavender of the setting sun. Anywhere but at the man who was telling her about his partnership with Mac and Cyrus and how they built the Circle C after the war with unclaimed stock they herded to Kansas from Texas. The man who captured her thoughts and attention like no other ever had.

Chapter 9

Sherman sat in the kitchen with the two men who had been his best friends for over thirty years. "What did you think of her?"

"That Hope's a mighty cute little gal." Mac's faded blue eyes twinkled.

"I meant Miss Casey." Sherman ran his fingers through his thick, auburn hair. "Did you like her all right?"

"She seems to be a fine, God-fearin' woman," Cyrus said.

"She is." Sherman took a sip of hot coffee before setting his cup on the table.

The three men talked about other things for several minutes, then Cyrus said it was time for him to turn in and excused himself. After he went out to the bunkhouse, Mac turned a speculative eye on the younger man.

"You interested in the schoolmarm in a romantical sense?" Mac always got to the heart of the matter.

"Miss Casey is the first woman I've felt an attraction for since Caroline's been gone." He rested his forearms on the table and leaned forward. "I have been thinking about inviting her to the Harvest Ball. Do you think I should ask her?"

Mac gave his question some thought before answering. "I don't see no reason fer you not to ask her."

"Do you think I should see what Carrie thinks first?"

"I kin tell you right now the little lady ain't goin' to like it. Not one little bit."

"Maybe I should forget the whole idea."

"You shouldn't do no sich thing." Mac gathered up their cups and limped to the sink. "Me an' Cyrus is gettin' up in years. We ain't gonna be here ferever, you know."

Sherman drew himself up to protest, but Mac cut him off before he could speak. "It's the way it's meant to be. Ever'thing dies in due season." He resumed his seat across from Sherman. "The little lady got her own family now. Someday she'll have young 'uns that will take up her time. Life kin get mighty lonely, Sherm. Miz Casey's a fine woman. But her an' thet little Hope is a lot alike. They've both been hurt real bad. If yer wantin' to win her heart yer gonna have to be mighty patient."

"Right now I only want to become better acquainted with her."

"Then you ast her to that ball, and if she says no jist don't give up. An' another thing, Sherm, don't worry none 'bout what the little lady thinks. I don't reckon she's gonna be too happy if she thinks someone else might take her place in yer affections, but she'll get over it."

"No one could ever take Carrie's place, Mac. You know that."

"Course not. Ever'one's got their own spot. The little lady may not realize thet yet." Mac scratched his chin with a gnarled forefinger. "We spoiled Carrie rotten, Sherm, but we never raised her to be selfish. If somethin' should come of yore friendship with Miz Casey, it might take a while, but she'll come round."

Sherman tried to catch Mariah's eye at services the following Sunday, but she kept her head turned away from him. After the meeting ended he headed in her direction, but Emily James intercepted him. By the time he was able to escape the Widow James, Mariah had left with Tom and Joanna Brady. He thought about stopping by her house on the way home and inviting her to the ball but decided it wouldn't be seemly to call on a lady who lived alone.

For the first time in her life women stopped Mariah on the street to chat about their children. They exchanged recipes and childcare tips. Despite the difference in their ages, she developed an especially close friendship with Joanna Brady.

Hope was a constant delight. Mariah had never felt more fulfilled as a woman. Yet every time she saw Carrie Nolan or her father, her stomach twisted with shame. She tried to avoid them—father and daughter—as much as possible. Carrie maintained her distance, barely acknowledging Mariah's existence. Sherman, however, was a different story. Several times Mariah barely escaped an encounter with him at church.

One Saturday afternoon in mid-October, Joanna Brady came calling. "It's such a beautiful fall day, I decided to go for a walk," she said, after Mariah invited her into the kitchen and put the teapot on. "Before I knew it, I was knocking on your front door."

"I'm so happy you stopped by," Mariah said. "Hope is taking a nap, and I was baking cookies. Oatmeal. They are her favorite."

"Mine, too." Joanna took a seat at the kitchen table.

"The last panful is about ready to come out of the oven." Mariah put several warm cookies on a plate and set them on the table. "Help yourself."

As soon as she removed the final pan of cookies from the oven, she poured them each a cup of tea and sat down across from Joanna.

Joanna stirred her tea before lifting the cup for a dainty sip. "This is the best tea I've ever tasted, Mariah. Wherever did you get it?"

"I blend my own." Mariah blushed at the compliment. "I'm glad you like it."

"I like it very much. You are an absolute wonder, Mariah." She set her cup down and helped herself to another cookie. "How is Hope doing?"

"Quite well." Mariah stirred a teaspoon of sugar into her tea. "She's extremely bright."

"Spoken like a doting mother," Joanna teased.

"I still have trouble believing God has given me this beautiful little girl," Mariah said. "I always dreamed of a large family. Of course it never happened."

"It still might."

"It's too late now. Besides, Hope is enough. I feel very blessed to have her."

"Hope is very blessed to have you. You are a wonderful mother, Mariah."

Mariah had received few compliments in her life and found Joanna's comments disconcerting. To cover her confusion she refilled Joanna's cup, then resumed her seat across the table from the younger woman. "I want to be a good mother more than anything in this world," she confessed, "but I fear I have no idea how to begin."

"Nonsense." Joanna smiled. "It's instinctive. God created women to be nurturing. Keepers of the flame, my father says."

"Not all women have that instinct." Mariah looked at the sweet-faced girl sitting across the table from her. Joanna was the only close friend she had ever had. In the short time she had lived in Cedar Bend she had come to love her. Now she trusted her with the dark secret of her heart. "My mother despised me."

"Oh no! That can't be true." Sympathy darkened the girl's eyes, and she reached out to cover Mariah's hand with hers. "I'm so sorry, Mariah."

"She never wanted me. I was a cruel disappointment to her. Those are her words, not mine." Mariah shrugged her shoulders. "It doesn't really matter."

"Of course it matters." Joanna's dark eyes filled with tears. "I'm so sorry for your pain."

"She never touched me when I was small. Never put her arms around me. Never read me a bedtime story. Never came when I was frightened and cried out for her in the night." Tears came to Mariah's blue eyes and rolled down her cheeks. "How can I be a good mother when I never had a mother?"

"Do you love Hope?"

"More than anything in this world."

"Do you read her a bedtime story and tuck her in at night?" At Mariah's affirmative nod Joanna continued. "If she was frightened would you go to her?"

Mariah blotted her tears with a napkin. "I would give my life for her."

"I know you would." Joanna squeezed Mariah's hand. "Because you are her mother. Don't you feel like just squeezing the stuffing out of her?"

A faint smile lifted the corners of Mariah's mouth. "Sometimes it takes all my willpower to keep from scooping her up and hugging her."

"Why don't you?"

Mariah's smile faded as she looked deep into her own heart and soul. She raised her head and met Joanna's gentle gaze. "I'm afraid she will push me away."

"Did your mother push you away?"

Mariah nodded. "She didn't like to be mussed."

"What about your father?"

Mariah took a sip from her blue flowered mug before answering. "Father had his church. His 'flock' he called them. They kept him busy. I know he cared for me, but there was always someone seeking his guidance."

"You know, Mariah, you are going to have to take the risk of reaching out." Joanna's dark eyes were serious. "Some people may reject you. That is the way life is. Most will accept you if only you stop holding them at arm's length. Except for church and the occasional Sunday dinner with us you never socialize. Why is that, Mariah?"

"I'm reserved like my father," Mariah said.

"I'm sure your father was dignified," Joanna replied. "That is how I visualize him. Stately, and very dignified. But he certainly wasn't reserved. He reached out to people."

"Father was a good shepherd. Everyone adored him."

"The people of Cedar Bend think highly of you, Mariah. They are eager to love you if only you'll allow them to." A sudden smile brightened Joanna's face. "I have a wonderful idea. It's time you were presented to society."

Presented to society! Mariah felt like a character in a romance as Joanna chattered on about what she must wear and how they could do her hair. Finally she held up a hand to stop the stream of words. "Don't you think I'm a bit old for all this? And besides, where did you plan for this unveiling to take place?"

"You aren't old, Mariah. My goodness, I hope I have a complexion like yours when I'm your age. You don't have a single wrinkle. The Harvest Ball is next Saturday night. I know you are a wonderful seamstress. Can you have a dress finished by then?"

"I have nothing from which to make a dress."

"We have plenty of time to walk to the mercantile and buy fabric, notions, everything you need. I'll help with the cutting and basting. Oh, Mariah, this will be such fun."

Joanna's enthusiasm was contagious. Mariah found herself almost believing that she could live her own version of Cinderella. Then reality settled in. She was a thirty-six-year-old spinster. Even if she went to the ball there would be no Prince Charming for her. No happily ever after.

"I'm afraid it's too late," she murmured.

"Nonsense." Joanna glanced at the clock on the shelf, then pushed her chair back and stood. "It isn't even two o'clock yet. Take off your apron, put on your bonnet, and let's go."

"I'd like to, Joanna," Mariah said. In a way it was the truth. Going shopping with Joanna, making the dress together that would transform her into the belle of the ball, it all sounded like such fun. Fun to think about but unrealistic. It was a relief to add, "But Hope is sleeping."

"Wake her up."

"I couldn't do that. Hope's naptime is very important to her."

Joanna sat back down. "Maybe she will wake up in a few minutes."

"Probably not. She only fell asleep shortly before you came. She will probably sleep a couple of hours."

Five minutes later Hope padded into the kitchen looking bright-eyed, rosy-cheeked, and positively adorable. "No more excuses." Joanna hugged Hope. "I'll put on her shoes while you get ready."

Mariah sighed as she untied her apron. "I can't go to this ball alone."

"Of course not. You're going with us. Daddy told me to invite you." Joanna took Hope's hand and led her from the room.

Mariah couldn't remember ever spending a more enjoyable afternoon. Joanna and Mrs. Harris insisted the deep rose-colored brocade the mercantile had received in its last shipment was perfect for her. When she protested that she was thinking more on the line of a serviceable gray, Joanna and Mrs. Harris shook their heads.

Back at Mariah's house the two women cut out and basted the rose-colored fabric. When Mariah tried on the basted bodice, Joanna studied her closely, then declared she looked lovely.

Mariah blushed when she saw her image in the bedroom mirror. The rose—while not something she would have chosen for herself—did bring color to her cheeks. Still, she could see nothing lovely in her appearance. "No matter what I wear I look like a mopstick."

"You are tall and elegant like Snow White." Joanna giggled. "I, on the other hand, look like one of your dwarfs. Hope, don't you think your mama looks like a princess?"

The little girl, who was sitting on Mariah's bed watching the goings on with wide eyes, nodded.

"Mama is going to be the belle of the ball, isn't she?"

Once more Hope nodded.

"Prince Charming will walk in the door. His blue eyes will scan the room. He will see a lovely lady dressed in rose. *Who is this beautiful stranger?* His heart will skip a beat. He will cross the room to where she is sitting. Bowing low before her, he will extend his hand and ask her to dance."

Joanna pantomimed her words. She scanned the room until her gaze rested on Hope; then she gasped and put a hand to her heart. She crossed the room to the bed and bowed in front of the child. "May I have this dance, beautiful stranger?"

Giggling, Hope slid from the bed and placed her tiny hand in Joanna's hand. Mariah sank into a chair and watched as Joanna waltzed around the room with Hope. Finally both girls collapsed onto the bed laughing until they were breathless. Mariah, still sitting in her grandmother's rocking chair, laughed with them until tears rolled down her cheeks.

Chapter 10

Time was running out. Since the afternoon Mariah and Hope spent at the Circle C, Mariah had avoided Sherman like the plague. Several times he tried to approach her after church only to be intercepted by someone. By the time he was free, she had vanished. As he rode to church Sherman determined this Sunday was going to be different. With less than a week remaining until the Harvest Ball, he was going to corner Mariah Casey and invite her to the fall gathering.

Sherman sat in the last pew instead of his accustomed seat. As soon as the final prayer was said and the service was dismissed, Mariah and Hope headed for the door. He remained in his seat until the last possible moment before stepping into the aisle, effectively blocking her exit.

"Miss Casey, I would like a word with you."

She reminded him of a cornered deer as her eyes darted from one side to the other looking for a means of escape. Finding no way out, she exhaled, and her shoulders slumped. "Mr. Butler, I am in a hurry. Sunday dinner is in the oven, and I have guests coming." Her eyes were fixed on his shirtfront. "May we please pass?"

"Not until you tell me what is wrong. What have I done to offend you?" He wanted to reach out and cup her chin in his hand. Force her eyes to meet his. "I had such an enjoyable afternoon the Sunday you came to the ranch for dinner. I thought you did, too."

For the briefest moment her eyes met his, and he saw the sheen of tears before she dropped her gaze. "I really must go, Mr. Butler. Joanna is waiting."

"If you would only allow me a moment. I wanted to ask you—"

"Papa, there you are." Carrie slipped her arm through his. "Hello, Miss Casey. Dr. Brady is waiting for you."

A crimson flush swept up Mariah's neck and stained her alabaster skin all the way to her hairline. Without a word she scooped Hope up, slipped past Sherman and Carrie, and hurried from the building.

"Well," Carrie remarked, "that certainly wasn't very polite. She never even spoke to me."

"Something is bothering her," Sherman said. "I only wish I knew what it was."

"Hmm," Carrie murmured as they stepped from the church into the sunny October afternoon. "Guess what Joanna told me? Her father is escorting Miss Casey to the Harvest Ball. You may lose your teacher after all, Papa."

Sherman stopped dead in his tracks. "Tom is escorting Miss Casey?" A keen sense of disappointment washed over him.

"I think from what I've been told it's quite serious," Carrie said as he handed her into the buggy beside Lucas.

"Quite serious." Carrie's words echoed in his head as he rode to the Circle C. Sherman Butler wasn't one to give up without a fight, but Tom Brady was his friend. It was Tom who had seen Caroline through her final illness. If Tom were interested in Mariah, he would respect their friendship and not muddy the waters by pressing his own suit.

Saturday afternoon Joanna appeared at Mariah's front door carrying a small black case. "Whatever are you doing here?" Mariah asked. She then added, "Not that I'm not happy to see you. It's only that I wasn't expecting you."

"I'm your fairy godmother, Cinderella." Joanna giggled. "I have my bag of magic to transform you."

"We are Christians, Joanna." Mariah frowned. "We don't believe in fairy godmothers or magic."

"I know we don't," Joanna agreed with a smile. "However, we do believe in transformations."

"Of the heart and soul," Mariah said. "Not of plain looks and dull features."

"Nonsense," Joanna scoffed. "You're beautiful as God made you. We are just going to emphasize that beauty. It's time you quit hiding your light under a bushel, Mariah. Now, shall we draw milady's bath?"

"Fine." Mariah laughed. There was something about Joanna's perpetual optimism that made her feel young and giddy. "You are about to discover you can't make a silk purse out of a sow's ear."

While Joanna entertained Hope in the living room, Mariah bathed in the kitchen. She felt positively decadent lounging in a hot tub in the middle of the afternoon. Mother would be horrified. The scent of lilac drifted up from the water. It smelled wonderful. *I don't care what Mother would think. I was a dutiful daughter while she was alive. Now, under God's guidance, I must be the mistress of my own destiny.* The warm water was so relaxing, her eyes drifted shut.

More asleep than awake, she imagined herself walking into the social hall of the Cattlemen's Association on Sherman Butler's arm. Everyone in the room turned to smile at her. She saw the affection in their expressions and knew they were her friends. Even Carrie Nolan smiled a greeting.

Mariah's eyes popped open. "Forevermore, Mariah Casey, have you taken complete leave of your senses?" She thought of Sherman Butler paying her court, and she thought of the way Carrie smiled at her in her dream with genuine affection. "When pigs fly," she muttered to herself.

Freshly bathed, dusted with lilac bath powder, and wearing her ratty old dressing gown, Mariah sat in front of her vanity mirror with Hope leaning against her knee.

"The first thing we are going to do is get rid of that bun," Joanna said.

Mariah's hands flew to the bun at the back of her head. "I've worn it this way since I was old enough to put my hair up."

"All the more reason to change it." Joanna began to remove hairpins. "Don't you agree, Hope?"

The little girl who was watching the proceedings in wide-eyed interest nodded her head in vigorous agreement.

"You two are impossible." Mariah smiled. She rested a hand on Hope's head. The first thing she had done after Hope came to live with her was get rid of those painfully tight braids. Now, except at night when her hair was loosely braided to keep it from tangling, Hope had ringlets that reached to her waist. Maybe it was time she changed her own hairstyle. When the last pin was removed, Mariah's hair tumbled around her shoulders.

Joanna had only been brushing a short while when she laughed.

Mariah glanced in the mirror to make sure her hair wasn't all falling out. It wasn't. "What's wrong?"

"It's your hair. The more I brush, the curlier it gets."

"I know," Mariah sighed. "Mother said it looked like sheep's wool. That's why I always wore it pulled back so tightly."

"It most certainly does not look like sheep's wool," Joanna huffed. "It's almost exactly like Hope's. Do you think her hair looks like sheep's wool?"

"Of course not." Mariah ran a gentle hand over the little girl's loose ringlets. "Hope has beautiful hair."

"And so do you." She stepped back and cocked her head to one side, studying Mariah intently. "Mmm," she murmured. "Mmm-hmm." She moved slightly to study her from a different angle. After about the sixth "Mmm-hmm," Mariah began to get nervous.

"I know it's hopeless." Her slender shoulders slumped. "Why not forget the whole thing and fix it like I've always worn it."

"Hopeless! *Au contraire, mademoiselle.*"

"Joanna, I didn't know you spoke French."

Joanna giggled. "You have heard my entire French vocabulary. I believe I read those words in a romance novel Mac loaned me."

"Mr. McDougal? He reads romance novels?"

"Indeed he does. Mac is an avid reader."

Mariah shook her head in wonder. If she had taken time to think about it, which she hadn't, she would have assumed the kindly little man was illiterate.

"That's what makes people so interesting, Mariah. Everyone has little things nobody knows about them."

"Do you have a secret, Joanna?" Mariah teased.

"No, my life is an open book." Joanna grinned at Mariah's reflection in the mirror. "Except for one thing."

Mariah, intrigued despite herself, couldn't resist asking, "What deep, dark secret are you hiding, Joanna?"

Joanna picked up the brush and ran it through Mariah's hair. "I'll tell you my secret if you'll tell me yours."

Mariah had been a shy, awkward child who had grown up to be a shy, reticent woman. She had never been close to anyone, but in spite of the difference in their ages she and Joanna had come to be close friends. She had a lifetime of confidences stored up. Which one could she share?

"It doesn't have to be anything embarrassing," Joanna prodded. "Well, not too embarrassing anyway."

Mariah thought of the beauty cream she had bought so many years ago. At the time it seemed tragic. Now in retrospect it was rather amusing. She was sure Joanna would enjoy it. "All right, I have one. When I was sixteen I realized I was never going to be pretty. At least not without help."

Joanna shook her head as if to argue, and Hope leaned comfortingly against Mariah. She continued, "So I saved my money and bought some beauty cream."

"Oh, Mariah, you didn't need that." Joanna slapped a hand over her mouth to stifle a giggle. "Did you notice any change?"

"Not really. I used it faithfully every night for months. Mother was snooping through my things one day while I was at school and found it. She was waiting for me when I got home. That was the end of the beauty cream."

"Your mother made you throw it away?"

"Mother had a temper and a tongue that could cut a person to shreds." Remembering the horrible, hurtful things her mother had said to her that long-ago day brought a rush of tears to Mariah's eyes. She quickly blinked them away, but not quickly enough.

Sympathetic tears filled Joanna's dark eyes. "I'm sorry, Mariah." She put her arms around Mariah's shoulders and hugged her tight.

Hope laid her head in Mariah's lap and patted her leg. "I sorry, Mama."

"Joanna, did you hear that?" Mariah scooped the little girl up into her arms and hugged her. "Hope, you can talk! I knew you could."

Joanna's smile was so bright it seemed to light up the room. "Aren't you something, young lady! You had a better secret than either your mama or me."

When the two women tried to persuade Hope to speak again, she hid her face against Mariah's neck and shook her head.

"At least we know she can when she wants to," Mariah said. "Although I am a bit disappointed."

"Don't be." Joanna patted the little girl's ebony curls. "I have a feeling once she starts talking, she won't stop. Besides, we've witnessed a miracle today."

"Of course we have," Mariah agreed. "Hope did speak and will again."

"True." Joanna grinned. "However, that isn't the miracle I was referring to. What are you doing, Mariah?"

Mariah's face was a study in confusion as she looked up at Joanna. Then the light of understanding brightened her features. She mouthed the words, "Hugging Hope."

"And what is Hope doing?" Joanna whispered in return.

The little girl's arms were wrapped tightly around Mariah's neck. She had reached out to Hope, and Hope hadn't pushed her away. The woman rested her cheek against the little girl's curls.

"Hope, you are going to have to sit on the bed and watch while I do your mama's hair. Okay?"

"Okay," Hope parroted as Mariah reluctantly released her. She slid off Mariah's lap and ran and climbed up on the bed.

Joy washed over Mariah as her heart struggled to break free of the walls that had imprisoned it for so many years. She felt as if she could soar right up to heaven. She wanted to sing and dance and praise the Lord. Since she only knew how to do one of the three, she whispered a prayer of thanksgiving to God for sending Hope and Joanna into her life.

"I have decided to give you a fringe." Joanna interrupted her prayer, bringing her back to earth with a thud.

"A fringe?" She noticed her friend had produced a pair of scissors from somewhere. "You mean cut my hair?" Mariah wrapped both arms around her head to protect her hair from the gleaming, extremely sharp-looking instrument in the girl's hand. "No. No. No, Joanna! I have never had scissors touch my hair."

"Don't be such a baby. A fringe will be very becoming." Joanna took hold of one of Mariah's arms and gently drew it down. "This won't hurt a bit."

"Isn't that what Delilah said to Samson?"

Joanna giggled. "You are a very witty person when you let your hair down. Now sit still."

When Joanna parted off and combed a thin layer of hair down over her face, Mariah closed her eyes. When she felt the cold steel of the scissors against her forehead she moaned. At the first cut, she whimpered softly. She held any other sounds back until she felt Joanna stop.

"Very nice," Joanna said.

Mariah opened her eyes a slit and took a peek. It didn't look bad. She opened her eyes all the way. Joanna laid down the scissors and went to work in earnest. Ten minutes later she nodded in satisfaction. "There! What do you think?"

The fringe and the short, wispy curls that surrounded her face softened the angles. She picked the hand mirror up from the vanity and turned so she could see the back. Her hair was a mass of elaborately pinned-in curls high on the back of her head.

Hope padded across the room and gently touched the fringe of hair on Mariah's forehead. "Pretty," she said.

Two warm tears rolled down Mariah's cheeks. "Thank you," she whispered.

"You are quite welcome." Joanna leaned down and kissed her forehead. "There's only one more thing before I leave. She reached into her bag and produced a small, squat jar. "A touch of this and you will be perfect."

"Face paint?" Mariah cringed. "I can't wear face paint. I'm a schoolteacher. Whatever will people think?"

"It's only a bit of rouge. No one will even know you have it on. Trust me." She added with a giggle, "It's not like it's beauty cream."

Mariah smiled and sighed in defeat. She allowed Joanna to add a bit of color to her cheeks and her lips. When Joanna was finished and Mariah turned back to the mirror, she could scarcely believe the transformation. Her face seemed to have come alive. Even her eyes had a sparkle that had never been there before.

Joanna was returning items to her bag. "You are all done except for putting on your dress. I'm going home to get ready. We will pick you up at six thirty." She stooped to kiss Hope. "Bye, sweetheart. See you later."

"Bye, sweethot. See ya lateah," the little girl said.

"My goodness." The young woman smiled. "You are becoming a regular chatterbox. Mariah, you know the old saying about little pitchers having big ears. We are going to have to start watching what we say around you-know-who. Our secrets may become town gossip."

"Speaking of secrets," Mariah said. "You never did tell me yours."

"Remember I told you about Clay Shepherd? The boy whose father was a drifter?"

Mariah nodded. "Yes, I remember. He left town right after you graduated from the eighth grade."

"We went early to the Christmas play practice. No one else was there. Clay kissed me underneath the mistletoe. That was my first, last, and only kiss from a boy." Joanna sighed and put a hand to her cheek, as if that long-ago kiss still remained there. "I was smitten. Isn't that silly?"

"I don't think so." Mariah escorted her friend to the door. "I think it was rather forward of young Master Shepherd, but I also think it is sweet."

"Clay liked Carrie a lot, but she steered a wide path around him. He was wild, and she said he was dangerous. Carrie was right about him, I suppose." Joanna sighed. "If I'd had a lick of sense I would probably have been afraid of him, too. But he was incredibly handsome, and without doubt the most exciting male I had ever met."

Mariah smiled sympathetically, but she thought it was a good thing that Clay Shepherd had left town before he broke her friend's heart.

She watched Joanna walk down the street, then closed the door and leaned against it for a moment. She had a friend to share confidences with. Hope could speak. No matter what happened at the Harvest Ball, this would still be the most perfect day of her entire life.

Chapter 11

Sherman Butler felt a small catch in his chest when he saw Mariah step through the door of the Cattlemen's Association meeting hall with Hope clinging to her hand. There was something different about her hair, and she was wearing a rose-colored dress. She stood straight and tall as she gazed around the room. That was one of the things that attracted him to her. Most tall women slumped in an effort to look shorter. Not Mariah. She was tall, proud, graceful, and beautiful. Her eyes meet his, then quickly shifted away.

While he watched, a group of chattering women surrounded Mariah and Joanna. Tom walked away to visit with one of the local ranchers. Then Carrie and Lucas arrived. With his daughter clinging to his side, Sherman forced his attention from Mariah.

———

Mariah saw Mr. Sherman Butler as soon as she stepped through the door of the meeting hall. Her eyes met his before she managed to look away. His daughter and son-in-law arrived shortly after that. Carrie was wearing a sparkling, emerald green dress that accentuated her auburn hair and flawless skin. She immediately took possession of her father, urging him toward the punch bowl.

Mariah tried not to look at them, but they were difficult to avoid. Even if Mr. Butler hadn't been the tallest man in the room, his and Carrie's copper-colored hair shone forth like beacons, distinguishing them from the crowd. She forced her mind away from the Butler family as a steady stream of her students and their mothers surged around to greet her.

Her cousin, Lucille Smith, and Lucille's friend, Gretchen Racine, rushed over to compliment Mariah's dress and becoming hairstyle. "Oh, Cousin Mariah, you look divine! I wish Mama could see you." Lucille rolled her big, green eyes. "Mama insisted on staying home with her grandson tonight. She practically forced Jed and me out of the house." She sighed dramatically and leaned close to Mariah. "She will be so happy when I tell her that I saw you tonight. Mama keeps saying that Kansas has been so good for you."

Kansas had indeed been good for her. Mariah smiled warmly. "Tell Cousin Gladys that Hope and I will stop in to see her soon."

For the next hour the friendly crowd mingled and visited as people gathered around the refreshment table. Promptly at eight o'clock the floor was cleared for the dance. This was the part of the evening Mariah most dreaded. She took a seat in one of the chairs that had been pushed back against the wall. Joanna sat on one side of her with Hope on the other, while the fiddler warmed up on a raised platform at the end of the room.

A tall, slender man Mariah recognized as the father of one of her first graders stepped up onto the platform. "Everybody choose your partner for the first set," he announced.

Little Karl Braun came over and asked Hope if she would be his partner. Mariah looked into her daughter's pleading eyes and nodded her permission. L. K. took Hope's hand, and the two of them skipped across the room to join a group of children.

"Well," Joanna said, "now I really feel like a wallflower."

"Little Karl always treats Hope so well."

Joanna laughed. "I declare, Mariah. You'll be making Hope's wedding gown before you make mine."

"Don't be silly, Joanna. Hope is only a baby." Mariah was watching the two children and didn't realize that Mark Hopkins had approached until she heard him ask Joanna to dance.

"Would you mind, Mariah?" Joanna's voice held a hint of apology. "I hate to leave you here alone."

Mariah turned her attention to the young couple. "Nonsense. Go ahead and have a good time. I'll be fine."

As soon as Joanna and Mark left, Tom Brady sat down beside Mariah. "Are you sure you wouldn't like to dance, Miss Casey?"

Before Mariah had time to reply, the fiddle player began a sprightly tune accompanied by the caller. The noise rendered conversation impossible. Both Mariah and the doctor turned their attention to the dancers who were divided into sets of eight.

"Choose your partner," Mr. Cox called out in a singsong rhythm. "Form a ring. Figure eight, and double-L swing."

The man certainly had a set of lungs on him. No wonder little Ezra Cox was so loud and rambunctious.

"Swing 'em once and let 'em go," Mr. Cox sang out. "All hands left and do-si-do."

Across the room Hope's dark curls bounced as L. K. swung her around. The tiny girl smiled up at her husky blond partner, and Mariah had a heart-wrenching vision of the future. She imagined her little girl as a beautiful, petite young woman with gleaming ebony curls smiling up at her burly, blond companion. She closed her eyes and shook her head slightly to clear her mind. *Goodness, Mariah*, she silently chided herself, *you know Joanna is only teasing. Besides, you want Hope to grow up and have beaux, and someday you want her to marry and have babies.*

"How will you swap?" Mr. Cox sang out, "And how'll you trade?"

She opened her eyes and saw that the children were changing partners.

"This pretty girl for the old maid?"

I certainly don't want her to be a lonely, old maid schoolteacher. Mariah's mouth twisted. *I'm not ready to lose her either. But that's years in the future.*

She felt a hand on her arm and turned her head to see concern in the doctor's dark eyes. He leaned over and spoke against her ear. "Are you all right?"

Mariah nodded in reply. "I'm fine," she mouthed to him.

He smiled and turned his attention back to the dancers, his foot tapping in time with the music. She scanned the room until her gaze came to rest on an auburn-haired man who stood head and shoulders above everyone else in the room. He was leaning against the wall, talking to Mr. Harris. She seized the opportunity to study him closely while his attention was elsewhere. He looked her direction, and she shifted her gaze to the children.

As soon as the final note of the fiddle faded away, the laughing dancers descended on the refreshment table for a glass of apple cider. When the caller announced the second set, Mariah insisted Dr. Brady join the dancers. He gave a token argument before asking the Widow James to be his partner.

Mac McDougal hobbled over and sat down in his unoccupied chair. "You look mighty purty tonight, Mariah."

She couldn't control the pleasurable glow that crept up her neck and assuredly stained her cheeks. "Thank you, Mac. I'm glad you think so."

"I ain't a flatterer, young lady. Yer a mighty purty woman, and I ain't the only one thet thinks so. How come yer feller is gettin' ready to dance with the widder 'stead of sittin' here with you?"

"My fellow?" Mariah's cheeks blazed. "What fellow? I don't have a—whatever are you talking about?"

"I heerd you an' the doc was courtin'. Ain't you?"

"The doc? You mean Dr. Brady?" Mariah put her hands to her burning cheeks. How many people besides Mac had heard that she was keeping company with Tom Brady? "I don't know who told you that Dr. Brady and I were—" She was so embarrassed she couldn't even bring herself to say the word. "It's not true. I never even thought of him as—"

"Then you an' him ain't courtin'?" Mac's faded blue eyes twinkled.

"Of course not," Mariah insisted. "I consider Dr. Brady a friend. That's all."

"I know somebody thet's gonna be mighty happy to hear thet," Mac murmured as the fiddle began to play another sprightly tune that almost drowned out his voice. "An' I know a young lady thet's gonna have a mite of explainin' to do when I get my hands on her."

The fiddle and Levi Cox's calling made further conversation impossible. Mariah turned her attention to Hope. Her tiny daughter was laughing as she skipped around a circle with the other children. The wonder that this child was hers brought a smile to Mariah's heart. So what if an absurd rumor was circulating about her and Tom Brady? Today, for the first time, Hope had called her *Mama*.

Sherman Butler watched Mariah from across the room. Her eyes were on the children, and there was a radiance about her that tore at his heart. He scanned the dancers until he found Tom Brady and Emily James, and his eyes narrowed. Everyone in town knew the widow was looking to replace her late husband. Why on earth would his friend want to spend his time with Mrs. James when he was courting the finest woman in town? *Maybe he isn't keeping company with Miss Casey.* The thought brought a sudden surge of hope. *Maybe Carrie misunderstood.*

As soon as the set ended, he approached Tom Brady and the widow. "I need to speak to you, Tom."

"Let me fill Mrs. James's glass first."

The widow dabbed at her flushed cheeks with a lace-trimmed handkerchief while the doctor filled her glass at the refreshment table. "I haven't noticed you dancing, Mr. Butler."

"I rarely dance, Mrs. James."

"What a shame." She rested a small hand on his arm. "You move so gracefully for such a tall man. I'm sure you are a wonderful dancer."

Sherman had met many women like the Widow James since Caroline passed away. Women who looked at a man with desperate eyes. Women who clung to a man's arm with all the tenacity of a drowning victim. He looked down at the rough, work-worn hand resting on his sleeve, and an unexpected wave of compassion washed over him. It must be frightening for a woman to be left suddenly alone with three half-grown children and a hardscrabble farm.

"Thank you, Mrs. James, but I'm afraid I'm not much of a dancer."

"Perhaps you haven't found the right partner."

Her eyes held a hint of sorrow, and Sherman thought she looked tired. His gaze drifted to Mariah sitting against the wall, talking to Mac. The widow was wrong. He had found the right partner. He only hoped he hadn't waited too long to declare himself.

"Here you are." Tom Brady pressed a chilled glass into the widow's hand. "Now, what can I do for you, Sherm?"

"I'd like to speak to you for a moment." He glanced at the woman sipping cider. "Alone if you don't mind."

"Certainly. Please excuse me, Mrs. James, and thank you for the dance."

Sherman led the doctor through the milling crowd and out the side door into a deserted alley. After a few steps he turned to his friend. "Tom, I want to know what your intentions are concerning Miss Casey."

"Miss Casey? The schoolteacher? Joanna's friend? I have no intentions regarding her. Why would you ask such a question, Sherm?"

"I just—" The big man ran his fingers through his hair. "I heard—someone told me—that you were courting the teacher. That it was serious."

"Well, someone was mistaken. I like Mariah Casey. She's an asset to our community. But no, I am not courting her."

A flood of relief washed over Sherman, bringing a smile to his face. "Are you seeing her home tonight?"

"Joanna and I are supposed to." The doctor cocked his head to one side. "Are you interested in Miss Casey?"

Sherman cleared his throat. "I might be."

"Why don't you speak up? Ask her if you can come calling."

"I would if she'd give me a chance. Tom, she runs from me like I was contagious."

"Mariah Casey is reserved, but I haven't found her to be unfriendly. If we put our heads together maybe we can come up with a way for the two of you to get better acquainted."

———

The last dance was being called when Mariah saw Joanna and her father talking to Sherman Butler. She hadn't seen either man for some time. Not that she'd been looking for them. It was only that they were conspicuous by their absence.

Hope, who was sleeping with her head cradled in Mariah's lap, stirred. She brushed the little girl's tousled curls back from her forehead and felt another crack in the hard shell that had enclosed her heart for so many years. *Thank You, Lord, for giving this precious child into my care. Help me to be the mother she deserves, and, Lord, give me the strength to become the woman You would have me to be. Help me dwell on whatever things are pure and lovely. Help me to be open and kind to everyone.*

When she looked up the Bradys were nowhere in sight, and Sherman Butler was heading her way. Her stomach flip-flopped at the sight of the handsome rancher, and she added a hasty postscript to her prayer. *Dear Father, please help me to remember who I am, and take away the feelings I have for Mr. Butler.*

"Miss Casey, Tom and Joanna had to leave unexpectedly—you know how it is with doctors—and they asked me to see you and Hope home."

For a moment Mariah felt as if all her dreams were coming true; then reality raised its ugly head. Mr. Butler might be—not *might* be—he *was* the most handsome man at the ball, but she was most certainly not Cinderella. She was a homely, middle-aged spinster schoolteacher whose foot would never fit a dainty glass slipper.

"You are ready to leave, aren't you?" Not waiting for her reply he leaned down and scooped Hope up. The little girl settled down against his chest, rested her head against his broad shoulder, and snuggled her face into his neck. Holding her with one arm, he reached his free hand to Mariah.

Ignoring his offer of assistance, Mariah rose. She had sat so long with Hope's head in her lap that her left foot and leg were asleep. Pins and needles shot from her foot to her knee, causing her to stumble. Immediately his hand was on her elbow, steadying her. "Careful there."

"I'm fine." She shook off his hand. "It is kind of you to offer to see us home, but it's only a few blocks. We'll walk."

"I have my horse so you'll have to walk." His dimples flashed. "But you aren't walking alone. I'm walking with you."

"It's kind of you to offer, but we will be fine. Now if you will just give Hope to me—" She put her hands on the little girl's waist and tried to lift her away from him. Hope murmured a few unintelligible words and slipped both arms around the man's neck, clinging even tighter.

"Hey!" A delighted grin spread across his face. "I didn't know she was talking. When did she start?"

"Today." For a moment Mariah forgot everything but the thrill of Hope's few spoken words. "She didn't say much, but what she did say was clear."

Mariah didn't see Carrie approaching, but suddenly she was there. "Papa, whatever are you doing?"

"The Bradys had to leave unexpectedly, and I'm going to escort Miss Casey home."

His smile was met by a frown. "You didn't bring a buggy."

Mariah knew that Carrie thought she was a desperate old maid who was out to snag her father. The young woman had made that clear when she showed her the portrait of her mother. Humiliation was no stranger to Mariah. She had been demeaned and mocked most of her life. Still, it hurt. She wished she could grab Hope and vanish.

"If you give me Hope, we'll leave." Mariah put her hand on the child. "It isn't far, and no one will harm us."

"You aren't walking home by yourself. I promised I would see you safely home, and that is what I'm going to do."

Mariah was beginning to realize Sherman Butler had a stubborn streak.

"Nonsense," Carrie snapped. "We will see her home."

So did his daughter.

"No!" The single word escaped before Mariah could stop it. She would walk a mile over hot coals before she would get into another buggy with Carrie Nolan.

Lucas Nolan had been standing quietly to one side. Now he put his arm around his wife's shoulders. "It's a warm night and there's a full moon. A moonlight stroll sounds like a good idea to me."

"Moonlight stroll!" Carrie sputtered. "No, it's not a good idea."

"Course it is, darlin'." He began to ease his wife away from them. "Good night, Miss Casey. Sherm. See you at church tomorrow."

Mariah was almost sure she saw Lucas wink at Mr. Butler as he led Carrie away.

Chapter 12

Mariah took off like she was going to a fire, only slowing her steps when Sherman made it obvious he didn't plan on being hurried. They walked in silence for a time, Sherman cradling Hope in one arm and leading his horse with the other hand, Mariah at his side.

Her profile was clear in the light of the full moon. Sherman wanted to know more about this woman he found so appealing. He cleared his throat. "Has it been difficult for you to adjust to life on the Kansas prairie?"

Mariah kept her gaze straight ahead. "Not at all."

"You don't miss Ohio then?"

"No."

"You never consider going back?"

"Had there been anything for me in Ohio I wouldn't have come here."

"You lived there your whole life. Surely you have friends that you want to see again. You must get homesick."

She turned her head to look at him. "I never had friends, Mr. Butler."

"In the short time that you have been here you've made a host of friends."

She turned her face away from him. "It's different here. I'm different."

He wanted to ask in what way she was different but felt it would be presumptuous to do so. "It's a beautiful night, isn't it?"

"Yes, it is." She pulled her shawl a bit tighter around her shoulders. "A bit chilly, perhaps." She lifted her face to the harvest moon. "I suppose that's to be expected this time of year."

Hope snuggled closer and burrowed her face into his neck. "I've seen some bad blizzards in October," he said.

"Yes. Cousin Gladys told me that the weather can be unpredictable."

Sooner than he would have liked, they were walking up the steps to Mariah's front porch. At the door she turned to face him. "Thank you for seeing us home, Mr. Butler. I'll take Hope now."

Sherman reluctantly released the little girl into Mariah's arms. "Before you go in, Miss Casey, there is something I would like to ask you."

He couldn't see her face in the shadows, but he felt her blue eyes on him. Beautiful blue eyes. He felt as shy as a boy with his first girl. Taking a deep breath, he plunged in. "I was wondering—that is, I thought—" This was more difficult than he remembered. He took a deep breath and slowly exhaled. "Would you and Hope come out to the Circle C for dinner tomorrow? After church, I mean."

Mariah's hesitation was a palpable thing. She put one hand on the doorknob. The door swung slowly open. He could hear his own heart beating in his ears.

"It's kind of you to ask, but I don't think so, Mr. Butler."

Disappointment coursed through the big man. "Do you have other plans?"

"It isn't that. It's. . ." She seemed to be searching for a reason to refuse his invitation. "It makes extra work for Mac having so many to cook for. There's your daughter and son-in-law as well as all the hired help. Mac needs a day of rest."

"He doesn't mind. Mac loves to feed people. Besides, Carrie and Lucas won't be there this Sunday. They are having dinner with friends. Mac thinks highly of you, Miss Casey, and he's fond of Hope. He'd love to have you. We all would. Please reconsider. Say you will come."

Mariah rested her face against the top of Hope's dark head. "I don't know. . . ."

"Say yes, Mama." The small, dark head lifted from Mariah's shoulder. "I wanna see my kitten."

After a moment of stunned silence, both adults laughed, releasing the tension. "Hope and I will be pleased to accept your invitation, Mr. Butler."

He ruffled the little girl's dark curls. "Well then, I'll see you tomorrow."

"Good night, Mr. Butler."

"Good night, Miss Casey. Hope."

He stood looking at the closed door for a moment before turning away. Whistling softly to himself, he walked to his horse and swung into the saddle.

Had Mr. Butler actually invited her to dinner? Mariah leaned against her closed front door until her heart resumed its normal rhythm. *"You are a fool, Mariah Casey."* Her mother's harsh voice spoke inside her head. *"Look at yourself, girl! Men like pretty women. Nobody wants a tall, gangly old maid."*

"Especially not a man like Sherman Butler." Sudden tears sprang to Mariah's eyes as she pushed away from the door and carried Hope to her bedroom. All those questions about whether or not she ever felt homesick. He probably thought she'd go running back to Ohio as soon as the school year ended. They hadn't been able to keep a teacher for longer than a year. Mr. Butler was only being nice to her so he wouldn't have to look for a replacement. She blinked back tears as she prepared Hope for bed.

By the time the little girl was in her nightgown, Mariah was inwardly fuming. How dare that man think he could flatter her into staying in Cedar Bend.

Well, she'd set him straight tomorrow after church. She would tell him Cedar Bend was her home, and she had no intention of going anywhere. He needn't waste his time wooing her. She had seen him talking to Emily James tonight. Let him court her.

She tucked Hope in and leaned over to kiss the little girl good night. Two little arms slipped around her neck. "I love you, Mama."

Another large chunk of the shell that encased Mariah's heart broke free and fell away. Mariah swept the little girl up into her arms. "Oh, Hope! I love you, too."

When a soft little kiss pressed against her cheek, Mariah burst into tears. A small hand patted her face. "Don't cry, Mama."

Knowing she mustn't frighten Hope, Mariah struggled to gain control of her emotions. "It's all right, honey. These are tears of joy."

The little girl snuggled closer. Mariah's heart twisted. She would gladly lay down her life for this child. She knew this was love. Pure, unmerited, *agape* love. For the first time she understood—at least as much as it was possible for a mortal to understand—the love that led Christ to the cross at Calvary.

Long after Hope was asleep, Mariah tossed and turned in her own bed. It had been the most emotionally exhausting day of her life. The sound of Hope's childish voice saying she loved her and the moist kiss the little girl had placed on her cheek moved her in a way she couldn't have imagined. Joy flooded her soul. No one had ever loved her before. *Thank You, Father, for bringing me to Cedar Bend. Thank You for bringing Hope into my life. Thank You for*— She felt herself drifting off to sleep, leaving her prayer unfinished. She knew God understood what was in her overflowing heart.

Sunday morning Mariah overslept. She knew she was going to be late for Sunday school. Then, when Hope dawdled over breakfast, she realized they were going to be lucky if they made it in time for morning services. They were a block away when the church bell started tolling. When Hope refused to be hurried, she scooped her up into her arms and ran. At the foot of the steps she stood the child down and tried to catch her breath. There wasn't time. Still huffing and puffing like a steam engine, she clutched Hope's hand. Feeling decidedly frazzled—she hadn't even had time to do anything with her hair beyond twisting it into a loose roll and pinning it up in back—she rushed up the church steps. They stepped through the door as the bell pealed its final note. Sherman Butler was standing in the vestibule, talking to the pastor.

Even though he was facing them, for one frantic moment Mariah prayed he wouldn't see her. That somehow, miraculously, she would become invisible. Today was evidently not the day for miracles.

"Miss Casey." His blue eyes lit up and his dimples deepened. "I was beginning to think something had happened to you."

"No," she gasped and was too winded to say more.

Hope pulled away from Mariah and grabbed Mr. Butler's hand. "Mama slept and slept." She swung on his hand and smiled up at him. "We had to run all the ways to church."

He lifted one eyebrow, and if possible the dimples were even deeper. Mariah felt the color sweep up her neck to her hairline.

"Miss Casey," he began as he took her elbow with the hand Hope wasn't clinging to, "they are playing the opening hymn. May I escort you to your seat?"

"I—I—suppose so."

As soon as they stepped into the main sanctuary, Joanna, who was leading the singing, smiled. Every head turned. Mariah shook off Sherman's hand. Head held high, she marched down the aisle a step ahead of him, past a gauntlet of faces. Some were smiling. Some, mostly the single women, were wearing a look of shocked disbelief. Thankfully Carrie Nolan was out of her line of vision.

She slid into the Jacobs's pew with a sigh of relief, leaving room for Hope to sit beside her. The little girl scrambled around Mariah and squeezed in between her and Gladys. Sherman, instead of continuing on to his accustomed seat, sat down in the space she had intended for Hope. It was a snug fit. Mariah was forced to scoot over as much as possible, but with the entire Jacobs family sitting on the other end of the pew, she couldn't move far. She lifted her chin. If Sherman Butler had set out to humiliate her, he was certainly succeeding.

They were barely seated when Joanna announced the next hymn and asked them to stand. Sherman took a hymnal from the rack on the back of the pew in front of them. Mariah never sang, but when he gestured for her to take one side of the book, she did. His arm brushed hers as they shared the hymnal, and her heart fluttered. *From all that running,* she assured herself. Though she had to admit, she did enjoy having him standing beside her. He was so big and tall that her eyes were barely level with his shoulder. Her hand, across the book from his large, callused hand, looked delicate. He wasn't much of a singer—a quality she found strangely appealing though what he lacked in skill he made up for in enthusiasm. She found herself singing softly.

When Sherman went to the front to assist with the offering, Gladys leaned across Hope and whispered, "What happened last night after the dance?"

Mariah shook her head. "Nothing happened. He saw us home. That's all."

"Me an' Mama's gonna go home with Mistah Butlah afta church." Hope's voice was a notch above a whisper, and Mariah felt the color rushing to her face even as she shushed the little girl.

"No, we are not!"

"You pwomised I could see my kitty." Hope's lower lip shot out.

Mariah had never seen Hope cry, but she'd seen enough tantrums in her life to recognize when one was forthcoming. She couldn't deal with that today. "All right, we'll go," she whispered. "I promised her she could see her kitten," she explained to her cousin.

"I see." Gladys sat back in her seat with a satisfied smile.

"You do not see," Mariah hissed.

Her cousin turned to whisper to Lucille, who was leaning so far forward she was in danger of falling out of her seat. Mariah closed her eyes. She felt a headache coming on.

She expected Sherman to take his place with the rest of the Circle C crew after the offering. To her surprise he slid back into the pew beside her. She thought briefly of asking him to go sit with Cyrus and Mac, then decided that would only attract more attention. Besides, his daughter would rush to his rescue before the final "amen" was uttered. Until then she would just have to endure his presence. When the congregation stood to pray, the coarse fabric of his jacket brushed against her arm. She clutched the back of the seat in front of her with both hands and implored God to please help her make it through this day.

Don't let me like this man, Lord. Please. My life is so good right now. The prayer that began as a plea became a disjointed litany of praise. *Thank You, Father, for Hope. Thank You for giving me friends. Especially thank You for Joanna who accepts me the way I am. And for Dr. Brady, too. And, dear Lord, thank You for sweet, funny, wise, little Mac. Thank You for my family: Gladys, Lucille, and Nels.* Carrie Nolan's face flashed across her mind. She took a deep breath and added one final, oft-repeated plea. *Help me to like Carrie. And please, Lord, help Carrie to not dislike me so much. In Jesus' name. Amen.*

When they sat back down, Mariah put her arm around Hope. The little girl snuggled close. Resting her head against Mariah's side, she fell asleep. Mariah leaned back in the seat and felt the coarse fabric of Sherman's jacket sleeve across her shoulders. Jerking upright she turned to glare at him. He grinned at her and leaned close to whisper against her ear. "More room this way."

Mariah sighed, then still sitting stiffly erect so as not to touch his arm, turned her attention to Pastor Carson. It was difficult to focus on his message with Hope's little head burrowing into her side. Not to mention the man sitting beside her with his arm resting on the pew behind her. If she could only lay Hope down. She cast a quick glance down the pew. The Jacobs had room to scoot over several inches.

She touched Gladys's shoulder with her fingertip. When the woman turned to look at her, she motioned for them to move down. Her cousin glanced pointedly at Sherman's arm and smiled, then turned her attention back to the sermon. She endured five more minutes of discomfort before laying Hope over and cradling her head in her lap. A few minutes later her back began to spasm. She shifted, trying to find a more comfortable position, at the same time avoiding touching the muscular arm resting on the back of the seat. After she squirmed a second time she knew she had to do something. She glanced at Sherman. He appeared to be absorbed in the sermon. If she leaned back it wouldn't be as though he had his arm around her. He was only resting it there so they would have more room. She slowly allowed her body to relax against the back of the seat.

She looked at Sherman out of the corner of her eye. His attention was riveted on Pastor Carson. Mr. Butler was totally oblivious to her. She only wished that she could be so unaware of him.

After church Mariah was surrounded by a group of chattering women. To her relief they were more interested in Hope speaking than they were in Sherman Butler sitting beside her in church. At least that's what they talked about. Mariah heard the stories about their children and the various ages they began to talk and embarrassing things they said. Suddenly, Hope was no longer with her, and she had lost sight of Mac.

"I have to go," she said. "Mr. McDougal is waiting for us, and I have to find Hope."

The other ladies drifted away to their own families, but the town seamstress and her two friends refused to allow Mariah to leave.

"We heard you had been invited out to the Circle C for dinner," Mrs. Wright said with a forced smile.

"Yes, Hope wanted to go." Mariah thought she would nip any gossip about her and Sherman Butler in the bud. "She has a kitten out there she wants to see."

"Oh! So you have been there before?" The seamstress had the avid look of a hungry vulture on her thin face. Her friends were ready to pounce on Mariah when Mrs. Braun broke into their conversation.

"Hope is with L. K., dear." Hilda Braun linked her arm through Mariah's. "I am so happy she is finally speaking, but if she's like most children, there will be days you'll long for silence." She gently urged Mariah away from the three gossips. "Don't let them bother you," she said softly. "They're lonely and they chatter, but they have good hearts."

Mariah knew what it was to be lonely. If she hadn't come to Kansas and been given Hope, she might have become a gossip had she had anyone to gossip with. Back in Ohio, she had begun marking the date on the calendar when a couple married, so she could count back from the date of their first child's birth. How despicable! She blushed at the memory.

"I know they mean well," she said. "But thank you for rescuing me."

"Mariah, it did my heart good to see Hope having such a good time last night. I had never seen her laugh before."

Mariah looked around the almost-empty room. "Where is Hope?"

"She's fine. She went outside with L. K., and Sherman and my Karl are with them. Mariah, Little Karl told me some time ago that Hope talked to him. I should have told you, but I didn't believe him."

Hope and L. K. had been inseparable since the first week of school. Mariah remembered all the times she'd seen the two children with their heads together. "I believe him," she said.

The two women stepped out into the chill October air. Mariah quickly scanned the almost-empty lot. Karl Braun and Sherman Butler stood talking beside the Brauns' large, two-seated surrey. The baby was in the front. Hope was in the backseat with the younger Braun children. The only other buggy was a sporty, dark blue phaeton she didn't recognize. Mac's black buggy was nowhere in sight, and neither was Sherman Butler's big bay gelding.

"Surely not," Mariah murmured.

"What is it, Mariah?"

"It's just that I thought—where is Mr. McDougal?"

"Mac has gone on home." Hilda Braun squeezed Mariah's arm. "Sherman told us you and Hope were going to have dinner at the Circle C."

"Yes, but I thought—when we went before, we rode out with Mac in his buggy. Mr. Butler always rides to church on that big red horse."

"Not today." Hilda laughed. "Don't worry, Mariah, you'll be fine. Mr. Butler is a gentleman, and you have a little chaperone."

Mariah's stomach was tied in knots as she allowed herself to be urged across the churchyard to where the two men were waiting. She felt so confused. What would she talk about on the trip out to the ranch?

Chapter 13

As it turned out, Mariah wasn't required to say much on the trip to the Circle C. Hope seemingly had stored up four years of questions against the day she would finally find her voice. And find it she had. Like water rushing over a broken dam, she asked questions. Lots of questions.

"How's come you only gots one horse, Mistah Butlah, an' L. K.'s daddy gots two?"

"Karl has a surrey. He needs two horses."

"Whatsa sarree?"

"It's like a big buggy."

"Oh." She took only a moment to digest this bit of information. "That's cause they gots lots of childruns."

"They have quite a few."

"Oh, look! See the jackrabbit, Hope?" Mariah felt as though her face were on fire.

"Wabbits has lots of babies, Mama. L. K. has a wabbit, and he says one day no babies, next day lotsa babies. Where you think all them baby wabbits comes from, Mama? Did God bring 'em?"

Mistah Butlah looked like he was about to explode. "Yes. I'm sure He did," Mariah answered.

Sherman snickered and Mariah glared at him. "Why don't you ask Mr. Butler? He's a rancher. He knows more about these things than I."

Hope looked up at the big man. He wasn't laughing now. "Mistah Butlah, how come the sky is blue?"

"Well, Hope—"

Mariah felt bad for putting Sherman on the spot and a little embarrassed at Hope's questions. She tried to help the rattled rancher. "Oh, look over there! Wasn't that a deer, Hope?"

"I don't see no dee-ah."

"I think he's over there in the tall grass. If you'll be really still maybe you can see him."

"How do you know he's a him?"

"Shh! You'll frighten him."

193

Hope was relatively quiet after that—even shushing the adults when they tried to speak. Still, Mariah breathed a sigh of relief when they turned in the lane leading to the ranch house. She was thrilled that Hope was talking, but tomorrow she would teach her the word *discretion* and its definition.

Sherman reached his hand out to Mariah to assist her from the buggy. When her feet were firmly planted on the ground, he turned and held his hands up for Hope. The little girl was standing on the seat. Before Mariah could react, Hope launched herself into his arms.

"Hope!" Mariah gasped. "I told you that was dangerous and to never do it again. What if Mr. Butler had dropped you? You could be seriously injured."

"Mistah Butlah won't dwop me." Her little arms tightened around the big man's neck. "Will ya, Mistah Butlah?"

"Well, certainly not intentionally. But your mama is right. If my reaction time happened to be a hair off, I could miss you and you could get hurt."

"So promise me you won't do that again, Hope."

The lower lip shot out, but only momentarily. "Okay, Mama. Kin I see my kitty now?"

"After dinner."

"Okay, Mama."

When they stepped inside the kitchen, Mac was hobbling around, putting the finishing touches to dinner. "Jist hang yore wraps there." He indicated a long coatrack beside the kitchen door. "It's gittin' a mite nippy out there, ain't it?"

"I think I can feel snow in the air." Mariah unbuttoned Hope's coat and hung it up beside her shawl and bonnet. "What can I do to help?"

"I'd reckon you kin mash these here spuds." He handed Mariah a large, white apron and a potato masher.

"While you're doing that, I'll take care of the horse," Sherman said.

"Kin I go with Mistah Butlah to take keer of the horse? Please, Mama!"

Mariah looked down into the pleading eyes of the little girl clinging to her apron. She was so tiny. One of those huge beasts could step on her. "I'm afraid you would be in the way."

"Carrie spent a lot of time in the barn with me when she was small," Sherman said. "If you don't mind her going, I'll watch out for her."

"Please, Mama."

Mariah sighed. "All right. But I want you to pay very close attention to Mr. Butler and do what he tells you."

"I will, Mama."

Sherman helped Hope into her coat, and the two of them went out the door.

When they were gone, Mariah allowed herself to relax in Mac's friendly approval as she mashed potatoes and then made pan gravy.

"I ain't in the habit of sharin' my kitchen with jist anybody, Miss Casey. But I know yer a mighty good cook. You make the flakiest pie crust I ever et."

"I started cooking when I wasn't much older than Hope."

"I'll teach you to make red-eye gravy one-a these days," Mac promised. "An' one-a these days soon I'll learn ya how to make chili. I learnt the receipt when we was down in Texas."

"I've never seen chili. But I'd love to try it."

"Thet's good." Mac chuckled. "Sherm loves my chili. As I told you already, I tried to teach Carrie how to cook afore she got married, but she never could git the hang of it. 'Course her ma couldn't cook neither."

"Mrs. Butler couldn't cook?" Mariah had assumed there was nothing Caroline Butler hadn't been a master at.

"Not a lick." Mac was piling thick slices of baked ham on a platter. " 'Course Caroline was raised to be a lady. An' she was. Tweren't nobody better at visitin' the sick an' comfortin' the afflicted than Caroline Butler. Joanna Brady is like thet. Good-hearted an' lovin'. Thet's what Caroline was. Good-hearted. Ever'body loved her."

"I had envisioned Mrs. Butler as being perfect."

"Ain't nobody perfect, Mariah, 'cept one and thet's the Lord Jesus Christ." He placed the platter of ham in the center of the table. "Caroline was jist a flawed human bein' like the rest of us mortals. But she did reach out to the needy. And she did love the Lord with all her heart."

Mariah took the gravy and put it on the table beside the mashed potatoes. "Was she a good mother?"

"Course she was. She loved Carrie jist like you love yore little Hope." He put a gnarled hand on Mariah's arm. "I know yore ma failed you, Mariah, but thet ain't keepin' you from bein' a good ma to thet little girl. Iffen she didn't love you an' feel secure with you, she wouldn'ta started talkin'. I see the way yore face lights up when she calls you Mama."

Mariah felt tears brimming up in her eyes. "Mac, if only you knew. I used to dream of the day I would have a family to love. I gave up that dream a long time ago. Then to have Hope given to me. . .It's just—I can't even find the words. It's a miracle that, after all these years, God would entrust this beautiful child to my care."

"I reckon He couldn'ta give 'er to anyone more deservin'." Mac pulled a red bandanna from his hip pocket and blew his nose.

The door opened, and Hope burst into the room followed by Sherman. "Mistah Butlah let me set on the horse."

"Hope, you have straw all over you. Here, let me pick it off. How on earth—"

"Mistah Butlah says I can wide. He says I'm a natchuwal—a natch—" She looked up at the man. "What did you say I was?"

"I said you were a natural horsewoman." He gave Mariah a sheepish smile. "Well, she is."

"I will not have my child on the back of some great beast."

"She wanted to sit on Tornado, and I didn't see any harm in it."

"Tornado! You put my little girl on the back of a horse named Tornado?"

"Her name's Tornado, but it's not what you think. She was born during a bad storm. She's gentle as a lamb. Besides, Hope wanted to."

Mariah was picking the last of the straw out of Hope's hair. "I suppose if she had wanted to jump out of the barn loft you would have let her." She looked from the straw between her fingertips to the man. Her eyes widened. "You didn't!"

"Carrie always liked to jump into the straw. There wasn't any way she could get hurt. Besides, she thought it was fun."

"*She* is a four-year-old who doesn't know the meaning of the word danger. You, on the other hand, are *supposed* to be a responsible adult."

Mariah rarely let her emotions get out of control. But the way Sherman Butler was standing there grinning at her made her furious.

"I'd reckon we'd better eat afore it gits cold," Mac said.

Cyrus had appeared from somewhere. She saw he was grinning, too. So was Mac. She took hold of Hope's wrist. "Come on, honey, and we'll wash your hands." She shot a scathing look at Sherman Butler. When she recognized that his amusement was directed at the situation, her irritation slipped away. No one was laughing at her. She straightened her shoulders and struggled to keep from smiling herself. "It's hard telling what *Mistah Butlah* let you get on your hands."

Mariah couldn't remember ever spending a more enjoyable afternoon. The two older men fussed over Hope, and she basked in their attention, while Sherman Butler engaged Mariah in conversation. Mariah forgot her shyness as she found herself sharing little anecdotes about her pupils back in Ohio. The big rancher hung on her every word as though what she had to say was important. When she told little stories that she found amusing, he laughed in all the proper places. She forgot that he was only being nice to her so he wouldn't have to look for another teacher in the fall. She even forgot that she wasn't pretty.

All too soon the meal ended. Mariah stood and began to help Mac clear the table. A gangly, teenaged boy Mac introduced as Andy Clark wandered into the kitchen. Mac took the stack of plates from Mariah's hands. "Andy'll do these dishes. This little lady wants to go see her kitten."

"She can wait until after the dishes are done."

"You an' Sherm take this here little gal to see thet kitten."

"Mama!" Hope's blue eyes pleaded. "You pwomised afta dinna I could see my kitty."

Sherman was buttoning Hope into her coat. "I feel guilty leaving you to clean up," Mariah protested, even as she draped her shawl around her shoulders.

"Pshaw!" Mac gave a dismissive wave of his hand. "You go on an' enjoy yoreself."

Mariah shivered as they followed Hope across the barnyard. Sherman stopped walking. "I'm going to run back to the house and get you a heavier wrap."

"I'm fine," Mariah insisted.

"I'm going to get a coat. I'll be back in a minute."

Before Mariah could protest further he was walking back toward the house. Hope snuggled against her. "Mistah Butlah gonna take keer of you, Mama, just like you take keer of me."

Mariah put her arm around the little girl and drew her close. "Mr. Butler is a very thoughtful man."

"I likes Mistah Butlah."

Mariah watched the big man disappear into the house. She liked Mr. Butler, too. She only wished she didn't like him so much.

It was late afternoon when Sherman Butler's buggy passed beneath the arched entrance to the Circle C and turned onto the main road heading back to town. Mariah snuggled deeper into the folds of the coat that sheltered her from the biting wind. Hope, cocooned in the heavy blanket Mac had wrapped around her, slept with her head cradled in Mariah's lap.

"I wouldn't be surprised to see snow before morning," Sherman said.

"It's cold enough," Mariah agreed.

After a few more offhand remarks about the weather, a silence as warm and comfortable as the borrowed coat she wore enveloped the buggy. Mariah's thoughts turned to Hope and the kitten in the barn. The small ball of blind, yellow fluff had turned into a hissing bundle of wildness with razor-sharp claws and wouldn't let any of them near enough to touch it. Nevertheless, Hope insisted she was going to bring it home with her. When Mariah told her she couldn't have the kitten, letting her ride Tornado had narrowly averted a tantrum.

Mariah knew the black mare with the streaked blaze was smaller than the other horses. Still, she looked huge with Hope perched on her back. At least she had forgotten the kitten. Mariah sighed. Now she claimed Tornado.

She turned her gaze to the man driving the buggy. Today, when he wrapped his coat around her, his touch had been gentle. She had seen that same gentleness when he led the black horse around the corral. She felt safe with him. His big hands were steady on the lines, and his eyes never left the road. Sherman Butler was a good man. She wondered what he was thinking.

———

Sherman's eyes were on the road, but his mind was elsewhere. He couldn't remember when he had spent a more enjoyable day. Hope had been on the verge of pitching a fit when Mariah told her she couldn't have the kitten. A smile tugged at his heart. She was a spunky little thing, considering how the Wainwrights had treated her.

Mariah was pretty spunky herself. He knew she had been nervous as a cat when he lifted Hope onto Tornado's back, but she'd kept her fears concealed from the child. Hope had taken to riding like a duck takes to water. He hadn't realized until today just how much he missed having a young one around.

He heard Mariah's soft sigh and glanced at her. She seemed lost in her own thoughts. He turned his eyes back toward the road. Today, when he came back from the barn, Mariah was bustling around the kitchen like she belonged there. Mac's kitchen was sacred ground. Except for his futile attempt to teach Carrie to cook, it was off-limits to outsiders. It had been all he could do to keep from laughing out loud. Then, when she started raking him over the coals for allowing Hope to jump out of the hayloft. . . Well, he had known for certain then. He wanted to spend the rest of his life with this woman.

———

Mariah turned when Sherman cleared his throat. "I suppose you will be having Thanksgiving with your family."

She turned her head to look at him. "I hadn't really thought about it. Mother and I never did anything special for the holidays."

"Your mother is gone." Sherman's voice was gentle. "You will want to start your own traditions now that you have Hope."

Mariah looked down at the blanket-wrapped bundle resting between them. "I want Hope to have a happy childhood."

"She will have. You are doing a wonderful job with her, Miss Casey."

"Thank you, Mr. Butler." Mariah sighed. "Raising a child is much more difficult than I ever imagined it would be."

"Being responsible for another person's life is never easy. It was tough with Matthew and Carrie."

"Matthew? I thought Mrs. Nolan was an only child."

"My son died three months before Carrie was born. He was almost three years old."

"I'm so sorry." Mariah's heart ached for the man. "I didn't know."

"It was a difficult time. First, I lost my son. Then I lost my wife." He hesitated, searching for the right words. "I wanted Caroline to have everything she'd given up when she married me. I never realized until it was too late that those possessions meant nothing to my wife." Mariah felt his eyes on her. "You know the man in Luke that kept building bigger and bigger barns to store his goods? That was me, Miss Casey. I was angry after Caroline died. I know it was irrational, but I was angry at God for taking her, and I was angry at her for leaving. Then one day I realized, like the man in the Bible with his big barns and many possessions, if my soul were required of me I would have nothing to give."

Mariah wanted to say something comforting, but even if she found the words, she doubted she could force them past the lump in her throat.

"I was raised in a godly home. But I never knew Christ as my personal Savior until after Caroline was gone. Shortly after my wife died, I took a Bible and a jug of water and went to one of the line shacks. Stripped down to the basics, I read and prayed until I met my Lord. I want you to know I'm not the same angry man I was back then." He paused and took a deep breath before plunging on. "I wasn't a good husband to Caroline—how could I have been? We were unequally yoked. I cherished the things of this earth. Caroline's treasures awaited her in heaven. The only thing on this earth that mattered to Caroline was my salvation."

He brought the buggy to a halt in front of Mariah's house. Sitting in the buggy seat, he turned to face Mariah. "I'm not the same man I was then, Miss Casey. I wasn't the husband I should have been to Caroline, but I would be a good husband to you and a good father to Hope." He took a deep breath before continuing. "We haven't known each other long, but I know that I love you and I love Hope. Will you marry me, Mariah?"

Mariah sat in stunned silence. Had she heard Mr. Butler correctly? Had he said he loved her?

"I won't press you for an answer right now. Six months from now, after a proper courtship, I will ask you again. May I court you, Mariah?"

For the briefest moment her mother's sharp words about her undesirability echoed through Mariah's mind. She took a deep breath and forced them from her mind. "Yes, Mr. Butler. You may."

Chapter 14

That night after Hope was asleep, Mariah sat in the chair in her bedroom. Bible in hand, she mulled over the happenings of the afternoon. Had Mr. Butler truly said he loved her? He had asked her to marry him. She knew that. But love? Was it possible Mother had been wrong when she told her no man would ever love her? That she wasn't pretty enough?

She sighed and rested her head against the high back of the rocking chair. Mr. Butler was a fine-looking man. He was kind and gentle. Besides that, he had a huge ranch. She supposed he was wealthy, although she had never really thought about it. He could have any woman he wanted. What was it Carrie said that first Sunday she went to the ranch? *"Other women have set their caps for Papa, but he's never been interested in any of them."*

What of Carrie? Does she see me as a threat? Is that why she dislikes me so intensely? Could that be the reason for the lecture in front of her mother's portrait? She's already lost her mother. Is she afraid of losing her father, as well?

Mariah closed her eyes. After all these years, did she even want to marry? She had Hope. Wasn't that enough? True, she'd prayed for a husband. But did she really want one now? Husbands made demands. Her mother had certainly told her enough about that in the years after her father died. She could still hear her mother's voice. *"I thought if I married an old man I wouldn't have to be burdened with children."* Mother's laugh was harsh. *"You are proof that I was sadly mistaken."*

Sorrow overwhelmed Mariah. Her mother had possessed everything. She was beautiful. She was an accomplished homemaker. Before the accident, she had friends. If only she could have shown the least bit of affection, their lives would have been so different. Mac said her mother was a foolish woman. And she had been. But more than that, she had been a woman trapped in the web of her own bitterness. What a waste!

As Mariah lifted her head and opened her eyes, the Bible slid to the floor. When she leaned over to pick it up she saw the corner of an envelope that had been hidden between the pages. She opened the Bible. Sherman Butler's letter. Had it been only two months since she received the offer of a position in Cedar Bend? She had been reading the twenty-ninth chapter of Jeremiah that day. As she looked down at the Bible, the eleventh verse reached out to her. She read the words of the Old Testament prophet aloud. " 'For I know the thoughts that I think toward you, saith the Lord, thoughts of peace, and not of evil. . . .' "

Mariah read the passage twice before leaning back in her chair. Had the last few months been ordered by God? Was it part of God's design for her life that she come to Kansas?

If I hadn't come to Cedar Bend, Hope wouldn't be sleeping in the other room now. Was that why God had brought her here? To be Hope's mother? Was it also in His plan for her to be Sherman Butler's wife? But what of Carrie? She couldn't accept Mr. Butler's proposal without his daughter's approval. She had been praying for the young woman since the day after her arrival in Cedar Bend. She recalled some of the prayers. In retrospect those entreaties had contained a preponderance of the pronouns *I* and *me.* Had she really been praying for Carrie, or had she been praying for herself?

The answer brought tears to Mariah's eyes. Except for the short plea this morning that she might come to like Carrie, most of her prayers had been centered on herself. Kneeling beside the chair in her bedroom, she asked God's forgiveness for her selfishness. Then she offered up the most heartfelt prayer of her life.

Every Sunday morning, Sherman drove Mariah and Hope to church, then out to the Circle C for dinner. Mariah told no one but Joanna of his proposal.

Mariah and Hope spent Thanksgiving Day with the Jacobses. After a bountiful meal, the men gathered in the parlor with the children. The women retired to the kitchen to face a mountain of dirty dishes.

"Well, are you going to marry him or not?" Gladys asked.

Mariah dropped a dish towel on the floor and bumped her head on the kitchen table when she bent to retrieve it. "About whom are you speaking, Cousin Gladys?"

"You know very well who I am talking about, young lady." The older woman held a damp cloth against the red spot on Mariah's forehead. "Sherman Butler, that's who."

Gladys's daughters were watching with wide-eyed interest. Mariah realized she was blushing. "Mr. Butler is a good friend."

"Good friend, indeed!" her cousin scoffed.

"Mr. Butler brings Mariah and Hope to church every Sunday morning," Lucille told Clara, her out-of-town sister. "He sits beside her, and" Lucille paused, seemingly for drama's sake—"he even puts his arm around her. It is so romantic!"

"Is Mr. Butler courting you, Cousin Mariah?" Clara asked.

"Of course he is." Gladys removed the cloth from Mariah's forehead. "If you could see them together you wouldn't have to ask."

"Oh, Cousin Mariah!" Clara threw her arms around her cousin. "I am so happy for both of you!"

Mariah returned her cousin's brief embrace before turning back to the dishpan.

"So have you accepted him yet?" Gladys persisted.

"I don't recall saying that he'd asked." Mariah slid a plate into the steaming rinse water.

"If he hasn't, he soon will." Gladys dried the plate and handed it to Lucille. "So you are going to accept him, aren't you?"

Mariah plunged her hands into the soapy water. "I don't know," she said honestly.

"Why ever not?" Clara asked. "Mr. Butler is quite a catch."

This was her family, and she knew they cared about her. Mariah took a deep breath. "Well, for one thing, there's his daughter. She doesn't like me."

"Carrie?" Lucille gave a dismissive wave of her slender hand. "I wouldn't worry about her."

"There are other considerations." Mariah rubbed at an invisible spot on the plate she was washing.

"Here." Gladys took the plate from her hands. "Let me have that before you rub a hole in it."

Mariah saw two little splashes in the dishwater. Lifting a soapy hand she swiped at her tears.

Gladys put her arm around her. "Sometimes a good cry puts things in perspective. Isn't that right, girls?" She led Mariah to a chair and urged her to sit down.

Through a blur of tears Mariah saw the concern on their faces. Not avid interest, like the three gossips at church, but genuine, loving concern.

She buried her face in the clean tea towel Clara pressed into her hand and released a lifetime of pain. While gentle hands caressed her back and shoulders, the last segment of the shell that had imprisoned her heart for so many years shattered and fell away. She wiped her face and blew her nose on the towel.

"Well, I guess we had better not dry dishes on that," she said.

They all laughed. Then Gladys pulled up a chair, facing Mariah. "Now, why don't you tell us what is really bothering you?"

Lucille and Clara pulled up their own chairs between Gladys and Mariah, forming a circle. They looked at her expectantly.

"First of all, I want to tell all three of you how much I love you. Secondly, I want you to promise you won't breathe a word of what I'm about to say to anyone."

"We will respect your confidence, dear," Gladys promised. "You should know that."

"Our lips are sealed," Clara said, while Lucille raised her hand to her mouth and pantomimed a key turning in a lock.

Mariah breathed a shaky sigh as she wadded the soggy dish towel in trembling hands. "Mr. Butler did ask me to marry him."

"I knew it," Gladys exulted. "I just knew it."

"Will the wedding be after school dismisses for the summer?" Clara asked.

"I don't know if there will be a wedding." Mariah twisted the dish towel. "I don't know if I can marry Mr. Butler."

"Why not?" Clara leaned forward. "Cousin Mariah, do you have any idea how many women have tried to snag Sherman Butler? Even I, before I met George, cast a speculative eye in his direction."

"Half the women in Cedar Bend have," Lucille said. "The other half are already married."

"Sherman Butler has never lacked opportunities," Gladys said. "But, until you came to town, I never knew him to give any woman a second glance."

"It's plain to see he is smitten by you," Lucille interjected. "The unmarried women of Cedar Bend are so jealous."

Clara put a hand on Mariah's arm. "You do love him, don't you, Cousin Mariah?"

"I don't know." Mariah pleated the dish towel between her fingers. "Until I came to Kansas I didn't know what love was. I admire Mr. Butler greatly, but love. . .I don't know."

"Surely you want a husband and children of your own," Clara said.

"I thought I did at one time. When I was younger I prayed for that very thing, but now—" Mariah looked down as her hands worried the dish towel. "God has given me Hope. It seems greedy to want more. Besides, there's the problem of Carrie. I will not come between Mr. Butler and his daughter."

Gladys took Mariah's hand in hers. "Carrie will come to love you once she knows you."

"She might," Mariah agreed, although her voice was laced with doubt. "But that's not my only concern." With her free hand she wiped a fresh tear from her face.

"Mariah, dear," Gladys said as she squeezed the younger woman's hand, "are you worried about the more intimate aspects of marriage?"

Mariah looked down at the dish towel in her lap. "Mother said it was horrible."

"Mariah, look at me!" Gladys put her fingertips under the younger woman's chin and lifted her head until their eyes met. "Mariah, your mother was wrong. The first marriage was performed by God in the Garden of Eden. Our heavenly Father decreed we were to be one with our husbands. This is not a curse, child. It's a blessing. A gift from God. Didn't Jesus say the Father gives His children good gifts? I know it is not proper to speak ill of the dead, but Margaret found no joy in anything but her own reflection in the mirror. I can only imagine what your life was like with that woman after she believed her beauty was gone." She pulled Mariah into a loving embrace. "You have nothing to fear from Sherman Butler, dear. He is a kind, gentle man. He would never do anything to hurt you."

"Mr. Butler is a handsome man. He deserves a pretty wife," Mariah murmured against Gladys's shoulder.

Gladys put her hands on Mariah's shoulders and pushed her away so she could look into her eyes. "You're beautiful, Mariah. I've noticed the way Sherman Butler's face lights up when he looks at you. I'd dare say in Mr. Butler's eyes you are *very* beautiful. As for Carrie—" She released Mariah and stood. "Well, we will all pray for her, and she'll come around. Now, girls, let's finish these dishes."

When the kitchen was finally in order, the women joined the men in the parlor. Clara's two children and Hope napped in Lucille's old room. Outside, the shadows were beginning to lengthen. Mariah sat on the sofa with Lucille's three-month-old son lying lengthwise on her lap.

"You're such a pretty boy," she cooed. He responded with a bubbly grin that made Mariah wish she could have held Hope when she was this age.

"Take his hands and pull him up," Lucille said.

"Don't I need to watch his head?"

"He can already hold his head up," Lucille said with maternal pride. "He's very advanced for his age."

"Of course he is." Mariah looked down at the baby in her lap. She imagined his fine, black hair as copper curls. Her face grew warm at where her thoughts were leading.

"I think we have company." Nels struggled out of his chair.

"I didn't hear anyone knock," Clara's husband, George, said.

"Daddy always sits where he can look out the window," Clara explained. "He must have seen someone coming."

Mariah heard the outside door leading from the porch into the front hallway open and close, but she was too involved with the baby to look up.

Nels opened the door before Sherman had a chance to knock. "Is Miss Casey still here?"

"She is." Nels swung the door wide. "Come on in out of the cold, Sherm. Let me take your coat and hat."

While Nels took care of his outer garments, Sherman sat down on a bench and pulled off his boots.

"The family is in the parlor."

Sherman stepped through the door behind Nels. He returned the Jacobs family's greetings, but his attention was on Mariah. She looked up and her eyes widened. "Mr. Butler, whatever are you doing here?"

"I thought I would come in and drive you and Hope home." He crossed the room and sat down on the sofa beside her. "This little fellow is growing like a weed, Lucille."

The young mother beamed. "You can hold him if you like, Mr. Butler."

"It's been a long time." Sherman took the baby from Mariah and lifted him to his shoulder. "But I reckon I need the practice for the day Carrie makes me a grandpa."

"Who knows?" Jed teased. "You might have one of your own before then."

Sherman looked at Mariah. She was mighty fetching in a sapphire blue dress that matched her eyes. "I just might."

Mariah's face flushed bright crimson. At the same time, Sherman felt a gush of warmth on his shoulder. Lucille sprang up, her face almost as red as her cousin's. "I'm so sorry, Mr. Butler." She grabbed her son.

Gladys appeared with a damp cloth, fretting at the milk stain despite Sherman's protests. Mariah put a hand over her mouth, her blue eyes danced, and her shoulders shook with merriment. It was worth smelling like sour milk if it made her laugh.

That night, lying in her bed, Mariah's thoughts were on the events of the day. Her heart had caught in her throat when she saw Sherman standing in his stocking feet behind Cousin Nels. She hadn't been the only one who was happy to see him. When Hope woke from her nap, she ran straight to Sherman and climbed on his lap.

Today in the kitchen with Cousin Gladys and her girls, I felt I truly belonged to a family for the first time. Sitting beside Sherman and Hope on the sofa, I felt complete. I do love him, Lord. Beyond any shadow of a doubt. If Carrie could accept me, I would marry him tomorrow.

Chapter 15

The week after Thanksgiving brought a foot of snow. On Monday morning, Mariah slogged through the drifts, pulling Hope on the sled Sherman had given her. Her thoughts were on the Christmas program. Some of the parts were going to be easy to cast. Mabel Carson with her dark hair and eyes would be perfect as Mary. Jay Braun would be Joseph. The angels and shepherds would be no problem. But what could Mark Hopkins do? The young man stood head and shoulders above her other pupils. In three months he had advanced to the fifth reader. She wouldn't leave him out for the world.

Mariah sighed. Joanna had offered to help her with the music and costumes. Perhaps she could come up with something.

"Mark will be perfect as the angel Gabriel," Joanna said, when Mariah broached the subject to her that evening.

"Of course!" Mariah exclaimed. "Why didn't I think of that?"

Joanna laughed. "Two heads are better than one. What are you going to do with the little ones?"

"Do you think anyone will be offended if they are sheep?"

"Why should they be?" Joanna asked. "After all, what is a shepherd without sheep?"

The next morning Mariah assigned parts. Since Pastor Carson would read the Christmas story from the book of Luke, there were few lines to memorize. That afternoon, she and Joanna began to transform the cast-off clothing they had collected into costumes. They only had a week until the first rehearsal.

"Everything is coming together beautifully," Mariah told Sherman the following Sunday as they rode back to town from the Circle C.

"Me an' L. K. is sheeps," Hope volunteered from her place between them on the seat of the open sleigh. "Mama made us sheeps hats out of a blanket."

Sherman smiled down at the little girl. "You look more like a little lamb to me. What do you want Saint Nick to bring you for Christmas, my little lamb?"

Hope giggled; then her small face turned serious. "I wants a daddy. Mistah Butlah, will you be my daddy?"

Sherman looked at Mariah. "I reckon you'll have to talk to your mama about that."

Mariah turned her head away, but not before Sherman saw the sheen of tears in her blue eyes. "What about it, Mama?" he asked gently. "This little lamb wants a daddy."

"You promised me six months," she said, with her face still averted.

"And I will honor that promise." There wasn't much more he could say in Hope's presence. Sherman shrugged his shoulders and turned his attention back to the snow-packed road.

The program was held at the Community Church the Sunday evening before Christmas. Joanna peeked around the makeshift curtains she and Mariah had hung to separate the stage from the rest of the building.

"The room is filled to overflowing," she whispered.

As soon as the children were in their places for the first scene, Mariah and Joanna sat down on the front pew. A visiting minister offered a lengthy prayer. Then Pastor Carson began to read. " 'And it came to pass in those days, that there went out a decree from Caesar Augustus that all the world should be taxed. . . .' "

When he read the final verses in the passage, two of the older boys pulled the curtains aside to reveal Mary and Joseph kneeling behind the straw-filled manger. Joanna stood to lead the congregation in singing "Away in a Manger."

The curtains closed at the end of the song. While Pastor Carson resumed reading, Mariah and Joanna slipped behind the curtain to arrange the next scene.

" 'And there were in the same country shepherds abiding in the field, keeping watch over their flock by night.' "

The curtains slid open to reveal shepherds and sheep while Joanna led "The First Noel." The little sheep were a bit fidgety. Hope kept looking around and waving to people in the audience. Mariah couldn't suppress a smile. At least the *friendly* sheep wasn't talking.

Soon the curtain closed for the final time. After the congregation sang the final Christmas hymn, the minister gave another prayer in conclusion. Then Mariah and Joanna stepped forward to thank everyone who had come. Joanna slipped away as parents surrounded Mariah, congratulating her on the program and voicing appreciation for her teaching.

Sherman watched Mariah accept the accolades she deserved. She was wearing a cranberry-colored dress he had never seen before. Dark curls framed her flushed face. Her blue eyes glowed as she talked to her students and their parents.

"Isn't she beautiful?" he murmured to Carrie, who was standing beside him.

"Who? Miss Casey?" Carrie shrugged her shoulders. "Getting rid of those drab clothes and that horrible bun improved her looks, I suppose. But I wouldn't describe her as beautiful. My mama was beautiful."

"I wish you would go up and say a few words to her, Carrie. You haven't been able to come to Sunday dinner for several weeks now." He patted her shoulder. "You don't want Mariah to think you are avoiding her."

"Mistah Butlah!" Hope pushed past several people to tug on his hand. "Did you see me? I was the sheep that waved at you."

"I certainly did, my little lamb." Sherman picked the little girl up. "You were the best one up there."

Hope wrapped one arm around his neck. "I waved to you, too, Miss Carrie. Did you see me?"

"I saw you. You made an excellent sheep."

"Well, my little lamb, would you like to help me pass out treats?"

Lucas put his arm around Carrie's shoulders. "Come on, darlin', let's go tell Miss Casey how much we enjoyed the program. And you, little miss," he said, squeezing Hope's hand, "have fun helping Mr. Butler pass out treats."

"I will." Hope leaned out of Sherman's arms to plant a moist kiss on Carrie's cheek. "Bye, Miss Carrie. Bye, Mistah Lucas."

"Your son is a delight to have in the classroom," Mariah told Mark Hopkins's parents. "If he continues to advance at this rate, he will graduate in April."

"Mark's a good boy," Mr. Hopkins replied. "I just want to thank you for all the time you've devoted to him, Miss Casey."

"I'm very fond of Mark, Mr. Hopkins. As I said before, he's a delight to work with."

After the Hopkinses moved on, Mariah turned and came face-to-face with Carrie Nolan and her husband, Lucas.

"I thought you didn't get involved with your pupils, Miss Casey," Carrie offered without preamble.

"Good evening, Mrs. Nolan. Mr. Nolan." Mariah briefly rested her hand on the younger woman's arm. "I want to apologize to you for what I said that day. It was rude and entirely uncalled for."

"We wanted to tell you how much we enjoyed the program," Lucas said.

"Thank you, Mr. Nolan." Mariah smiled. "But I can't accept all the credit for that. I couldn't have done it without Joanna's help."

"Mac told me you and Hope will be spending Christmas Day at the Circle C."

"We were invited," Mariah said. "You will be there, won't you?"

"The Circle C is my home, Miss Casey. Nothing, and nobody, will keep me from celebrating Christmas with my family."

Mariah longed to put her arms around the younger woman. This was neither the time nor place. She smiled and told them she was looking forward to seeing them Christmas Day.

As Sherman drove Mariah and Hope home after the program, the still-excited girl chattered about the program. "I was the bestest sheep," she said. "Mistah Butlah sayed so. So's did Uncah Mac an' Uncah Cy'us. Evahbody sayed I was."

"I think I'm going to have to teach someone the meaning of the word H-U-M-I-L-I-T-Y," Mariah said.

"I hope you have better luck than you did with D-I-S-C-R-E-T-I-O-N." Sherman laughed.

"Mama, you know what I gots in my sack?" Hope clutched the treat bag to her. "I gots an apple an' some peppahmint sticks an' a o'ange thing. What is that o'ange thing, Mama?"

"The orange thing is an orange, Hope." Mariah hugged her close. "Mr. Butler had them shipped all the way from Florida."

Before Mariah could stop her, Hope took a bite of the orange. She made a face and spit the piece of peeling out. "I don't like o'anges," she said.

"It's supposed to be peeled," Mariah explained. "When we get home, I'll peel it for you. Then I think you will like it."

Hope returned the orange to the sack and folded the top down. "I'll eat my apple, Mama. You kin have the ol' o'ange."

Sherman chuckled, then said, "You did a good job on the program, Mariah. I was proud of you."

"Thank you, Mr. Butler." She strained to see his face in the dim glow of the sleigh's lanterns. "I couldn't have done it without Joanna."

"Didn't I see Joanna with your star pupil after the program?"

"Mark escorted Joanna home," Mariah said. "He's exhausted the library at school. Joanna has been loaning him books."

"I thought they might be keeping company."

"No," Mariah said. "Mark and Joanna are friends. That's all."

"Ma'k's sweet on Aunt Joanna," Hope interrupted. "Julie told me so."

Julie was Mark Hopkins's six-year-old sister and a prominent member of Hope's growing circle of friends.

"I believe Julie is mistaken," Mariah said. "Mark and Joanna have been friends for years. Nothing more."

"From what I've seen, Hope and Julie are right," Sherman said. "That young man's got that certain glow in his eyes when he looks at Joanna. The same glow I get when I look at you, Miss Casey."

A pleasurable warmth enveloped Mariah. "What a thing to say, Mr. Butler," she scolded. "Especially in front of the C-H-I-L-D."

"I's not a child, Mama," Hope said. "I's a girl."

Sherman chuckled. "How well can she spell, Miss Casey?"

"Obviously better than I thought she could." Mariah laughed. "I knew she was learning to read, of course. And I knew she loved books, but I thought she mostly looked at the pictures."

When Sherman walked them to the door, he bent down and whispered in Mariah's ear. "I love you, Mariah."

Mariah stood in the open doorway with Hope at her side and watched through swirling snowflakes as he climbed into the sleigh. She could still feel his warm breath on her ear. *I love you, too, Sherman Butler.*

She didn't go inside and close the door until the sleigh and its driver were swallowed up by darkness.

On Christmas Eve, Mariah and Hope had dinner with the Jacobses. As they exchanged gifts, Mariah looked around the parlor at her family: Nels, Gladys, Jed, and Lucille with baby Lawrence. She then hugged Hope, who was snuggled on her lap. She felt a sense of belonging she had never experienced before coming to Kansas. This was her family. She loved every one of them. And she felt secure in their love for her.

Later, after Jed had driven Mariah and Hope home, she sat on the edge of Hope's bed and read Clement Moore's poem, " 'Twas the Night Before Christmas," to her. After she closed the cover of the book, the questions began. What was a kerchief? What was a sugarplum? What? Why? Where? When? How?

When Hope ran out of questions, Mariah said her prayers with her then kissed her good night. After the little girl's eyes closed, Mariah went into her own bedroom. She took from the wardrobe the doll she had made for Hope. It wasn't pretty like the china dolls at the mercantile, but it was soft and durable, and every stitch was sewn with love. A little girl could hug this doll and sleep with it and feed it strawberry jam and love it without fear of it breaking. Mariah smoothed the flannel gown that was fashioned from leftover scraps of Hope's gown. There were three outfits made of scraps from Hope's dresses still hidden in the wardrobe. Tomorrow she would give them to her.

Mariah lifted the covers and slipped the doll in beside the sleeping child. Hope, who slept like a rock, never stirred. Mariah kissed one of her rosy cheeks and tucked the quilts around her. Hope would be so surprised when she woke tomorrow and found the doll. Mariah smiled and went to her own bed.

"Mama! Mama! Look what I gots." The excited little girl stood beside Mariah's bed, clutching the doll. "Did Saint Nick bwing her, Mama?"

Mariah lifted the covers. "Climb in with me before you freeze."

Hope snuggled next to Mariah under the covers. "Where did her come fwom, Mama?"

"Do you like her, Hope?" Mariah waited while Hope examined the doll's embroidered face and stroked her dark brown yarn hair.

"I love her, Mama." She hugged the doll close. "Did Saint Nick bwing her? Or did God bwing her?"

"What do you think?" Mariah hugged Hope as tightly as she was hugging her new doll.

Hope's small face twisted in concentration as she mulled the question. "Mrs. Harris say every good an' perfect gift comes fwom God." Her expression relaxed. "Saint Nick isn't weal, Mama. The story you wed to me is make-believe. Weinde-ahs can't weally fly. God is weal, Mama. He gived me you. An' He gived me my dolly."

Mariah blinked back tears as she kissed Hope's smooth forehead. "However did you get so smart in only four years, honey?"

Hope giggled. "You teached me."

Mariah gave the little girl a final squeeze. "You stay here with your baby while I build up the fire."

Mariah slipped from the bed, slid her feet into cold slippers, threw on a robe, and ran across the icy floor. While she waited for the kitchen to warm up, she looked out the frosty kitchen window. Last night's snow had added six inches to what was already on the ground. A few snowflakes still hung in the frigid air. In the east the sun was rising, dispelling the few clouds that remained. It was going to be a beautiful day.

Chapter 16

Mariah bustled around the kitchen helping Mac put the finishing touches on dinner. The roaring fire in the fireplace combined with the heat from the big, black range warmed the large room. Mariah felt comfortable in Mac's presence. As she had from their first meeting, she shared her deepest feelings with him.

"Before last night at Cousin Gladys's I never celebrated a family Christmas," Mariah said. "There was something so special about gathering with family to share a meal and exchange gifts." She touched the brooch pinned in the froth of white lace at the throat of her cranberry red dress. "Joanna gave me this. It is my first Christmas gift. Actually, I believe it is my first gift ever. Not that the gifts are the important thing," she hastened to explain. "What makes it special is the love we share. Before I came to Kansas I didn't know what—" Her voice broke off as she turned and saw Carrie standing in the doorway.

How long had she been there? How much had she overheard? Mariah set the dish of sweet potatoes on the table. "Mrs. Nolan, is Hope all right?"

"Hope is fine. Lucas and Papa are entertaining her." She stepped into the kitchen. "Mac, is there anything I can do to help?"

Mac raised a bushy eyebrow. "I reckon you kin set the table in the dining room, little lady. Then you kin help us git the grub on the table."

"All right. I can do that." Carrie started to leave, then turned back. "Where are the dishes you want me to use?"

"Caroline Abigail Butler, you lived in this house fer nineteen years. You know as well as I do thet the good chiner's in the sideboard."

"Oh! That's right!" Carrie turned on her heel and left.

"Thet girl's as useless around the kitchen as her ma wuz," Mac grumbled. "Course Caroline had an excuse. She wuz raised to be a lady. Her pa had folks hired to wait on her hand and foot. She never had to lift a finger to do nothin' afore she married Sherman. The little lady is different. Carrie was born right here. I tried to learn her, but I don't know—" The old man shook his head. "Mebbe bein' a lady is jist bred into her. You know my ma always said you cain't beat out of the bones what's born in the blood."

Mariah moved to the stove. "You have all done a fine job raising her," she said. "Mrs. Nolan is a secure young woman, and she certainly has many talents." Mariah stirred the gravy. "She's as comfortable on horseback as most people are in a rocking chair."

"Carrie kin ride all right." Mac deftly transferred the roasted goose from pan to platter. "You oughta see her at the roundup."

Mac cast a speculative look in Mariah's direction. "I jist had me an idee. Why don't you come with us on the spring roundup?"

"Oh, my! I couldn't do that." Mariah poured the gravy into a large gravy boat. "I have school. Then there's Hope. Besides, horses make me nervous and cows frighten me. What would I do on a roundup?"

"Help me with the cookin'." Mac put a gnarled hand to the small of his back. "My rheumatiz is actin' up. You know I ain't as young as I once was, an' feedin' thet crew is a lot of work. I sure could use yore help, Mariah."

"I would like to help, Mac. But there's school and—"

"School will be out jist afore roundup," Mac said. "And Hope kin come right along with you. The two of you kin ride out with me in the chuck wagon. You kin sleep in the wagon, too. Carrie done it ever since she weren't no bigger than Hope."

"I don't know, Mac. It would be an adventure. But there are other considerations besides school and Hope."

"You think on it, Mariah. You got plenty of time to decide. It ain't 'til April."

Mariah promised Mac she would let him know as soon as she arrived at a decision. Then Carrie came back to the kitchen, and she didn't think about the roundup again that day.

Later, gathered in the living room in front of a blazing fire, Mariah gave Carrie and each of the men a small, beautifully wrapped package. The four men immediately ripped the paper from their gifts.

Sherman, Lucas, and Cyrus were so lavish in their praise of the woolen socks that Mariah blushed. Only Mac remained silent. He examined the heavy brown socks for so long Mariah was afraid he didn't like them. She was on the verge of apologizing for her poor choice of gifts when he cleared his throat and looked up.

"Well, would you looka here! Wool socks. Did you knit these yerself, Mariah?"

Mariah nodded. "It's a small token of my affection."

"I ain't had a pair of hand-knitted socks since the war." Mac pulled a red bandanna from his hip pocket and blew his nose. "My Emily knit socks fer me afore I went away."

A wave of remorse swept over Mariah. Without thinking, she rose from the couch where she was sitting with Hope and Sherman. Two steps and she dropped to her knees beside Mac's chair. "I'm sorry. It wasn't my intention to bring back sad memories. I recall Mrs. Dodd—she was one of the older members of Father's flock—talking about sending her husband wool socks when he was in the war. I should have known your wife knit socks for you." Mariah put her arms around the old man she had come to regard as a dear friend. "Please forgive my foolishness."

"My memories of Emily an' my little boy ain't sad ones, Mariah. You know thet. I'm mighty proud of these socks." Mac patted the arm that encircled him. "Now you go back an' set with Sherman an' yer little girl."

Mariah had an urge to kiss Mac's bristly cheek, but she wasn't quite brave enough, so she gave him a hug and returned to the couch. Sherman's big hand squeezed her shoulder. Mariah looked over Hope's head and into his clear, blue eyes. He had told her twice that he loved her, but the tenderness reflected in his eyes spoke more eloquently of the depth of his feelings than words ever could. With all the strength she could muster, Mariah turned her head.

Seated on the couch across from them beside Lucas, Carrie was staring at her. Mariah would have expected to see hatred, or even the usual disdain on the young woman's face. What she saw was pain so deep it tore at her heart. The young woman's gaze moved to her father, and the expression deepened to heart-wrenching agony.

"Aren't you goin' to open your gift, Caroline?" Carrie had put the small package aside when Mariah handed it to her. When she showed no indication that she intended to unwrap it, Lucas nudged her gently with his elbow. "Come on, darlin', let's see what Miss Casey gave you."

For a heartbeat Mariah thought the younger girl was going to refuse. Then, her movements lackadaisical, Carrie removed the wrapping and looked down at the delicately embroidered, hem-stitched set of linen collar and cuffs. Tears welled up in her eyes. "Please! I need a drink of water. Don't wait for me."

She handed the package to her husband and fled the room.

"I'd reckon I'd better go see about her," Lucas said.

"No, I'll go." Sherman patted Mariah's shoulder. "We won't be long."

Sherman found Carrie sitting at the kitchen table, her head down, a full glass of water in front of her. "Caroline Abigail, you owe Miss Casey an apology," he said without preamble. "I want you to march right back in there and thank her, and I want you to apologize for your rudeness."

"How could you, Papa?" Carrie raised a tearstained face to him. "I saw the way you looked at that woman. How could you do that to Mama?"

Confronted with the evidence of her misery, Sherman's anger fled. "I'm not doing anything to your mama, little girl." He pulled out a chair and sat down beside her. "I love Mariah, Carrie."

"You told me no one would ever take Mama's place." Carrie's tear-filled brown eyes accused him. "You lied to me, Papa."

"I didn't lie to you, little girl. Mariah isn't taking your mama's place; she has a place of her own." Sherman placed his hand over Carrie's clenched fist. "I have asked Mariah to be my wife."

Carrie pulled her hand from under his. A sob tore from her throat. "How do you think Mama would feel knowing you were marrying another woman?"

"Your mother would be happy for me. It's your behavior that would shame her." Suddenly Sherman saw what had been right in front of him all the time. The reason Mariah wouldn't marry him was sitting at the table beside him. He sprang to his feet and loomed over the child he cherished more than his own life.

"I know you and Mariah got off on the wrong foot, but you have never given her a chance. You have been rude and hateful to her from the beginning."

"*I've* been rude!" Carrie's temper flared. "I told you how she behaved that day at school. Demanding a key, telling me the room was improperly organized, saying she didn't get involved with her students. Besides that she jumped all over me because I was late."

"Well, you were late," Sherman retorted. "As for the key, Mariah didn't come from a small place like Cedar Bend where people can be trusted. And she is an experienced teacher, Carrie. She knows how a classroom should be arranged. I have no idea why she said she didn't get involved with her pupils. She spends hours working with the children. She is fond of them, and they all seem to love her. You know that."

"She's pretending to be different." Carrie pushed her chair back and stood to face her father. "And now I know why."

"What exactly is that supposed to mean?"

"She's just trying to snag you. I'll bet she couldn't say yes fast enough when you asked her to marry you."

All the anger drained out of Sherman as quickly as it had come. "She didn't say yes, Carrie."

The astonished expression on Carrie's face would have been amusing if the circumstances had been different. "She didn't say anything. I promised her time to think about it."

"Why wouldn't she say yes?" Carrie frowned. "There must be a reason."

"Yes, there must be," Sherman agreed. "Why don't you think about it, little girl, and see if you can figure out why Mariah would reject my proposal?" He put an arm around her and drew her close. "Honey, all I ask is that you give Mariah a chance. All right?"

"All right." Carrie buried her face against his shirt. "I will for you, Papa."

Sherman pushed her gently from him. "Wash your face, and as soon as you feel able come back to the living room." He turned at the door. "And, Carrie, it would be nice if you thanked Mariah for the gift."

Mariah looked up from where she was sitting on the couch with Sherman and Hope when Carrie rejoined them. Sitting down beside Lucas, Carrie picked up the discarded gift. After carefully examining the delicate embroidery and neat hemstitching, she lifted her head, and her gaze shifted from her father to Mariah.

"Thank you, Miss Casey." Her eyes were swollen and red, her voice little more than a whisper. "You must have spent hours on these."

"You are welcome, Carrie." Mariah's heart ached for the young woman. "I enjoyed making them for you."

That evening, on the way home, Mariah and Hope nestled under a buffalo skin robe. With the moon reflecting off the thick blanket of snow it was as light as midafternoon. The first mile or so Hope chattered about her gifts, then clutching the rag doll Mariah made for her—the doll she had named Jake for some inexplicable reason—she fell asleep. Silence as deep as the night that surrounded them enveloped the sleigh.

Mariah didn't object when Sherman carried Hope into her bedroom and laid her on her bed. While he went outside to finish unloading the sleigh, Mariah pulled the covers snugly around the little girl and the doll she refused to relinquish even in sleep. After she kissed Hope good night and whispered a prayer over her, Mariah, still wearing her coat, went into the parlor. Sherman was building a fire in the parlor stove.

She watched him close the stove door and adjust the damper. He had never been in her home before. She saw the room as she imagined he must see it. The needlepoint, the crocheted antimacassars and doilies, the hooked rugs. All the fussy, meaningless froufrou she had created on thousands of empty evenings. And she saw how he filled her parlor with his presence.

Mariah's house was pretty much as Sherman had imagined it. Spotlessly clean and feminine, but homey. Hope's books were scattered about. A small stocking was draped over the arm of a chair. A large, black Bible lay open on a chair-side table. He turned away from the stove. Mariah was standing in the doorway. The soft lamplight shadowed her face, but her luminous blue eyes spoke to him.

He cleared his throat. "I've got your fire going."

Her gaze shifted, then came back to rest on his face. "Thank you."

"I put Hope's things over there." He gestured to the corner. "I wasn't sure where you would want them."

"That's fine." Mariah looked at the small rocking chair, the wire-wheeled wagon, and an assortment of smaller gifts. "Everyone was so generous. I know this is a Christmas Hope will never forget." A slight smile touched the corners of her mouth. "Don't you think the horse was a bit extravagant, Mr. Butler?"

"Nope." Sherman chuckled. "Did you see the expression on her face when we took her out to the corral, and she saw Tornado with that big red bow tied around her neck? She hugged me so tight she liked to choke me."

"She's a very exuberant child." Mariah crossed the room and plucked the stocking from the chair arm. "She is also messy."

Sherman took the stocking from her hand and tossed it into the chair. "Mariah, I have something for you." He put his hand in his pocket and drew out a small, velvet bag with a drawstring. "I didn't want to give this to you in front of everyone."

"Oh, Mr. Butler, I can't—" Mariah ran her palms down the sides of her coat.

"I want you to know that I love you more today than I did yesterday, and I reckon I'll probably love you more tomorrow than I do today." He turned the small bag around in his big hand. "Anyway, I'm not going to ask you to marry me again. I reckon once is enough for that."

Mariah clasped her hands together. "I don't know what to say."

"I know you don't. That's why I'm giving you until after the roundup to give me your answer." He took her hand in his. "I want you to take this. When you make up your mind, if the answer is yes, put it on your finger. That way, I'll know."

He placed the bag in her hand and closed her fingers around it. Leaning down he brushed her lips with a light but fervent kiss. Then he left the warmth of the house, but the warmth in his heart remained with him all the way home.

Chapter 17

In mid-February, a blizzard raced across the Kansas prairie dumping two feet of snow and forcing the cancellation of school. Mariah and Hope were housebound for two weeks. Mariah spent most of the time praying and reading her Bible.

One night, while Hope slept, she clutched the small, black velvet bag that contained the fulfillment of all her dreams as she read from the black, leather-bound book. She turned to the verse that had come to mean so much to her. *"For I know the thoughts that I think toward you, saith the Lord, thoughts of peace, and not of evil, to give you an expected end."*

Mariah reflected over the past few weeks. She and Hope had spent the first day of 1894 at the Circle C. The Nolans were there, too. Mariah had accepted Mac's invitation to join them on the roundup. When Mac shared the news with everyone else, Carrie looked crestfallen.

After New Year's Day, Lucas and Carrie were always at the ranch for Sunday dinners. Occasionally Mariah would catch Carrie watching her with pain-filled eyes. At those times, Mariah's heart ached for the young woman. God in His infinite mercy and boundless love had given Mariah much more than she had ever dreamed possible. Hope would be enough. As much as she loved Sherman Butler, and she did love him, she would not come between Carrie and her father. Kneeling beside her chair, she thanked God for Hope. Then, with tears streaming down her face, she released the only man she had ever loved. She arose, and with a new determination, she sat at the small writing desk in her parlor and penned a short letter to the principal of her old school in Ohio.

Two days later, after some of the snow had melted, Joanna came to visit. Sitting in Mariah's kitchen with teacups in hand and a full plate of sugar cookies between them, they caught up on the last two weeks.

"Not much happened." Joanna took a second cookie. "You make the best cookies in the state of Kansas. Anyway, as I was saying, not much happened, so I did a lot of thinking. You know what we need in Cedar Bend, Mariah? A library."

"A library?"

"Mmm-hmm. I think we should start a library." Joanna brushed cookie crumbs from her fingers. "So what do you think?"

"I think it's a wonderful idea." Mariah thought of the small library at school. "What books we have at school are excellent, but there are so few of them. Mark has already read everything."

"That's one reason I thought of a library. I've loaned Mark almost every book we own. The only ones left are Daddy's medical books." She took another cookie. "Mariah, would you please put those away before I eat the whole plateful? Anyway, learning to read has opened a whole new world for him. Can you believe he's halfway through the Old Testament?"

"Mark is a very bright young man," Mariah commented as she transferred cookies from the plate to a cookie jar. She put the lid on and got up to place the jar on the counter. Sitting back down across from Joanna, she smiled. "I hear he's sweet on you."

"Sweet? On me?" Joanna's rosy cheeks flushed a shade darker. "Whoever told you that?"

"A certain little pitcher with big ears."

"And an even bigger mouth!" Joanna exclaimed. "I told you when she started talking we would have to be careful what we said around her."

"It seems Mark's little sister told her that he is really sweet on you." Mariah grinned. "Mr. Butler says he has noticed a special gleam in Mark's eye when he looks at you."

"I guess Mr. Butler would recognize that gleam if anybody would," Joanna teased. "Daddy says he wishes you would marry the poor man and put him out of his misery."

Mariah's face flared bright red. She returned to their original subject before Joanna had a chance to say more. "About this library. Where would we put it?"

"I'm not sure." Joanna's expression was thoughtful. "We need a building, and that will take money. Then we'll need to buy books. I thought you might have some ideas. You are going to help me with this, aren't you?"

"I would like to, but I'm not sure I'll be able to be of much assistance." Mariah folded her hands on the table. "I may not be here after this school year ends."

"Oh, Mariah, why not? I thought you would marry Mr. Butler and stay in Cedar Bend forever."

"I would like to stay, but I'm not sure I'll be able to." She felt two tears slide down her cheeks.

Joanna's brown eyes brimmed. "Tell me about it."

Mariah told the younger woman everything, concluding with her struggles of the last week. "I love him with all my heart, Joanna, but I can't marry him. I can't build a life with Sherman on the ashes of Carrie's unhappiness. Yesterday I wrote to the principal of my old school and asked if they have an opening. If I receive a favorable reply from him I will take Hope and move back to Ohio."

"You can't go back, Mariah." Joanna dabbed at her tears with a napkin. "You have no friends in Ohio."

"But I will have," Mariah said with a confidence she didn't completely feel.

"But they won't love you like we do."

"My dear friend, before I came to Kansas I didn't know what love was."

"But you do now."

"Yes, I do." Mariah covered Joanna's hand with hers. "From you I have learned the love of a friend. With Gladys and her family I have experienced the love of family. With Hope I have come to understand one of the most precious loves of all, the love of a mother for her child. And, with Sherman, I have been allowed a glimpse of the love between a man and a woman. I wouldn't take anything for the time I have spent here, Joanna."

"You can't leave, Mariah," Joanna protested tearfully. "You have so many friends in Cedar Bend. Your students adore you. Mark thinks you are the most wonderful teacher on the face of the earth. You have no one in Ohio."

"Joanna, there is a verse in Jeremiah that says God has our future planned. I read that verse the morning I received the offer of the teaching position here. It didn't mean anything to me then, but now it does. I know God brought me here, and if it is His will I go back to Ohio, then I know He must have a reason." She squeezed Joanna's hand before releasing it. "Now, let's dry our tears and start planning your library."

A half hour later, when Hope wandered into the kitchen clutching Jake in one arm and looking for a snack, Mariah and Joanna were busy making lists. The little girl climbed up on Mariah's lap and shared her cookie with the doll.

Mariah and Joanna took their plans for a library to Gladys Jacobs a few days later. Under her able guidance, the project began to take shape as winter neared to a close.

One morning Mariah spotted a fat robin in her front yard. Spring had finally arrived. The days passed quickly as Mariah tried not to dwell on her impending move back to Ohio. Before she knew it, April arrived.

The school year ended with a graduation ceremony for Mark Hopkins, Jay Braun, and Fred Carson. Since the school was too small to accommodate the crowd that was expected to attend, closing exercises were held in the church.

With Mabel Carson at the piano, the students of Miss Mariah Casey stood at the front of the room and sang "Battle Hymn of the Republic." At the conclusion of the song, Dr. Tom Brady gave a short speech praising the accomplishments of the three young men. Then Sherman Butler, acting as school board president, handed out their diplomas. When he shook the hands of Jay and Fred and congratulated them, the applause was long and loud. Then Mark walked up, and the crowd rose to their feet to give the young man a thunderous ovation.

Sherman raised his hands, and the roar gradually died out as the crowd sat down.

"We are proud of what all three of these young men have accomplished," Sherman said. "They all received high marks in all subjects this year. The other young men have elected Mark Hopkins to speak in their behalf."

As the young man stood in front of the crowd, Mariah's heart swelled with pride. Six months ago when Mark walked into her classroom, he knew his alphabet but little else. He had completed eight grades in one school year, an almost unbelievable accomplishment.

"From the time I was a little shaver it was my dream to learn to read," he said. "After the crops were planted last spring, Pop took me aside and told me he wanted me to go to school. For many years I had prayed for this day. Now that the time had come, I knew it was impossible. Like Moses I could look into the Promised Land, but I couldn't enter. Do you know what stood in my way?" The young man laughed. "Pride, folks. It didn't overly bother me that I would be sitting at a table beside my six-year-old sister. But I could not abide the thought of someone I had known all my life—someone younger than myself—teaching me to read."

His gaze settled on Carrie. "I know you were a fine teacher, Carrie. But I was mighty happy when Lucas took you out of the schoolroom." Laughter rippled through the crowd. "Carrie and I have been friends for years." Mark smiled. "I hope we always will be."

Carrie nodded an affirmation before Mark continued. "Jeremiah 29:11 says, 'For I know the thoughts that I think toward you, saith the Lord, thoughts of peace, and not of evil, to give you an expected end.' That verse is certainly true. Last September, God answered my prayers and sent me a miracle. When I saw Miss Casey at the dinner the town held to welcome her to Cedar Bend, I knew she would be the one to teach me to read. And I was right. I couldn't even tell you how many recesses and lunch breaks she gave up to teach me to read and write.

"Today I want to thank three very special people who made it possible for me to realize my dream. Mom and Pop, thank you for making the sacrifices and sending me to school.

"Miss Casey, on behalf of Fred and Jay, I want to thank you for the time you devoted to the three of us. You make learning an adventure. Would you please say a few words?"

Mariah rose and moved to stand beside Mark. The crowd erupted in applause. She waited patiently until the room grew still before attempting to speak. "For eighteen years I taught second graders. Facing a roomful of children of varying ages was an overwhelming experience. I didn't know how I would ever teach such a diversified group.

"I want you all to know that this last school year has been the most rewarding of my career. You have wonderful children. I have come to love every one of them. Teaching these young people has been a delight." Knowing this was the last time she would stand before the people she had come to love, Mariah ended abruptly. "I wish to thank you all for being here today to honor these three young men."

She returned to her seat. Pastor Carson offered the closing prayer. The congregation sang "God Be with You." The program was over.

Mariah was immediately surrounded by her students and their parents. After the crowd thinned out, Joanna hugged her and whispered, "You are leaving?"

Mariah blinked back tears and nodded. "I got a letter from Principal Sterns yesterday."

"Have you told Mr. Butler?"

"No, not yet. I thought I would after the roundup."

Tears welled up in Joanna's brown eyes. "Don't go. Please, Mariah, don't go."

Neither one of the women knew Sherman was there until he spoke. "Don't go where?"

They both looked up at the tall rancher. "Nowhere," Mariah said. "We were talking about the roundup, and one thing and another."

"I see." He put his arm around Mariah's shoulders and gave her a brief hug. "I'm proud of you, Miss Casey."

"Thank you, Mr. Butler." Mariah managed a shaky smile. "Your approval means more to me than you will ever know."

Hope chose that moment to run up and fling her arms around Mariah's legs. "Mama, Miss Carrie says when she was a little girl like me she wore overnalls on the roundup. Can I have overnalls? Pul-eeze, Mama."

Mariah glanced at Carrie standing behind Hope, then smiled down into the little girl's upturned face. "I made you some divided skirts. Remember?"

"But I wants overnalls." Hope released Mariah and grasped Carrie's hand. "I wants to be a cowboy like Miss Carrie."

Mariah sighed. "If Harris's has overalls your size, I'll buy you a couple of pairs. All right?"

"Thank you, Mama." Hope flung her arms around Mariah. "I gots to tell L. K. and Julie I gets overnalls."

Mariah watched her daughter run off to join her friends.

"She's an adorable little girl," Carrie said. "You have done wonders with her, Miss Casey."

"Thank you, Mrs. Nolan."

"Since we are going to be spending the next week together, don't you think you should call me Carrie?"

"Yes, I would like that." Mariah hesitated for a heartbeat. "If you will call me Mariah."

"I have to go. Lucas is waiting for me." Carrie smiled. "I'll see you bright and early in the morning, Mariah."

"Yes. Good afternoon, Carrie."

Carrie actually smiled at her! Could Sherman's daughter actually be accepting her? Mariah turned to share this small victory with Sherman and found he and Joanna had both wandered away while she was talking to Carrie. Well, never mind. She couldn't allow her thoughts to stray in that direction anyway. She had already made up her mind to leave Cedar Bend. Right now she had to collect her daughter and go to the mercantile. Hope needed *overnalls*.

Chapter 18

The night before the spring roundup, Mariah and Hope slept in Carrie's old bedroom at the Circle C. It was still dark outside when Mariah rose and dressed. With Hope still sound asleep, she joined Mac in the kitchen. After a hastily prepared and eaten breakfast, she went back to the bedroom. Hope barely stirred when she scooped her and Jake up and carried them to the chuck wagon she and Mac had stocked the previous day.

As soon as Hope was settled on the bed inside the wagon, Sherman assisted Mariah onto the high seat beside Mac. "You look mighty fetchin' this morning, Miss Casey." His lips brushed against her ear.

Mariah blushed. She still felt uncomfortable in the divided skirt Joanna had insisted she make for the roundup. "Thank you, Mr. Butler."

Cyrus and the other men rode on ahead, while Sherman, Lucas, and Carrie rode beside the chuck wagon for a while. Then, tiring of the slow pace, they, too, rode on. Mariah hadn't slept well, and sitting beside Mac as they jostled and creaked across the prairie, she fought to keep her eyes open.

"Don't go, Mariah." Mac's sudden outburst jerked Mariah awake. The little man and Joanna were the only ones Mariah had told of her plans to leave Cedar Bend. "Sherm needs you."

"Mac, we've discussed this before." Mariah blinked back tears. "You know how I feel."

"Whut about how Sherm feels? He loves you, Mariah. Why, his face jist plum lights up when he looks at you. I ain't never seen him as happy as he has been these last few months."

"Please, Mac, there is no need to discuss this further. Didn't you tell me what can't be cured must be endured? That's what I'm trying to do, endure. Please help me to get through this."

Mac grumbled a bit under his breath, but the remainder of the trip passed in silence.

———————

The eastern sky was a symphony of pink and gold when Mariah and Hope set out with a bushel basket to collect cow chips.

Hope wrinkled her nose when Mariah bent to pick up the first dried chip in a gloved hand. "Pew-eee! You know what them things is, Mama?"

"They are fuel for our fire." Mariah added a second chip to the one in the basket.

"Uh-uh. Them is not fool. You know where them things come from?"

"Hope, where they came from is not important. People living on the prairie had to adapt. The brave pioneers who settled our land used what was at hand in order to survive. Why don't we pretend we're pioneers?"

"Uh-uh." Hope had insisted on having her hair braided like Carrie's. When she shook her head, the single, long braid switched back and forth. "I don't want to be no pie-neer. Does you want to be a pie-neer, Jake?" She consulted the doll clutched in the crook of her right arm. "Jake don't want to be no pie-neer neither. Me an' Jake wants to be cowboys like Miss Carrie."

"We'll see." Mariah picked up the basket, which was now full. "Let's go back to camp. Mac needs our help."

Hope trudged along at her side. "Mama, when Mistah Butlah is my daddy, he'll let me an' Jake be cowboys."

Mariah glanced down at the little girl. How was she going to tell Hope that Mr. Butler would never be her daddy? A month after the roundup they would be in Ohio. All the people they loved would be left behind in Cedar Bend. How could Hope—how could she—go on without Sherman and Mac and Joanna? And what of her family? What would she do without Gladys? And Carrie? Hope adored Carrie. *What can't be cured must be endured.* How, oh how, were they ever going to endure being separated from everyone they loved?

Every day Mac and Mariah loaded up and moved the chuck wagon to a new location. The roundup was noisy and dirty. The milling of hundreds of cows and horses kept an almost constant dust cloud rising over the camp. At night Mariah tumbled into the bed in the chuck wagon beside Hope, so tired she barely had strength to pull off her boots. At four o'clock in the morning, she forced herself from bed to begin all over.

The third morning they were out, Mariah stood behind a long table helping Mac serve breakfast. When she handed Carrie her plate, the young woman turned chalk white. Clapping a hand over her mouth, she stumbled away from the table, with Lucas close on her heels. That morning Carrie stayed in camp with Mac and Mariah. By the time the men brought in the first catch, she seemed to have recovered enough to go out and round up strays.

The same thing happened the following two mornings. After lunch, Carrie rode out with Lucas. Hope was taking the afternoon nap her mother insisted on, and Mac and Mariah were preparing for the final move of the roundup.

"I am concerned about Carrie," Mariah said. "She is so sick in the morning. I don't think she should be out in the afternoon in all that dust and heat."

"She probably ort not," Mac agreed. "But I wouldn't worry too much 'bout the little lady."

"She's so sick, Mac."

"I seen this sickness afore." Mac grinned. "Ain't nothin' time won't take keer of."

"You don't think what she has is contagious, do you?"

"I don't reckon so." The little man chuckled. "I'd reckon in 'bout seven months er so the little lady is gonna be a ma."

"You mean Carrie is—oh, my!" Mariah blushed bright crimson. "Carrie is with child? Oh, Mac! How wonderful! Do you think she knows?"

"I'd reckon not. If she did, she wouldn't be lookin' so woebegone."

"Maybe you should tell her." Mariah shook her head. "No, that wouldn't be proper. Somebody should tell her."

"I'd reckon she'll figure it out in due time."

The next morning, Mariah saw that Carrie was sick, again. After helping serve the noontime meal, she moped around camp instead of going out with the men to round up the last of the strays. While Mariah and Mac washed the last of the tin pie plates, she sat on a low stool, watching them.

Mariah excused herself to put Hope down for a nap inside the chuck wagon. When she rejoined Mac and Carrie, they were deep in a conversation that ceased as soon as they saw her. Mariah expelled a deep breath as she sat down for some much-needed rest before beginning supper preparations. "I have never worked so hard in my life."

Mac smiled. "You've did a fine job, Mariah."

"Mariah, would you like to go down to the creek with me?" Carrie asked. "We could take a bath while the men are gone."

"My hair feels like it has ten pounds of dirt in it." Mariah ran a hand over the coronet of braids that encircled her head. "But I don't want to wake Hope. She is a regular little bear if she doesn't have her nap."

"I'll watch Hope," Mac offered. "You go on with the little lady."

Mariah put up only a token argument before going to collect a towel, a blanket, a bar of scented soap, and a change of clothes.

On the banks of the shallow creek, the two women stripped down to their sleeveless, knee-length, cotton-knit union suits and walked into the water. After they bathed and washed their hair, they waded to shore. Concealed by the blankets, they changed to fresh underwear, then dressed. After spreading the blankets in the sun, they sat down to dry their hair. Fortunately, Carrie had remembered to bring a hairbrush.

"I have been trying to get up the courage to talk to you." Carrie turned to face Mariah, the sun glinting red-gold off her damp hair. Tears sparkled in her dark eyes. "I have been so rude to you, Mariah. Can you ever forgive me?"

"Oh, Carrie! There is nothing to forgive. I'm the one who should be begging forgiveness. I was so hateful when I came to Cedar Bend. The first time I saw you I thought you were so beautiful. You reminded me of my—of someone I once knew." Tears welled up in Mariah's own eyes, and she hastily blinked them away. "I could make all manner of excuses, but I won't. My behavior was inexcusable."

"You are such a good teacher. Everyone was always bragging on you. I was so jealous." Carrie sniffled. "It all seems so unimportant now."

"I've been a teacher for many years, Carrie. After only one year, you couldn't expect to know everything it took me eighteen years to learn."

"I know." Carrie wiped the tears away with her fingertips. "I couldn't stand it when I saw that Papa was falling in love with you. I thought he was being unfaithful to Mama."

Mariah took a deep breath. "I would never do anything to come between you and your father, Carrie. Surely you know that."

"You love my papa, don't you?"

"Yes, I do. Very much."

Two drops of liquid crystal rolled down Carrie's cheeks. "Mac told me you were going back to Ohio. Is that true?"

Mariah glanced down before raising her head and looking directly into Carrie's tear-filled eyes. "Hope and I will be leaving shortly after the roundup ends."

"Don't go, Mariah." Carrie threw both arms around the older woman. "Please stay. Papa loves you so much." She burrowed her head into Mariah's shoulder.

Mariah put her arms around Carrie and held the young woman close while she sobbed. "I have never been sick in my life. Never." The words came amid heartrending sobs. "I'm so sick. I know I'm going to die. I don't want to leave Lucas and Papa and everybody else, Mariah. But I know I'm going to have to. After I'm gone Papa is going to need you."

Mariah held Carrie and patted her back until the sobs became occasional hiccupy shudders, then died away. The young woman pulled away and wiped at her eyes with the backs of her hands. "I'm trying to not be afraid, but I can't help but be. Mama died young. I remember how sick she was. I think I may have the same illness."

"Carrie, listen to me! You aren't going to die." She took the young woman's hand in hers. "If what Mac suspects is true, your illness isn't about death. It's about life."

"Life?"

"Life." Mariah smiled and squeezed the younger woman's hand. "A new life. Mac believes you display all the symptoms of being with child."

"With child?" A glorious smile lit Carrie's face. "I'm going to have a baby! Lucas and I are going to have a baby! Of course. I remember how sick Lucille was. And Gretchen says she thought she was going to die for a month or so. Oh, Mariah!"

"Carrie, I won't be here when the baby's born, but will you write and let me know about him?"

"Won't be here?" Carrie turned a wide-eyed gaze on the older woman. "What do you mean you won't be here? Aren't you going to marry Papa?"

Mariah picked at her skirt. "I told you I wouldn't come between you and your father. Now that you know you aren't dying—well, I thought—"

"The selfish little brat that said all those terrible things to you deserves to lose you, Mariah. But not my baby. He needs a grandmother. And not Papa. Papa needs a wife. I need you, too, Mariah. Please say you will stay and be my baby's grandma and Papa's wife and my friend. I want you with me when my baby is born, Mariah. Please say yes. Please say you will stay here with us."

"For I know the thoughts I have for you, saith the Lord." Drops of saltwater fell on Mariah's hands. Tears of joy. "Yes," she said, looking into Carrie's dark eyes. "Yes, Carrie, I will stay."

That evening after supper the cowhands gathered around to sing and swap tall tales. Mariah left Carrie to watch Hope. Then she asked Sherman to go for a walk with her. As they wandered along the banks of the creek, he took her hand in his.

"Have you made a decision, Mariah?"

"Yes, I have." Inside the pocket of her skirt Mariah ran her thumb around the band of gold that encircled her finger.

They stopped walking. Sherman put his fingers under her chin, lifting her face until their eyes met. "Will you be my wife, Mariah?"

Mariah withdrew her left hand from her pocket and held it up. A moonbeam glanced off the diamond on her finger.

"Ya-hoo!" Sherman hugged her so tight she thought her ribs might crack. A shower of kisses rained down on her face before his lips met hers. She clung to him and returned his kisses with all the love in her heart.

When they walked into camp hand in hand, Mac smiled. "Wal, have you got somethin' you want to tell us?" the little man asked.

"I have an announcement to make." Sherman grinned and put his arm around the woman at his side. "Miss Mariah Casey has finally agreed to be my wife. The wedding will be Sunday afternoon, May 14, at the Community Church. You are all invited."

The men gathered round laughing and congratulating Sherman. Carrie hugged her father, then put her arms around Mariah. Hope tugged on Sherman's pant leg. He lifted the little girl into his arms.

"Are you gonna be my daddy?" she asked.

"I sure am."

"Good." Hope planted a wet kiss on his cheek. "Can I be a cowboy?" She batted her big blue eyes. "Pul-eeze, Daddy?"

Epilogue

W hite satin?" Mariah laughed. It seemed she laughed a lot these days. "Don't you think I'm a bit old for white satin?"

"There is no reason you shouldn't wear white, Mariah." Carrie shook her head firmly as if to emphasize the words.

"I think you will be beautiful in white." Joanna wrote on the pad of paper as if the matter was settled. "White satin. All right." She looked around Mariah's kitchen table at the other three women gathered to help plan Mariah and Sherman's wedding. "What else shall we put on our list?"

"A veil," Lucille said. "You need a veil, Cousin Mariah."

"Really, girls! Veils are for young brides. If I agree to the white satin, will you agree to a simple hat?"

The three young women looked at her; then Carrie said, "I have a wonderful idea. You can wear my veil. I wore Mama's wedding dress, but my veil was my something new. It can be your something borrowed."

"Perfect," Joanna exclaimed. She made a note on the pad of paper. "Now, what about flowers for the bridal bouquet?"

Mariah sat down with a soft plop in the chair behind her. She let her gaze linger on each girl before her and smiled as they continued to chatter, making plans for her wedding without her input. Hope wandered into the kitchen and stopped beside Mariah's chair. As she leaned against her, Mariah slipped an arm around her and drew her close. *For I know the thoughts that I think toward you, saith the Lord, thoughts of peace, and not of evil, to give you an expected end.*

———

Mariah walked down the aisle with slow, measured steps behind Hope. Her daughter dropped rose petals with precision, keeping her head bent to the task. Mariah lifted her gaze to the front where Sherman stood waiting, tall and handsome. Her breath caught in her throat as her old insecurities tried to gain a hold. Then she saw the love-light in his eyes as he met and held her gaze with his and knew that for whatever reason, Sherman Butler loved her as much as she loved him.

When he took her hand in his, Hope stepped to the front pew and sat down. Mariah smiled at her beaming face, then turned with her hand sheltered in

Sherman's to take the vows that would forever bind them together.

"You may kiss the bride." Sherman enclosed Mariah in his arms and claimed her lips under his. When he lifted his head, his smile was wide as his arm kept her close to his side.

"May I introduce to you, Mr. and Mrs. Sherman Butler." The minister's joyous words brought smiles and laughter as the congregation stood and Hope joined her parents.

With Hope leading the way, Mariah walked beside her husband past their friends and family while Carrie and Lucas followed. In less than a year she had gone from a friendless, bitter woman to a bride with more friends than she could count.

The dearest man on earth loved her. She had two beautiful daughters and a wonderful son-in-law. In a few months she would become a grandmother. *"For I know the thoughts that I think toward you, saith the Lord, thoughts of peace, and not of evil, to give you an expected end."* What a wonderful God she served! Mariah's soft laughter brought a smile from her new husband.

JOANNA'S ADVENTURE

Dedication

In memory of my sister, Jean Norval, who encouraged me to never stop writing.

Chapter 1

Cedar Bend, Kansas, May 14, 1894

I, Mariah Casey, take thee, Sherman Butler, to be my lawfully wedded husband."

Joanna Brady blinked back tears as she stood beside the bride in Cedar Bend Community Church and listened to her friend repeat the vows that joined her life to Sherman Butler, one of the richest cattle ranchers in western Kansas. At first Mariah had argued that at thirty-seven she was too old for a traditional church wedding with all the trimmings. Joanna and Carrie Nolan, Sherman's married daughter, finally persuaded her otherwise. Joanna smiled through her tears, glad that Mariah had agreed at last. She looked radiant in white satin.

"Are we married yet?" asked Hope, Mariah's young daughter who sat between Lucas and Carrie Nolan in the front pew, her voice carrying across the church.

Carrie put a finger across the four-year-old's lips and shook her head. "Not yet," she whispered.

Hope squirmed in the seat before she sighed deeply. Joanna suppressed a giggle. In the few short months Hope had lived with Mariah, she had changed from a mute, frightened little girl into an exuberant, headstrong chatterbox. Joanna could not imagine what had moved Felicia Wainwright to give her unwanted orphaned niece to Cedar Bend's schoolteacher, but she thanked God every day that she had done so. Mariah and Hope were destined to be together just as Sherman and Mariah were meant for each other.

"I will love, honor, and obey you as long as we both shall live."

Mark Hopkins, sitting across the church from the Nolans, caught Joanna's gaze and smiled. She returned his smile, hoping he didn't read more into it than she intended. She loved Mark. Had for as long as she could remember. But she was not in love with him. He was comfortable to be with. There were no surprises with Mark. No excitement. No romance. He bore no resemblance to the heroes in the romance novels she read. Mark was too predictable for that. Joanna's entire life had been comfortable and predictable. And boring. Like a parched flower thirsting for water, Joanna craved excitement and romance.

"Sherman, you may kiss your bride."

Joanna watched as Mr. Butler lifted the veil from Mariah's beaming face and kissed her with love and reverence. Joanna sighed while time rolled backward in her mind.

Seven years ago, at thirteen, Joanna hadn't thought much about boys—until Clay Shepherd walked into the one-room schoolhouse and took a seat in the last row. Like most of the girls in eighth grade, Joanna couldn't help noticing the older boy's dark good looks.

With glistening black hair and olive skin setting off his pale blue eyes, he had only to lift the corners of his mouth, and the girls fell over themselves trying to get his attention. Except for Carrie Butler. She said he had a wild streak a mile wide.

Joanna didn't listen to Carrie. Oh, she didn't follow Clay around like some of the girls, but she spent a fair share of time daydreaming, fitting him into the plot of her life as her hero. He did odd jobs for her doctor father and listened politely when her mother talked to him, giving motherly advice, so she saw him often, yet he never paid much attention to her. That's probably why he took her by surprise at the Christmas play rehearsal.

She still remembered arriving early at the schoolhouse only to find no one there yet. She started to leave when Clay stepped through the door. His quick grin when his gaze darted to the mistletoe hanging above her head then back to her face had her heart pounding. Before she fully understood his intentions, he grabbed her upper arms and pulled her toward him. His grin disappeared as he closed the remaining few inches to place a kiss on her upturned lips.

He'd laughed then and said, "That's what you get, Joanna, for standing under the mistletoe."

She had been so shocked she could only stare at him in silence. But she had never forgotten her one and only kiss.

"Are we married now, Carrie?" Hope's loud whisper brought Joanna back to the present. She turned to look at the little girl.

"Yes." Carrie kissed Hope's rosy cheek. "We are married, little sister."

An hour and a half later in the back room of the Cattlemen's Association Hall, Carrie and Joanna helped Mariah change into a buttercup-colored suit.

"I probably should have chosen a more conservative color," Mariah fretted. "The stagecoach is so dusty."

"Not this time of year," Carrie reassured her.

"With last night's rain you shouldn't have a thing to worry about." Joanna set a small matching yellow hat atop Mariah's elaborately arranged ebony curls.

"You are a beautiful bride, Mariah."

"Thank you." Mariah's cheeks flushed a becoming pink. "Carrie, are you sure you'll be all right with Hope?"

"We'll be fine." Carrie hugged her new stepmother. "Don't you waste one minute of your wedding trip worrying about Hope. I always wanted a sister. We are going to have so much fun."

"Oh dear." Mariah pulled on snug-fitting white gloves. "I feel as though I'm being pulled in two directions. I want to go. And I want to stay. Do I look presentable?"

"You look beautiful." Carrie laughed. "Please don't take offense, but the first time I saw you, I never imagined you could be so. . .so. . .human."

"I was a real old maid, wasn't I?"

"You certainly were." Carrie stretched up to kiss the taller woman's cheek. "I love you, Mother."

"Oh, Carrie." Tears rimmed Mariah's blue eyes as she hugged the younger woman. "I love you, too."

Joanna brushed away her own tears. "We'd better go before we all start blubbering." She thrust into the bride's hand the bouquet of yellow roses Mariah had carried down the aisle. "Don't forget you are supposed to throw these."

"Joanna, my dear friend." Mariah brushed a final tear from Joanna's cheek. "A true friend is a gift of God. When I arrived here last year, I knew no one except my cousins. You were the first to become my friend, and I thank God every day for the gift of your friendship."

"And I thank Him for bringing you to Cedar Bend. My life has been greatly enriched by knowing you, Mariah. Now, we must go. Your husband is waiting for you."

"So he is." Mariah opened the white-beaded handbag she carried. "I have something for you, Joanna. This is a gift from Sherman and me." She pressed a paper into Joanna's hand. "It's the deed to my house. I have removed everything I want to keep. The rest is yours for the library."

"I can't take this." Joanna looked at the deed in her hand. "It's too much."

"Nonsense. Sell it and use the money to build your library. Or turn your house into a library. It's an ideal location."

"Not *my* library." Joanna shook her head. "It's *our* library."

"It will be Cedar Bend's library." Mariah leaned down to kiss her young friend's cheek. "I love you, Joanna."

Later, Mariah and Sherman ran to catch the stagecoach through a hail of rice.

They waved out the window as the stagecoach pulled away.

"Mariah!" Gladys Jacobs's voice rose above the cheers of the assembled townsfolk. "Throw your bouquet."

Mariah leaned farther out the window and tossed the yellow roses. They arched through the air and landed in Joanna's outstretched hands.

Mark Hopkins stepped close to Joanna and whispered in her ear, "Well, looks like we're next."

Am I supposed to consider myself engaged? Joanna backed away to look at Mark. She knew him well enough to know that this was more than likely his idea of a proposal. She could marry Mark and live with him the rest of her life—she could give birth to a dozen little Hopkinses—and never once hear a romantic phrase from his lips. She'd loaned him one of her romance novels hoping he would get the idea of a proper courtship. He said he'd read all he could stand before he finished the first chapter, and then he laughed. "Real men don't talk like that," he'd said. Mark was about as romantic as a stick.

Now she said, "I don't know, Mark. Catching the bouquet is just a silly tradition. I don't think it means anything, really."

Then, without thinking of the consequences, she prayed, *Please, Lord, bring a dashing, romantic adventurer into my life. Send me someone exciting and unpredictable and a tad dangerous.*

Chapter 2

Western Nebraska, a few days later

Clay Shepherd knew when he signed on as a wrangler at the Crooked S that they were a rough bunch. After he had been there less than a week, he noticed most of the cows had altered brands. A bit of rustling didn't bother Clay—long as someone else did the rustling—but he for sure wanted nothing to do with robbing a bank.

"Count me out," he said when Bob Simms approached him with the ill-conceived scheme. "I don't want any part of it."

"I thought you was game." Simms scowled. "You a yellowbelly, Shepherd?"

"I'm no coward," Clay retorted. "But I'm not a fool, either. Robbing a government payroll in broad daylight will buy you a place on Boot Hill."

"I ain't aimin' to get shot." Simms's hand strayed to the gun tied low on his right hip. "Neither is the rest of the boys."

"If you're dead set on doing this, why don't you do it after dark when nobody's around?"

"Wouldn't work. That payroll will only be there one night. The way I figure it, they'll have guards posted. We'll hit 'em around noon when they ain't expectin' us."

Simms was shy a few marbles, although Clay couldn't say that to his face. The town would be teeming with cavalry. Not to mention the sheriff and his deputies. The Crooked S gang would be lucky to escape the bank alive. Clay had no intention of dying just yet, but with the way Simms eyed him while toying with his six-shooter, Clay figured he'd be a dead man right quick if he refused to ride with them. That little fact didn't give him a whole lot of choice.

"Sounds as though you've come up with a brilliant plan," he finally said. "Count me in."

A grimace that passed for a grin crossed Simms's thick face while his hand moved from the stock of his pistol. The two men shook hands. "Glad you decided to join us, Shepherd. You understand, bein' as how you're new and all, I can only give you ten percent of the take. Me and the other two boys will divvy up the rest. That agreeable to you?"

Clay noticed Simms's burly hand hovering around the stock of his gun again. "Sounds more than generous to me," he agreed.

"Good!" Simms started away then turned back. "By the way, I can't let you go in the bank with us, neither. Your job will be to hold the horses in the alley behind the bank. You agreeable to that?"

"Yes sir, Mr. Simms. It will probably be for the best. Seeing as how I have never robbed a bank before."

Clay grinned as he watched Simms walk away. He had no intention of getting himself killed. Escaping Simms and his gang was going to be easier than he first imagined. While they were in the bank—most likely getting themselves blown to kingdom come—he'd be lighting a shuck out of town.

Texas. I haven't been in Texas for a while. I'll head south. In case any of the Simms gang survives, they'll never find me there.

Clay whistled as he headed for the bunkhouse.

———

Almost a week later the sun beat down on the men's heads and shoulders as they rode to town with a cloud of dust rising behind them. Simms passed a bottle around, and all the men except Clay took a hefty swig. When his turn came, he lifted the bottle to his lips but only pretended to drink. By the time they rode into town, Clay was the only clearheaded member of the gang.

They split up just outside town, going in by twos so they wouldn't attract attention. Simms stayed with Clay. As they ambled down the main street of town, Clay noticed the sheriff leaning against a storefront across from the bank. A guard stood outside the bank's door.

He pointed out the two men to Simms, certain there were more he hadn't seen. "Sure you want to go through with this?"

"You ain't gettin' lily-livered, are ya?" Simms sneered.

"Nope." Clay figured he'd better not push the issue. "Just thought you might have changed your mind."

"Not a chance."

They took their time riding through town then doubled back to the bank at high noon where they met the other two gang members.

"You wait fer us here, Shepherd," Simms said as soon as they were in place behind the bank.

The men dismounted and handed Clay the reins to their horses. "Soon as you hear the signal, you ride 'round front with our horses like I told you."

"Yes sir, Mr. Simms, I'll do that," Clay said. "What was that signal again, just so's I don't forget?"

"One shot." The husky outlaw stumbled. "I reckon I oughta not have let you share our bottle. Can't even remember a simple signal. Come on, boys. Let's go."

Clay watched the three men slip around the corner of the brick building. One of them tugged his bandanna into place. They would be lucky if they even got inside the bank before they were shot.

Clay dropped the lines to the three horses entrusted to his care and slapped the nearest horse across the hindquarters. The horse ran a few paces away before stopping to take a bite of tall grass by the side of the alley. The other horses milled around, then bolted at the sound of yelling and gunfire. Clay swung into the saddle and patted his stallion on the neck. "Reckon that's our signal, Lucky?"

A volley of gunshots rang out. Clay winced and nodded. "Yep, that must be it."

He kneed his mount, and they rode slowly out of town in the opposite direction from the way they had entered.

———

Two days later Clay crossed into western Kansas heading south. The air had been heavy laden with humidity all day. Now, as late evening approached, the sky became a green-tinged yellow bruise. Nothing stirred, and that fact concerned Clay as much as anything.

"There's a twister coming for sure." Clay patted the black stallion's gleaming neck. "We'd better find shelter, Lucky, if we don't want to get blown back to Nebraska."

They had been following a winding creek. Clay dismounted and led Lucky down a shallow embankment to the water's edge. After both man and beast had drunk their fill of the clear, tepid water, Clay turned to leave, spotting a rock overhang facing east. He led the stallion to the shelter nature had carved high in the creek bank. Deep enough to be a cave and well out of the water, it provided the protection he and Lucky needed.

Clay removed his saddle and rubbed Lucky down before laying out his bedroll. He built a small fire in the mouth of the cave and settled back on his bed just as the wind picked up. The tongues of his campfire danced to the whining tune of the wind, but most of the moist air rushed past his hideout, making Clay glad he had sought shelter when he did. Rain splattered at first then came down in torrents as the shrieking wind turned into a deafening roar. Within twenty minutes the rain stopped, the wind died down, and the black sky filled with twinkling pinpoints of light.

Clay stood and stroked the black stallion's muzzle. "Well, Lucky, looks like we missed the worst of it."

He gave the horse one final pat before crawling onto his bedroll. In minutes he fell asleep.

Clay headed out the next morning at daybreak. He saw evidence of the storm all around, in the flattened grass that had reached Lucky's underbelly the day before. Near midmorning he came upon some scraps of milled lumber. Not far beyond, he saw the battered homestead. A large tree in the backyard had been pulled from the ground, its branches chewed to stubs then dropped on the roof of the house. His first instinct was to ride on by when he saw no evidence of life. After all, he reasoned that anyone in what remained of the small cabin would be either dead or close to it. Still, someone might need help, and if not, there might be something worth salvaging among the wreckage.

He rode up to the homesite and dismounted beside the destroyed cabin. The roof had caved in with the weight of the old oak tree, but the front two rooms seemed to have escaped serious damage. Clay entered to shuffle his way through the debris left from the storm.

He called out, "Hey, anybody here?" He listened and heard nothing, so he began sifting through the mess, looking for anything of value. When he opened a cabinet door, he heard a faint sound coming from the rubble at the back of the house.

He lifted his head and listened. There it was again. Sounded like a kitten. He'd always been a sucker for the helpless, so he turned toward the mewing sound. Probably the little thing had gotten caught in a corner and couldn't find its way out. He pushed aside enough debris to enter the bedroom then stopped short. A heavy beam had fallen across the walnut bedstead. The man and woman sleeping there never had a chance. He bowed his head in a moment of respect.

Again he heard the mew of the kitten. A few feet from the bed a door had fallen across what looked like a cradle. The mewing sounds seemed to come from there.

Clay lifted the door and tossed it to one side. "What in the world—" He stood looking at the red-faced occupant of the cradle. The baby's eyes were squeezed shut with its mouth wide open, exposing toothless gums. The mewing he'd heard before sounded full force, like that of a squalling infant now.

"You are one ugly little person," Clay said over the annoying sound.

The baby hushed in midshriek. Little eyes opened and regarded Clay with a light blue gaze.

"What's the matter, buddy? Are you hungry?" Kitten or baby, Clay couldn't walk away.

A crock in the kitchen, sitting untouched on the sideboard, held milk. Clay rummaged through the debris until he gave up finding a bottle with a nipple to feed the infant. When the baby's cries finally seemed to be growing weak, he decided to try spoon-feeding. He'd done it with a kitten, so why not with a human baby? After a few tries with the baby still in the crib, he decided he'd have to find a place to sit and hold the little guy so the milk would go down better.

He brushed dust and pieces of the ceiling from a kitchen chair then carried the baby wrapped in a blanket into the next room. By holding him in a reclining position, Clay found he was able to get a steady supply of milk down.

"Is your tummy full now?" Clay asked when the baby seemed to lose interest. "I sure hope so."

He carried the baby into the bedroom and put him back in the crib.

"What am I supposed to do with you?" He stood looking down at the wriggling tyke while considering his options. He could walk away. Leave him here. Probably wouldn't take a kid this size long to starve.

The baby looked up at him with a wide-eyed stare, almost as if he expected him to solve his problems. "Sorry, kid. You can't go with me. I travel alone."

A soft sigh lifted the baby's chest.

"I know, kid. It's a tough world. Your ma and pa are both dead. My ma died when I wasn't much older than you. Of course I had Pa. He's dead now, too."

The baby's eyelids appeared to be too heavy to remain open. "Reckon that makes us both orphans."

Clay watched the baby fight against sleep and felt a kinship with the little one. He couldn't walk away knowing a death sentence awaited this innocent little one. What he needed was a mother. Someone to care, like Mrs. Brady had cared for him long ago when he was an unlovable teen. A slow grin crossed his face.

"You know, kid, I just had an idea. We can't be much more than a day's ride from Cedar Bend." Clay studied the sleeping infant's face. The kid wasn't so hard on the eyes when he wasn't screaming. "There's a woman in Cedar Bend who would take real good care of you. She's a doctor's wife, so you'd be in good hands. I'll take you to her."

Clay foraged around in the kitchen until he found a covered tin container. He filled it with milk, hoping it was fresh from the night before and would keep a day or two. He put it in his saddlebag along with some cans of beans for himself and went back for the baby. The kid's diaper hung halfway to his knees, heavy and wet. Clay removed the diaper and confirmed the baby was a boy. He held the baby's kicking feet out of the way and put on a clean diaper. He didn't do much of a job pinning on the replacement, but he reckoned it would hold until they got to Mrs. Brady.

After digging one large grave, he buried the man and woman, saying as much as he could remember of Psalm 23. Funny, he hadn't thought of any scripture verses in years. Not since he left Cedar Bend and the woman who'd been as much a mother to him as he'd ever had. He hadn't thought of the Bradys in a long time, but he knew without a doubt they would welcome the orphaned baby just as they'd welcomed him when he needed their friendship.

He took baby clothes, blankets, whatever he could find that looked like it belonged to the little guy, and stuffed it all in his saddlebags. A few more canned goods went in after that. He found a family Bible with names inside and decided the kid would like to have it when he was older. Then he tied half a bedsheet around his neck, devising a sling to carry the baby. He mounted Lucky with one hand holding the baby against his chest and headed south.

Chapter 3

Joanna set a platter of sausage, eggs, and oatmeal on the table in front of her father and a bowl of oatmeal across the table for herself. She bowed her head while her father prayed then picked up her spoon and dipped it into the oatmeal sitting in front of her. That with a glass of milk made up a satisfying breakfast for her now.

Her friendship with Mariah Casey had given Joanna more than just someone to talk to. Although seventeen years apart in age, the two women had grown close soon after Mariah moved to Cedar Bend. They both had nursed their mothers through sickness and grown up with little time for friendships. They found they had much in common in spite of the years separating them. Joanna also found she had lost some weight and felt better after following Mariah's example of eating fewer sweets.

"When are Sherm and his new wife due back home?" Dr. Brady asked.

"In the next few days, I suppose." Joanna took a sip of milk. "They've been gone almost two weeks already. Carrie said she got a card from them just yesterday, and all it said was they were having a wonderful time."

Joanna giggled. "I don't think Carrie quite knows what to make of her father off on a honeymoon. She's being a good sport about it, though."

"She'll do fine." Dr. Brady loaded his fork with egg then stabbed a small piece of sausage. "So what are your plans for the day?"

Joanna watched him slip his fork into his mouth and felt no desire for the greasy food she had once craved. If her mother were still alive, she knew she would be so proud of her accomplishment in controlling her appetite. Sometimes she missed her mother with an almost physical pain, even after two years. "I'm going to have a good look at Mariah's old house. I still can't believe she gave it to me. Well, actually to the town. I want to see what needs to be done to turn it into a library."

"Sounds like a worthwhile project." Her father nodded and took a drink of milk.

"Oh, it is." Joanna felt the inner glow that always warmed her at the thought of the library that would soon become a reality. "I'm sure as word spreads others will want to become involved as well."

Dr. Brady wiped his hands on his napkin and smiled. "While you are at the library, I shall be making my rounds. Mr. Hartley is my first stop, and the Danville boy is due to have his cast taken off."

"How is Mr. Hartley doing with his skin condition?" Joanna stood and began gathering dishes. She cleaned the kitchen while her father filled her in on the health of his patients.

Several minutes later, with a ray of sunlight peeking from behind a cloud, Joanna secured her bonnet and waved to her father as he set off in his buggy. She closed the kitchen door and headed on foot toward town, being careful to skirt mud puddles left from the overnight rain they had received. The air smelled fresh and clean after the rain. Droplets of water still clung to leaves, creating an occasional shower when she walked underneath.

She and her father lived at the edge of town. Behind their house the prairie spread all the way to the horizon on gently rolling hills, while their front yard faced the dirt road that led past the Cattlemen's Association Hall to a handful of stores, two churches, and a one-room schoolhouse. Mariah's house sat on Main Street, an easy walk from the cluster of buildings that made up the business district of Cedar Bend.

But it was Mariah's house no longer. Joanna felt the thrill of her dream soon becoming reality. Before too many days passed, the entire town would think of the little bungalow as their library. She smiled as she set a brisk pace down the side of the street, waving and speaking briefly to those she met.

She slowed when she neared Conway's Feed Store at the corner of Main and Pine streets. Mark Hopkins had started working for Jack Conway as soon as he entered his teens. She searched for a glimpse of him when she came abreast of the old white board building and then hurried past. As much as she cared for Mark, she didn't feel like talking to him today. He'd been trying to get her to go on an outing with him for the last two weeks, and she couldn't say yes with a thankful heart. But today Mark was nowhere in sight, so Joanna again set a steady pace.

Two blocks later, she opened the gate to Mariah's house and started up the walk, stopping after several steps to look at the small house that belonged to her now. Flowers stood in a stately row on either side of the walk to the front porch. So much like Mariah. Joanna smiled as she thought of the woman who had become her best friend. She'd be glad when the Butlers returned from their trip. Always efficient, Mariah would be a great help with the library. If she wasn't too busy with her new family, that was.

Joanna crossed the porch and pushed the front door open. Except for the few special pieces taken to her new home, Mariah had left her furniture to be used in the library. Joanna looked around the front room as her imagination placed a desk near the door. The librarian would need to be handy to greet patrons and check books as they went out and came back. Shelves could be built in each room, maybe three or four freestanding with the ends secured to one wall. That would leave room for a couch in the corner opposite the desk so people could sit and read at their leisure.

Giving a little twirl in the center of the room, Joanna smiled in satisfaction. She could just see Cedar Bend folk pouring into her library. Their library. A place of learning and culture and dreams set free.

A sharp knock at the door brought Joanna back to earth. She turned as Carrie Nolan poked her head inside. Gleaming auburn hair framed her pretty face and wide smile. "Are we open for business yet?"

Joanna laughed while her friend stepped inside followed by Hope. The child ran across the room to give Joanna a hug. "I love you, Aunt Joanna."

Returning the little girl's hug, Joanna felt a rush of warmth fill her heart. Hope always brightened her world.

"I love you too, Hope."

"My mama's coming home." Hope stepped back and looked at Joanna with wide, serious eyes. "We not leaving my new daddy's house, though, so you can have this old house. Him told me we gonna stay forever and forever."

"My, that's a long time." Joanna stood and shared a smile with her friend while Carrie's little stepsister explained that forever meant as long as Mama, Papa, and she should live.

Carrie said, "We were on our way to town and saw the door open. Are you getting ready to start work on the library?"

"Oh, I wish I could." Joanna sighed as she glanced around the room again. "It will take a while to get this place in shape. We need shelves and the right furnishings. I'd like to have an area rug in each room and different curtains at the windows. We have to buy books—lots of books."

"You are right." Carrie tapped a slender finger against her lower lip as she studied the room. "What we need is some way to raise money. And not just to get the library itself ready. There needs to be money on an ongoing basis. What about a salary for the librarian? And don't forget the expenses."

Joanna turned toward the wood-burning stove in the corner and groaned. "Oh no, I never even thought about that. There's a pump for water in the kitchen, but if I can't find a donor for wood, I'll have to buy some, at least in the winter."

"Will you leave the kitchen as it is?" Carrie stepped across the floor to peer through the open doorway into the next room. As Hope ran past, Carrie rested her hand across her flat stomach in an unconscious gesture of protection toward her unborn child.

Joanna joined Carrie and watched Hope circle the oak table that took up the center of the room. She smiled at the little girl's antics as Hope climbed into one chair after another.

Carrie called to her, "Hope, be careful. I don't want you getting hurt."

"I not get hurt, Carrie." Hope stretched to reach a chair set back from the others, gave a little hop, and landed safely on it.

Joanna giggled when she heard Carrie's breath rush out. "She'll be all right."

Carrie and Joanna moved back into the living room while Hope continued playing on the chairs. "I'd just hate for Mariah to come home and find bruises on her daughter."

A burst of laughter from Joanna brought a smile to Carrie's lips before she, too, laughed and said, "This has been an experience for Luke and me. I think I have a better idea of what being a mother will be like."

"I heard about a man who married late in life." Joanna leaned against the doorframe to tell her story. "When their first baby was born and then started crawling, he took every bit of furniture that was not padded out of the house. That child grew up afraid to play games with the other children because she feared getting hurt. Any new experience was something to be dreaded. She missed so much of life because of too much fear."

"How terrible," Carrie said.

"Yes, I think so." Joanna looked out through the front window as if she could see beyond the small Kansas town set in the middle of the prairie. "I want some excitement in my life. I've never told anyone this before, but I'd love to have an exciting adventure. Do something daring for a change." She grinned as she brought her gaze back to Carrie. "Maybe something just a tad dangerous so I could tell my children and grandchildren about my adventures someday."

"I don't know, Joanna." Carrie shook her head. "Our foreman, Cyrus, always says you should be careful what you wish for because you just might get it."

"Then I shall wish for excitement and pray for it, too." Joanna giggled. "Actually, I already have been."

Carrie looked beyond Joanna through the open door leading outside. "Does Mark Hopkins have anything to do with the answer to your prayers?"

"Mark Hopkins! Why would you think. . . ?" Joanna's voice trailed off as she realized Carrie was looking at something. She turned just as she heard the first footstep on the wooden porch.

Mark lifted a hand to knock. What was the use in hiding from him? She couldn't avoid him forever, and she really did like Mark. As a friend. If only he didn't want more. If only her knight in shining armor would ride into town and sweep her off her feet.

"Good morning, Mark," Joanna called out before he could knock. "Come on in."

"I saw you go by the feedstore." He smiled. "Figured you might be headed this way."

"Carrie and I have been discussing ways to raise money for the library." Joanna turned away from Mark. "Carrie, I never did answer your question about the kitchen. I really don't know. I guess we could leave it as a kitchen in case it's needed, at least until we need the room for more books. What do you think?"

Carrie's curious glance from Mark to Joanna said she thought there might be more under the surface than Joanna wanted to admit. But she kept her counsel on that subject. "It never hurts to build gradually. We could have a box supper to raise money. And we could ask for book donations. Maybe folks around town would be willing to share any books they might have."

"Those are wonderful ideas, Carrie." Joanna, feeling guilty for excluding Mark, turned to face him. "Don't you agree, Mark?"

He shrugged. "I came by to tell you that I'll pick you up for the church social at six o'clock Saturday night."

How typical of Mark. Joanna couldn't remember him inviting her to attend the social with him. Instead, he just assumed they would go together.

She started to tell him just what she thought of his assumptions when a small streak rushed past her skirt.

"Mark!" Hope launched herself into Mark's arms. He lifted the little girl above his head and gave her a little toss. Her delighted squeals brightened Joanna's mood, and she again saw Mark for who he was—a good man with good intentions. So what if he took her for granted? He was solid and reliable. Shouldn't those be the traits she looked for in a husband? Who needed exciting and unpredictable? Who needed romance? She did, but she wasn't likely to get what she needed, so she might as well take what she had.

As Mark set Hope back on the floor, Joanna forced a smile. "All right, Mark. I'll be ready at six."

He gave her a quick nod. "I'll walk you home."

Carrie took Hope's hand and stepped toward the door. "We do need to get to town before Luke comes looking for us. He's taking us to the hotel dining room for lunch. We'll get together again, Joanna, to discuss our ideas for the library."

"Yes, that will be good." Joanna watched her friends go down the walk and turned to Mark. "Would you like to look around and see what I'm planning?"

She took his shrug as agreement and began explaining what she would like to do with the living room. As they went through the house, Mark had little to say but seemed determined to stay until she finished. Finally, she said, "All right, Mark, I'm ready to go."

Mark crossed the road before setting off at a brisk pace, and Joanna fell into step beside him.

Their conversation consisted of Mark's work and the house he planned to begin building soon. Joanna tried to steer away from talking about his house, because she knew he intended for her to live there with him one day. But each attempt at bringing the library to the front was ignored until Joanna gave up.

"I've been storing materials in my dad's barn," Mark said as they stepped off the boardwalk.

Joanna stopped. Mark plowed ahead through the muddy road, leaving a good impression of his boot soles with each step. She looked around and realized they were on the opposite side of the street from the way she had come earlier. That's how she had missed the mud before.

As she tried to decide what to do, Mark stopped on the other side of the road and looked at her. "Aren't you coming?"

Clenching her teeth in frustration, Joanna wondered if he were blind. How could he not know that a woman's shoes were not as sturdy or waterproof as his boots? She lifted her skirts just enough to keep them from dragging in the mud and picked her way carefully around the huge puddle until she had crossed the road.

Mark took her arm when she reached his side and helped her step on the boardwalk, as if that made up for not helping before. She felt like jerking her arm away but didn't.

"I guess we could have gone a different way," he said. "I didn't think about the mud being a problem."

"It's all right, Mark. I'm across now."

What difference did it make? Mark would never change.

Lord, I don't even want to change Mark. He doesn't need changing. He just needs someone more suited to him. But what about me, God? Isn't there someone out there who can see past the end of his nose? Don't you have someone You can send that will be gallant, ready to step between me and danger? Even if it is just mud. Please, Lord. Send me someone who will set my heart racing.

Chapter 4

Clay figured on making good time. He'd never ridden with a baby strapped to his chest before, but it wasn't too bad. They'd already gone several miles. The kid bounced a lot, which was fine with Clay as long as he kept quiet. Kids liked that rocking motion, didn't they? Yep, he was doing just fine.

He had no sooner congratulated himself when a funny gurgling noise came from the baby. He looked down as a spray of what looked like clabbered milk shot from the kid's mouth. In the next instant, a squall that nearly burst Clay's eardrums sounded. At least the kid had a good set of lungs.

That high-pitched wail was the most annoying sound he'd ever heard. When Lucky faltered, Clay figured he'd better do something fast before his horse had a nervous fit and hurt them all.

"Whoa," he said to Lucky. "Reckon we'd better take a breather."

He swung from the saddle and wrinkled his nose. A breather was definitely in order. Soured milk and something else accosted his nostrils. Something that reminded him of an outhouse.

"Yuck." Clay lifted the crying baby from the sling and held him out at arms' length. "What I wouldn't give for a woman right about now."

He looked around the grass-covered prairie, but no woman materialized. He could see clear to the horizon in all directions, so he didn't figure one would come walking up anytime soon. Only a broken-down cabin broke the view. Looked like he was on his own, and at the moment that didn't sit so well.

"Should have left you back there in that cabin when I thought you was a kitten." Blue eyes looked across at him trustingly. Misplaced trust, but at least the kid had stopped crying.

"You know, I'd much rather wrestle a wild bear than mess with you." The baby regarded him with a solemn expression.

When Clay looked around for a place to lay the kid, his gaze hit the front of his duster where a stream of clabbered milk clung. "Hey, what'd you have to go and do that for?"

Figuring his duster had already gotten the worst of the milk attack, he held the baby in one arm and shrugged out of the opposite sleeve. Shifting sides, he let his duster fall to the ground. Laying the baby on it, he rummaged through his saddlebag for a fresh diaper and gown. Using drinking water and another diaper, he swiped most of the milk from his duster first and the baby next. He stepped back and looked down at the little one. His face scrunched and his mouth puckered just before the squalling started again.

"Hey, stop that. I know I ain't finished the job. But give a little slack here. You're my first. Got any hints on this thing?" He held the clean diaper up and looked it over. The one he'd changed at the cabin had been folded. This one just looked like a square piece of cloth to him. He looked at the dirty, soaked diaper still on the baby. The thing was bunched up between the kid's legs. He looked back at the cloth in his hand and wondered why they didn't come formfitting like trousers. No man should have to tackle a job like this.

He knelt again by the baby and touched one finger to the pin holding the diaper in place. A rumble of thunder sounded in the southwest. Clay looked up. Clouds were rolling in. They needed to take shelter and hope another tornado didn't blow through the area.

In a hurry now, Clay unhooked the pin and pulled the diaper back. He gagged at the contents but used the dirty diaper to wipe most of the grime from the baby. After several attempts to make a triangle, he folded the clean diaper into a rectangle and hoped it would fit. It didn't, but it would have to do. He tugged it together in front and pinned it.

"You sag here and there, and I don't reckon a woman would have done it this way, but you'll do until next time." Clay just hoped there wouldn't be many next times until he reached Cedar Bend. He slipped the gown over the baby's head, glad it was roomy enough to move around when the kid held fists up by his shoulders and wouldn't give.

Clay worked the sleeves on anyway, amazed at how hard dressing an infant was. "You're a lot stronger than I thought you'd be. Shame you'll probably grow up to be a doctor like Doc Brady. With those muscles, you could wrangle horses with the best of 'em."

Joanna Brady's face appeared in Clay's mind. "Reckon you'll have a big sister. She'll know how to take care of you a lot better than I do."

He grinned, remembering the day he'd surprised her under the mistletoe. He'd taken a kiss, too. He knew now it hadn't been much of a kiss, but he hadn't forgotten it—or her. He couldn't help wondering if he'd see her when he got to town. Naw, she wouldn't want to see the likes of him. He'd just drop the baby off and run. She was probably married with a kid of her own by now, anyhow.

A splat of water hit his duster. He didn't bother checking the sky. He didn't figure he had time. Settling the baby back in his sling, Clay grabbed his duster, threw it on, and swung into the saddle. Turning Lucky's nose toward the dilapidated cabin he'd seen in the distance, he hoped they could reach it in time.

A few minutes later, Clay slid from the horse and, holding his duster over the baby, ran to the house through a pelting rain. He banged on the door and listened, keeping his shoulder hunched to shield the baby. Only the drumming sound of rain against the roof answered. Hoping he didn't startle any varmints of the four-legged kind, or two-legged for that matter, he pulled his six-shooter from the holster on his hip and shoved the door open.

The heavy oak door swung back with enough force to hit the wall. Something small and gray darted behind a cupboard in the corner. Clay scanned the one room before stepping inside. He shoved his gun back in place as he let his muscles relax. The *plink* of water hitting the wooden table before splattering onto the floor sounded loud in the otherwise quiet room. A musty smell greeted him. Clay looked up at the dripping ceiling.

"Hey, buddy, what do you say? Think this place will do?" When the kid didn't answer, Clay said, "Come on now. It's not that bad. Just one leak if you don't count the broken window. And there's a bed in the corner. Which side do you want?"

Clay figured he'd better shake out the bedcovers before laying the kid down. Wouldn't do to find something alive hiding in their bed. From what he could see in the dim room, the table looked like the cleanest place. He swiped his finger through thick dust on the dry end and shrugged. At least it had been wiped off once, even if not lately.

"Hey, a little dirt never hurt anyone, did it, buddy?" He slipped the sling off and laid the baby on the table. The little guy looked at him as if trying to understand this new experience. "Tell you what. You stay right there and don't move. I have to get the saddlebags and take care of Lucky. You do that and I'll get you some more milk. Okay?"

When the baby didn't cry, Clay figured that meant he'd better get a move on. He just hoped the kid didn't decide to scoot over or roll off the table. For a guy so little, three feet or so would be a long way to fall.

Clay ran from the cabin to his horse. He led Lucky up the one step to the porch and tied him to a corner post. If the wind didn't blow too hard, Lucky should have shelter there and still be able to reach the tall grass growing against the cabin. Clay patted the horse's neck and rubbed his long, sleek nose. Although his duster took the brunt of the rain blowing under the porch roof, a shiver moved across his shoulders. He unhooked the saddlebags and lifted them from the horse. When he tossed them inside the door, he checked on the baby and saw two little fists flailing in the air. At least he hadn't moved. And he was quiet. Couldn't ask for more than that.

Clay's stomach rumbled. Since he was hungry, it was a pretty safe bet the kid would be, too. And that meant he might start crying at any time. The thought of listening to any more of those ear-piercing cries had Clay moving faster than usual. Finished outside, he closed the door against the rain.

Ignoring his own stomach, Clay opened the container of milk and set it on the table. He pulled an old wooden rocker from the wall and settled in it with the baby. While the kid swallowed each spoonful of milk, Clay set the rocker into motion. He'd sure hate for one of his cowboy buddies to see him rocking a baby, but to tell the truth, he didn't mind the doing of it one bit.

After a while, the infant started wheezing, like he couldn't breathe right. He kept taking the milk as if nothing was wrong, but Clay didn't like that sound at all. A couple more spoonfuls and he decided something must be caught in the kid's throat. His heart pounding with fear for the little one's safety, Clay slung him over his shoulder. He pounded the little guy's back, hoping to dislodge whatever blocked his airway. After three or four firm, open-hand swats in the middle of the tiny back, a belch that would have done any cowboy proud sounded in Clay's ear.

He pulled the baby back and looked at him. His breathing sounded fine, but his face scrunched up just like it always did before he cried. Clay tucked him back in the crook of his arm and poured another bit of milk into his mouth before he could let out a sound. He didn't wheeze anymore, and he didn't cry after he finished eating. Instead, his eyes drifted shut and he went to sleep. That's when Clay felt something warm and wet spread over his lap.

Later, in the darkest part of the night, Clay dreamed he had just lassoed a young steer. He threw him to the ground, dust rising in a choking cloud as he tied the short rope around the calf's feet. He smelled sweat and—outhouse? The calf looked up at him with a baby's light blue eyes and puckered his mouth just before he bawled. Clay sat up, confused when the calf's bawling turned into the baby's cries.

He rubbed his eyes and looked toward the bed next to the wall. Buddy lay on his back. Both little fists and two little feet fought the air where the covers had been. Red-faced and squalling at the top of his lungs, the baby demanded attention.

Clay gained a new respect for the female gender as he changed the fourth diaper in less than ten hours. He couldn't wait to get to Cedar Bend and would have headed out right then except the rain still beat a steady tattoo against the tin roof.

With a clean diaper more or less covering his roommate, Clay thought his job was done. But the kid kept crying, arching his back as if he were having a mad fit. When his fist hit his mouth and he sucked on it, Clay got the message.

"Why didn't you say you were hungry, buddy? I reckon milk runs out of a little half-pint belly quicker than solid food goes through my gallon-sized one." He worked quickly to get the milk and spoon out as he spoke over the cries that didn't give any sign of letting up. As soon as he had everything ready, he picked up the baby and settled back in the rocker.

This time Clay's eyes drooped lower with each rock until he stopped altogether. Forcing himself to stay awake so he didn't drop the baby or miss his mouth with the spoon, Clay thought of Cedar Bend, Kansas, and the Brady family.

"You'll like Doc and Mrs. Brady. Reckon you'll like Joanna, too. She's a mighty pretty girl. Sweet as they come. A boy called her fat once, but I set him straight pretty quick." Clay chuckled, remembering. "He went crying home to his mama with a bloody nose. Never heard him say anything bad about Joanna after that. If we'd been older, I might have come calling on her. 'Course, a girl with a fine family like that wouldn't want to pal around with the likes of me. Reckon I'd better stop walking down memory lane, don't you think, buddy?"

The baby looked up at Clay with a serious expression. If Clay didn't know better, he'd think the kid understood everything he told him. When that wheezing sound started this time, Clay was prepared. He felt like an old hand when the baby belched just like before. This time he lowered the little guy and stuck the spoon back in his mouth before a single cry sounded.

By the time Clay felt his arm go numb, Buddy's eyes closed and his breathing evened out. Holding the little guy close, Clay stood and crossed to the bed. He gladly laid his burden on the far side and crawled in beside him. He yawned as he tucked the covers around the baby. First light would come too soon for his liking, but he needed to get to the Bradys' as soon as he could. He didn't know beans about taking care of a baby, and he'd be glad enough to be rid of him.

Clay jerked awake when something hit his side. He grabbed for his six-shooter and realized he'd left it in the holster hanging on the back of a chair eight feet away. He must have been awfully tired when he went to bed to do that.

Sunshine streamed through the dirty window beside him, lighting the cabin. A quick glance around the unkempt room brought Clay to full awareness, as did another kick in his side. The baby had turned crossways on the bed and was using him for a target.

"Hey, buddy, what're you kicking me for?" Clay put a hand on either side of the little guy and looked down at him. "Think it's past time to get up, do ya?"

Both little arms flailed in the air and a baby smile brightened the little one's face while gurgles and coos sounded like real words.

"Well now, I didn't know you could talk." Clay found himself smiling down at the baby. He touched a finger to the smooth skin just under the tiny chin.

The baby gurgled again, and Clay figured he knew what his little friend was trying to say. "I know, buddy. I overslept. 'Course I reckon that might be because I had to get up in the middle of the night and feed someone. We won't even mention that diaper. We'd better get on the road, though. We don't want Mrs. Brady to get away before we get there, do we?"

By the time Clay had the baby fed and changed, he'd given up on arriving at the Bradys' before breakfast. In fact, the sun had traveled well into midmorning by the time he saw the first sign of Cedar Bend. On the trip in, he'd given his errand a bit of thought and decided he might not be as welcome as he had been all those years ago. After all, he was a grown man now rather than a motherless boy. So he circled the town and came in across the open range to the back of the Brady house.

Clay spotted the barn first and headed toward it. He spoke to the baby. "Reckon we'd better lay low until we can see what's going on around here. What do you think about that idea, buddy?"

Sliding from his horse and slip-tying him to a tree near the back corner, Clay took the baby out of his sling and carried him into the barn. As his eyes adjusted to the muted light, Clay took inventory of his surroundings. Tack and tools hung from the weathered walls with a wide empty space where he assumed the buggy usually rested.

Doc Brady must be out making calls on his patients. Maybe that was for the best. He liked the doctor, but it was Mrs. Brady he remembered with fondness. Still, his heart pounded against his chest at the thought of seeing the woman who had been the closest to a mother he had ever known.

"Reckon I'd better not stop in and say howdy to your new ma, buddy." Clay looked into the baby's blue gaze. "For sure I'd be a big disappointment to her. You'll understand one of these days when you do something wrong and wish you hadn't 'cause you don't want to hurt your ma."

Clay dipped the last of the milk out and fed the baby. An idea took root in his mind when he saw an empty crate leaning against the far wall. As soon as the baby had given his customary belch, Clay wrapped him in a quilt and made a bed for him in the crate with all of his belongings, including the Bible. While the baby went to sleep, Clay tore the paper label from the crate and went in search of something to write with. When he'd about given up on finding what he needed, he saw the doctor's toolbox. Rummaging through it, he found the stub of a pencil.

Holding the paper against the doorframe, he thought about what he wanted to say. Finally, he printed a note and replaced the pencil. "Good thing you're a sound sleeper." He spoke in a soft voice as he unpinned the baby's diaper and pinned it back with the note attached.

Carrying the crate with the baby nestled inside, Clay slipped from the barn and approached the side of the house facing the drive. Hoping Mrs. Brady didn't appear before he could get away, Clay set the crate down on the porch, gave three quick knocks on the door, and dashed across the yard to hide in the barn. He had a good view of the house and road from where he stood near the open door facing the house. Shouldn't take long for Mrs. Brady to answer her door, but Clay intended to make sure his little buddy was taken care of before he went on to Texas.

Chapter 5

Clay stared at the closed door, willing it to open. Maybe no one was home. Could be Mrs. Brady and Joanna had gone with the doctor someplace. Maybe Joanna didn't live here anymore.

That last thought didn't sit well with Clay. For a reason he didn't understand, he wanted Joanna to be just the way he remembered her. Well, not exactly the same. A little older wouldn't hurt.

He shook his head and muttered, "Better toss that notion out real quick. Won't do any good to get sentimental about something that'll never be."

He concentrated on the door that remained stubbornly closed. Surely the Bradys hadn't moved. He saw the sign announcing the doc's services in the front yard facing the street. He'd clipped grass from around the posts enough times to know where to look for it.

A wagon rumbled down the dirt road, splashing water from a mud puddle before turning the corner and rolling toward town. Clay looked back at the crate on the porch. A tiny hand reached above the wooden side, and the baby's soft mews sounded. Clay knew what that meant from experience. Wouldn't be long before some real squalling started. Maybe he'd better do something.

Clay started to move out of the barn just as a buggy rolled into the lane leading to the house. He jumped out of sight.

A tall man stepped down first. He wore cowboy boots and a wide-brimmed Stetson. Didn't look like he'd done any cowboy work in that fancy leather vest and creased denim pants, though. He lifted a little girl from the seat and then helped a lady climb down. Clay tried to remember the couple and couldn't. Every muscle in his body tensed when the family headed toward the porch and the crate.

The baby's cries intensified at that moment. The little girl ran ahead and bent over the crate. Her childish voice carried to him.

"Mama, Papa, look what I founded." She clapped her hands and turned to face her parents. "Can I keep it? Please, Papa, can I?"

"Oh, Sherm, it's a baby." The woman joined the little girl. "What do you suppose. . ." Her voice drifted off as she picked up the crying infant.

Clay watched as she cradled the little guy in the crook of her arm and gently swayed with him in a rocking motion. His cries stopped, and Clay knew his little buddy would be inspecting these new people with that intense look in his blue eyes.

The man knocked on the door, his voice a low rumble that Clay couldn't distinguish. Maybe Mrs. Brady would come now at his knock. Clay watched, holding his breath. Then he heard the woman again as she held up the paper he'd torn from the crate. "There's a note. It says his ma and pa are dead. Someone left him for Mrs. Brady. Oh, that's so sad. Who would have done this?"

The man and woman lowered their voices then. Probably so the little girl wouldn't listen, but Clay couldn't hear either. He was ready to reveal himself at any time in defense of the little guy, but the way the woman cuddled and soothed the baby, that didn't seem necessary. They found the Bible and looked through it, then finally gathered up the baby's things and headed back to the buggy. Clay watched the woman climb in with the baby held close, as if she were laying claim to his little buddy, and he felt a sudden, unexplainable sense of loss.

As soon as the buggy turned back onto the road, Clay raced for Lucky and leaped into the saddle to follow them. No way would he let his buddy get away until he knew he'd be all right.

Joanna placed the freshly bathed and warmly wrapped infant in his mother's waiting arms. While her father cleaned his instruments and stored them in his bag, Joanna opened the bedroom door to call to the new father.

"Mr. Dugan, you may come in now and see your wife and child." She stepped back as the young father barreled past her.

He turned midway to the bed. "Is Margaret all right?"

Joanna giggled as the young mother spoke from the bed before she could answer. "I'm fine, Jerry. Just tired. You would be, too, if you'd done what I just did. Harder than puttin' in a day's washing, I'll tell you now."

Smothering another giggle, Joanna crossed the room to her father's side. "Dad, I think I'll walk back to town if you don't mind."

Dr. Brady snapped his black bag closed and looked at his daughter with raised eyebrows. "You sure? You've been on your feet since before daylight."

"Standing around mostly, just waiting. It's only a couple of miles. A brisk walk should do me good."

A smile crossed her father's pleasant face. "You've made some good changes, Joanna. I'm proud of you. Your mother would have been, too."

Joanna swallowed the lump that formed at the mention of her mother and smiled. "Thanks. Now, if you don't need me anymore, I'll go on."

With her father's permission granted, Joanna congratulated the Dugans and left. There'd been more rain the night before, but sunshine now streaked across the land, brightening the world in a riot of spring colors. Drops of water glistened on the new leaves of the trees and undergrowth along both sides of the road. A fresh, clean scent permeated the country air, and Joanna breathed deeply as she walked along, being careful to stay off the softer parts of the road.

She walked down Main Street, waving and speaking to one person or another as they met. She passed the future library and thought about going inside but decided she wanted to go home and change her clothing first. A couple of blocks farther brought her to the feedstore. She saw a wagon parked in front but didn't see anyone outside until Mark stepped from behind the vehicle.

"Joanna, I didn't know you were coming by today."

He made it sound as if she had come to see him. "I'm on my way home. I just helped Dad deliver a baby."

"A baby." Mark smiled. "Maybe someday we'll have our own babies."

Joanna instinctively stepped back. "I don't know, Mark. I don't think unmarried people should have children."

Mark laughed. "That's what I like about you, Joanna. You've got a real sense of humor. I meant after we're married. Isn't it about time we set the date?"

Joanna sighed. How could she come right out and tell Mark she didn't want to marry him? How could she hurt him that way when marriage to him, more than likely, was exactly what the future held for her?

A buggy rolled down the street, and she turned to watch it as an excuse to ignore Mark's unwelcome question. She recognized the buggy at the same time she saw Mariah Butler sitting on the front seat. Mr. Butler drove quickly down the street, and neither he nor his wife looked to the side. They drove away before she had a chance to call out a greeting. How strange. She hadn't realized they were home, but they must have come in the day before. She thought she saw Hope sitting between them.

Disappointed she had missed seeing her friend, Joanna scarcely listened to Mark as his voice droned on. She turned from watching the Butlers' buggy and caught sight of a lone rider going the same direction.

"Joanna, are you listening to me?" Mark asked.

"Yes, Mark, of course I am." As the horse and rider drew alongside the wagon Mark had been unloading, Joanna's breath caught in her throat. The man's white cowboy hat sat low on his forehead, with coal black hair curling beneath. His forearms and hands, strong-looking and tanned, contrasted with his light blue rolled shirtsleeves. A flood of memories filled Joanna's mind. Memories of a teen boy sitting in the back of the classroom. His smile seeming so personal when his pale blue gaze rested on her face. The same boy working for her father, cutting grass, chopping wood, running errands for her mother. Joanna's heart fluttered before reason returned.

It couldn't be Clay Shepherd. He wouldn't be riding down the streets of Cedar Bend. He probably wasn't even in Kansas. She would know, wouldn't she? As often as he filled her dreams, she would know if he were anywhere near. Surely she would.

Clay caught up with the buggy just before it reached the business part of town. He held Lucky back. No need to let the man know he was being followed. They rode past the church Clay remembered attending a few times just to please Mrs. Brady. That was before he'd gotten interested in the things he heard and continued attending for his own benefit. The minister had preached about promises from a loving heavenly Father that Clay wished were true, such as granting the desires of his heart and adopting him into the family of God. The preacher claimed God was always with His children in good times as well as bad. Clay figured God wouldn't take a cowboy into His family who'd stumbled over the right and wrong line so many times he couldn't stand straight anymore. He'd never walk on those streets of gold.

Clay hadn't thought of the things he'd learned in Cedar Bend, or of the people who lived there, for a long time. Oh, sometimes he'd dream of a cute little girl who grew right along with him in his mind. But he figured she wouldn't remember him if she saw him. When his pa moved him from one ranch to another so often he couldn't keep friends, he'd learned to not even try. Only when they'd stayed in Cedar Bend a whole year had he let his guard down. And look what that had gotten him—a glimpse into heaven and a glimpse at a true family. Two things he would never experience for himself.

When Clay worked for Dr. Brady, he saw firsthand what home and family meant. Although he never let them know, he watched Joanna and her parents in their daily lives. What he saw made him envy Joanna and yet fall in love with her at the same time. He envied her because she had both a mother and father who loved and cared for her. He fell in love with her because of her gentleness, caring, and obedience to her parents.

Then Pa said it was time to move on, and Clay left Cedar Bend without ever letting Joanna know how he felt about her. He knew he would never stand a chance with a lady of Joanna's caliber. He remembered watching and listening to her sing at church. He'd never heard another voice so pretty as hers. He'd never seen anyone else who enjoyed singing as much as Joanna either. A smile always hovered around her lips when she sang, and he was certain the angels in heaven must have looked down in approval. He thought surely that's exactly the way she felt, because when she sang, Clay felt a presence of love and peace that must be God descending to take Joanna's offering.

Clay sharpened his attention on the buggy ahead when it turned onto a country road. They must be getting close to their destination. But they traveled several miles more before turning again. As Clay reached the second turn, he had a good idea where he was. When he saw the wooden arch that spanned the road, he knew. Burned on the cross board above his head were the words CIRCLE C RANCH. Clay rode in as if he'd been planning a visit all along.

He knew three men owned the Circle C and that this was one of the largest spreads in western Kansas. One of them had a daughter that had been in his class at school. He remembered she had auburn hair and kept away from him as if he might contaminate her, but he couldn't remember her name.

That didn't matter to him. He made a quick decision as he guided Lucky toward the buggy that had stopped near the ranch house. He needed a job and a place to stay. One ranch was as good as any other to him, but this one had his little buddy, so he couldn't move on just yet. He'd talk to the boss. See if the Circle C needed a good wrangler. Just until he was sure the baby would be taken care of. Then he could go on to Texas.

Chapter 6

Joanna waited until midmorning Wednesday before her father's buggy was available for her to take out to the Circle C.

"Don't stay long, Joanna," her father cautioned. "You never know when an emergency may come up."

"I won't."

Joanna pulled the door open and stepped onto the front porch just as a buggy pulled to a stop in the drive. She laughed and waved then stuck her head back inside. "I'm not going, Dad. Mariah's here."

Joanna turned back to watch Mr. Butler help Mariah from the buggy. She seemed to have something clutched in her arms as she stepped carefully down. No sooner had he turned Mariah loose than Hope leaped into her father's arms. Joanna could hear Mariah scolding the little girl. She giggled when Mr. Butler assured his wife he was capable of catching a four-year-old. Then he pulled Hope back and looked into her eyes with a stern expression. His voice drifted across the yard to Joanna.

"However, young lady, that does not give you license to jump at me before I'm ready. You must always be certain I know what you have in mind, or you may find yourself in a heap on the ground with a broken arm. Is that clear?"

Hope nodded her head, dark ringlets swaying. "Yes, Papa. Now can I go see Aunt Joanna?"

He turned to his wife. "How about it, Mama? Shall I let this one go?"

Mariah's laughter sounded of happiness and contentment. "By all means."

Hope's little legs churned as soon as her feet touched the ground, and she called out, "We comed to see you, Joanna, 'cause I finded us a new brohver on your porch."

"On my porch? A new brother?" Joanna scooped the little girl up and gave her a hug. "Whatever are you talking about now?"

"We comed to talk to you. Can we keep him forever and ever?" Hope's little arms squeezed Joanna's neck. "Mama says he's yours so we haves to ask you."

Joanna turned her attention from Hope to watch Mariah and Sherman approach. Her eyes widened. Mariah indeed carried a baby wrapped in a soft blue blanket. "Mariah, what is she talking about?"

Her friend smiled as she stepped up on the porch. "May we go inside? If your father's here, I'd like to include him."

More than a little confused, Joanna nodded. "Yes, he's home." She opened the door and stepped back. "Please, go on in."

Joanna followed Mariah into the house and then called her father from his office.

While the Butlers settled on the sofa and her father took his favorite chair, Joanna set out cookies and poured coffee for the adults and a small glass of milk for Hope. When everyone had been served, Joanna sat in a wide, overstuffed chair next to the sofa. Within seconds, Hope climbed up to snuggle next to her, a cookie clutched in each hand. Joanna turned her attention to her friend and said, "All right, I'm about to burst from curiosity. Whose baby is that? Where did you get him?"

Mariah looked from Sherman to Tom Brady and back to Joanna, "We stopped by here yesterday morning about ten o'clock because I wanted to let you know we had returned home. Obviously, we missed you."

"Yes," Joanna said, "I helped Dad deliver the Dugan baby. We were gone most of the night and morning."

"Oh, how wonderful." Mariah smiled. "Are they all right?"

Joanna nodded. "Yes, they have a healthy baby boy. But so do you, and you still haven't told us where he came from."

Mariah laughed. "I assure you I'm still trying to figure that out for myself."

"I finded him." Hope squirmed in the chair. "I wants to keep him forever and ever. Can I, Aunt Joanna? Please?"

"I really don't know, Hope. Maybe if your mother tells us where she got him, we'll know more." Joanna looked at Mariah, but Sherman was the one who spoke.

"A crate was on your side porch in front of the door. Hope had already discovered the baby nestled in a bed of straw and wrapped in a quilt by the time we got to the porch. Someone left him there."

Mariah turned to Dr. Brady. "We were hoping you would take a look at him, just to make sure he's all right. Would you mind?"

"Of course not." Tom stood. "Why don't you bring him into my examining room, and we'll see what we think?"

After everyone filed into the next room, Mariah handed the baby to the doctor and then watched as he laid him on the table. His examination didn't take long, but the tiny boy woke and started to cry until the doctor spoke to him in a soothing voice. The baby's expression became serious as he studied the man's face above him.

Dr. Brady wrapped him up and handed him to Mariah. "You've got yourself a fine little boy there, Mrs. Butler. He seems healthy and well cared for to me." He looked from Mariah to Sherman. "Have you tried to find the parents?"

"Oh, I forgot to tell you about the note." Mariah handed the baby to her husband who cradled him close in his arms while she dug in her handbag.

Mariah handed Joanna a folded piece of paper and watched while she opened it and read aloud, "Mrs. Brady, another boy needs your mothering. His ma and pa died in a tornado a day's ride north of here."

Joanna looked at the others, but no one spoke. Were they thinking the same thing she was? Probably not. They hadn't seen Clay Shepherd riding down Main Street yesterday. Excitement stirred in her heart at the thought of Clay outside on her porch.

Another boy needs your mothering. But even if he had written the note, where could he have gotten a baby whose parents were dead? The man she saw yesterday probably wasn't Clay anyway. Sometimes her imagination distorted her common sense, and that's more than likely what happened. Especially with Mark pressuring her to set a date for a marriage she had never agreed to in the first place.

"Joanna, is anything wrong?" Mariah's voice brought her back to the present.

"No, of course not." Joanna handed the note back to her friend. She giggled. "Here you are just back from your wedding trip, and you bring a baby. You certainly have changed from that stuffy, old-maidish schoolteacher Carrie remembers, Mariah."

"That I have." Mariah laughed, and the men laughed with her. She sobered as she touched the blanket that covered the baby then smiled up at her husband. "I wouldn't go back to those days for anything, Joanna. I thought I had passed the age for a family of my own. Now look at what all God has given me."

She gave a quick laugh. "Just think, we will soon be grandparents, and here He has brought us an infant we've already come to love as if he were our own. Do you think it would be wrong for us to keep him?"

Joanna looked at her father. He shook his head. "I don't know why it would be wrong as long as there is no family."

Sherman nodded. "I've got Luke looking into that."

Tom met the gazes of his friends. "Sherman, Mariah, I can't think of any other couple who would make better parents for this little fellow. If my wife could, she would tell you to take him into your home and into your hearts and raise him as your own son. He needs a mom and a dad, and I believe your hearts are big enough to fill that role."

Joanna felt as if her father's words of approval were a sort of benediction on the Butlers becoming the baby's parents. She dabbed at moisture in the corner of her eye and giggled. "Since we are all agreed that God has given you another child, why don't you tell us what we can call him? Young Master Butler will be too much to say when he starts toddling around getting into things, don't you think?"

Mariah laughed and gave Joanna a quick hug. "My dear friend, you do know how to lighten a mood, don't you? There was a family Bible in the crate with him. In the family pages there is an entry for Daniel S. Jacobs who was born on February 3, 1894. That makes him nearly four months old. I think that's our baby, don't you?"

"Oh, how wonderful that you have that for him. I wish we could find out who brought little Daniel, though."

As Sherman shook hands with Dr. Brady and thanked him for his help and approval, Mariah told Joanna that since they didn't know his middle name, they were hoping to turn his middle initial into Sherman.

"Then he'll truly be yours." Joanna smiled. "And we can call him Danny until he's older."

Mariah laughed and said, "We could call him Buddy, I guess. That's what our new ranch hand called him when he asked Sherman for a job."

Joanna's heart jumped as her imagination brought to mind a young man with coal black hair and pale blue eyes astride a fine-looking black horse. She imagined him offering a gentle finger for the baby to grasp and turning that half smile she had never forgotten on the little guy before he called him Buddy. Still, as much as she wanted to, she could not bring herself to ask Mariah their new employee's name.

Later, Joanna busied herself getting lunch ready for her father. After they ate and he left, Joanna thought of Mariah's baby and wondered if Clay really had come back. She tried cleaning the house but gave up when she realized she had dusted her mother's occasional table three times.

"I'll go to town." She put the dustrag away, changed into a clean dress, and straightened her hair before tying on a matching bonnet. Satisfied that she looked presentable, she started out on foot.

Sunshine flooded the land around her, and she welcomed its warmth even though she knew the hot days of summer were just ahead. When she reached Hutchinson's General Store, she crossed the street and opened the door. The bell jingled to announce her presence.

"Good afternoon." Mrs. Hutchinson looked up from some trinkets she had been arranging in a display. "How are you, Joanna?"

"Just fine."

"May I help you with anything?"

Joanna started to say she wanted to make a quilt for Mariah's new baby but stopped just in time. Mariah and Sherman would have to spread their own good news. Instead, she asked, "Do you have any batting? And I'd like to look at your fabric."

"Going to make a quilt, are you?" Mrs. Hutchinson led the way down one aisle.

Joanna smiled at how quickly one's business became public, no matter how inconsequential. "Yes, I've been thinking about making one."

Mrs. Hutchinson glanced over her shoulder as she stopped by the fabric. "Why don't you pick out the prettiest ones while I get your batting?"

"Thank you." Joanna began looking through the bolts of fabric.

"So is this for your hope chest?" Mrs. Hutchinson hadn't left as Joanna hoped. "You and Mark Hopkins haven't set the date, have you?"

Joanna shook her head. "No, nothing like that. I just found a little time on my hands this afternoon and decided to start a quilt."

Obviously discouraged by Joanna's lack of information, the woman turned away. "I see. I'll be getting that batting then."

By the time Joanna had purchased enough fabric and batting for a full-size quilt, plus several pieces of soft cotton, she had a large, bulky package to carry home.

"Sure you can handle that?" Mrs. Hutchinson asked.

Joanna grasped the bag with both arms and nodded. "Oh yes, it isn't heavy, just burdensome. I'll make it fine." Without thinking about her route home, Joanna stayed on the same side of the street as the store and soon came to the mud-hole that she'd had to wade through the other day while Mark waited on the other side. She stood looking at the muddy street. Granted, the sun had dried the standing water, but she still hated to walk through mud, no matter how shallow. Clumps of sticky clay always seemed to cling to the soles of her shoes.

A whistle sounded behind her. Joanna swung quickly to see a grinning Clay Shepherd swaggering down the street toward her. Surely a figment of her imagination.

"Miss Joanna Brady. Been a long time since I've seen you. Least ways I'm hopin' you're still a miss."

His grin widened, and her heart stopped pumping blood to her brain so that she lost all rational thought. Before she realized this was the real Clay Shepherd and not one of her dreams, he swept her up in his arms, bulky package and all. She let out a shriek that should have brought the entire town running as her arm found the only hold available—a tight clutch around Clay's neck. Before she could gather her wits, Clay strode across the mud and deposited her on the other side on dry ground.

A bit late, she found her voice. "You can't carry me. I'm too heavy."

Clay took her package from her, then stepped back and let his gaze drop to her shoes and back to her face while that half grin she had always loved lifted the corner of his mouth. He shook his head. "If that's so, I sure didn't notice. Seems to me, Joanna Brady, you've grown up into a mighty fine-lookin' woman."

Chapter 7

Joanna saw the appreciative glint in Clay's eyes, and warmth flooded her cheeks.

"Hey, Joanna, you all right?" A man who had probably seen the entire incident called from across the street.

"I'm fine." She waved and realized he wasn't the only one who had been watching. A couple stood just outside the general store staring at her. Another man rode by on a horse, his neck craned to look back. If these people were any indication, the entire town had indeed been ready to come to her aid.

She grabbed for her bag, which Clay skillfully kept from her reach. "Give me that. Everyone is staring at us."

Clay stepped around her to take his place between her and the street. His wide grin said he didn't mind the attention, but he enjoyed her discomfort. He extended his elbow for her to take and gave a short bow. "In that case, my lady, don't you think we'd better be on our way?"

"What do you think you are doing, Clay Shepherd?"

"Aha, then you do remember me." He shook his head. "For a second there, I thought you might not."

If he mentions that kiss, I know I'll die of embarrassment. Lord, is Clay the answer to my prayer? There certainly is nothing boring about him. My heart is pounding as if I've just run a mile. And he thought I had forgotten him. Little does he know how often he's visited my thoughts in the last six years, but even more so in the last two days.

Lifting her head high, Joanna started down the street toward home. How else could she get away from the stares still directed toward them? "Of course I haven't forgotten you, Clay. You worked for my father, after all."

"That's right, I did." He fell into step with her as he swung her package onto his shoulder and held it there with one hand. "How is the doctor?"

"He's fine." Joanna wondered if her heart pounded from Clay's proximity or from embarrassment over the scene he had caused in the middle of town.

"Reckon he's keeping busy doctorin' everyone?"

"Yes, he is."

Clay chuckled. "You're real talkative today, ain't ya?"

When Joanna didn't respond, he said, "Since you didn't ask, I got a job here and plan to stay for a while. You'll be seeing me around, I promise."

The breath caught in Joanna's throat. What kind of promise was that? Did he mean anything by it? She turned to see a teasing light in his clear blue eyes. Time hadn't lessened Clay's appeal. In fact, he had matured into a heart-stopping and very appealing man.

"The Circle C needed a wrangler, so here I am."

"You are the Butlers' new help? Mariah said they hired someone."

"You friends of theirs?" Clay asked.

Joanna tried to read his expression, which seemed curious, as he waited for her answer. She nodded. "Yes, Mar– Mrs. Butler is a very dear friend of mine."

"Mrs. Butler," he repeated. "I heard they just got married."

"That's true. They were married two weeks ago."

He looked forward as if in thought before he spoke in a musing voice. "I reckon that means her first husband died leavin' her with two little kids to raise."

Joanna giggled.

Clay looked at her with a wide grin. "What? I must have said something funny."

"It's just that Mariah's never been married before."

"Ya don't say?" Clay's eyebrows lifted. "Then those two little ones must belong to Mr. Butler."

Joanna giggled again. She couldn't help feeling especially lighthearted with Clay striding alongside her, carrying her package on his shoulder. If she didn't know better, she would think all her dreams had just come true. But Clay Shepherd wouldn't stick around. She imagined he was like his father, drifting from one place to another, never content to settle down like regular folks. He didn't know anything else. She couldn't expect any more from him. And wouldn't. But why not enjoy this little respite from her too-quiet life?

Looking up into Clay's handsome face, Joanna resisted the nervous urge to giggle yet again. Instead, her smile matched his as she said, "I know it sounds a little strange, but Mariah seems to attract children. I mean, she was a schoolteacher for a long time, and then she moved here to teach, and the next thing we knew, Mrs. Wainwright. . .I don't know if you remember the Wainwrights, but they were raising her niece. When they moved away, she decided she didn't want her anymore. Hope, I mean. The niece. Mrs. Wainwright always resented her sister, Hope's mother. She took Hope in when her sister died, but she never treated her right."

She shut up as soon as she saw Clay's amused expression. Why did she have to giggle and then rattle on like a magpie just because he looked so appealingly handsome?

"So Mrs. Wainwright gave Hope to Mrs. Butler?" Clay encouraged her to continue.

"No, to Mariah." Joanna flushed when he lifted his eyebrows. "I mean she wasn't Mrs. Butler then. She was still teaching school. And now she has a new baby boy that someone left on our doorstep. Probably because my dad's a doctor. But the Butlers found him, and now they want to raise him as their son. We think that's wonderful, don't you?"

"Yeah, sure."

Clay watched the color come and go in Joanna's smooth cheeks. Her eyes, large and dark, showed her feelings as much as the soft giggle that sounded like music to him. He had never forgotten her, but his memories were nothing compared to the real woman beside him. She was small and feminine, yet he sensed strength in her that he didn't remember. She'd grown up mighty pretty, too. Prettier than he'd expected.

They turned onto the road that led to the Bradys', and Clay wished they could walk without end, but that wouldn't happen. He needed to get back to the ranch. He had just come into town to pick up some personal things he needed. Besides, he'd see Joanna again. He'd make sure of that.

When no mention had been made of Joanna's mother before her house came into sight, Clay wanted to ask about her. But he couldn't, in case he didn't want to hear the answer. It didn't seem right that Mrs. Brady hadn't kept the baby. The woman he remembered wouldn't have handed over a stray dog to anyone else, let alone an orphaned baby. Something was wrong, but he didn't want to hear what it was.

Clay's feet slowed and so did Joanna's as he told her a little about his work on various ranches from Texas to Nebraska. He didn't tell her about his recent experience with bank robbing, but kept his stories to the ordinary workday. Still, her eyes sparkled with interest, and he decided she was the prettiest girl he'd ever seen.

Before he wanted to, they crossed the street and stepped into the short drive leading to the Brady house. He stopped and turned to face her. "Joanna, do you reckon I could—"

"Joanna!" A man's voice yelled. Pounding footsteps sounded from the direction they had just come.

Clay heard Joanna's intake of breath as she turned to see who had called her name. He thought he heard her mutter, "No, not Mark now."

He looked, too, and saw a husky young man running toward them at full speed. Joanna's muttered words didn't make sense until he recognized an older and bigger Mark Hopkins. Years ago they'd had a few run-ins. Mark had even tried to bash his fist against Clay's face a time or two. Although Clay never stepped back from a fight he couldn't avoid, he preferred to use his quick mind and feet to get out of those he could. Especially when the odds were stacked against him like they always had been with the heavier, more muscular Mark. The same man who at the moment reminded Clay of a bull pawing the ground with both nostrils flaring. And that bull was running straight at him.

Mark crossed the road in record time, and Clay imagined he could see smoke rising from each footprint he left. "Joanna, are you all right?"

Mark stopped just short of them and pulled Joanna toward him while glaring at Clay. "Jack said he heard you scream and then go off with some man he didn't recognize. If you've hurt her, I'll—"

Clay grinned, shifted Joanna's package to his left shoulder, and offered his right hand to Mark in a gesture of friendship. "Howdy, Mark. Been a long time, hasn't it?"

Mark stared at him without touching his hand. Clay figured he hadn't recognized him yet. He felt a bit of satisfaction when he saw Joanna squirm away from Mark and step closer to him.

She crossed her arms and gave a little stomp with her foot. "Mark Hopkins, you have no right chasing after me this way. Clay didn't hurt me. I was just surprised, that's all."

"Clay?" Mark's eyes narrowed. He glanced down at Clay's outstretched hand and back to his face. "Clay Shepherd, isn't it?"

"Sure enough." Clay kept his friendliest grin in place. "I'm workin' out at the Circle C now. Reckon you'll be seein' lots of me. Just givin' Miss Joanna here an escort home from town."

Mark spit to the side before turning back to glower at Clay. "Stay away from her. You hear me, Shepherd? Joanna and me are getting married."

"That so?" Clay lifted his eyebrows in a questioning look toward Joanna.

Again her foot stomped the ground. "No, it isn't so. Mark and I are friends, that's all. I've never agreed to marry anyone."

Mark's brows drew together in a heavy dark line. He looked as if the wind had just been knocked out of him. "Joanna, you can't mean that. What about my house? Who did you think I was building a house for?"

"I'm sorry, Mark." Her voice softened. "I never wanted to hurt you, but you just assumed I felt the same about you that you did me. I love you as a friend, Mark, not as a future husband."

Tears sprang to her eyes, and she grabbed her package from Clay before turning away. She ran to the house without looking back, but her voice drifted toward them. "I'm so sorry."

Clay didn't feel the sense of victory he had when she first told Mark off. He felt deflated somehow, like Mark looked. "Hey, man, I'm sorry. I didn't know—"

Mark's head jerked up at Clay's apology, and his eyes blazed with anger. "Just get out of here, why don't you? Face it, Shepherd, you don't belong anywhere near Cedar Bend. You never did. All you ever did was stir up trouble. Joanna's my girl, and I am going to marry her. If you come near her again, I'll rearrange your pretty-boy face for you. I promise you that."

Chapter 8

Joanna slammed the door and stood in the middle of the parlor while hot tears ran down her cheeks. She threw her bundle of quilting material at the sofa where it sat for a moment before slowly falling to the floor. She swung to the window and looked out.

Clay and Mark still stood where she left them. Mark was talking, or yelling. She couldn't understand his words, but she could hear his voice. Then he turned and stomped back toward town. Clay watched him for a moment before looking at the house.

Joanna ducked out of sight, her heart pounding. Surely he wouldn't try to talk to her, not now. She ran straight to the mirror in her bedroom. She looked a sight. Pouring a little water into the washbasin, she wet a washcloth and washed her face.

When no knock sounded at the door, Joanna laid the cloth down and crept with silent feet across the parlor to stand beside the window. She pushed the curtain aside and looked at an empty yard. Her heart sank. Clay had gone without speaking to her.

She crossed the room to sit in the wide, overstuffed chair by the sofa. As she leaned her head back and closed her eyes, she reached out to the One who had promised to be with her always. *Lord, I'm beginning to think Carrie is right. She told me I shouldn't wish for an exciting adventure because I might get more than I want. I can't believe Clay came today, just like in my dreams. Lord, is it wrong to want someone like Clay?*

Joanna searched her heart for the answer, but none came. She wondered why Clay had shown up just when she'd been praying for excitement. Surely God would not send him to her if He didn't want them to be friends. Or maybe even more.

She thought of the way he had carried her across the mud as if she weighed no more than a child. She couldn't stop the giggle the memory brought. Clay Shepherd had certainly swept her off her feet, and he'd given her more excitement in one afternoon than she remembered having in her entire life. If she must one day marry Mark, what would it hurt to have a little fun first? She certainly would have very little afterward.

At the thought of Mark, Joanna grew sober. She had hurt Mark, and she hadn't wanted to. She did love him, but only as a friend. Why couldn't he understand that? Why did he assume she would jump at the chance to be his wife?

She bowed her head and prayed. *Lord, please forgive me for hurting Mark. If possible, could You send someone else for Mark to love? Someone who will appreciate his goodness and loyalty. He's a dear friend, and I love him in that way, but I just can't marry him. Not even someday in the future like I've always thought. I'd rather be an old maid. So please send a good wife for Mark. And Lord. . .*

Joanna stopped. How could she pray that Clay would be the one for her when she didn't know if she even wanted him? But she'd loved Clay from the first day she'd seen him when they were just children, hadn't she? Still, he was so wild. He carried an air of mystery and romance about him that called to her desire for adventure even while warning her away. She certainly would never know what to expect with Clay the way she did with Mark. Maybe that wasn't good. When they were in school, Carrie hadn't thought so, but now Carrie had found her knight in shining armor. Lucas Nolan had been just as wild and unpredictable as Clay a few years back. He'd led Carrie on a merry chase before he'd found what he was looking for.

"Come unto me, all ye that labour and are heavy laden, and I will give you rest."

The words from Matthew 11:28 spoke to Joanna's heart, convincing her. Lucas had settled down and become a regular family man after he filled the emptiness in his heart with God's love. She should be praying for Clay's salvation rather than praying for his attention.

Joanna stood and grabbed her bundle of fabric. She needed to get started on the quilt for Mariah's baby. Tomorrow would be soon enough to apologize to Mark for telling him in front of Clay she didn't want to marry him. His pride might be hurt, but he would get over her. When he met the woman God had picked out for him, he'd thank her for turning him down. As for Clay, Joanna didn't know what to do, except begin praying for him.

Clay stopped at the general store and picked up the things he'd come into town to get. Then he walked to the livery where he'd left Lucky. But his mind wasn't on Lucky so much as it was on Joanna. He couldn't forget the way she'd said she was sorry and then run into the house. At first he thought her feelings were hurt, but the sound of that door slamming made him wonder. Did he say or do something that made her mad, or had her anger been directed at Mark? Maybe she was angry at both of them or maybe just herself.

Clay shrugged. He'd learned long ago that women couldn't be figured out. Soon as you thought you understood them, they'd turn the tables on you and you had to start all over again. They kept a man guessing, that was for sure. Of course he wouldn't mind studying Miss Joanna Brady one little bit. He sure was glad to know that she had never married, although he knew her marital status shouldn't matter to him. He didn't plan to stick around long enough to renew any friendships. He just wanted to make sure his little buddy had found a good home before he went south.

He paid for Lucky's stay and headed toward the Circle C. At the ranch, Clay turned Lucky toward the corral where he unsaddled him and rubbed him down. He watched the big stallion run a short distance away before turning back to whinny.

"You'll be fine." Clay grinned at the horse that was all the family he had. At the sound of his voice, Lucky trotted back for another pat. Clay obliged, then slipped through the gate and hooked it before walking toward the bunkhouse with his saddle thrown over his shoulder.

He had already spent one night at the Circle C and found the other hands to be quiet for the most part. They seemed to be a praying bunch, and he wasn't used to that. Last night and again this morning they had all gathered in the big ranch house to eat. Fifteen men sat around the long table and bowed their heads while the foreman prayed. He'd never seen anything like it. If anyone had tried that at the Crooked S back in Nebraska, they would have been laughed off the ranch. Still, these men were friendly enough without pushing past the limits he set. He hoped Lucky found his roommates as easy to get along with.

"Mighty fine-lookin' horse you got there."

Clay turned at the sound of the foreman's voice. "Howdy, Cyrus. I didn't realize anyone was around."

"I figured you'd be back about now, and I wanted to talk to ya." Cyrus fell into step with Clay. "Go ahead and stow your saddle. We can talk out here on the porch."

Clay nodded and went through the door while Cyrus sat in one of the wide, wooden chairs on the porch. One thing Clay liked about the Circle C was the cleanliness. A porch ran the entire length of the bunkhouse with white painted chairs sitting here and there. The place looked comfortable and inviting. Might be a good place to settle down if a man wanted to stay. He let his saddle and bags fall to the bare wood floor at the head of his bed and then returned outside.

He sat in the chair next to Cyrus, rested his ankle across his opposite knee, and waited. The older man leaned back and folded his hands behind his neck before he spoke. "Thought I'd give ya the lay of the land around here." He chuckled. "Reckon ya already figured out our eatin' arrangements."

Clay nodded with a grin. "First thing I usually check out is where to fill my belly."

"Can't fault ya none for that." Cyrus narrowed his eyes as he looked at Clay. "I remember your old man."

"That so?"

"Yep, kept to hisself mostly. Never caused no trouble that I can recall. Never heard any complaints about him." He nodded as if satisfied. "Reckon you're proud ta be called his son."

"I reckon so." Actually Clay hadn't thought one way or the other. He'd accepted his pa's ways, figured moving from one ranch to another was normal. He'd done the same after his father's death. Work a job until your feet get restless and then move on. That had seemed like a good philosophy to him up until now. Someone always needed a ranch hand. Like the Circle C. He looked across the yard toward the sprawling ranch house and wondered what it would be like to stay for a change. Cedar Bend was the closest to home he'd ever known. Might be a good place to put down some roots.

"Got a few broncs ta break. You done much of that?" Cyrus asked.

Clay turned from his thoughts of growing roots and faced his foreman. "Sure, I've done my share, I reckon."

"Good." Cyrus nodded. "Tomorrow we'll let ya take a turn riding fence, makin' repairs, and lookin' for trouble. Haven't had much of the two-legged kind for more'n ten years, but ya never know on a spread this size. The four-legged ones keep us plenty busy anyhow."

"How big is the Circle C?"

"Let's just say you could ride all day before comin' to the other boundary, and if ya kept goin' around the entire property, it'd take ya another three days to get back to the startin' point."

Clay whistled through his teeth. "That's a lot of land."

Cyrus chuckled. "Yep, the finest spread in Kansas. Think you'll like it here?"

"I sure hope to."

"Fine." The older man used his hands to push himself out of his chair.

Clay stopped him. "Cyrus, can you tell me something?"

"What's on your mind?"

"Just curious." Clay didn't look at Cyrus, so he wouldn't know how much his answer mattered. "I used to work for the doctor. What happened to his wife?"

Cyrus rubbed the back of his neck. "She got sick. Was an invalid for a while. She died about two years ago."

The news didn't surprise Clay, but he still fought the pain it brought. He stood, being careful to keep his feelings private. "She was a good woman."

"That she was," Cyrus agreed before he changed the subject. "Hope you stay awhile. I'll get ya started with those broncs."

Clay put aside his feelings of loss as he let the excitement he always felt before riding a wild bronco glimmer deep inside. He barely listened to Cyrus and found himself nodding before he realized what he had agreed to do.

"We leave around nine to make it on time."

"On time?" He focused on the foreman's face.

"Yep, Sunday school starts at half past nine."

"Sunday school?" Clay hadn't been to Sunday school since he'd left Cedar Bend. Had he just agreed to go with Cyrus?

The old man nodded. "And church. Most everyone here goes. 'Course we take turns stayin' and workin' on Sundays so no one has to miss too often."

Clay remembered that Joanna used to sing in church. Maybe she still did. He grinned as they reached the breaking corral and another sort of excitement caught up with him. "Sure, I'll be ready at nine come Sunday morning."

"And don't be forgettin' the annual church social Saturday night." Cyrus leaned against the corral fence. "Everybody's sure to be there. Fact is, so many come that they've taken to havin' it at the Cattlemen's Association Hall. Biggest place in town."

"That so?" Clay figured that meant Joanna would go. He grinned. "I'll be plannin' on it then. Thanks for lettin' me know."

He stepped on the first rung of the fence and jumped the rest of the way over, landing on his feet. Facing a wild bronco should be easy compared to a jealous Mark Hopkins come Saturday night. Clay chuckled at the thought. Good thing for him they'd be at a church social.

Chapter 9

Joanna had no sooner cleaned the kitchen on Friday afternoon than a knock sounded at the front door. She dried her hands on her apron as she crossed the parlor. Mariah and Carrie stood on the porch, with Hope peeking around her mother. Mariah held her new baby son close.

"Come in." Joanna started to step back but stopped when Hope launched herself against her and held tight. "Why, sweetheart, what's the matter?"

The little girl looked up as Joanna bent to lift her into her arms. Her lower lip trembled while her large dark eyes filled with tears. "We's come to give my brohver back."

"What?" Joanna looked up at Mariah with wide eyes. "Why would you do such a thing?"

Mariah and Carrie looked just as shocked as Joanna felt. Mariah spoke first. "I have no idea where she got that idea."

Joanna turned and carried a now sobbing Hope into the parlor and sat in the overstuffed chair where she could hold the little girl on her lap. "Hope, you don't have to give little Daniel back. Your papa had Luke check into it. They even went to the house where your new wrangler said he'd found your brother. Luke said it's all right for you to keep your brother forever."

"Huh uh." Hope shook her head. "Mama said we has to bring him back."

Joanna looked at Mariah, who seemed to be speechless at the moment. "Do you have any idea what you might have said?"

Mariah shook her head and leaned toward her little daughter. "Hope, exactly what did I say that made you think I wanted to give Daniel back?"

Hope sat up and turned a frown on her mother. "You telled Papa we's gonna go back to see Aunt Joanna, and you's gonna take my baby brohver back, too."

"Oh no, honey." Mariah reached out to touch the little girl. "I didn't mean we were going to take him back and leave him. I just meant that I wanted to come back to see Aunt Joanna even though we had been here only two days ago. I love little Daniel as much as I love you and Carrie."

Mariah smiled at the young woman beside her. "None of you were born to me as most mothers have children, yet you each have been born in my heart in your own special way. I will never, as long as I live, stop thanking God for giving me such wonderful children."

She turned back to Hope. "I love you, Hope. You are my own special little girl. Carrie is my special young lady and good friend who will soon make me a grandmother." Mariah shared a smile with Carrie and then said, "And Daniel is our very special baby boy whom I already love much too much to give back."

Hope's tears stopped, and she scooted from Joanna's lap to lean against her mother's knee. She patted the baby's tiny arm. "Is we gonna keep Daniel?"

At her voice and touch, the baby opened his eyes and focused on her face. His mouth spread into a sweet baby smile as he cooed to his big sister.

Hope brightened. "Him loves me."

Mariah laughed with Joanna and Carrie. "Yes, he does." She sighed. "Oh my, I had no idea how difficult motherhood could be."

Joanna giggled. "You are doing a wonderful job, Mariah. Remember, I told you once that it was instinctive."

Carrie rested her hand on her stomach. "You make it sound so easy, Joanna. I have my doubts, though. I'm so glad Mariah is going through this now, so I'll have someone to ask questions to later."

Mariah shook her head. "I fear, Carrie, that we shall have to learn together."

The three women laughed while Hope and Daniel talked and cooed to each other. Joanna watched her friends and longed for the day when she would share their so-called problems. She couldn't help wondering if her babies would have brown eyes like hers or pale blue eyes like—

"What do you think, Joanna?" Joanna's mental image of Clay cuddling their baby burst into a thousand pieces at the sound of Mariah's voice.

"I'm sorry. What did you say?"

Mariah laughed. "We were discussing plans for the library. The last time we talked, you had mentioned wanting to raise money at the town's Fourth of July celebration. Carrie just suggested we incorporate a rodeo put on by the Circle C. We'd charge an admission price and award a purse to the first three winners."

Joanna nodded. "Yes, that sounds like a very good idea. All the ranches nearby could take part. We could charge admission for the spectators, too, couldn't we?"

Mariah and Carrie exchanged amused looks. Carrie said, "That's the idea, Joanna. If we put up posters ahead of time, we should draw a good crowd."

"Back in Ohio, box suppers were quite common," Mariah said. "Do you think we could have one here?"

"Yes, we've had them before." Carrie nodded. "We'd need an auctioneer, maybe Mr. Braun."

Joanna noticed Hope had grown restless. She handed her a couple of picture books she'd had since she was a child. When the little girl settled on the floor to look at the books, Joanna leaned back and listened to her friends. The ideas they discussed could bring in a sizable income for the library if they were carried out in the right way. She had dreamed of this for so long. Now with Mariah's generosity and help, her dreams could very well become reality.

When Mariah paused for breath, Joanna said, "I want you two to know how much I appreciate all you are doing to build a library for Cedar Bend. This has been my dream, but I believe you, too, have caught the vision of what can be. However, I'd like for our library to belong to the entire town, and for that to happen, I think we need more people involved."

"Maybe we could form a sort of club with open membership to anyone interested." Mariah's eyes sparkled with enthusiasm.

"That's a great idea," Carrie said. "The more people involved the better."

Excitement grew in Joanna as she thought of the women in the community who would join. Although the library had been her idea and part of her hated to give up control, she realized she couldn't handle such a big project alone. Hard as it might be, she would have to step down and become just one of many working for the betterment of Cedar Bend.

"However," Carrie continued. "I think we need to make it clear from the start that Joanna is in charge."

"Yes, of course," Mariah agreed. "I took for granted that she would be."

Joanna met the smiling faces of her friends, and her heart filled with love for them both. What did anyone ever do without friends? How could Clay drift from place to place without forming attachments? She shook off the invasive thoughts of Clay Shepherd that continually plagued her and concentrated on Mariah's voice.

"We could have a quick meeting at Saturday evening's social when everyone is together. Our first order will be to make Joanna our official librarian." She lifted a questioning gaze to Joanna. "That is unless you have any objections."

"No, no, I don't suppose I do." Joanna turned to her friend. "Do you think I can handle the job? I've only been to one actual library a long time ago."

Mariah laughed. "I think you'll do fine."

"Great." Carrie stood. "Since that's decided, Hope and I have business elsewhere."

Hope jumped up from the picture books and ran to Carrie, taking her hand. "We's gonna go on a secret."

"Yes, we are." Carrie placed a finger across Hope's lips. "Let's not tell or it won't be a secret."

"Awright." Hope nodded and pulled Carrie toward the door. "Bye, Aunt Joanna. Bye, Mama. Bye, baby brohver."

Joanna and Mariah both told her good-bye and watched as Carrie closed the door behind them. Mariah stood with the baby. "I believe my son has gone to sleep. Would you mind if I lay him down?"

Joanna jumped up. "No, of course not. You may put him on my bed. Does he roll over yet?"

"Not yet. But let's put a pillow on each side just in case."

After they settled the sleeping baby on the bed and tiptoed from the room, Joanna asked Mariah, "Do you know what your daughters' secret is?"

Mariah laughed. "I have a good idea. I'm sure they are on a mission to buy a gift for a certain little brother they both dote on without shame."

"Oh, how sweet." Joanna smiled. "Carrie has certainly had to make some adjustments in her life, hasn't she? Going from an only child to having not only a stepmother but two young siblings in less than a month must make quite a difference."

"I'm sure it does." Mariah sat at Joanna's table and accepted the cup of tea she offered. "She called herself a selfish little brat once, but I haven't seen any selfishness manifested lately. She loves Hope and treats her as if she's always been her little sister."

"God had great things in store when He brought you to us, didn't He, Mariah?"

"Oh yes, God and Kansas have been good to me." Mariah smiled. "But enough about me. I want to know what's troubling my dear friend."

"Me?"

"Yes, Joanna, you. I'm not blind, deaf, or dumb. I've been watching you slip off into a world of your own even as we visited this afternoon. Something is on your mind, and it isn't just the library, as important as I know that is to you."

Joanna giggled. "My, but you are perceptive. However, I really couldn't say that anything is wrong. On the contrary, so much is right. The library is off to an absolutely marvelous start, thanks to you. I've lost weight and feel better than I can ever remember. I have the dearest friend anyone could ever ask for. How could anything be wrong?"

Mariah sipped her tea and gave Joanna an assessing look. Joanna lifted her own cup and took a long, bracing sip. How could she feel so guilty when she hadn't lied? She just hadn't confessed the whole truth. But did she have to? Did she have to tell her friend of the longing in her heart for excitement? Carrie hadn't understood, and Carrie was her age. How could an older, wiser, more settled friend understand the restless feelings that sometimes seemed to overwhelm Joanna?

Finally, under Mariah's steady gaze, Joanna looked up and giggled. "You know me too well."

"It isn't hard to see you have something on your mind."

Joanna sighed. "It's nothing really. I just feel so restless sometimes. Mark Hopkins thinks I'm his girl, and he's even building me a house."

"That's wonderful. Mark is such a nice young man." Mariah's quick smile faltered as Joanna shook her head.

"But it isn't wonderful, and that's part of the problem." She sighed again. "I don't love Mark. I mean, I do, but only as a friend. I told him that. The other day when Clay walked me home from the store. I told him right in front of Clay that I don't want to marry him."

Joanna covered her face with both hands until she heard Mariah's soft laughter.

She looked up to see a teasing light in her friend's eyes. "Why, Miss Joanna Brady, I do believe you lead a more exciting life than I knew. Would this Clay you mentioned be Sherman's new wrangler?"

Heat filled Joanna's cheeks as she nodded.

A light seemed to ignite behind Mariah's expressive eyes, and she laughed aloud. "Oh, I can't believe this. Clay Shepherd. I am so dense to not put two and two together when I first heard his name. Don't I recall being told a secret story about a first kiss under the mistletoe?"

"Mariah, don't breathe a word." Joanna's eyes widened at the thought.

"Of course I won't." Mariah reached across the table and covered Joanna's hand with hers. "What you tell me in confidence will always remain between only the two of us." She smiled. "Clay Shepherd is a very handsome young man, Joanna. And you say he walked you home?"

Joanna nodded. "I'm going to tell you something, Mariah, in confidence. I've been praying."

When she paused, Mariah nodded in encouragement. "That's always a good thing, Joanna."

"Maybe. I mean, it could depend on what you pray for." Joanna pushed her teacup from one hand to the other before she finally spoke. "I've been praying for God to send me someone exciting. Someone dashing and romantic."

Joanna lifted hesitant eyes to look at her friend who sat staring at her. Finally, Mariah said, "You mean someone like Clay Shepherd?"

"Oh yes." Joanna released the words on a rush of breath she hadn't realized she'd been holding.

"Oh, my dear." Mariah again touched Joanna's hand. "Are you sure the young man is a Christian?"

Joanna's gaze dropped to her cup and to her friend's hand on hers. Now that Mariah had voiced her secret concern, she knew she would have to face it. How could Clay be a Christian when he'd led the life of a drifter, going from ranch to ranch with no place to call his own? Yet, why couldn't he be? She had prayed so hard. God could not make a mistake. He would send the very best, and He had sent Clay, hadn't He?

When Joanna didn't answer, Mariah's soft voice spoke to her heart. "My dear friend, be very careful. Don't allow the enemy to attack your Christian faith through this man. No matter how appealing he may seem, no matter how exciting, you must be certain that he is a child of God first. I will be praying for you."

Chapter 10

By Saturday afternoon Joanna had seen neither Mark nor Clay since the afternoon Clay had walked her home from town. Using a large package of dried apples, she made a couple of pies for the church social that evening. When the top crust turned golden brown, she pulled the pies from the oven and set them in the middle of the table to cool.

A glance at the clock told Joanna she needed to start getting ready. After a relaxing bath, she dressed in a new royal blue dress she had made herself. The color complemented her dark hair, making her skin appear smooth and unblemished. She brushed her hair until it shone then put it up, leaving short ringlets to hang down on either side.

When she looked in the mirror she scarcely recognized herself since she rarely took such pains with her appearance. She batted her eyelashes at her reflection. "Why, Miss Brady, you take my breath away."

"Mine, too." Her father's voice sounded behind her.

Joanna turned with an embarrassed giggle. "Don't you dare make fun of me. I was just complimenting myself since I don't even know if I have an escort."

Her father frowned. "No escort? For the loveliest girl in town? I assumed you would be going with Mark."

"Yes, so did I." Joanna shrugged as if she didn't care. Which she didn't really, except that she didn't like the idea of going alone, and she didn't want Mark's feelings hurt. If she saw him tonight, she would make certain to apologize. Now she answered the question in her father's eyes. "We had a few words the other day, and I haven't seen him since."

"Oh, that's too bad, especially if you have to go with your old dad." Tom Brady turned from her open door. "I'll hurry and get changed. By the way, were those pies on the table for the social?"

"What do you mean *were*?" Joanna hurried toward the kitchen. "There had better be two uncut pies still on the table."

Her father's laughter told her before she saw the pies that he had been teasing her.

She decided to return the favor. She smiled at him. "I see you are in a good mood. Does this mean you have a date for the social tonight?"

His dark eyes danced with merriment. "From the way you've been talking, I may have to escort my own daughter."

"You mean you didn't ask Mrs. James?" Joanna tried to keep her expression innocent.

"As a matter of fact. . ." her father began then stopped.

Joanna's eyes widened. He wouldn't.

The doctor grinned as he finished his long, drawn-out pause. "I didn't."

"Oh, Dad. Can't I ever get the better of you?"

His laughter drifted to her as he turned toward his room. "Not if I can help it."

Joanna had the pies packed in a box and her father was just coming out of his bedroom when someone knocked at their front door. "I'll get it," he called to her.

When the door opened and she heard the murmur of men's voices, Joanna went into the parlor. Mark clutched a spray of white daisies, which he held out to her with a wide smile on his face.

"Here, I thought you might like these."

Mark had brought her flowers? Joanna took the daisies and held them while she fought the urge to feel Mark's forehead for fever. "Thank you, Mark. I'll put these in water."

"I'll help you."

When Mark followed her to the kitchen, she thought about telling him she didn't need help, but then she remembered the pies. He might as well carry them. Besides, this would give her a chance to talk to him in private.

She took a glass from the cabinet and pumped water into it. While she arranged the flowers, she said, "Mark, I want to apologize for the other day. I shouldn't have spoken to you the way I did. I could have waited until we were alone to tell you how I feel."

"Don't worry about that, Joanna. I know you were just upset." Mark leaned against the counter. His smile seemed as confident as ever.

Didn't he understand? What could she say to get through to him? She started to speak when her father called to them to hurry, or they'd be late for the social.

"Mark, do you mind carrying the pies?" Joanna slid the box across the table.

"Course not." He sniffed as he picked up the box. "Mmmm apple. Did you make these for me?"

"Just be glad she made them." Dr. Brady spoke from the doorway. "If I'd baked them, you wouldn't want even a taste."

Mark laughed with the doctor, and Joanna swept past the men and out the door. At least Mark appreciated her pies. Not that it did anything to endear him to her. She had spent the last three hours making herself presentable for the evening's activities and not one word or even a noticeable look of appreciation did she get. Only her pies were worthy of that honor.

Since the Cattlemen's Association Hall had been built on the edge of the business district within an easy walk of the doctor's house, they decided to leave the horse and buggy at home. Mark balanced the box containing the pies while he walked beside Joanna. Her father trailed behind.

With Mark talking about a recent increase in the cost of grain and how that affected the farmers and cattle ranchers, Joanna relaxed. She might be bored, but at least he wasn't trying to push her into marriage.

The streets were lined with wagons and buggies, and several families and couples on foot headed toward the hall. Joanna and Mark spoke to nearly everyone as they joined those going inside the large lighted building.

Joanna took the pies from Mark, thanked him for carrying them, and headed for the already groaning table of food.

"Here, let me clear some room." Mrs. James smiled at Joanna before moving several pies and cakes closer together. "This looks like one of our largest turnouts."

"There's certainly enough food." Joanna looked at all the pies, cakes, and other goodies on the table. She saw meat dishes and vegetables. There were more bowls of potato salad than she wanted to count.

"And more coming in, but your pies are always my favorite." Mrs. James patted Joanna's arm. "I hope I get a piece."

"Why, thank you, Mrs. James." Someone jostled against Joanna, and glad for the interruption, she turned to greet another woman from church. She liked Mrs. James but always felt uncomfortable with her. While she wouldn't mind if her father remarried, she wanted him to find someone he could love, and she hadn't noticed that he had special feelings for Mrs. James, although the woman obviously admired him.

As Joanna moved away from the ladies gathering around the food table, she looked across the room. Why her gaze landed on a tall, dark-haired young man with an appreciative glint in his eyes and a half smile on his face, she didn't know. Why Clay Shepherd was in attendance at the church social, she also didn't know. She certainly hadn't expected to see him. Her heart tripped in her chest, and she looked away.

"Hello, Joanna."

She started at the sound of Mariah's voice, and a flood of color filled her cheeks. Joanna hoped Mariah hadn't noticed where her attention had been.

"Hi. I didn't realize you were here. Where are your children?"

"Daniel is with Carrie, and Sherman has Hope." Mariah glanced across the room where Clay stood with a couple of men from the Circle C before her gaze met Joanna's. "I see our new wrangler is here."

"Your new wrangler?" Joanna looked up at her friend with wide, innocent eyes. "Oh, you mean Clay Shepherd."

"You knew perfectly well who I meant. And you knew he was here, too."

Joanna sighed. "Yes, I suppose I did."

"Just please be careful. You are a dear friend, and I don't want you hurt." Mariah glanced back toward the men. "Mr. Shepherd is a very handsome young man, and he has just the right amount of cowboy charm that could easily capture a young lady's heart. I saw him break a wild bronco the other day. There was something about man and beast that seemed to fit. Maybe the same wild streak runs through both, making them resist the confining reins."

"I know you're right. I promise to be careful." Joanna felt as if her heart might break. She had been infatuated with Clay and his free spirit for so long. She had never forgotten him, and she never would. She almost wished he had not returned. He had been only a childhood memory before, while now he stood less than thirty feet away, an appealing man who seemed as aware of her as she was of him.

She chanced another peek at Clay and wished she hadn't when his smile widened and he winked. Joanna's heart pounded so hard against her rib cage that she had to take a deep, calming breath. If she could just keep from looking at Clay, she'd be all right.

"Joanna, I wanted to tell you"—Mariah slipped an arm around Joanna's shoulders and turned her away from Clay— "Carrie and I have already spoken to several of the ladies, and they seem quite interested in our plans for the library."

"That's wonderful." Joanna tried to concentrate on Mariah's voice as she suggested that Joanna set up a planning meeting while the ladies were interested.

She promised she would. Just then, Pastor Carson's booming voice welcomed everyone. After he prayed, he said, "We'll start off tonight with some games. If you don't want to join in, please remain outside the circle so no one gets hurt. For those who would like to play, let's gather in the middle of the room and start a brisk game of 'Captain Jinks.' "

Mark appeared beside Joanna at that moment, ready to whisk her off to play in the musical games.

Pastor Carson's voice rang out. "Grab a partner, and let's all sing together."

As soon as the circle formed, those playing and several standing to the sides of the large room joined their voices in singing, "Captain Jinks of the horse marines, we clap our hands beyond our means."

At that point everyone brought their hands together in one loud clap. The next stanza had the men swinging their partner.

"And swing that lady while in her teens, for that's the stout of the army."

Next they all joined hands and skipped to the left in a circle as they continued to sing. Then the words "Captain Jinks, the ladies' knight, the gentleman changes to the right" had the men and women changing places, which gave Joanna a new partner. This man, one of the cowboys from the Circle C, swung Joanna before they promenaded around the circle.

The game continued in the same way until Joanna found herself next to Clay. He swung her around, and they began the promenade. Although she had been well aware of him, she had lost track of how quickly they would become partners. He grinned at her, and while everyone else sang, he leaned close and said, "I thought you'd never get here."

Joanna tried to ignore the flutter his words caused in her midsection and kept her gaze on the couple in front of them. She tried to remember Mariah's warnings instead of letting herself give in to the thrill of being so close to Clay. Granted, he was at their church party, but that didn't mean he was a Christian, and she needed to remember that fact.

"Will you be my partner for the next game?" Clay asked.

Joanna missed her step, and Clay tightened his hold on her.

She looked across the circle at Mariah, but her friend didn't seem to notice her predicament. She glanced into Clay's blue eyes fringed with long, black lashes and thought she had never seen any man so handsome. Why would he waste his time on her? She gave up trying to sing and nodded. He grinned.

When the promenade stopped and they all clapped their hands, Clay leaned close and said, "You sure are pretty tonight, Miss Brady."

With the loud clap ringing in her ears, Joanna thought she might have misunderstood his words, but she recognized the admiration in his eyes. He slipped his arm around her waist to swing her, and she forgot to say thank you as she had intended. Instead, she stared up at him, holding his left hand with her right and clutching his shoulder with her left.

She followed the motions as they skipped. The words came from memory, so she sang with the others, but she and Clay might as well have been alone, for that's the way she felt. Then Clay switched to her right side and she had another partner.

When the original partners were back together, Pastor Carson called a pause.

———

Clay stayed back, letting Mark monopolize Joanna during the break. He'd watch, see how things were between the two of them. After all, if Joanna really cared for Mark, he wouldn't step between them. But the second time Joanna looked his way while Mark talked to her, Clay decided he had waited long enough.

He saw Pastor Carson stand and figured he was about to call for another game, so he crossed the room and stopped by Joanna. "Looks like the next game is starting."

Joanna took a step back and told Mark she had promised to be partners with Clay for the next game. Before Mark had a chance to react, Joanna took Clay's arm and pulled him away.

Clay figured Mark would have liked nothing better than to bloody his nose at that moment, so he flashed his friendliest smile at the angry guy and followed Joanna. They played "Skip to My Lou," and Clay kept a close eye on Joanna after the first skipper tried to steal her from him. To play the game right, he couldn't hold Joanna's hand, but he thought about breaking the rule when Mark ended up in the center of the circle. As expected, Mark tried to steal Joanna, but Clay blocked him so he had to move on to someone else. Clay ignored the glare Mark sent his way and grinned because Joanna didn't seem to notice.

Clay hadn't had so much fun in a long time. Associating with church people wasn't so bad. He might even enjoy going to church in the morning. After all, Joanna would be there.

When the game ended and Pastor Carson prayed a short prayer over their dinner, Clay took Joanna's elbow and steered her toward the table. "I've been eyeing that food. Reckon we can get a bite of something?"

Joanna giggled. "We'd better hurry or it might all disappear."

"You think so?" Clay smiled at her. He wouldn't mind just looking at her instead of eating. He couldn't remember ever seeing a prettier girl. Her eyes were like two drops of shiny dark chocolate with beautiful, long, dark lashes. In contrast, her skin was smooth and olive toned with a touch of color in each cheek. She had put her hair up in some fancy style, and while he couldn't find any prettier in the room, he liked it better hanging down to the middle of her back and swinging free. Of course, he knew better than to tell her that. In fact, she'd probably be shocked if she knew what he was thinking.

They got in line, and Clay helped Joanna fill her plate, although she said she couldn't eat so much. "I'll be as big as the side of a barn if I eat everything you're trying to put on my plate."

Clay laughed and dropped the mound of potato salad on his plate instead of hers. He spoke low so no one else could hear. "Reckon it don't matter how much you eat, darlin'. You're still the prettiest girl in this hall."

Color flooded Joanna's cheeks, proving to him that he was right. He could look the world over and never find a more beautiful woman. Nor a sweeter one. Yep, Miss Joanna Brady could wrap him around her little finger without half trying.

"Joanna," a middle-aged woman stepped between them. "Mariah's been telling me you intend to start a library here in town. Is that right?"

"Yes, it is."

Joanna turned to the woman, and Clay stepped back. He didn't see them coming, but as soon as Joanna moved away from the table, five or six other women surrounded her, all talking about a library. He glanced to the side, trying to find a place to get away where he could eat. Then he saw Hopkins bearing down on Joanna from across the room.

"How will you display the books?"

"Won't you need a sign put out front so everyone will know the house is a library?"

"What about renovations on the house?"

Clay heard the ladies as he watched Mark weaving his way closer. Then Clay got an idea that would be sure to win Joanna's attention. He stepped back to her side.

"Excuse me, ladies, but I couldn't help hearing your conversation." Clay turned his most charming smile on the older ladies before letting it rest on Joanna. "I've done some carpenter work before. If you are in need of shelving, I'd be glad to donate my time to such a worthy cause as a library."

At the same time that Mark reached the group, Joanna turned and smiled at Clay. "That would be wonderful. As soon as we get some lumber, you can get started."

With the approving voices of the older ladies surrounding him, Clay almost forgot Mark stood glaring at him. He looked into the smiling face of the woman he just might care for enough to put down those roots he'd been thinking about and grinned.

Chapter 11

Joanna couldn't have been more pleased. The library would soon become a reality. Her love of reading had been the catalyst that spawned the idea to provide Cedar Bend with enough books to satisfy everyone in the area. Now many others had joined her cause. Even Clay.

"Back off, Shepherd." Joanna turned at Mark's growl. The scowl on his face looked almost frightening. "You're just trying to get in good with Joanna. If she needs anything done for her library, I'll do it."

Clay simply shrugged with an amused expression on his face. "Reckon that's up to Miss Brady."

Joanna was vaguely aware of the startled reaction coming from the women surrounding them. Several of them stepped back. Some gasped. Mariah had been standing to the side listening while Joanna talked with the ladies. Now she stepped forward.

"Mark, I'm sure there's plenty of work to share for the library."

"I don't intend to share with the likes of him." Mark scowled.

Clay grinned.

Joanna wondered if he ever took anything seriously. Had Clay breezed back into town only to have some fun at their expense? Maybe his attention had just been a big joke after all.

"You want to step outside and settle this?" Joanna heard the threat in Mark's voice.

Clay didn't seem to. He looked down at his heaping plate of food with a wistful expression before looking back at Mark. "Well now, Hopkins, to tell the truth, I'd much rather eat my dinner."

"You scared I'll mess up your pretty face?"

"Mark Hopkins, you stop this right now." Joanna turned toward her long-time friend. "There's no need to fight. Like Mariah said, we'll have plenty of work for everyone to do."

"Sorry, Joanna, this thing's between me and Shepherd. Doesn't have anything to do with your library. This has been building for a long time."

Mark's angry gaze never left Clay's face. Joanna wondered how Clay could act so unconcerned. He kept a pleasant expression as he tried to talk his angry rival out of making a scene. "You know, maybe we oughta drop this, Hopkins. Seems to me a church social just ain't the right place to settle differences."

"He's right, Mark." Mariah tried to intervene again. "Let's calm down and forget this unpleasantness ever happened."

So far the men had kept their voices low so only those standing close enough to hear knew of the confrontation. Joanna didn't know what she would do if Mark didn't back down. Clay obviously didn't want to fight. He'd tried being friendly, and he'd tried to talk Mark out of fighting. But Mark refused to give up. If she'd had any doubts before about her feelings for Mark, she didn't now. If he ever calmed down enough to see reason, she planned to tell him straight out that she didn't want him pursuing her ever again. She'd had enough.

Mark gave Clay one last hard glare and nodded toward the back door of the hall, not far from where they stood. "I'm going outside. We'll soon see if you're man enough to follow."

When Mark took off for the door, Clay let out a sigh and shook his head. He grinned at Joanna as he handed her his plate. "Can you hold this for me, Joanna? I'm powerful hungry, but I reckon I still will be when I get back."

"You aren't going out there, are you?" Joanna took the plate and balanced it with her own. "He's angry, Clay. You might get hurt."

Clay shrugged and looked from Joanna to the other ladies. "I apologize to all you nice ladies for this. But I don't reckon your friend's gonna cool down much standin' around waitin' on me. Might as well get this over with instead of putting it off." He started away, then glanced over his shoulder with another grin and said, "I don't reckon Mark ever did like me much."

Joanna watched the back door close behind Clay and click with a decisive sound. She let out a strangled cry and shoved the two full plates onto the corner of the food table before running to the door.

———

Mark stood in the back alley behind the hall. Clay saw him as soon as he stepped outside, even though the sun had already set. He paused on the landing before stepping down the stairs. "Hey, Hopkins, we don't have to do this, you know."

"If your yellow streak's showing, just say so," Mark taunted him.

"Well, it isn't that I'm exactly scared," Clay drawled. "I'm just thinking about Joanna and how she might feel. Have you stopped to think that these churchgoing ladies might not like having a fight break out at their evening social? Could put a damper on their fun, don't you think?"

Clay kept moving toward Mark as he talked, trying to reason with the other man. Mark had hit him once when they were kids, and Clay figured the husky man had grown even more powerful through the years. He really didn't relish getting his face bashed in, but he figured he could stand pretty much anything for Joanna. Besides, maybe if Mark worked off some anger, he might also work out whatever it was that had been bothering him since he'd first laid eyes on Clay more than six years ago.

By the time he realized his talking wouldn't do any good, he was standing just outside Mark's reach. He saw Mark coming as the heavier and slower fellow lunged with his fist doubled. Having the advantage of being quick on his feet, Clay sidestepped, and Mark walked past without touching him.

Trouble was, Mark didn't like to miss, so he grew even angrier. Clay didn't want to hit Mark unless he had to, so he kept dodging the other man's big fists. Maybe in time his anger and the force he put behind each thrust of his fist would wear him down if Clay could keep a close eye on him and stay out of his way.

Mark and Clay had danced around in a circle so that when the back door of the hall burst open Clay had a clear view of the landing. For just a moment, Joanna stood framed by the doorway with the light from the room spilling out behind her. He paused, unable to look away as she ran down the stairs.

He started to call out to her to stay back. In his anger, Mark might accidentally hurt her. But at that moment a big fist blocked his view and pain exploded in his head.

In an instant, Joanna brushed past Mark and knelt beside Clay. "Are you all right?"

Clay tried to focus on her voice. Joanna wasn't nearly as pretty with her face blurred, but her voice still sounded like music to him.

"He's fine, Joanna. Why don't you step back and let me take a look. This isn't the first time a man got a black eye." Dr. Brady knelt beside Clay. "You go on over there with Mariah and Carrie."

Clay's thinking seemed as fuzzy as his vision, but he answered the doctor's questions and let him look in his eyes. He figured Mark would claim Joanna since he'd won the fight. Of course, maybe she wouldn't let him. After all, she had run to Clay first thing. That must mean something.

"Doesn't appear to be too bad. Didn't even get knocked out, did you?" the doctor asked.

Clay started to shake his head, but the movement didn't help either his vision or the pain. He grinned. "My pa always said my head was hard."

Dr. Brady laughed and helped Clay stand with Sherman Butler's help. "I'll get a cool compress for that eye. We expect to see you in church in the morning," he told Clay.

Cyrus spoke up. "He done agreed to that."

"Good." The doctor turned to Pastor Carson, who stood watching. "I think the show's over. If you can get your congregation back inside, the party can go on."

"Well, boy, you want ta tell me what happened out here?" Cyrus took Clay's arm and led him away from the others who were heading inside.

Clay saw Mark with Joanna, although they didn't seem very happy. When the door closed behind them, he turned to Cyrus. "Would you be satisfied if I said I walked into a fist that had a little more punch than I expected?"

"Nope."

Clay sighed. "I didn't figure you would. The fact is, Cyrus, I don't rightly know what happened. Hopkins might have a better idea. If he even knows."

"Wouldn't be over a girl, would it?" Cyrus persisted. "Maybe Doc Brady's daughter?"

Clay's grin turned into a grimace as the pain shot to his eye. "Miss Brady is mighty pretty, but like I already said, I don't know. Mark never went to school when we were kids, but I saw him at Doc Brady's some when I worked there. Maybe he wanted my job."

Cyrus nodded. "Or maybe the doc's daughter."

The door opened and Dr. Brady stepped out. Clay watched him descend the stairs, glad his vision seemed to be coming back. "I would like to apologize for my part in the ruckus. It wasn't my idea for anyone to get hit."

"Least of all yourself, huh?" The doctor laughed. He applied a cool, damp cloth to Clay's eye. "Hold this against the swelling for a while. When you get home, you might want to apply another cold compress. You going back inside?"

Clay looked toward the hall and thought of Joanna with Mark. He gave a little shake of his head. "Nah, I'll head on back to the ranch."

"Well then, I'll get back inside. My daughter is mad as a hornet. I imagine we'll go home early."

"Mad?" Clay couldn't resist asking. "At who?"

The doctor laughed. "Right now either a couple of young men or the entire state of Kansas. I'm not sure which it is."

When Clay fetched his horse, he felt comfort in Lucky's welcoming whinny. He'd sure made a mess of the evening, although he wasn't sure what he'd done wrong. A fight with Hopkins hadn't been in his plans. He'd just wanted to see Joanna again. He'd wanted to play some games with her as his partner and get a glimpse of what it meant to live a normal life where people stayed in one place. Where they got to know each other and developed friendships that lasted a lifetime.

Maybe putting down roots wasn't for him. He remembered Mrs. Brady told him once that God had a plan for everyone. Did that include him? Did God care if he ever had a family, or was he destined to ride the range for the rest of his days, moving from ranch to ranch and from state to state just the same as his father had done?

He patted his horse on the shoulder and swung into the saddle. "I don't know what's down the road for us, Lucky, but I'm sure glad I've got you to carry me there."

Chapter 12

Clay sat on the backseat at church the next day and watched Joanna lead the singing. She'd always had the prettiest voice he'd ever heard, and that hadn't changed. What had changed was that she had grown into a beautiful, confident woman.

She looked up and turned toward him as her voice carried clearly to the back row. He started to smile, but she quickly looked away almost as if she didn't want to see him. She probably didn't. After the ruckus he and Mark had caused the evening before, she might never want to see him again. He figured the church people were being mighty forgiving to let him inside their church. Of course, they probably thought he needed to be there even more after the mess he'd made of their party.

After Joanna sat down, Clay concentrated on what the pastor had to say. Since he didn't have a Bible, he listened while the minister read several verses from the third chapter of John. One that stuck in his mind said, "Verily, verily, I say unto thee, Except a man be born of water and of the Spirit, he cannot enter into the kingdom of God."

Pastor Carson explained that the kingdom of God meant heaven and all of eternity that would follow. He said man had been born in sin and that made him a sinner from the minute he came into the world.

Clay looked at the Butlers who sat near the front. He could see his little buddy with his head against Mariah's shoulder while she patted his back. He'd kept an eye on him every chance he got and could already see the tiny baby thought the Butlers were his ma and pa. Clay had seen their little girl give the baby a kiss more than once and knew she loved him. Mr. and Mrs. Butler did, too. He felt sure of it. Even Carrie and her husband treated him as if he'd been born into the family.

The minister's words reached him again. "And how can we be born again? In John 14:6, Jesus said, 'I am the way. . .no man cometh unto the Father, but by me.'"

Clay listened as the old message of salvation became a new idea in his mind. He'd done his share of sinning, he knew that. He'd found little forgiveness from those he'd wronged, though. So the idea that the Creator of all would freely forgive him for every wrong thing he'd ever done if he would only ask just didn't make sense. Sure would be nice.

When the preacher stopped talking, Joanna stepped forward to lead another song. Clay enjoyed singing, but he mostly watched Joanna as she sang "Just as I Am," her sweet voice rising above the congregation's.

When the song ended, the pastor prayed and people began leaving. Clay hesitated when he saw Mark head for the front and Joanna. But when Joanna stepped to the far side of the piano to speak to the pianist, Mark turned and started back down the center aisle. Clay slipped out the door into a bright early June day.

"Ridin' back out with us?" One of the ranch hands walked past with a friendly smile.

"Nah," Clay shook his head. "I'll be out later."

"All right. See ya then."

As Clay started toward Lucky, a cat ran past with a mongrel dog hot on its trail. He grinned at the sight and at the racket of the cat's yowls of alarm and the dog's barking. But his grin disappeared when the cat darted between the legs of a horse hitched to a wagon. The horse let out a frightened whinny and reared, jerking the reins from a woman who appeared to be alone. Clay broke into a run and hoped the horse didn't bolt before he got there.

The horse came down with a twist and headed straight toward Clay. Five running steps brought Clay close enough to grab the horse's neck and swing onto its back. Leaning forward, he grabbed the reins and soon had the runaway horse under control.

"Thank you, mister." The woman ran to the side of the wagon.

Clay slid from the horse. "No problem, ma'am."

He ran his hand down the horse's front leg and lifted its foot. Just as he thought. A shoe had come loose. He looked up at the middle-aged woman. "This needs to be taken care of."

"Oh dear," she glanced down the road. "Brother Landon has already gone. I hate to take him from his Sunday dinner."

Several men and women stood watching and offering advice, although none had the necessary equipment to fix the horseshoe. Clay released the horse and handed the reins to the woman.

"That's all right. I'll stop on my way and let Landon know. I'm sure he'll come right away." Clay gave the woman a reassuring grin as he turned away.

Ten minutes later, Jack Landon, Cedar Bend's blacksmith, headed back to the church while Clay turned his horse in the opposite direction. Lucky ambled down the dirt road that led through the business part of town, and Clay thought about the woman he had helped. A sense of satisfaction warred with his restless spirit. He wondered why he didn't just turn south at the next street and keep on going. Texas still waited with plenty of ranches and a bunk for sleeping. He could stop by the Circle C and pick up what little he had there. Shouldn't take long.

Then he remembered those roots he'd been wanting to put down. He thought of his little buddy and wondered how it would be to have a son of his own. One thing was for certain. If he had a son, he wouldn't want him raised the way he had been—always on the move and never able to retain a lasting friendship. He'd spent only one short year in Cedar Bend, yet he'd lived here longer than he'd lived in any other place. Long enough to make an enemy.

He chuckled as he thought of Mark's frown when he'd seen him walk into church with the other cowboys. Reckon Mark wouldn't miss him if he left. Probably no one would. Joanna's wide brown eyes entered his mind accusingly. Okay, so maybe he'd made one friend. Joanna might miss him for a while, but it wouldn't be long until she married Hopkins anyway. Just save him the trouble of seeing it happen if he left.

A woman walked ahead of him down the road. He stopped Lucky and sat watching. A slow grin spread across his face, and he nudged Lucky forward until he rode beside her.

"Mornin', Miss Brady." Clay grinned down at the sweetest sight he'd ever seen. "Or is it afternoon already?"

Joanna's face registered surprise, delight, and then a slight frown within the space of only a moment before she turned away. "I believe it's straight up noon."

"That so?" Clay kept pace with her. He liked sitting above her where he could watch the sunlight brighten the red highlights in her dark hair. "Sure is a pretty day."

"That's because it's early June. You won't like the bright sun in another month when there's no rain."

Clay laughed. "Reckon not. Good thing I'm not a farmer."

Joanna turned to face him with her fists planted on her hips. "Clay Shepherd, why are you following me?"

Clay admired the flash of anger in her dark eyes. A strong emotion he refused to name filled his heart. All he knew was that he wanted his future sons to have dark brown eyes just like the ones currently glaring at him, which were the prettiest he'd ever seen.

"Why, Miss Brady, I'm not following anyone. Lucky here just decided to walk along beside you." Clay shrugged while a half grin sat on his lips. "He's a smart horse. Knows a pretty woman when he sees one."

"Well, I wish you would just move on." Joanna started walking away as quickly as she could.

A little nudge had Lucky beside her again. "You aren't mad at me for some reason, are you?"

Joanna swung back to look at him. Stomped her foot. "Yes." With that one word, she started on again.

"Mind tellin' me what I did?" Clay raised his voice without moving forward.

She kept walking faster than before, but her voice reached him easily enough. "You got a black eye."

Clay stared at her retreating form for a second and then laughed aloud. He let her get almost to the next cross street before he nudged Lucky forward. If he died of old age, he would never understand a woman.

He didn't stop this time but rode slowly past with a wave and a smile. "I'll see you about ten in the morning, Miss Brady, at the library. Reckon I might as well see what you need done, so I can get on it like I promised."

He didn't wait for her answer, but turned Lucky down the cross street and rode out of town.

Joanna spent the first two hours after breakfast Monday morning debating. Should she go to the library, or should she forget Clay Shepherd had returned to town?

Like she could do that. She collapsed into her favorite chair as her breath rushed out. What should she do? She had thought to ignore both Mark and Clay, but that didn't seem possible. Clay wouldn't let her.

She stood with a sigh. Maybe Carrie had a point. She'd prayed for excitement, and she'd gotten more than she expected. Now she might as well go face the answer to her prayer.

The warm summer sun shone down on Joanna as she walked across town. She purposely picked the path across the street from the feedstore and was glad when she didn't see Mark. When she arrived at the little house that would soon become Cedar Bend's library, she saw Clay's horse grazing in the side yard. He lifted his head and whinnied at her when she opened the gate and started up the walk to the porch.

Joanna pushed the front door open and stepped inside. The cooler, stale air of the closed house greeted her. Then Clay stepped out of the kitchen with a grin on his face and a wooden ruler in his hand.

"Good morning, Miss Brady."

She clenched her jaw. "Why are you trying to irritate me?"

His dark brows rose. "Irritate you? What are you talking about? I've come to help you."

She resisted the urge to stomp her foot. She hadn't thrown a temper tantrum since she was a child, but lately she had come close more than once. Clay Shepherd had a knack for bringing out the worst in her. Now she folded her arms and lifted her chin. "You know exactly what I mean. Calling me 'Miss Brady' yesterday and today."

Mischief twinkled in Clay's eyes. He took a step closer to her. She felt crowded although half a room separated them. She couldn't look away from his eyes when the mischief faded, replaced by an intensity that frightened her.

He spoke in a soft voice. "I'd rather call you darlin'."

"No." She threw her hands out in a gesture to keep him away. "We shouldn't even be here alone like this. I don't know what I was thinking."

"Joanna, don't." Clay crossed the room before she could get the door open.

He didn't touch her, but he leaned against the door to block her escape. "Forgive me, please." She had never seen such a serious look on Clay's face, and it frightened her. "I didn't mean anything disrespectful. I'm sorry. I'm sorry for getting a black eye. And mostly I'm sorry for not bringing a chaperone today, because you tempt me more than any girl I've ever met. You always have. I never forgot you, Joanna."

His quick grin took her by surprise. "I never forgot the mistletoe, either."

Joanna's face flamed at the memory of her first and only kiss. She would never forget that mistletoe. In fact, she still had it. That day long ago she had taken the green sprig and pressed it between the pages of one of her father's large medical books. She kept it in her treasure box tucked safely away in the drawer of her bedside table.

Clay stepped away from the door and motioned toward the opposite wall. "I assume you'll want some shelves here coming out into the room with one end attached to the wall. The libraries I've seen usually have shelves to the ceiling with a divider in the middle so you can put books on both sides."

"You've been to libraries?" This was a side of the wild, fun-loving cowboy that Joanna hadn't expected.

He shrugged. "Sure, ropin' and brandin' and bustin' wild broncs is a physically drainin' job. Nice to relax with a good book once in a while." He waggled his eyebrows at her. "You did know I can read, didn't you?"

Joanna giggled. "I seem to recall from our school days that you used to read fairly well."

Clay laughed. "Glad to know your memories don't exclude me."

Oh, if he only knew. Lord, I don't know what's happening here. Joanna breathed a prayer even as she recognized the serious meanings behind Clay's jokes. *Every time I'm with him, I become more entangled in my feelings for him. But I can't fall in love with him, Lord. I know he went to church yesterday, but I don't think he's a Christian. Mariah is right. I can't let myself love the wrong man. Please, Lord, bring Clay to salvation.*

Chapter 13

As soon as Joanna told him what she wanted done, Clay opened the door and told her he'd handle it from there. She walked back home feeling as if she'd just been sucked into a whirlwind and thrown back out.

The next few weeks were busy for Joanna as she met with the library committee and made plans for the upcoming rodeo and box supper at the Fourth of July community celebration.

For the most part, she kept her distance from both Mark and Clay, although she saw them in church. Mark tried to approach her several times, but she managed to either sidestep him or speak briefly and move on.

Clay seemed to be biding his time, or maybe he no longer cared. Joanna missed his admiring looks, as he seemed more interested in the pastor's sermons than he did in winning her affections. She knew she should be glad, because she had been praying for his salvation. And truly she was glad. In fact, encouraged by his apparent interest in spiritual things, she prayed even harder. But that didn't stop the longing deep in her heart for something she probably shouldn't have. After all, she felt as if the adventure she had prayed for had ended before it began.

One evening in late June, several from the community and from the ranch met at the future library to work. As Joanna and her father arrived, she saw three farm wagons and another buggy stopped along the street. Mariah's cousin, Gladys Jacobs, called a greeting as she and her husband turned in at the gate.

Joanna and her father followed the Jacobses to the door. Gladys stopped to speak. "We couldn't be more proud of you, Joanna, for the work you are doing here."

"Thank you, Mrs. Jacobs." Joanna smiled. "But I'm not doing much. Everyone has pitched in to help. We wouldn't have a library without Mariah's generosity and her work."

At that moment Mariah appeared in the open door. She greeted her cousin with a hug then slipped an arm around Joanna. "Come on in. We couldn't wait to get started. I hope you don't mind."

"Of course I don't mind. That's less work for me." Joanna watched her father disappear around the corner of the house where some men were setting up a sawhorse. She wondered if Clay was there but decided it didn't matter. He probably wouldn't talk to her anyway.

Inside, Joanna spoke to Carrie and Lucille, Gladys's daughter. Both young married ladies were expecting, Carrie for the first time, Lucille with her second baby. They had been given the job of corralling the young children and were heading outdoors to play in the grass.

Hope grabbed Joanna for a quick hug as she passed. "I gots to help Carrie take care of my baby brohver. Bye. I love you."

With a quick wave, the little girl ran out the door almost before Joanna could respond. She and Mariah laughed.

"Oh, Joanna, there's someone I want you to meet," Mariah said. "I think she's in the kitchen."

Joanna stopped short when she saw Mark's broad back. He stood in the middle of the kitchen talking to someone and effectively hiding the person from Joanna's view.

"Mark, I hate to interrupt, but I'd like to introduce Liz to Joanna."

At Mariah's voice, Mark turned. His gaze caught and held Joanna's while a strange feeling swept through her. He looked—guilty.

He held out a hand, palm toward her. "I was just talking to Miss Cramer, honest."

The truth hit Joanna like a slap in the face. Mark did feel guilty. He looked like a little boy who'd been caught taking something that didn't belong to him. Joanna wanted to laugh and cry at the same time. Instead, she stepped into the room, eager to meet the woman who made Mark feel as if he needed to explain a simple conversation.

"Joanna, I'd like for you to meet Cedar Bend's new schoolteacher, Miss Elizabeth Cramer. I left the schoolchildren of Cedar Bend high and dry when I married Mr. Butler." Mariah laughed. "We are glad to have a replacement arrive so early in the summer. Liz will have time to become acquainted before school begins this fall."

From the corner of her eye, Joanna watched Mark slink out the back door and wondered how a man so large could move so quickly without making a sound.

"Liz, this is Joanna Brady. Her father is our doctor, and Joanna is the librarian and our boss tonight."

Miss Cramer looked scarcely old enough to teach. She had large blue eyes and a halo of blond hair with loose curls that she wore tied back at the nape of her neck and falling to her waist. She stood at least two inches shorter than Joanna and a good ten pounds lighter. No wonder she had been hidden behind Mark. She wore a simple, everyday dress, and her smile seemed genuine as she extended her hand.

"Miss Brady, I have been hearing your praises since I arrived in town almost a week ago. I'm so glad to meet you." Liz gave Joanna's hand a firm shake before she glanced around the kitchen. "What you are doing is wonderful. Every town should have a library. The gift of reading is a precious thing that should be encouraged."

"Yes, I think so." Joanna felt tongue-tied in front of the nearly perfect schoolteacher.

"I hope we can become the best of friends." Liz smiled sweetly. "Cedar Bend is such a friendly town. Everyone I've met has been helpful. Mark"—her cheeks colored—"I mean Mr. Hopkins was the first to lend a helping hand. He happened by when I arrived and carried my trunk upstairs at the boardinghouse. I couldn't believe how easy it looked for him to carry such a heavy load."

"Is that right?" So that's why she hadn't seen Mark all week. "I'm sure he didn't mind. He enjoys helping."

"I guess you know him pretty well, then." Liz laughed. "But of course you do. This is a small town. You probably know everyone here."

"That's true, but Mark and I go way back. We've been friends forever." Joanna felt like the dog that looked into a pond at another dog with a bone. Wanting that new bone so much, he opened his mouth to steal it away and lost the one he had. Had she wanted Clay only because he was a new bone? He was exciting and dangerous just as she had prayed. He'd always been mysterious and unpredictable. Had she only wanted him because he seemed unattainable? Had she lost Mark when she should have kept him?

At that moment the back door opened and Clay walked in. Joanna's heart raced in a way that it never did around Mark. He looked at her and grinned while all her doubts flew away. Clay was no reflection in a pond.

Mark followed Clay inside with several cut boards in his hands. His gaze flew first to Liz and then to Joanna. At that instant, she knew what she had thought all along. She loved Mark, but only as a friend.

She looked back at Clay and smiled. She had fallen in love with Clay when they were children in school. When he left, she had set that love aside to become a dream and a memory. Now that he had returned, her longings had been set free to become reality. No wonder she had wanted a man that was a tad dangerous and mysterious. Since her heart had longed for Clay all along, he was the one she had prayed for.

Suddenly her dreamworld crashed at her feet. She couldn't love Clay. Although he went to church, and she knew many were praying for him, he might never make a commitment to serve God.

"Hey, Joanna," Clay called to her. "Are you ladies going to paint that wall before we attach the shelving unit to it?"

"Yes, of course," Joanna answered and then looked to Mariah for guidance. "Do you know if they've already started on that?"

Mariah laughed. "I'm afraid we've been standing around gabbing while everyone else has been working. Let's go see what they've done."

While the ladies moved on to the next wall, Joanna held boards for Clay to secure together into shelves.

"Here, hold this one like this." Clay took Joanna's hands and placed them where he wanted her to hold the board.

At his touch, her blood stirred, but she kept her hands steady so he wouldn't guess how she felt.

Scarcely paying attention to the activity around her, Joanna helped Clay and listened to the account of his life at the Circle C. He seemed to like working on the ranch. "There're some mighty pretty spots out there. Maybe someday I'll take you out for a picnic."

Joanna tried to sound as if she didn't care. "That should be fun."

"Then we'll count on it." Clay gave her a quick smile that set her heart pounding.

When they finished putting a row of shelving together, Clay went outside and Joanna saw Mariah heading her way.

"So what's going on between you and Mark?" Mariah spoke with the bluntness of close friends.

"Mark?"

"Yes, Mark. I thought you two were pretty close not that long ago."

Joanna thought of Mark and the friendship they had shared for so many years. She said, "I guess you're right, Mariah. Something has happened. I always took for granted that Mark and I would marry someday. Now I don't think so. Actually, I wonder if he doesn't feel the same way. I've scarcely seen or spoken to him since the church social when he and Clay fought."

"Clay." Mariah repeated the name as if it left a bitter taste in her mouth. "I wonder if Sherman made a mistake in giving that young man a job."

"Why do you say that?" Joanna's eyes widened in surprise. Mariah always seemed to love everyone. Why would she pick on Clay?

"Because he isn't a Christian. Because his good looks and his wild reputation have turned my best friend's head." Mariah touched Joanna's arm. "Please, be careful in forming too close a friendship with him. Surely you know I want the best for you. I thought that was with Mark, who is a good, Christian man."

"Mariah, I would never marry a man who does not share my Christian beliefs." She gave a short laugh. "This is all hypothetical anyway. Clay has been a perfect gentleman and has never indicated any interest in a lasting alliance."

"I'm glad to hear that, Joanna." Mariah smiled. "Remember I am praying for you."

Joanna watched Mariah turn away to check on her children. She thought of Clay, and a smile touched her lips. She couldn't stop the warm glow that filled her heart when his image appeared in her mind. What would it hurt to be friends with him? Surely a few days of fun could not be wrong.

Joanna ignored the fact that Clay already held her love, and if he crooked his finger, she would be powerless to resist.

As Clay went outside, he met Mark and Mr. Butler carrying a load of boards into the house. They said they would put them together, so he stepped over to the corner of the house where Lucas Nolan, the local sheriff, sat on an overturned bucket taking a break.

"Hey, Shepherd," Luke greeted him with a grin.

Clay nodded and asked, "Could you spare me a minute?"

"Sure, what's on your mind?"

Clay crouched down to sit on his heel. He picked up a pebble and tossed it back. "I've been seeing you in church every time I go, so I reckon you're no stranger to God."

Luke nodded. "We're on pretty good speakin' terms, yeah."

"I've been hearing some things." Clay gave a short laugh. "I mean they aren't exactly new ideas. I went to church when I lived here before, but I reckon I never understood about being saved. Isn't that what you all call gettin' right with God?"

Luke nodded.

Clay shrugged. "Looks like there oughta be more to it than just saying I'm sorry."

"You're right." Luke said. "Every one of us has sinned. I suppose you'd be lying if you said you didn't already know that."

Clay grinned. "That part I haven't had any problem understanding."

Luke chuckled. "Good, because that's the first step. Next you need to confess all your wrongdoings to the Lord."

As Luke talked, Clay listened without interruption. Finally, Luke said, "I reckon the bottom line, Clay, is this: Do you want to continue living your own way, which takes you down the road to destruction, or are you ready to accept God's salvation and the freedom to live for Him?"

"And spend eternity in heaven," Clay added. He looked down at the twig he had snapped into several pieces before he tossed them aside and stood. "Sounds like a big decision to me. Reckon something like that shouldn't be entered into without thinking it through. Thanks for talking to me."

"Don't think too long, Clay," Luke cautioned. "When Jesus knocks on your heart's door, that's the time to respond. Seems to me He's knocking now. Don't turn Him away."

Clay nodded. "I understand. I'll keep what you said in mind. Thanks, Luke."

With that, Clay went back inside the house.

Chapter 14

Cedar Bend's Fourth of July community celebration turned out even better than Joanna had expected. Surely everyone in town and for miles around had shown up. Horses grazed in the vacant lot across from the feedstore where farm wagons, buggies, and a few surreys had been parked.

Booths selling crafts and homemade jellies and preserves were set up along either side of Main Street. The aroma of barbecue beef roasting over an open pit tempted the appetites of those who walked by.

Less than a block away, in the city park, several musicians had gathered in the bandstand to play rousing patriotic songs that could be heard all over town.

Since her father had been called out to tend to an injury, Joanna decided she would walk to town. Her father promised to meet her before noon so they could eat together. After he left, Joanna set off on foot. Now she walked past the busy booths while the band played and a dozen conversations sounded around her. She called out greetings to the men and women running the booths as well as the townsfolk who were spending money, making the day a success.

As she walked on, she sniffed the air appreciatively. The Circle C had pulled their chuck wagon in and set it up on the corner. A couple of tables and benches sat off to the side. A little old man wearing denim pants and a red plaid shirt bent over a couple of huge iron pots above an open fire, stirring first one and then the other.

"Hey, Mac," Joanna called to him.

He looked up with a welcoming grin on his leathery face. "Howdy, Miss Joanna. Got some books fer ya in the wagon."

"For me or for the library?" Joanna stepped closer and peered into one of the pots. "Mmmm, this looks as good as it smells."

Mac chuckled. "If you're hintin' fer a sample, cain't oblige. This here's fer barbecue beef sandwiches. The books in the wagon's fer you ta read. Put 'em in the library when yer done."

"Good." Joanna smiled at her friend and fellow romance book lover. She often traded books with Mac. He seemed to enjoy the stories as much as she did.

"Jist don't ferget ta git 'em before we leave here tonight," Mac cautioned her.

"Oh, don't worry. I won't. I'll be back for one of those sandwiches, too." She laughed. "I probably should pack a couple in a box for the supper this evening. That way I'd be assured of my box selling."

Mac gave her a sharp look. "I heard about them two fellers fightin' over you."

Joanna felt the color rise in her cheeks, but she shook her head. "I don't think so, Mac. They were fighting over some silly grudge from when they were boys. I don't think either of them even know what it was."

"Reckon they'll be biddin' on your box anyhow."

"Thanks, Mac, but it doesn't matter. I just want to raise a lot of money for the library. That's what's important."

Joanna watched Mac stir the beef before she moved on down the street. She hadn't gone far when someone fell into step with her.

"Hi, Joanna."

She looked up into clear blue eyes and lost the ability to think. Finally, she remembered to answer. "Hi, Clay."

"I've been hearing some pretty nice comments about you."

"Really?"

"Yep. Makes me proud to be your friend." Clay looked down into Joanna's eyes. "We are friends, aren't we, Joanna?"

Friends. How could she resent such a nice word? But she didn't want to be friends with Clay. Not when there was so much more they could be to each other. Then Joanna's conscience pricked. Unless he accepted Christ's love and sacrifice as a free gift, they would have to remain only friends.

She nodded. "Yes, of course we are, Clay. Friends for life."

He looped her arm though his and grinned. "Good, then why don't you come with me to the park. Someone is getting ready to make a speech. A state representative, I think. Wonder how we rated his attention."

"It wasn't too hard." Joanna giggled. "He's the mayor's cousin."

After listening to the speech, visiting with the Butler family, and watching a ball game in progress, Clay and Joanna headed back toward Main Street where they met Dr. Brady.

"How's the little Johnson boy?" Joanna asked.

"He's fine. Just a sprained wrist when he jumped from a tree. His mother thought sure he'd broken his arm, but when I wrapped his wrist and told her he'd be fine, she bundled the kids into the wagon and came to town."

"Wonderful. Are you hungry, Dad?" Joanna glanced up at Clay, who stood quietly behind her. "We were just thinking about those barbecue sandwiches

Mac's got cooking. I've been smelling them all morning, and I'm about to starve."

"Is that right?" Dr. Brady seemed interested in something beyond his daughter. A quick smile touched his face. "I know we planned to eat together, but Clay's here and I see a friend. I believe I'll let you go ahead without me, if you don't mind."

As her father hurried off, Joanna turned to watch, but all she could see was Mrs. James with two of her children standing a few feet away. Surely he wouldn't. . .

"Clay, do you see that?"

Clay chuckled. "What's wrong, Joanna? Don't you think your father should have a lady friend? Are you jealous?"

"Of course not," Joanna protested. "I know they're friends. I've seen them talk at socials for the last year or so. My mother died about the same time Mr. James was killed in that accident. They have a lot in common I guess."

Clay laughed. "You know your father isn't ancient, don't you? What is he, about forty years old?"

She nodded. "Yes, he's forty-two."

"I always wished my pa would remarry. That was one of my dreams when I was a kid. But he never did. Said no one else could measure up to my ma. Maybe he was right." Clay took Joanna's hand. "Come on. Let's get something to eat. You aren't the only one who's starving."

After they ate, Clay and Joanna spent the afternoon together watching the contests in the park. Everything from prettiest baby to frog jumping had been planned.

She saw Mark a few times, but he never tried to speak to her. She didn't know whether to be glad or hurt. Once she saw him with the new schoolteacher. They seemed deep in conversation, and she wondered if anything might develop between the two of them. She remembered her prayer for someone to love Mark and offered another that if Liz was God's choice, Mark would be able to see her in the right way.

"I'm riding in the rodeo." Clay made the announcement as they sat on a park bench listening to a group sing gospel songs from the bandstand.

Joanna wanted to tell him he could get hurt riding a wild bronco, but somehow she knew he would just laugh at her. So she said nothing.

"That means I've got to go get ready." Clay shifted closer to her. "Will you watch me ride, Joanna?"

She nodded. "Of course I will."

Clay stood. "Come on. I'll walk you back to the Circle C's booth. I imagine

Mariah and Carrie will be there since Luke is riding, and the ranch is sponsoring the event."

Joanna let him hold her hand as they walked. It felt so right. They had spent almost the entire day together, and not once had she wanted to leave him. In fact, she found the thought of being separated from Clay during the rodeo almost unbearable. Of course, that was probably because of the danger involved. She tugged him to a stop as they neared the chuck wagon.

He looked down at her. "Something wrong?"

"No. . .yes. . .maybe."

Clay grinned. "Ain't nothin' like knowin' how you feel about something, is there?"

Joanna sighed. "That's the problem. I do know." She met his amused gaze with a frown. "I just don't want you to get hurt."

His chuckle did nothing to relieve her worries. He brushed a wisp of hair from her cheek and smiled at her as if he really cared. "Joanna, I've been riding a horse since I could sit in the saddle. I'd already broken my share of wild horses before you ever met me. This is something I do all the time."

"Do you mean you've never been hurt?"

"Now I didn't exactly say that." He grinned. "Don't reckon you need to worry, though, not with your pa there. I hear he's got the prettiest nurse west of the Mississippi to help him sometimes, too."

"Clay Shepherd!" Joanna stomped her foot. "If you get hurt I'll help him all right, and I'll make sure the cure is worse than the injury."

Clay laughed and gave Joanna a kiss on the forehead so quickly she wondered if she'd dreamed it. He turned her toward the corner. "You do that, darlin', and I'll come back every time a horse throws me just so I can watch your beautiful brown eyes shoot sparks at me."

A half hour later, Joanna sat with Mariah and Carrie to watch the rodeo. She saw her father walk past with Mrs. James. He listened to something she said and then laughed. An uneasy feeling twisted Joanna's stomach. Certainly her father was not old, but still, he didn't need to make a spectacle of himself in front of all their friends.

Then a rider shot through the gate, and Joanna lost interest in her father. Glad that she scarcely knew the cowboy, who at that moment flew through the air and landed in the dust before rolling to his feet, she tried to relax. Clay stood inside the fence, his blue shirt and white Stetson easy to find. Of course, she figured she could pick him out of a line of identically dressed cowboys a thousand paces away without half trying. Her heart would lead her to him every time.

Several more riders hit the dust, but some stayed on the entire eight seconds, including Luke Nolan. Carrie whistled through her teeth when he walked away from his ride. The next cowboy didn't do as well.

"Too bad," Carrie said. "That one didn't stay on long."

"How do you stand it?" Joanna asked her friend. "When Luke rides, aren't you afraid for him?"

"Of course I am." Carrie rolled her eyes. "But this is nothing compared to the wild steer Luke rode before we were married. I think he was trying to impress me, although he won't admit it."

"Oh my." Joanna couldn't stop the image of Clay on the back of a wild longhorn steer. She thought horses were bad enough, but at least they didn't have horns, and they generally stepped over the cowboy unlucky enough to land near their hooves.

Carrie smiled. "He was supposed to ride for five seconds, but he stayed on for ten before he jumped off. When I saw he was safe, I felt so weak I couldn't even stand up."

"Oh my." Joanna couldn't think of anything else to say even though her friends laughed at her. She turned back to watch and saw that Clay now sat on the back of a fidgeting horse in the chute. She saw him give a nod to the men surrounding him, and then the gate opened and the horse shot through.

Joanna watched the bronco lower his head and lift his back, twisting first one way and then the other while Clay held one gloved hand high and stayed with the horse as if he anticipated every move. Each second seemed an hour to Joanna as she watched Clay ride. Then the whistle sounded and Clay jumped to the ground, running a few feet away with both hands raised in victory.

Those watching cheered, but no shouts were so heartfelt as Joanna's. She stood clapping while tears ran down her cheeks. Clay was safe. He had not been bucked off. He had not been trampled to death. She saw his wide grin and knew he felt good about his ride. He saw her and waved. She lifted her hand and waved at him, although what she really wanted to do was smack him for scaring her so much.

When the rodeo ended, Clay and Joanna walked to the city park where the bidding on the ladies' boxes would take place. They had spent a long day together, and the sun hung low in the western sky by the time they reached the park. If she could, Joanna would pull the sun back a few hours so her time with Clay wouldn't have to end so soon.

As the bidding started, one box after another found a home. Married women seldom had competition for their boxes. But several unmarried men bid the other boxes up to a hefty price.

As the new schoolteacher stepped forward, Joanna was surprised at the bids. But what surprised her even more was the fact that Mark Hopkins was one of the most energetic bidders.

Not sure how she felt about Mark's switch of affection from her to Elizabeth, she watched the bidding reach almost ten dollars before it stopped with Mark as the winner. Surely he had just spent every cent he had.

Clay chuckled and gave Joanna a hug while he spoke close to her ear. "Don't tell me you're jealous."

She jerked away just enough so he dropped his arm. "Of course not. Why would I be?"

"Can't think of a single reason." He took her arm and pulled her back next to him as he spoke for her ear alone. "You're a sight prettier than that little blond schoolteacher anyhow."

Joanna walked to the front and picked up her box with more confidence than she'd had when Liz's box brought so much. Even if Clay's bid was all she got, she wouldn't mind.

"Now here's the lady who got this box supper together for us. And that's not all. The profits go toward the new library Miss Brady is building for Cedar Bend." Karl Braun, serving as auctioneer, said, "Let's give Miss Brady a big hand for all the work she's done for our town."

If her confidence had faltered before, it soared now. Joanna couldn't stop smiling as her friends and neighbors stood and clapped. A few whistled and cheered. When someone called for a speech, the clapping faded into silence.

With the flush of embarrassment staining her cheeks, Joanna lifted her chin and said, "Thank you all so much, but I don't deserve your praise. Without each of you coming out and giving of yourself and your hard-earned money, today would have been wasted time. So many of you have put in more time and talent to make our celebration a success than I did. The Butlers, the Nolans, the Jacobses, Mrs. James, the Brauns. I shouldn't have started naming, because there are so many, but you all know."

She lifted her fingers to her lips and threw a kiss to everyone. "Thank you for today and for all the work you've already done on the library. And please remember that Cedar Bend's library is your library."

After that, Mr. Braun had more bids than he could keep up with. Joanna's box passed ten dollars, and she worried Clay wouldn't have enough. An easy smile sat on his face, so she figured he either had a pocket full of money or he didn't care if he lost. Then the bidding stopped with Clay's offer of eleven dollars and fifty cents.

Joanna spread her blue and white checked tablecloth on the grass, and Clay set her box in the middle. As they sank to either side to unpack their supper, Joanna said, "I'm afraid I didn't pack enough."

Clay grinned. "For my appetite or for my money?"

"Neither. I mean for the money you used to have."

His chuckle let her know he didn't mind. "Darlin', you're worth every penny."

Chapter 15

With their library money safely deposited in the bank, Joanna opened her home to the library committee one warm day in the second week of July. While their children played in the yard outside, several women crowded into the Bradys' parlor to look over some publishers' lists Mariah had received in the mail.

"We have enough money to get several books, don't we?" Gladys Jacobs asked.

Joanna nodded. "Yes, but we've already been accepting donations of used books. I've made a list of what we have to date. That way we won't duplicate when we order."

Mrs. James looked up with a smile for Joanna. "You've done a wonderful job, dear. How soon do you think the door will be open for business?"

After she had gotten over the shock of seeing her father with another woman, Joanna decided she liked his choice. Mrs. James never pushed her way on anyone, yet she was friendly and helpful. All four of her children were well behaved and seemed to accept the doctor as part of their family. Joanna had made the decision that she would accept the James family into their family just as graciously, if that was what her father wanted.

She smiled at Mrs. James. "Thank you. I'm not sure when we can open. Mariah, how soon do you think our new books will come once we order them?"

"I would allow at least a month." Mariah lifted her five-month-old baby son to her shoulder and patted his back. "We have to consider the time for the order to travel to the publishers, shipping time for the books, and processing of the orders."

"Wouldn't it be nice if the library could open about the same time school starts this fall?" Liz smiled. "That would give us even more to look forward to."

Mariah smiled at the young teacher. "I understand. I taught for many years, but not once did I approach the opening of school without a great deal of nervous anticipation."

Liz looked around the group and sighed. "Oh dear, here I sit with three of Cedar Bend's former teachers. I feel like such a novice. This is my first year to teach. I can only hope I will be able to fill your shoes."

Carrie and Lucille exchanged amused looks and giggles. Carrie reached over and patted Liz's hand. "Don't even try to fill mine. I only taught one year. If I did anything right, it was an accident."

"Me, too," Lucille said. "I'm only too glad to pass on the banner."

"Just be careful," Mariah added, "that you don't follow our examples. We each taught only one year here. My husband, who is on the school board, says Cedar Bend is destined to replace its teacher each year."

Carrie and Lucille giggled again before Carrie said, "What Mariah is saying, Liz, is that if you have any desire for marriage, you've come to the right place."

Liz's face turned an attractive shade of pink as she shook her head. "Oh no, I would never break my contract."

Mariah smiled. "That's all right, Liz. The contract is only for one year, and if what I saw on the Fourth of July is any indication, you've already caught the eye of several of our most eligible bachelors. Maybe one in particular."

Joanna watched Liz blush and deny that anything was going on between her and any of Cedar Bend's bachelors. She waited for the familiar feeling of loss and jealousy to hit her, and when it didn't, she knew she had completely given up Mark. She no longer felt as if he belonged to her. She no longer assumed that someday she and Mark would marry. Clay had taken that notion from her. And left her empty inside.

Feeling more than a little disgruntled, not because she had lost Mark, but because Clay was not hers either, Joanna said, "Maybe we should let our new schoolteacher mind her own romantic affairs while we pick out some books for our library."

As the women returned to the catalogs, Joanna noticed the concerned expression on Mariah's face before she looked away. When the other women left, Joanna would ask her friend to stay. She had to talk to someone before she made a complete mess of her life. Who better than her best friend?

———

"Thank you for coming." When the last lady went out the door, Joanna turned to Mariah, the only one remaining. "I hope you didn't mind staying for a few minutes."

Mariah sat on the sofa. She leaned forward with her hands clasped in her lap. "Why do you suppose I sent Daniel and Hope home with Carrie? I'm not so insensitive that I can't see when my dear friend is hurting. Why don't you tell me what's troubling you?"

"Would you like some more tea first?" Joanna started toward the kitchen. Now that the time had come to confess, she just wanted to run away.

"Joanna." Mariah's voice was soft but firm. "Come and sit down. We'll have some tea later."

Retracing her steps, Joanna sank into her favorite chair near the sofa. "All right."

"Why don't you tell me what's troubling you? Does this have anything to do with the conversation we had with Liz? We were teasing her, but you know as well as I do that there is an element of truth in everything we said. I know you saw her with Mark on the Fourth of July, and you couldn't have missed noticing they sat together in church last Sunday."

"I noticed." Joanna crossed her arms. Why she felt so cold in ninety-degree temperatures, she didn't know, but a chill moved through her body. "And I'm glad. I've been praying for Mark to find someone special. I think Liz is perfect. At first I thought she was too perfect to be real, but I like her. Really, I do."

"So you wouldn't mind if Liz takes over that house Mark was building for you?" Mariah's question sounded blunt to the point of being tactless, but Joanna knew she simply wanted a straight answer.

She shook her head, meeting Mariah's searching gaze with a steady one of her own. She tried to smile. "No, I honestly hope that is exactly what happens. Mark deserves someone as wonderful as Liz. I hope they do fall in love and get married."

Mariah sighed and leaned back against the sofa. "I assume that means your problems come from a different direction then."

"Yes." The word came out in a whisper. "I've done exactly what you told me not to."

When Mariah remained silent, Joanna looked at her and said, "When I was thirteen years old, Clay moved here with his father. Carrie said he was too wild, but I didn't think so. He became a symbol to me of everything romantic. He kissed me under the mistletoe, and I fell in love. With him or the idea of a boy actually kissing me, I don't know. I just know I loved him. Then he moved away. As the years passed, the memory I carried of Clay became my dream."

Mariah didn't move or speak.

"When I caught your wedding bouquet, Mark said we'd be next. That's when I prayed for God to send me someone exciting. I asked for an adventure, and God sent Clay. I assumed I'd marry Mark after my adventure ended, but I didn't know I'd fall in love again."

Mariah's intake of breath stopped her for a moment. Joanna wiped a drop of moisture from her eye. "I know. I shouldn't have. Carrie told me I needed to be careful. I didn't listen to either of you."

Joanna gave a short laugh. "Well, it's been an adventure, that's for sure. I think Clay is beginning to care for me. I've tried to just be friends, but I love him so much it hurts. He isn't a Christian. Oh, he goes to church, but that isn't enough. Mariah, what should I do?"

"Besides doing some serious praying, I think you know the answer to that, my dear friend." Mariah gave Joanna the hint of a smile.

Another tear slipped from Joanna's eye, and she wiped it away with her finger. "I have to break off my friendship with Clay, don't I? Mariah, will you pray with me?"

"Hey there." Clay fell into step with Joanna after Sunday morning service. His horse followed along behind while he held the reins. "Care if we walk with you?"

Her heart did a funny little flip before she could stop it. She shook her head. "No, of course not."

"Where's your pa?"

Joanna smiled. "He's taking someone home from church."

Clay gave her a searching look. "Reckon you got over that jealous streak."

"Jealous!" She threw him a disdainful look. "I was never jealous. I don't get jealous."

"So you wouldn't mind if Lucky and I take that pretty little schoolteacher for a ride out in the country this afternoon. Is that right?"

Skidding to a stop, Joanna stared at Clay. Surely he wasn't serious. "Together? On the same horse? There isn't room."

Clay laughed. "For the right woman I'd borrow Sherman's buckboard."

Joanna crossed her arms as her brows drew together. "And I suppose Liz Cramer is the right woman for you."

"I never said she was. I just said you were jealous." Clay's eyes danced in amusement.

"I am not."

"Methinks the lady doth protest too much."

"Oh!" Joanna's foot hit the dirt road, raising a puff of dust. "You are impossible."

"I know, but I'm still not taking Miss Cramer anywhere." Clay took Joanna's arm and headed her back down the road.

She lifted her chin. "I never thought you were."

"'Course not," Clay said. "Mark wouldn't let me."

Joanna met his teasing gaze and couldn't stop the laughter from bubbling. Even as she laughed, pain sliced through her heart. How could she ever give him up? She'd prayed with Mariah, but she hadn't been able to relinquish her feelings for Clay. She loved him and always would.

"Since I'm not giving the schoolteacher a ride this afternoon, how would you like to have a picnic?"

"A picnic?" Would it hurt to go on one last outing with him? Surely God had provided this time, so she could tell Clay their friendship would have to come to a close. How she could possibly tell him without hurting his feelings, she didn't know, but she must try. She could not continue subjecting her heart to this torture of loving him yet knowing she could never be his.

"Yeah, there's a real pretty place I want to show you out on the Circle C. Tell you what," Clay said. "I'll borrow the buckboard from Sherman and have Mac pack a lunch from whatever he's got ready. Then I'll pick you up as soon as I can get back into town. How's that sound?"

As they crossed the yard to her house, Joanna smiled at Clay and nodded. "That sounds fine. Dad is eating at Mrs. James's today. I'll just leave him a note so he'll know where I am."

"Great." Clay's grin looked so happy Joanna felt like crying. What would he think if he knew what she planned to do? She'd eat one last meal with him and store away another wonderful memory, then probably break both their hearts when she told him she couldn't be his friend anymore because she loved him too much. He wouldn't understand, and she didn't blame him. How could he when she scarcely understood herself?

Clay watched Joanna run up the porch steps and disappear inside her father's house. If he'd been a little quicker, he'd have given her a kiss to take with her. He turned and patted Lucky's neck before swinging into the saddle.

"Reckon the kissin' can wait." He headed toward the ranch, whistling the tune to a song they'd been singing in church that morning.

"She's the woman for me, Lucky. What do you think? Will she say yes when I ask her?"

Lucky answered with a whinny and a nod of his head.

Clay laughed. "Glad you agree, because if I can convince Miss Joanna Brady that I'm a good catch, she'll soon be part of our family."

A smile sat on Clay's face as he thought of Joanna. He loved her wide brown eyes that shot sparks at him when she was angry. For the last month, he'd been holding a tight rein just to keep his hands from touching her thick dark hair when she wore it down her back. Her smooth olive skin and full rosy lips were a temptation he could scarcely resist. Just holding her hand sent his blood pulsing through his body, but he hadn't fallen in love with her because she was beautiful.

Truth be told, there were plenty of beautiful women around, but none who possessed the inner beauty Joanna had. The woman he loved had strength of character. She wouldn't let anyone run over her, yet she freely gave of herself to the entire community. Her work for the library proved that if helping her father on his rounds didn't. Besides, she represented the stability he craved. He wanted to settle down right here in Cedar Bend, and he wanted to spend the rest of his life with Joanna by his side.

Clay gave Lucky his head as he picked up speed at the outer edge of town. Settling into an easy run for the big horse, they headed home.

Chapter 16

Joanna wrote a note for her father telling him she would be with Clay on a picnic at the Circle C. With her heart heavy, she went into her bedroom and changed into an everyday dress. Then she walked past the mirror and stopped. Reaching for her brush, she loosened the bun at the back of her head and brushed her long hair. Bringing the thick mass to the nape of her neck, she secured it with a ribbon, letting it hang free down her back. She washed her face and patted it dry.

Joanna walked into the parlor and sat in her favorite chair. Her Bible lay on the table beside the chair where she had dropped it when she came in earlier. She picked it up and ran her hand over the leather cover. She had been neglecting her Bible reading all summer.

Holding the book in her lap, Joanna opened the cover, letting the pages fall open near the middle. Psalms, without doubt, was her favorite book of the Bible. She glanced down and began to read from the thirty-seventh chapter. "Fret not thyself because of evildoers. . ."

She read through the third and fourth verses and then read them again, "Trust in the Lord, and do good; so shalt thou dwell in the land, and verily thou shalt be fed. Delight thyself also in the Lord: and he shall give thee the desires of thine heart."

Then the fifth and sixth verses said, "Commit thy way unto the Lord; trust also in him; and he shall bring it to pass. And he shall bring forth thy righteousness as the light, and thy judgment as the noonday."

Joanna looked up, letting God's promises speak to her heart as conviction rushed in. She had wanted the desires of her heart without trusting in the Lord to bring them to pass. When was the last time she had delighted herself in the Lord? No wonder Clay had not accepted salvation as she'd prayed. She had not set a godly example before him. Her righteousness had not been brought forth.

"Lord, please forgive me." Tears filled Joanna's eyes as she cried out in a heartfelt prayer of remorse that started her on the journey back to a right relationship with her Savior.

———

"Can you smell that chicken?" Clay grinned at Joanna as she sat beside him on the buckboard seat. He flicked the reins, and the horses picked up the pace.

She sniffed the air and smiled. "Yes, Mac makes the best fried chicken of anyone I know."

Clay chuckled. "Mac can cook, that's for sure. I've never eaten so well. Makes a man want to stay around." He flashed her another grin. "Maybe settle down."

Joanna sucked in her breath, unsure if special meaning lurked behind his words and ready grin. She tried to smile. "That would be nice, Clay. I mean, everyone should have a place to call home."

She thought of the verses she'd just read. As the scripture said, she would wait upon the Lord and rest in Him. Surely He would bring His will to pass. But right now she wanted to enjoy the picnic with Clay, to store up memories for later.

As they turned toward the Circle C, Joanna relaxed. She and Clay talked about the perfect summer day, the wildflowers growing beside the road and scattered across the fenced-in fields on either side. They even talked about the cattle grazing some distance away on a slight rise.

"I'd like to have a spread of my own someday." Clay turned the buckboard onto a side road and looked out over the vast land before them as the horses moved forward. He chuckled. "Not necessarily this big. Actually, I wouldn't mind starting off with a small farm. I just want something of my own."

When Joanna only smiled at him, he veered off the road and pointed toward the distant hill. "Over that rise the land slopes down to one of the prettiest spots you'll ever see. There's a natural stream flowing through a stand of timber. The grass is thick and green, and at one place the bank runs right down almost level with the water. We should be able to find a bit of shade for our picnic."

"It sounds wonderful." For Clay's sake, Joanna wanted to be happy, to laugh and talk as if she didn't have a care in the world, but she couldn't.

He reached over and took her hand. "You're mighty quiet today. Got a lot on your mind?"

She nodded.

He grinned. "Me, too."

He gave her hand a gentle squeeze and then drove over the rise. As the buckboard lumbered down the hill, Joanna saw a dense stand of trees that seemed to go on to the horizon. Since they followed a meandering line about a hundred yards wide, she assumed the stream of water Clay had mentioned would be somewhere in the middle of the trees.

Clay brought the buckboard to a halt at the edge of the woods. "Sorry, but we'll have to hike to that pretty spot I told you about."

Joanna smiled at him. "I don't mind. I like to walk."

She wondered if she would be walking home after she told him what was on her mind.

Clay unhitched the horses and tied them so they wouldn't wander. He lifted Joanna from the buckboard and then pulled out the picnic basket. Holding the basket in one hand, he linked the fingers of his other hand through Joanna's, and they entered the cooling shade.

As they walked, Joanna noticed the trees were not so close together as she had thought, but were just far enough apart to create a comfortable setting. A breeze stirred, ruffling her hair and cooling her face. Their footfalls made a crunching sound, and the scent of pine lingered as they passed an evergreen tree. Birds chirped in the tops of the trees, and small animals scurried away from them.

In a small clearing, Joanna saw what Clay meant by the prettiest place she would ever see. A cleared patch of grass gradually sloped to the clear, blue-tinted water. She stopped. "Oh, Clay, you're right. It is beautiful."

He grinned as if he had ordered the spot just for her. "I knew you'd like it."

"I do. Thank you for bringing me here." If only she didn't feel like crying. If only she could forget what she had to say.

Clay set the basket down then lifted a large tablecloth from the top and started to unfold it. Joanna took the cloth from him. "That's my job."

She shook the cloth open, and it billowed out in the breeze before settling down on the grass. She sank to one side and looked at Clay. "Is this all right?"

His gaze never strayed from her face. The intensity in his eyes held her motionless. Then he smiled, and she breathed again. He answered, "It's perfect."

Clay sat beside her and put the basket between them. He took both her hands in his and said, "Will you pray before we eat? I'm not on the best speaking terms with the Almighty."

Which was exactly the problem. She wanted to yell at him, tell him he had to become a Christian. Because if he didn't, she couldn't go on any more picnics with him. She had already lost her heart to him; she was determined not to lose her faith, too.

Instead, she bowed her head and offered a short prayer of thanksgiving for food that she knew she probably wouldn't taste. Mac McDougal was considered one of the best cooks in the county, and the fried chicken he'd packed for Clay proved his expertise. On some level, Joanna knew the chicken and mashed potatoes tasted wonderful, yet they might as well have been cooked by her father, who thought boiling water was beyond him. Clay kept up the conversation, and Joanna contributed as much as she could.

Finally, Clay put his plate back in the basket and took Joanna's from her.

"Joanna, I've got something—"

"Clay, I need to—"

They both started and stopped at the same time. "You go ahead," Joanna said, glad for a reprieve.

Clay set her plate in the basket. He turned and, taking both her hands in his, looked into her eyes with a serious expression. When Clay got serious, Joanna got nervous.

"Joanna Brady, I love you."

"Oh, Clay." She tried to pull her hands away, but he wouldn't let her.

"No, please, hear me out." She saw the love in his eyes, and she couldn't move because she loved him, too.

"I guess I fell in love with you when we were kids. I didn't know what it was then, but I know now. Joanna, will you marry me? I don't have much, but I can support a wife. Please say yes."

"Now ain't that the purtiest proposal ya ever did hear?" The man's gravelly voice and rough appearance as he stepped from behind a tree several feet away would have been enough to frighten Joanna, but the gun he pointed at Clay tore a scream from her lips.

"Mr. Simms." Clay stood quickly, placing himself between the man and Joanna. "I'm surprised to see you this far south."

"I reckon you are." The man spit a stream of tobacco juice to the side. "Thought you'd run out on us and never see us again, didn't ya?"

"I can't imagine what you are talking about." Clay held his hands out to the sides, hoping the outlaw he'd left in Nebraska wouldn't shoot an unarmed man. He took a few steps to the side. If possible, he might draw the man's attention away from Joanna.

"Even you ain't that stupid." Simms waved the gun. "One shot. That was the signal. Remember? Ya done asked, and I told ya twice. Where'd ya go when ya heard the signal? Ya run out on us, that's what ya done."

"I didn't run out on you, Mr. Simms." Clay shifted again. He hadn't run out; he'd let Lucky walk out of town. "I heard that first shot. Really I did. Then there were so many, I didn't know what had happened. You know, those horses you picked weren't real good for a bank job."

"What d'ya mean by that?" Simms swayed, and Clay figured he'd been drinking.

Clay took a step to the side. "All I'm sayin' is that those horses took off in three different directions with all that shootin' goin' on. With you not there to tell me what to do, I figured you'd want me to go after the horses. Never did catch 'em, though."

"Stand still." Simms growled at Clay. He lifted his gun so it again pointed at Clay's chest in a sort of wavering circle. As unsteady as Simms seemed, Clay feared he might aim at him and still hit Joanna.

"Yes, sir, Mr. Simms." Clay shifted again.

"Them two boys with us didn't make it. I got taken in. Spent a month in jail before I got away. Been trackin' you ever since. Gonna make ya pay fer what ya did."

"Mr. Simms, even if the horses hadn't run off, I couldn't have helped much. That place was crawlin' with the law. Don't reckon we had much of a chance anyhow."

"Don't matter. Ya run out on us. And yore gonna pay." Simms grasped his gun with both hands.

Clay glanced at Joanna. She sat where he'd left her, watching with large, frightened eyes. If he had to die, he wanted to save her. That's all that mattered.

"Don't ya move no more. I'm done talkin'."

Clay heard the click of Simms's gun being cocked, and he froze in place.

Joanna's scream and warning came in rapid succession. "Clay, look out."

Clay tried to turn, but he never saw what hit him as the crack of impact against his skull sounded at the same time pain exploded in his head. He crumpled to the ground.

Chapter 17

Joanna sat on the tablecloth transfixed, unable to move. She watched the man who had hit Clay with the butt of his six-shooter kneel and put a finger to Clay's neck. He then looked up at Simms with a grin. "Hit a man too hard one time. He never got back up. This one's fine, though."

"He better be." Simms growled and holstered his gun. "I didn't come all this way so's you could kill 'im. Well, tie 'im up, Burton. What ya waitin' fer?"

Joanna wanted to scream. She wanted to cry. Mostly she wanted Clay to get up, hold her close, and tell her it was all a bad dream. But Clay lay in a crumpled heap on the ground. She watched the man called Burton roll Clay over and tie his hands behind him. Next he tied his feet together, and then the two men lifted Clay into a sitting position and leaned him back against a tree, tying him in place.

Simms placed a big dirty boot on Mac's clean tablecloth, and before Joanna knew what he had in mind, he grabbed her by the arm and hauled her to her feet. She jerked and twisted, trying to get away from him, but he just laughed and tightened his grip.

"What are you doing? Let me go." She tried to stomp on his foot and missed. He wrapped an arm around her and held her against his filthy shirt. She gagged at the smell of sweat, horse, and liquor that radiated from Simms's body.

"Settle down, sister. You're comin' with us." She saw Burton dip his hat in the creek and toss water on Clay as Simms dragged her across the clearing.

He stopped by the tree where he had hidden earlier and, holding Joanna in front of him, sneered at Clay, who was coming around. "Hey, Shepherd, I'm takin' yer girl. Hope ya don't mind. You come and get her if ya want her."

His cruel laughter grated on Joanna's already raw nerves. "I promise I won't kill her till you show up. That is, iffn ya want her back and iffn ya can find us. I figure the two of you 'bout evens the score fer them two boys you let get killed."

As Simms tugged her around the tree, Joanna saw Clay jerk against the ropes binding him, and she knew he had regained consciousness.

Clay yelled, "Let her go, Simms. This ain't her fight. Why don't you face me like a man?"

Simms just laughed again and pulled Joanna with him. By the time they reached Simms's horse tied to a sapling, Joanna felt as if she had already prayed more than she had all summer. Her heart pounded, and she looked around, desperate for a means of escape. But even her struggles as the big man lifted her to the back of his horse did no good. He mounted behind her and, keeping a good hold around her waist, headed out. As they broke out of the trees and started across the prairie, Burton caught up. They rode for a while before they finally reined in and stopped on a small rise where they could see for miles in all directions.

"We're stoppin' here." Simms climbed down and dragged Joanna with him. She stumbled to gain her balance on muscles weak with fear and prayed silently. *Lord, please save me. Let someone find Clay and help him. Forgive me. I didn't know this would happen when I prayed for an adventure. I almost got Clay killed.*

As she realized what she was praying, the blood drained from her face. *Oh, Lord, they are going to kill us, aren't they? Both me and Clay when he comes after them. Please confound our enemies.*

The verses she had read in Psalms came back to her mind. *Fret not thyself because of evildoers.* Of course, that might be easier said than done, but she could try.

Simms gave her a shove. "Sit over there and don't try anything." He stuck his gun under her nose. "Your days were numbered the minute you hooked up with that yellow-livered Shepherd. Reckon ya know I'm gonna shoot ya first so's he can watch. Then I'm gonna shoot him."

Burton started toward Joanna. "If ya need her watched, I wouldn't mind at all." His leering expression left little doubt to his intentions.

"Get yourself away from her. She's bait and that's all." Simms dug a bottle out of his saddlebag and popped the cork. He took a long drink before handing it to the other man. "Here, take a swig of this. It'll calm yer nerves."

"I ain't nervous." Burton took the bottle and tipped it up then wiped his mouth with his sleeve. "I told ya when I took this job, I could kill a man easy as anyone."

He might not be nervous, but Joanna couldn't seem to keep her hands from trembling, and his bragging didn't help. She sank to the grass when her legs wouldn't hold her. She bowed her head and closed her eyes. *Lord, I know I've done a foolish thing. I love Clay, but he's not mine to love. For all these years I've remembered his wild, free spirit and thought of him as my hero. In all the books I've read, Clay became the dashing, exciting hero who won the maiden's heart. I thought that was what I wanted. I didn't know it would be like this, but You knew, didn't You?*

Tears filled Joanna's eyes as she thought of Clay. He didn't know the Lord.

If he died because of her foolishness, he would die without Christ. She prayed for him, that he wouldn't come, although she didn't understand why the men thought he would after they'd tied him to a tree. The prayer she had prayed before she left home that afternoon had brought her closer to the Lord. She prayed now for forgiveness, for putting her desires above God's best for her and Clay.

Lord, please deliver us from this evil. Bring Clay to You so he will know the joy of Your salvation and have the promise of a home in heaven one day. And please forgive me for my discontent. Just, please Lord, save us and let us stay safe from now on, even if our lives are boring.

Clay struggled against the ropes holding him as he watched Simms drag Joanna through the trees. He saw her fighting the big man and worried that she might be hurt. Then the trees blocked them from his view. When he heard the sound of hoofbeats going away, he knew they had taken her with them.

He renewed his efforts to free himself and found the rope went around his hands in a way that he could pull one hand back if he didn't struggle. With one hand free, he easily slipped the rope off his other hand and untied his feet. Obviously the man who tied him didn't know what he was doing.

On the other hand, maybe they intended for him to get free after they had a head start. He knew Simms had been drinking, so he probably hadn't been thinking clearly, but why didn't he just kill him while he had the advantage? After all, he knew Clay wasn't armed. Why take Joanna and give Clay a chance to get his guns and track him down? It didn't make sense, but then he didn't figure Simms ever made much sense.

Clay stood and waited for his head to clear before heading toward the horses he'd left tied at the edge of the trees with the buckboard. Whoever hit him had left a knot the size of a walnut on the back of his head and a throbbing pain to boot. He untied one of the horses and hoisted himself on bareback. His instinct was to head after Simms, and he figured Simms was counting on that, but he had no weapon and no plan. He'd have to get some help.

Turning the horse toward the ranch house, Clay pushed the plodding animal into a run for Joanna's life. When he reached the house, he jumped from the horse and ran to the back door. Concern for Joanna took the place of his manners as he pulled the door open and stepped inside.

"Mr. Butler!" he called from the empty kitchen. Surely someone was here. "I need help!"

"In here." He heard Sherman's voice and followed the sound. The tall, broad-shouldered man met him just outside the parlor door, a concerned look on his face. "Clay, what's happened?"

"Joanna's been kidnapped."

"Joanna Brady?" The doorway filled as Mariah, Carrie, and Luke Nolan joined Sherman.

"Yes." Clay briefly explained Simms forcing him to hold the horses while the three men robbed the bank in Nebraska. Then he said, "I'm to blame for this. I should have known my past would catch up with me. They won't touch her until they have me, but I'm afraid they plan to kill Joanna, too. Please, help me get her back to safety. Then when she's safe, if I'm still alive, I promise I'll ride out of her life, and she'll never see me again."

"Don't worry, we'll get her back." Luke Nolan stepped into the hallway with Sherman. "Sherm, we need to round up a posse. How about some of your boys? Think they'd ride out with us?"

"Sure thing." Sherman nodded. "I'll go get Cyrus to tell the boys." He stopped long enough to place a fatherly hand on Clay's shoulder. "We'll get Joanna out of this. Just do whatever Luke says. He rode with the Texas Rangers, and he knows what he's doing. Later we'll talk about this notion of you running away. Best thing to do with your past is to face it head on."

Clay didn't answer as he followed the two men from the house. He ran to the bunkhouse and strapped on his six-shooters, grabbed his rifle, and made sure all the guns were loaded.

Cyrus soon created a stir among the cowboys as they came in and armed themselves in like manner. For the first time since he saw Bob Simms step from behind that tree, Clay felt as if Joanna might be safe. He didn't care so much about his own life, but he didn't want anything to happen to her.

Chapter 18

Twelve men gathered outside the bunkhouse and formed a semicircle around their boss. Sherman Butler explained the situation.

Then he said, "Men, you all know Joanna Brady. Clay says this outlaw has little respect for anyone, including women. He says he's pretty sure the man was drinking, and there's at least one more man with him, maybe a hired killer. The situation doesn't look good, but we know Someone who cares and is able to confound the evil deeds of such men. Let's go to Him now and ask for His help."

Clay watched the men bow their heads before he followed their example. As Sherman led a prayer for Joanna's safe rescue and their successful capture of the outlaws who had taken her, Clay felt a presence of comfort sweep over them.

Please, don't let them hurt her. Although he didn't speak aloud, he added his request to the others. From the moment he watched Simms drag Joanna away, Clay had been pleading in his heart for her safety. Whether he prayed or only gave words to his fears, he didn't know. But now, as he again pleaded for Joanna, he felt as if Someone might be listening.

Sherman brought the prayer to a close and waited while Luke looked around at the men, saying, "I can't promise your safety. We are dealing with outlaws who more than likely live by the gun and would kill as quick as they'd look at a man. If anyone wants to back out, not a word will be said."

He waited while the men either voiced their determination to bring Joanna back or simply stood with a nod and a stubborn expression.

"All right, men. Let's ride then." Luke gave the order for them to mount up.

Clay rode Lucky between Sherman and Luke. The rest of the men rode behind and to the side of them. They were all regular churchgoers and knew Joanna. Most had told Clay they would get her back and make sure Simms went to prison for a long time. They seemed to like and respect Joanna. Clay figured they had volunteered to go for her sake rather than for his, but he didn't mind. The important thing was that she be rescued from the lowlife who had taken her.

Clay pointed out the direction Simms had gone, and they soon found the trail easy to follow through the tall dry grass. After a few miles, Luke lifted his binoculars. He held up his hand as a signal to stop.

"There they are." He pointed to a distant rise where Clay could see dark spots against the background of brown and green grass.

Luke laughed. "They are sitting out in the middle of an open prairie without cover. Did they expect you to come after them alone?"

Clay nodded. "I never said Simms was smart."

"We can't take them by surprise. Not from where they are." Luke shrugged. "A full frontal approach is our only choice. Does that sound all right to you, Sherm?"

Sherman nodded. "Looks like the only thing we can do."

"We'd better spread out then." Luke turned to give orders to the others. "We're going to ride straight on, and I want plenty of space between every horse. Those on the ends go ahead a few paces so we form a large semicircle around them. They may try to run when they realize Clay hasn't come alone, so be prepared to give chase. I want those men brought in. Unless I missed someone, there are only two men. Let's go get them."

Clay would have liked to surprise Simms, but he knew Luke was right. They had to approach the outlaws in clear view. If he saw so many riding toward him, would he kill Joanna?

Please, Lord, keep Joanna from harm.

This time Clay knew he had prayed, and he sure hoped God was listening. He nudged Lucky into line near the center of the semicircle and rested his hand on the gun at his side. With Luke's order to follow his lead ringing in his ears, Clay leaned low in the saddle and guided Lucky to run straight toward Simms.

Joanna sat on the ground praying just as she'd been doing for what seemed like hours. Simms and Burton sat a few feet away, watching her and sharing their second round of liquor. She felt as bound as if she had ropes around her hands and feet because she knew they would catch her if she tried to get away.

After a while, Burton lay back and appeared to be asleep. Joanna prayed Simms would do the same, although she didn't know how anyone could sleep as hot as it was. The afternoon sun beat down on them without mercy, causing prickles of sweat to run down Joanna's back and neck. The grass under her scratched, and she shifted.

Simms had leaned back with his eyes closed but at her movement mumbled, "Jist sit still, girl. Your boyfriend'll come for ya soon enough. And then we'll put ya both ta sleep."

She cringed at the cruelty in his laugh and looked away. That's when she saw a dark line that seemed to stretch clear across the horizon. She glanced at the men. Both appeared to be sleeping. She prayed they were. Because, if she wasn't dreaming, that rapidly approaching line of horses meant help was on the way. She prayed the vibration of the horses' hooves against the ground would not alert the outlaws.

The riders were close enough for Joanna to recognize Clay on Lucky near the center of the line when she heard Simms let out a stream of cursing.

"Get up ya lazy, no good—"

Joanna scrambled to her feet, and so did Burton. She tried to ignore the filthy language coming from the two men as she whispered over and over, "Thank you, Jesus."

Then Simms grabbed her, jerking her in front of him like a shield. "Get a gun and start shootin'," he yelled at Burton.

"You stay and get yourself killed. I didn't hire on to fight an army." Burton jumped on his horse and took off. A man from either end of the line broke away and gave chase.

Her rescuers stopped in a circle that had Simms covered on all sides. Clay nudged his horse forward another step. "Let her go, Simms. You haven't got a chance."

Joanna felt the cold, hard metal of Simms's gun as he pressed it into her side. His laughter sounded crazed against her ear. "Not so fast, Shepherd. I got my ticket out of here. You let me go or she dies now."

"If you hurt her, you'll be a dead man, Simms. Take a look. You're surrounded." Clay nodded toward Luke. "The sheriff is here. Let her go and you'll get a fair trial."

"I ain't goin' back ta jail. Now let me out of here."

"Turn her loose, Simms."

"Do I look stupid?" The big man twisted to look from side to side, keeping Joanna against him. "Soon as I let her go, you'll shoot me."

"No we won't, Simms." Luke held his hand up and spoke to the other riders, "No one fires if he lets her go." Then Luke said, "It might interest you to know that some of the best shots in Kansas have you in their sights right now. Every one of them knows and respects Miss Brady, and they intend for her to leave here unharmed. They are just waiting for my signal. If you don't let the lady go, I'll let them cut you down."

Joanna felt the gun that was pressed into her ribs move. She held her breath, not knowing what Simms might do. She knew he was scared. So was she.

"Put the gun down, Simms," Clay ordered.

But he didn't. The outlaw lifted his gun and pointed it straight at Clay. "If I go, I'm takin' ya with me, Shepherd."

She'd been afraid before. Now she felt anger rise to push the fear aside. How dare this horrible man threaten Clay! He wouldn't get away with shooting the man she loved if she could help it.

Joanna sank the heel of her shoe into the arch of Simms's foot with as much force as she could muster. At the same time she leaned forward slightly to give more power to the jab of her elbow in his ribs. As she straightened, she felt the back of her head make contact with what she assumed was Simms's nose. Purely an accident, but not one she regretted.

Joanna heard the boom of the outlaw's gun go off as he howled and released her. She sank to the ground and curled into a ball, afraid to look.

A few more shots rang out, and then all was quiet.

"Clay's been hit."

Joanna heard Mr. Butler's voice above the others that called out orders as they took Simms into custody. She ignored the outlaw screaming words she didn't want to hear. She scrambled to her feet and pushed past those who stood between her and Clay.

He lay on the ground, his eyes closed in a face as white as the cuff on her sleeve. A crimson stream poured from the wound in his head. "No–o–o." Her cry became a wail. "Don't die, Clay. Please, don't die."

Cyrus knelt on the other side. He placed a folded white handkerchief on the blood and pressed. "He ain't dead, Joanna. Just knocked out."

When she only looked at him, not understanding, he went on in a calming voice. "Reckon you saved his life. I saw what ya done. Stompin' that feller's foot and bashin' his nose is what kept him from shootin' our boy here down."

"But he did get shot." She held Clay's limp hand in hers while tears ran down her cheeks. "I don't want him to die. Cyrus, please, don't let him die."

Cyrus chuckled. "Thought you was the nurse 'round these parts, Miss Joanna. Ain't you never seen a flesh wound before?" He lifted the blood-soaked handkerchief. "See here? Clay got his hat knocked off and his hair parted, that's all. The bleedin's already slowin' down."

"But he's unconscious."

Cyrus grinned. "Not for long, he ain't. He's comin' 'round now."

Joanna scarcely noticed the commotion around them as she watched Clay's eyes flutter open while color returned to his cheeks. She knew some of the men rode off, but she didn't bother looking up. Instead, she watched Clay's eyes widen and rest on her face. A faint smile touched his lips, and the strength returned in his hand as he squeezed her fingers.

"Are you an angel?"

At first Joanna thought his whispered question came from a fuzzy mind. Then Cyrus laughed and said, "Reckon our boy here thinks he's died and gone to heaven."

Clay's grin widened. "Anywhere Joanna is would be heaven."

Cyrus patted Clay's shoulder. "You'll be all right. Feel like sittin' up?"

"Yeah." Clay didn't take his gaze from Joanna as she helped Cyrus raise him into a sitting position.

Clay rested his arms across his knees and looked at Cyrus. "What hit me this time?"

"Just a little ole bullet." Cyrus picked up Clay's hat and handed it to him. "You might want to go bareheaded for a couple of days. Doc Brady should take a look at that and the knot on the back of your head soon as we can get ya to town. He'll give ya something for that headache. His nurse is too shook up to be much help."

Clay grinned at Joanna. "Sure am glad to see you're still breathing. Don't reckon Simms expected you to fight him. Last thing I saw was you stomping his foot."

He looked around with a frown. "What happened to Simms anyway?"

"Luke and some of the boys are takin' him in. They got the other fellow, too." Sherman stopped beside them and looked down at Clay. "That was a close one. I believe we owe the Lord a big thank you for saving your life. He and Miss Joanna here." He smiled at her. "Joanna, it took courage for you to do what you did. God answered our prayers and saved not only your life, but Clay's as well. Why don't we thank Him now?"

Clay struggled to stand, so Cyrus and Sherman helped him. Joanna let him take her hand in his and watched him bow his head while Sherman prayed. She felt as if her heart might break. How could she give Clay up now? Surely the Lord asked too much of her.

Chapter 19

Clay couldn't remember ever having such a headache. He clung to Lucky on the way back and fought the nausea rolling in his stomach. Any other horse might have dumped him, but Lucky stepped carefully as if he knew his master could scarcely hang on.

Joanna rode double with Mr. Butler to one side of Clay while Cyrus stayed abreast on the other side. Clay knew they kept a close watch on him, probably expecting him to fall off his horse. By the time they finally rode into the yard at the ranch, he felt so tired he could scarcely slide from Lucky. He desperately wanted to crawl into his bunk and sink into a sleep free of pain. But even more than that he wanted to see that Joanna got home safely.

Carrie ran out of the house with little Hope following. Mariah came right behind them with her son in her arms. "Joanna, are you all right?"

"I'm fine." She hugged them all and picked Hope up to hold her close. After assuring the little girl the bad man hadn't hurt her, she told her friends, "But Clay's been shot."

"Shot?" Mariah swung to look at him.

He held to Lucky's reins, letting his horse hold him upright, and forced a grin. "Nothin' to worry about, ma'am. Just got my hat knocked off."

"Oh my." Mariah turned back to her husband. "Sherman, Clay needs to see a doctor. The men rode through here several minutes ago. Did they take those outlaws in? Did they get all of them?"

Mr. Butler slipped an arm around Mariah and held her close as he told her what had happened. Clay felt a pang of envy for the love that seemed to pass between the two of them. He'd give everything he had if he could experience that sort of love with Joanna. But this encounter with Simms had taught him a valuable lesson. Joanna didn't belong with him.

He scarcely listened to the others talk as he watched Joanna with Hope and knew his time with her was coming to a close. As soon as he felt well enough, he'd be moving on to Texas just as he'd planned. He couldn't stay around and endanger her life again.

His gaze shifted to his little buddy who had grown so much in the short time they'd been in Cedar Bend. Maybe he'd done something worthwhile by coming here, at least. Little Daniel had a good home with a loving family. He wouldn't have to grow up without a mother's love. Mr. and Mrs. Butler were the best parents any little fellow could hope for.

A jingle of harness and creaking of wood announced the arrival of the buckboard that Clay had borrowed. One of the ranch hands drove it around to the barn and through the wide-open doors. Clay was glad to see it had been returned without damage. Another man drove the family buggy and stopped beside the Butlers.

"We'd better get Joanna home and have Tom Brady take a look at you," Mr. Butler said to Clay. "Why don't we let Ben take care of your horse so you can ride with us?"

Clay knew Lucky wouldn't like someone else caring for him, but he knew Ben was good with horses, so he agreed. "He's a little skittish around anyone else. I can brush him down when I get back."

Ben grinned. "Don't worry about this big guy. If he won't let me do more than get the saddle off, I'll let you know. Otherwise, I'll take care of him."

"Thanks, Ben." Clay patted Lucky. "You go on with Ben here, and I'll be back quick as I can to check on you."

Lucky sidestepped and whinnied when Ben led him away, but he settled down as the man talked to him and stroked his neck. Clay, relieved to know Lucky was in good hands, let Joanna help him to the buggy. Carrie stayed behind with the two small children. She and Hope stood in the yard waving as the others left.

Joanna sat in the backseat beside Clay on the way to town. Clay wanted to put his arm around her and hold her close, but he knew if he did he wouldn't be able to let her go. He couldn't think right now. His head hurt too much. He knew he didn't want Joanna to go through anything like what had just happened ever again. There might be other fellows bent on getting revenge. He didn't know. He couldn't remember. His past hadn't been a Sunday school picnic, though. Of that he was certain. A heavy weight of guilt and helplessness sat on his heart.

At Joanna's house, Clay climbed from the buggy feeling like a train had run over him. Sherman and Mariah went inside with them. Clay sat in the nearest chair while the others looked for Dr. Brady.

"Tom?" Sherman called to the empty house and received no answer.

Joanna went into the kitchen and came out carrying a slip of paper. "Here's the note I left telling him I would be gone. He hasn't been home."

"Maybe he was called out," Mariah suggested.

"No," Joanna shook her head. "He went to Mrs. James's house for dinner."

"Is that right?" Sherman grinned. "I saw them talking after church this morning. That wasn't the first time, either." He looked at his wife. "Didn't we see them together at the Fourth of July doings?"

Mariah smiled and nodded. "Ruth James is a wonderful woman, Joanna. Your father couldn't do better."

Joanna sighed. "I know. I don't have any objections, except I wish he'd get home and take a look at Clay." She walked over and touched Clay's forehead. "Are you all right?"

Her fingers felt cool and soft against his skin. He grinned at her, wishing he could keep her standing beside him, touching him. "I've been hurt worse and lived."

"Oh Clay, I'm so sorry."

"This wasn't your fault, Joanna." Clay leaned his head back against the chair and closed his eyes. Her hand dropped to her side. "I'm to blame for signing on with a bunch like that in the first place."

"Whoso keepeth the law is a wise son: but he that is a companion of riotous men shameth his father." Mariah's soft voice brought rebuke to Clay's heart.

He opened his eyes and looked at her. "That's from the Bible, isn't it?"

She nodded. "Yes, from Proverbs 28:7."

"I reckon I can be thankful my father doesn't know what kind of man his son has become. He never stayed put in one place, but he was a law-abiding man."

Sherman pulled a straight-backed wooden chair close to Clay and straddled it facing him. "Clay, there isn't a one of us can claim that we've lived our whole lives without sin and be telling the truth."

Clay shrugged. "Maybe." He hesitated and then said, "I mean no disrespect, sir, but I've not lived a charmed life. I haven't had a home that I could remember. My companions, like Mrs. Butler said, were riotous men for sure. I don't think you realize just how far into sin I've gone."

Sherman chuckled. "At one time, Clay, I might have been one of those riotous men you've known if you'd lived in Texas about thirty years ago."

"You?" Clay stared at the gentleman rancher. Everyone knew Sherman Butler was an upright citizen, member of the church, and wealthy rancher.

"Yep, me." Sherman nodded. "Once, before I met the Lord, I had a pretty bad reputation in Texas as a gunfighter. I grew up in the North, and I hated Southerners because of what a couple of them did to my mother during the war. You see, the war didn't end for me in '65. I kept it alive with my riotous living. Then one day I met Someone who took that hatred away. Jesus Christ gave His life for me. When I accepted His gift of salvation, He gave me a new life. Clay,

He can do the same for you."

"I don't know." Clay looked at Joanna. She and Mariah sat across the room quietly listening. She gave him an encouraging smile.

At that moment the door opened and Dr. Brady walked in. "Well, what have we here? A library committee or"—he took a second look at Clay—"or a head wound? Sherm, can you help me get the young man to my examining room?"

Clay pulled himself forward and stood with Sherman's help. "That's okay. I can walk."

As Dr. Brady cleaned and bandaged Clay's head, Sherman filled him in on the afternoon's events. The doctor mixed some white powder in a glass of water and handed it to Clay. "That should fix you up. Drink this, and it should knock away some of the pain. I want you to take a couple of days off work, and Sherm, have someone check on him through the first night. Wake him up about every two hours. He's got a concussion. Send someone for me if there's a problem."

———

On Wednesday morning Joanna walked to the library. She'd spent the last two days doing nothing but thinking about Clay and reliving the horrible experience they'd gone through. Her father had seemed to understand her need to recover, and although he didn't say anything, she knew he worried about her and had been praying for her.

But this morning she decided she had to get on with her life. She couldn't hold on to what would never be while hiding away in her room until she grew old and slowly lost her mind.

She pushed the front door of the library open and went in. Wiping a trickle of perspiration from her face, she crossed the front room to the shelves Clay had installed for her. She ran her hands over the smooth wood and knew she would never forget him. As long as she had the position of librarian, she would have a bit of Clay with her in the work he had done.

She opened a box that had been dropped off and retrieved the top book. She might as well get to work stocking the shelves. She hadn't heard from Clay since Sunday, except her father said he was recovering nicely. She hurt even though she hadn't expected him to contact her. Not after what had happened. He probably wished he'd never asked her to marry him. Maybe it was best she had been unable to give him an answer.

Joanna had been working for an hour or so when the door opened and Carrie rushed inside. "Oh, Joanna, I'm so glad I've found you! I didn't know where else to look when you weren't home."

"What's wrong?" Joanna scrambled to stand from her sitting position on the floor. "Is it Clay? Did he take a turn for the worse? Can't you find my dad?"

"Whoa." Carrie held up both hands to stop Joanna's flow of questions. "Clay's fine. I just wanted to tell you he's leaving."

"Oh, is that all?" Joanna turned to straighten a book on the shelf. "I suppose we always knew he would. It's probably for the best anyway. He doesn't stay in one place long, you know."

Heavy footsteps on the porch caught their attention. Mark stepped through the open doorway. "Joanna, are you all right? I heard about what happened Sunday, and I've been wanting to come see you ever since but didn't know if I should. Then I saw you walk past the feedstore a while ago and decided it would be okay. Everyone said you were all right, but I just wanted to see for myself that you aren't hurt."

Joanna forced a laugh. "I'm fine, Mark. Nothing happened really. Not to me anyway. They caught the men, so all is well."

"Oh, that's something else I wanted to tell you," Carrie said. "Luke got word just this morning about those men. He held them overnight here and wired the U.S. marshall. They were charged with kidnapping and two counts of attempted murder plus a list of other crimes they've committed. Anyway, when the marshall was taking them to the county seat to be tried, Simms almost got away."

Joanna's eyes widened. She visualized the huge, filthy man who had held her prisoner, and her heart pounded. "He's free?"

"No, I'm sorry, Joanna. I didn't mean to scare you. He tried to get away from the marshall, but his hands were in cuffs behind his back and he couldn't control his horse. The horse fell in the chase, and Simms broke his neck. He died instantly."

"Oh, that's terrible." Joanna felt a rush of pity for the man who had probably never been taught right. "I mean, I'm glad he won't bother us anymore, but I didn't want him to die."

"I understand."

"Well, I don't." Mark frowned. "The guy deserved to die after what he did to you."

"I suppose," Joanna said. "But we all do wrong, Mark. I never expected anything like this to happen, but I've learned my lesson well. I'll be content with the life God gives me. And I'll be more careful whom I associate with from now on."

"Are you saying you've decided Shepherd isn't the man for you?" Mark asked.

A sad smile touched Joanna's lips. She shook her head. "I guess Clay never was for me. Carrie says he's leaving now anyway, so it doesn't matter. I've resigned myself to being an old maid librarian."

"Why don't you go tell him how you feel?"

Mark's question couldn't have surprised Joanna any more if he'd asked her to marry him after all she'd done to him. "What are you talking about, Mark?"

Mark shrugged. "Maybe I'm learning a little about romance now that I've found someone who really cares for me." He smiled. "I owe you, Joanna, for nudging me in the right direction. Now it's my turn. You love Clay. You always have. I saw him kiss you way back when we were kids. You remember. I can see it in your eyes. You never knew I was there because I didn't stay after what I saw. But I hated Clay after that. I was jealous. That's all."

"You aren't anymore, are you?" Joanna saw her answer in the contented expression on Mark's face before he answered.

He shook his head. "Nope. I love you, Joanna. Guess I always will, but now I know the difference between having a friend and having a woman to stay with for the rest of my life. I don't know what will happen with Liz, but I hope to give us a chance. I think you need to give Shepherd that same chance."

Mark took Joanna's hands in his and looked into her eyes with a slight smile. He leaned forward and kissed her cheek. "I wish you and Clay the best."

Joanna watched him leave through a sheen of tears. She turned to Carrie with a shaky smile as she wiped the moisture from her eyes with the tips of her fingers. "I've had a productive summer, haven't I? Here I am, twenty years old, and I have no prospects for marriage because I've run off two of the best men around."

Carrie gave Joanna a sympathetic hug before she stepped back and searched her face. "Tell me what's going on between you and Clay. You went on a special picnic Sunday afternoon, and now you aren't even speaking to each other. He's packing to leave, and you say good riddance."

Joanna felt silent tears run down her cheeks, but she ignored them. "I don't know what Clay's problem is. He asked me to marry him just before Simms stepped out from behind the tree. After that everything changed. He acts now as if he never proposed. At least that's the way he acted Sunday. I haven't seen him since."

"And what's your problem?"

Joanna sighed and blotted her face with her sleeve. "Clay isn't a Christian, Carrie. I can't marry someone who doesn't believe. I know he goes to church, but will he later? You know the Bible says we should not be unequally yoked together with unbelievers. I've struggled this summer in my faith because of Clay. I let him come first before God. I can't do that anymore."

"What if I told you that isn't an issue now?"

Joanna stared at Carrie. "What do you mean?"

"Last night Clay accepted Christ. My dad and Cyrus had a talk with him. They said he prayed through to salvation. Joanna, Clay still thinks his past is a problem. He thinks he isn't good enough for you because of the things he did before. That's why he's leaving. If you love him enough, you won't let him get away."

Joanna's surprise and delight brought a wide smile to her face. She swiped at a new source of tears and laughed. "I do love him."

"Then come on. I've got the buggy outside waiting."

"Can you take me by my house first? Will we have time?"

"Sure, if it's important." Carrie shoved Joanna out the door and closed it after them. "Let's hurry, though. He isn't leaving until after lunch, but he doesn't have that much to pack."

After a quick trip to the house, Joanna had what she needed to convince Clay she loved him. Carrie pushed the horse, and they covered the ground quickly. Joanna jumped from the buggy as soon as it came to a stop in the yard at the Circle C. Carrie told her to look in the middle bunkhouse where Clay stayed with three other hands, so she ran in that direction.

The door stood open and Joanna looked in. Clay stood with his back to her, stuffing a bag with clothing. Her heart sank. He really was leaving, and he wouldn't have told her. What if she couldn't convince him to stay?

She stepped into the long room that held four bunks. "Clay."

He stiffened and then slowly turned, the expression on his face cautious. "Joanna? What are you doing here?"

"I came to stop you from leaving." She took a step forward.

"I can't stay. You of all people should know that." He turned back to his bunk.

"Okay." Joanna felt her heart break. What more could she say? "If you have to leave, I'll try to understand, but I've brought you a going away gift."

"You didn't have to—" Clay stared at the dried mistletoe she held up.

She continued moving closer to him as she talked. "Do you recognize it, Clay? I was standing under this mistletoe seven years ago when you kissed me. I fell in love with you then. I haven't stopped loving you since."

Before she lost her nerve, Joanna lifted the mistletoe and held it over Clay's head. He didn't move as she stepped close enough to touch him. He didn't move when she touched her lips to his. He started to pull away as she wrapped her arms around his neck. Then with a sound deep in his throat, he crushed her to him and took control of their second kiss.

The love in his eyes when they pulled apart nearly took away what little breath Joanna had left. She smiled, and he smiled at her.

"I haven't forgotten that you asked me to marry you, Clay. I didn't get to answer Sunday, so now I'm saying yes. If you are leaving, you will have to take me and my mistletoe with you."

Clay grinned and took another kiss before he answered. "Are you sure you want to hook up with someone like me?"

Joanna nodded. "I'm not afraid of your past, if that's what's worrying you. Carrie told me you accepted the Lord. Don't you know He's able to take care of us just like He did Sunday?"

"Yeah, I guess that's right. He's already started working in my life. By the way, you aren't the only one who fell in love under that mistletoe. I love you, Joanna, with all my heart. So when can we get married?"

Joanna giggled. "Are you busy this afternoon?"

Clay grinned. "Sorry, I've got to get my job back. Let's take enough time to find a place to live and let you fix all the frills you want. How's that sound?"

"Perfect." Joanna couldn't say anything else as Clay claimed her lips once more.

Epilogue

The trees lining Main Street had burst in autumn's brilliant colors of red, yellow, and orange before Joanna and Clay were married in the little church in Cedar Bend, Kansas.

Joanna stood beside her father at the back of the church, holding Hope's hand. As matron of honor, Mariah Butler followed the bridesmaid, Elizabeth Cramer, up the center aisle where they took their places to Pastor Carson's right.

Mariah had confided in Joanna just the day before that God was going to bless the Butlers with another little one. Only this one would come the conventional way. Next spring Mariah would give birth for the first time at the age of thirty-eight. Joanna breathed a prayer for her friend and the unborn baby.

She glanced at Carrie and Luke Nolan, sitting near the front with their baby son. He had been born only two weeks ago, and Joanna had been privileged to help with the delivery. Luke held Daniel, who at nine months of age tried to steal the show with his happy smiles and baby babbles.

Ruth James sat just behind the Nolans with her four children. Last week Joanna's father had asked her to be his wife, and she had accepted. He had teased Joanna, saying he had to have someone to cook for him now that she was leaving him. Joanna knew the truth. He had fallen in love with Ruth, and she was glad because Ruth seemed to be just as much in love.

Sherman Butler stood in front beside Clay. Next to Sherman, Mark Hopkins stood with a pleasant look on his face. He seemed to be watching the bridesmaid more than anyone else. Joanna didn't know the outcome of Mark's romance with Liz, but she expected a wedding would take place when school dismissed in the spring. Both Mark and Liz had been helpful in getting the library off to a good start, and they had become some of Clay and Joanna's closest friends.

Joanna released Hope's hand and bending low said, "Okay, now you can go. Do you remember what you are to do?"

The little girl looked up at Joanna with big brown eyes shining and lifted her basket. "I just got to throw these flowers on the ground."

Joanna smiled and gave Hope a gentle push forward. "That's right. And then go sit with Carrie and Luke in front."

"I know, Aunt Joanna. I'm a big girl." Hope stepped forward, taking a handful of flower petals then tossing them in front of her. She watched them settle to the floor before taking another long step and repeating the process.

By the time Hope reached the front, Joanna no longer watched her as her gaze moved to Clay. He smiled, and Joanna smiled in return.

"Are you ready for this?" Her father spoke beside her.

She turned to give him a brilliant smile. "Oh yes, Dad. This is the adventure I wanted all along."

"Then let's go."

As they stepped forward, Joanna watched Clay's smiling face and thanked God for giving her the desires of her heart and bringing her even closer to Him in the process. Maybe praying for an adventure hadn't been such a bad idea after all.

A Letter to Our Readers

Dear Readers:

In order that we might better contribute to your reading enjoyment, we would appreciate your taking a few minutes to respond to the following questions. When completed, please return to the following: Fiction Editor, Barbour Publishing, Inc., P.O. Box 719, Uhrichsville, OH 44683.

1. Did you enjoy reading *Prairie Hearts* by M. J. Conner?
   ❑ Very much—I would like to see more books like this.
   ❑ Moderately—I would have enjoyed it more if _____
   _____
   _____

2. What influenced your decision to purchase this book?
   (Check those that apply.)
   ❑ Cover   ❑ Back cover copy   ❑ Title   ❑ Price
   ❑ Friends   ❑ Publicity   ❑ Other

3. Which story was your favorite?
   ❑ *Circle of Vengeance*   ❑ *Joanna's Adventure*
   ❑ *Mariah's Hope*

4. Please check your age range:
   ❑ Under 18   ❑ 18–24   ❑ 25–34
   ❑ 35–45   ❑ 46–55   ❑ Over 55

5. How many hours per week do you read? _____

Name _____

Occupation _____

Address _____

City_____ State _____ Zip _____

E-mail_____

If you enjoyed

PRAIRIE HEARTS

then read

MOUNTAINEER DREAMS

If you enjoyed

PRAIRIE HEARTS

then read

PAINTED DESERT